THE
Web of Days

THE
Web of Days

by

EDNA LEE

NEW YORK & LONDON
D. Appleton-Century Company, Inc.

PRINTED IN THE UNITED STATES OF AMERICA

FOR WALTER

AND LEE

AND HARRY

For in the time we know not of
Did fate begin
Weaving the web of days that wove
Your doom, Faustine.

—SWINBURNE

THE
Web of Days

Chapter One

WHEN we are confronted by the unknown, the known—however disagreeable—attains new value in our eyes. As I stood on the deck of the steamer *Captain Flint,* which was thrusting her blunt prow along the Altamaha River, and watched the wavering line of Georgia coast move toward me, I knew a sudden fondness for the boat. Her rail as I grasped it for steadiness might have been the hand of a friend. Yet I had never laid eyes on the boat until I had come aboard at Savannah the night before. Now she had become the last link binding me to my past.

It is not a comfortable sensation for a young woman to feel alone in the world, and bound for a destination of which she has no knowledge, yet lacking a place to which she may return if that destination fails to please.

And already I knew that this green land of muddy rivers weaving through wide sea marshes, cut by salt creeks, broken by islands with mysterious names, was as foreign to me as though it lay across the sea. The need which had driven me toward it, seeking for something stable and enduring in my heretofore unsure and unstable life, now seemed to have brought me to circumstances less favorable than those I had wished to escape.

The trip through the war-scarred country had disillusioned me. I had imagined a land of white-columned mansions standing in wide acres, and a way of life which even war and defeat had not entirely robbed of grace—a land where everyone through necessity must start anew. Because of this it offered equal opportunity for all. But little grace had I found in the arid pine barrens, in the shanties crouching desolately, or in the down-at-heel towns where shiftless Negroes and indolent whites gathered

1

at depot or wharf as if the arrival of train or boat constituted the main event of their day.

Yet even these had been preferable to the scene which had met my eyes since the *Captain Flint* left Savannah. Here was nothing but mile on mile of low reedy shores, fields of withered cane and sedges that whispered as the boat crawled its twisting way down the sinuous curve of creek or inlet. A sad, lifeless land, I told myself, so strange that it lost reality. I myself felt unreal, as if I might lose my grasp on life and become merged with the inanimate pattern.

Even the town of Darien, which was my destination, repelled me. It sprawled untidily on the bluff that rose above the marshes, its wharves and shabby shrimp boats clustering at its feet. Yet it was not these that brought me distaste—to me these were familiar sights. It was the tangle of palmetto scrub and live-oak that matted island and coastline in a twisting, writhing mass. It was the gray moss that trailed, the yellow water that reached about the islands and into the forests on the coast like sallow fingers.

That there was a sort of charm in the riot of lush green, in the quiet marshes whose quivering grasses were not unlike the watered silk of my best dress, I could not deny. But it was a weird charm and I suspected that on the humid floor of land and marsh were poisonous creeping things, and that bolder things lay coiled across the cypress knees which thrust themselves, gray and gnarled, above the low-lying landscape. Standing by the boat's rail I knew the disappointment which one feels when mirage yields to reality; and I knew that if in the unsure past there had been one sure refuge to which I could return, I would never leave the *Captain Flint*.

When we reached Darien it did not take me long to realize that those who were supposed to meet me were not on the wharf. I scanned each face closely—and received many curious glances in return—but no one approached me, and I knew a twinge of uneasiness. For even now the bluish haze which is a forerunner of night in these parts was settling over land and water. Looking toward the town of Darien I found no assurance there. It seemed, I thought, a poor place with its few rude shops, its scattering of small houses standing forlornly on the expanse of white sand. There was no promise of a night's shelter for a young woman traveling alone.

Now the boat's captain came down the gangway followed by a Negro roustabout who bore my box on his shoulder.

"Here's your box, ma'am," he said, and lifted his cap gallantly.

I had been aware since boarding ship that a young woman traveling alone provides cause for comment and that the doughty little captain's attentions to me had bordered on the oversolicitous. Heretofore I had repulsed these attentions. But now it dawned upon me that he, no doubt, could give me information regarding the place for which I was bound. So when the roustabout had placed my box on the ground and slouched away, I turned to the captain with a friendly smile.

As if encouraged by my smile he lingered. "Your friends ain't here to meet you, ma'am?"

I pretended a confidence I did not feel. "Not yet, captain. Probably they are detained."

"No doubt that's it, ma'am." His pudgy forefinger toyed with his mustache. "You're stopping at Darien a spell, ma'am?"

Still smiling I nodded in assent and he expanded into garrulous familiarity. "Well ma'am, you'll find it mighty interesting country down here. I've worked every waterway east of the Mississippi, but none that runs through land like this."

"You know the country well, captain?"

"Every sinkhole in it, ma'am. Brought the first boat down after Lee surrendered."

"Then perhaps you can give me some information."

Reaching into my reticule I brought out the letter which I had perused so many times and which told me no more of what I wanted to know in the last reading than in the first.

"This letter, captain, written by Mr. Saint Clair LeGrand, states I should land at Darien and would be met by the house boat. Can you tell where the LeGrand place stands, sir?"

"You are going to Seven Chimneys, ma'am?"

"Seven Chimneys?"

"That's the LeGrand plantation, ma'am. They say the Indians named it so."

"Then you know the place?"

"Everybody around here knows Seven Chimneys, ma'am. You—you're going there?"

I nodded. "But still I do not understand, captain. Is the place —Seven Chimneys, I believe you call it—on an island?"

"No, ma'am, it ain't. But I can see how it would be confusing to a stranger. All boats stop at Darien, ma'am, and a lively port it was before the Yankees razed it. But to reach one of the islands or further down the mainland you must go from Darien by canoe."

"Is Seven Chimneys on the mainland?"

"Yes, ma'am. It stands down about where the Altamaha joins the Sound, back in the forest a bit, looking out on the marshes." There was speculation in the gaze he bent upon me. "So you are going to Seven Chimneys?" His voice was thoughtful. "Are you intending a long visit, ma'am?"

With another smile and a shrug I pretended to take him into my confidence. "I am not a guest, captain. I am to be governess to Mr. LeGrand's son."

For a moment he surveyed me steadily, then abruptly became his talkative self again. "Well, ma'am, the LeGrand plantation used to be one of the finest in these parts. I remember as well as if it was yesterday—"

I stopped his flurry of reminiscence with another question. "You know the family then, captain?"

Interrupted, he paused and cleared his throat. "I know 'em and I don't know 'em, ma'am." His eyes turned speculative again. "Do you know 'em, ma'am?"

I designated the letter in my hand. "Our arrangements were made by letter."

"I see, ma'am. Well," he stared across the water, "Saint Clair LeGrand travels between Darien and Savannah with me regular. And he is what I would call a cool customer, a very cool customer indeed. Not but what he wants the best," he added quickly, "and pays for it. The best at any price—that's his ticket."

I would have liked to hear more. But the captain, as if reminded by the quiet which now pervaded the wharf and which had followed the activity of loading and unloading goods for Darien, glanced at his pompous silver watch. Then turning he looked over the stragglers on the wharf as carefully as I had on arrival.

"I don't see any of the Seven Chimney folks, ma'am. But I

tell you what you'd better do. Go to Angus McCrackin's store on the main square. There's a bench where you can sit. You might have to wait a considerable spell. I'll post old Zabo on the shrimp boat yonder to keep an eye out for the Seven Chimney folks. He'll tell 'em where to find you."

I held out my hand with a feeling close to friendliness for the little man. "Thank you, captain. You are most helpful."

He shook my hand energetically. "Always glad to oblige a lady, ma'am," and touching his cap he strode off, his finger at his mustache again.

Asking a loitering Negro urchin to carry my box, I made my way toward the main square of Darien. A drab square it turned out to be. There was a sign that read: DR. TOITTANT—DRUGS & SIMPLES, a scattering of other ramshackle buildings, their character nondescript, and Angus McCrackin's store standing flat to the ground, its door open. It was deserted when I entered except for a dour-faced man who counted eggs behind the pine counter. He glanced up without faltering in his work. "Do you want something?"

He listened, looking at me unblinkingly through reddish eyes, while I explained that I had been directed there by the captain.

"There's a bench by the stove," he said briefly and went back to his egg-counting.

I crossed to the rusty iron stove—empty now of fire. The Negro placed my box on the floor. I thanked him and sat down on the wooden settle—but not, you may be sure, until I had dusted it with my kerchief. For assuredly I had no intention of trusting my new dolman to the dust and grime which covered the place. Crockersacks of potatoes sifted their earth to the floor; overalls and piece goods on the counters were tumbled and shopworn. And from the barrels of pickles and sauerkraut spilled an acrid odor that mixed unpleasantly with the stale devitalized air of a place never thoroughly cleaned.

Depression, which I had fought off with fair success until now, would no longer be suppressed. Doubts regarding this venture of mine, which heretofore I had refused to recognize, would not be denied. Had I been overhasty and impractical to advertise through a Savannah newspaper for a position as governess in a southern family? Had my decision to seek new faces and new circumstance been but futile reaction against the mediocrity which had bound my life since I could first remember?

Back home I had told myself that any life was better than the one I knew, the one I had known. Even now I shuddered at the memory of the unceasing toil, the loneliness, the insecurity. Yet sitting in the dusty little store, watching Angus McCrackin mount a chair to light the dirty oil lamp suspended from the ceiling, I doubted if anything in my old life had been half so unpleasant as the uncertain future which confronted me now.

The yellow lamplight sprang to life and I realized that as I had sat there lost in thought, darkness had come to press its soft face against the flyspecked windows. From outside came the chant of frogs and the call of the whippoorwills, their three plaintive notes repeated with maddening persistence; and I began to wonder. If no one came to meet me—could Darien offer decent shelter to a young woman traveling alone? I spoke to the storekeeper.

"Is there no way to reach the LeGrand plantation except by boat?"

He turned his dour face toward me. "Joe Jud poles a raft over the river at daybreak," he said. "There's a trail that picks up there and leads by Black Banks. You wouldn't want to go that way, would you?"

I was annoyed at his churlishness, yet I knew it was the nature of the man to be caustic and disagreeable. So courteously, as if I had met with courtesy, I tried to draw what information I could from him.

"If necessary could I get a night's lodging in Darien? Is there a hotel or a decent lodginghouse?"

He shrugged. "Sure. We've got a hotel. But if you're worrying about 'em not meeting you, you needn't. Like as not they're already in Darien."

"In Darien?"

"Yeah—swilling rotgut licker. The Seven Chimney niggers don't get to town often."

Uneasiness, like a light warning hand, laid itself upon me. Liquor! Negroes! The combination sounded perilous for a night's trip down a swampy waterway. I was seized by the temptation to remain in Darien overnight and take the steamer back North in the morning. But when I reminded myself that I would be faced with the necessity of seeking another situation and would be forced to live on the few dollars I had so painfully saved until that situation materialized, the temptation passed. No, I told myself, I had believed that a new life awaited me in the South. I would not relinquish that belief yet—I would go on to Seven Chimneys.

Emerging from my revery I found the storekeeper's reddish eyes upon me. "Would you like a cup of tea?" he asked, and though his voice was sullen as before I thought I caught gruff kindness in it.

I told him nothing would be more welcome. With a curt nod he crossed to a rear door and opening it spoke to someone in the back room. "Flora, there's a young lady here who could do with a cup of tea."

The woman who came to the door drying her hands on her apron was a hard, worn little thing but her eyes were as friendly as a child's. "If you'll step this way, ma'am."

I began to protest. I did not wish to impose. If I might have just a cup of tea—

The storekeeper cut across my words. "There's a charge of fifteen cents for tea."

Relieved, I followed Mrs. McCrackin—as I supposed her to be—into the rear room where I found a cookstove glowing orange and a table spread with a red and white checked cloth. The room I saw served as kitchen as well as dining and sitting room. It was much crowded, but it had a sort of homely comfort. And when I had eaten of the fresh-raised bread and had drunk my tea, which was hot though strong to bitterness, I felt in a more cheerful frame of mind.

Mrs. McCrackin was all polite attention but I could see that she looked at me with curiosity. "You're from the North, ain't you, miss?"

"Yes. But how did you know?"

"Oh, folks from up there are just different somehow." She fingered the stuff of my skirt. "Is that one of those new walking skirts I've heard about, ma'am?"

I told her that it was and her eyes widened with amazement

when she discovered that it stopped at my ankle. "Think of that!" she gasped.

She refilled my cup from the earthen pot. "Are you aiming to stop at Darien a while, ma'am?"

I told her I was bound for Seven Chimneys, and she surveyed me with unbelieving eyes, the pot motionless in her hand. "Seven Chimneys, ma'am? You are going to Seven Chimneys?"

"Yes. Do you know the place?"

"Oh, everybody knows Seven Chimneys, ma'am."

My interest grew. Perhaps, I conjectured, from this simple, friendly woman I could learn something about the house.

"Come," I said, "sit down and tell me about it. You see, I don't know the place at all."

She crossed over slowly and sat in the chair facing me. Picking up her apron, she rolled it meditatively in her roughened fingers.

"What do you want to know, miss?"

"What sort of a place is it? Is it big, is it small? Why is it called Seven Chimneys? Why does everyone say, 'Oh, everybody knows Seven Chimneys'?"

Her eyes lifted in surprise. "But everybody does know it, ma'am."

"Yes. But why?"

"Well," she said thoughtfully, "it's always been here you see."

"Oh, come now," I smiled, "not always."

She nodded vigorously. "Leastways as long as anybody round here can remember. The first LeGrand came here long ago. I've heard my mother tell it many a time and she heard it from her mother. He came over with some other Frenchmen. Real fine aristocrats they was, she said. The others built on Sapelo. But he built his house back on the marsh and fetched gew-gaws from all over the world for it."

"Then they must be genteel folk," I suggested.

Her eyes lifted and dropped. "Genteel?" she repeated doubtfully. "Why, yes, ma'am, I reckon so. But they're strange too."

"Strange—how are they strange?"

She was apologetic. "I don't know as how I can say about that, ma'am. And it's just people's talk most likely. You see, the LeGrands don't mix with Darien folks—not even the gentry." Her voice sank. "They say the mistress is strange."

"You mean—?" I touched my head significantly.

"I don't know a thing, ma'am, but what people say—" she began, then broke off nervously as her husband thrust his head through the door. "Flora," he ordered, "stop your gabbing," and his fox's eyes rested on me meaningly before he withdrew.

Rising, I laid fifteen cents on the table. "Your tea was delicious," I told her.

"Thank you, ma'am."

I started to go back into the store, but at the door I could not resist turning. "Mrs. McCrackin—"

"Yes, miss?"

"Tell me, what does Saint Clair LeGrand look like?"

She faltered. "Why, I don't know, ma'am."

"Is he an old man?"

"Oh no, ma'am. He ain't old."

"Then is he a young man? Is he well-favored or ugly?"

She eyed me wonderingly. "Why, I couldn't say, ma'am. I haven't ever thought about it one way or—"

"But you must have some idea," I persisted.

She stared at me, her little face puckered with the effort of thinking. Then, sighing, she shook her head. "No, ma'am," she insisted, "I couldn't really say."

I decided that she was the stupidest woman it had ever been my fortune to meet, and turning, laid my hand on the doorknob. But she spoke again.

"All I know, ma'am," she said dryly, "is that Saint Clair LeGrand walks like he thinks he is God A'mighty hisself."

I went back to the settle by the stove. How long I waited—if the time passed swiftly or at a snail's pace—I do not know. All the tiresomeness of my journey, the steamcars, the boats, the coach trip from Waynesborough to Charleston, seemed to culminate in the wooden settle which bored achingly into my flesh. The thought of bed became an anguish so exquisite that only by the greatest exertion of will could I hold my eyes open.

How much later I was startled to sudden wakefulness I have never known, but there was a rush of thudding hoofs past the window, a man's voice exclaiming, "Down, Sans Foix!" and a second later a young man strode through the door. He advanced to the counter and threw a coin upon it, demanding tobacco.

Whether it was because he was young and personable, or whether it was because he was so unlike anyone I had seen so far in the South, I do not know, but he caught my interest immediately. In the proud lift of his head, the arrogance of his aquiline features, even in the cloth and cut of his worn clothes, I saw race and breeding. And certainly little of these had I seen.

He lounged against the counter slashing the toe of his boot with his riding crop, restlessness and impatience in every line of his body. He was not unlike a hawk, I thought, pausing in flight, but eager to be on the wing again. But when Angus McCrackin, fetching his tobacco, leaned over the counter and whispered in his ear, I saw the riding crop slow to stillness. Bending his head that he might hear the better, the newcomer listened closely to the storekeeper's murmuring.

I did not know then that their conversation had to do with me; that I know it now is a part of that dark knowledge the possession of which was to change the whole aspect of my life. Even when the young man turned and looked at me, I realized only that he had caught me staring at him. Embarrassed, I turned my head and gazed out of the window beside me, though all I could see was my own pale reflection in the pane.

It was only when he spoke that I turned to find him at my side.

"You are going to Seven Chimneys, miss?"

I answered in the affirmative.

"You are waiting for the boat to meet you?"

Again I answered, "Yes."

"You will not have to wait much longer now," he said swiftly, and wheeling he was gone out into the night.

I addressed the storekeeper. "Who is that young man?"

"Him?" He threw me a sharp glance. "That's Mr. LeGrand."

"Mr. LeGrand? You mean—Mr. Saint Clair LeGrand?"

"No, that's the young one, Mr. Roi, Mr. Saint Clair's brother."

"Does he live at Seven Chimneys?"

His whinnying laugh held some hidden meaning. "No'm, Mr. Roi don't live at Seven Chimneys. Not him."

I would have liked well to ask him more. But I caught myself up sharply. Unbecoming it would be, I knew, for me to pry into the affairs of my employer. Instead I asked dryly, "And does the fact that he is Roi LeGrand give him the privilege of addressing young women without a proper introduction?"

He shot a sly and knowing grin in my direction. "The LeGrands do what they want to do, I reckon." He broke off and looked toward the door. "Here's Vene from Seven Chimneys come to fetch you." The grin spread on his face.

But already I had seen the tall, sinewy mulatto who stood unsteadily in the doorway. His eyes, filled with drunken mockery, traveled over my figure. "Is you Miz' Snow, ma'am?" he asked, his not unmusical voice furred and thick.

"Yes." I spoke sharply to hide the cold knot of dismay that was gathering within me. "Kindly take my box."

Obediently enough, but lurching as he came, he crossed the floor and with a single lithe movement hoisted my box to his shoulder. "This way, ma'am," he said thickly.

I turned to thank the storekeeper for his hospitality and found his reddish eyes fastened upon me curiously. "Ain't you scairt?" he asked.

"Why should I be scared?"

His eyes held a grudging admiration. "Well, I've always heard that you Yankee schoolmarms ain't scared of man or devil."

I found small comfort in his words as I followed Vene across the road to the wharf, now a dark and deserted blot against the water. And when I saw the canoe bobbing on the river, it looked so frail that I had no liking, notwithstanding my brave words, for this trip with a drink-befuddled Negro. When he scrambled into the boat and turned to assist me, instinctively I recoiled.

A voice behind me spoke. "Is something wrong, miss?"

Even before I turned I had recognized the voice of young Roi LeGrand.

"This man is in no condition to handle a boat, sir," I told him sharply.

Without further ado he stepped lightly into the boat and shoved Vene unceremoniously toward the bow. "Get back there, you trifling devil," he ordered. "You ought to be whipped for this!" Turning, he held out both hands to me. "Come, miss, I will see you safely to Seven Chimneys."

I sat in the middle of the canoe as he told me. Without speaking, he took up the paddle, braced it against the wharf and pushed the craft out onto the river. In silence we went down the dark expanse of water, a dank odor of crushed reeds and grasses rising on the air as the boat pushed through them. Behind me Vene began to snore, but his snoring was only a lesser quietness that merged with the plap-plap of the paddle and the monotonous chick-chack of the frogs.

I shivered in my dolman. Against the black void of sky and water our canoe seemed so insignificant—we three within it so unimportant and lost. For reassurance I fixed my eyes upon the figure of Roi LeGrand, but I could distinguish only the light blur that was his face and the darker blot of his body as it swung with the movement of the paddle.

The silence was becoming uncomfortable and I cast about in my mind for something to say.

"Sir, I have not thanked you for your kindness."

His body swung left-right.

"It is of no importance, miss."

"Indeed it is. You have saved me from an unpleasant experience."

He laughed. "I think you would have made out well enough. You strike me as a most competent young woman."

"And because you thought me competent you came to my aid? I am afraid you underrate your good intentions."

"I offered to see you to Seven Chimneys because it happened to please me," he spoke carelessly, as if the matter did not merit further talk. "Please don't try and saddle me with good intentions."

"Perhaps you were going there anyway," I suggested.

"I never go to Seven Chimneys."

"But did not the storekeeper tell me it is your brother's home?"

"It was also my home once," he said briefly. "I do not go there now."

There was that in his manner which prevented me asking

more, and so I fell silent again. It was he who broke the silence
next. "Since the fact that you are young and—er, quite at-
tractive"—his voice was a light and mocking sound against the
night—"doesn't furnish, at least for you, sufficient reason for
my 'kindness,' perhaps I'd better tell you my real reason for
seeing you to Seven Chimneys."

Although he was hidden by the night, I could sense the
masculine confidence in his eyes, the expression, half-appraisal,
half-admiring, on his face. Instinctively I stiffened and tried to
frame what I felt would be a suitably crushing reply to this
audacious young man. But before I succeeded, he spoke again.

"I'd like to know why *you* go to Seven Chimneys."

I held my voice to coolness which matched his own. "To be
governess to the son of Mr. Saint Clair LeGrand. To earn my
living."

He laughed. "To earn your living," he repeated. "That's
something new to hear. I've never heard a woman say it before.
A southern woman would die before she admitted it, even
if it were true." He paused and laughed again. "So Rupert is
to have a governess! You have your work cut out for you,
Miss— Miss—?"

"My name is Hester Snow."

He repeated that too. "It is a cool, calm name. It is like you.
I knew when I saw you in Angus' store that you were cool
and quiet, that you would never cry over a fickle beau or
throw a tantrum over some trifle you couldn't have. But I
didn't know you were one of the Yankee schoolmarms that
have descended on the South like a plague of locusts. Have
you come to find a husband too, Miss Snow?"

By now I was angry and I spoke tartly to the young man.
"Whatever my reasons, you may be sure that finding a husband
is not one of them."

"Good," he said, "for you would find no husband around
here that you would want. Most of our young men died in
the war and our old ones are too weary for the effort of
bridegrooming."

I disliked the bantering mockery of his words as much as
the false position in which they placed me. So determined
to put an end to both I leaned toward him earnestly. "Mr.
LeGrand," I said, "I do not believe that you intend rudeness

but you are rude nevertheless. Let me make myself clear to you."

His voice coming through the dark was edged with surprise. "Certainly, Miss Snow."

"I am not making a bid for sympathy when I tell you that I am alone in the world, that kith or kin I have none. It is a fact. I have accepted a position in your relative's home—I believe the storekeeper said you were brothers—because I must work. But I do not see—and I am considered intelligent, sir—why that should give you the right to treat me with disrespect."

For a space he did not speak and the only sound was the splash of the fish jumping in the shallows. When he did reply his voice had lost the mockery which had angered me.

"Forgive me, Hester Snow," he said.

"You are forgiven," I told him coldly, "but do not let it happen again."

His laughter rang out in the night. "How like a schoolmarm you sounded then. Almost I feel like a boy again back in old Marriot's classroom." And then his laughter died and he became engrossed with the handling of the boat which he turned with great dexterity up the channel that left the coast and ran inland. "We are in the channel that leads to the house now, Hester Snow. You are but a short ways from Seven Chimneys."

Had I been a timid woman (which I was not) that trip up the channel would surely have filled me with terror. The darkness was impenetrable under the smothering canopy of the trees, and the gray moss trailed its dead dry fingers across our faces. Great birds darted past us with swift-thrumming wings, and bullbats swept over us with their quivering cries. I held my kerchief to my nose to shut out the fetid feverish smell of the swamp which rose like a dreadful miasma all about us.

I pulled my dolman close about me to keep out the unhealthy night air, but if I thought the first LeGrand had been a fool to build his house in this forsaken spot, I kept my own counsel. Only once did I speak, and that was when from somewhere in the night there came a great trumpeting roar that might have emerged from the throat of some antediluvian monster. It seemed to shake the very water on which we traveled.

"What is that?" I asked of Roi LeGrand.

"There is nothing to fear," he answered quickly.

"I am not afraid. I am curious. What is it?" The roars were increasing. Where there had been one tremendous bellowing now a dozen could be heard.

"It's the bull 'gators down at Black Banks. But that's a long way from here."

"You mean alligators?"

"Yes. They come up the creek from the great inland swamp, but they are harmless unless annoyed."

This seemed to me but poor reassurance, but the trumpeting roars died and so I said nothing. I might have told him I had no intention of annoying alligators and that my opinion of the first LeGrand—already poor enough—had depreciated still more. And so we moved in silence up the channel which had narrowed until now I could reach out and touch the bank on either side. At length I spoke to Roi LeGrand. "Isn't it pointless to come by boat when there is land for walking?"

"The land on either side of you is quagmire. You would sink to your armpits. Once when I was a boy I had a mare—I shall never forget standing helpless while she was sucked down."

"But why would anyone ever choose this place to live?" I cried.

His body swung back and forth with the oars. "The first LeGrand was a refugee from France," he laughed. "He wanted a place in which he could not be found."

"Why did he flee from France?"

"That he never told, Hester Snow. When a man flees his native land and comes to a strange one, it is to escape something in the past. You may be sure he tries to forget it." He laughed scornfully. "Pioneers," he scoffed.

"Would you have me believe that pioneers are only people that run away?"

He laughed again. "Aren't they?" he asked lightly. "Aren't they merely people who cannot accept whatever hardships life has put upon them?"

I was about to deny this with vigor, but my own situation flashed before me vividly. Had I not run away from my past because I could not accept its disagreeable burdens? Was it not human nature to seek an escape when life became too difficult?

But there was not time for further meditation upon the subject, for now we scraped against the wood of a landing pier. Roi LeGrand tied the boat fast, and reaching back, his hand found mine in the darkness and guided me up the landing steps onto the wharf.

"The house stands a short distance away," he said.

I waited under the canopy of trees while he shook Vene awake and gave him orders about my box. Then taking my arm he led me up the path which ran twisting and turning through a labyrinth of trees and undergrowth and brought us finally to the house.

I knew a great sense of relief when I saw the house. It stood sturdy and high, topped with a square turret. There were indeed seven tall chimneys silhouetted against the sky. Yet I could perceive even in the darkness that it was far different from my expectations. For this was no gracious mansion with white columns rearing proudly. It was a house of dark brick and but for the lights which gleamed through the long high windows on the front and the reflection of firelight that danced on the porch, it was gloomy and somber.

At the front steps Roi LeGrand halted and released my arm gently. "I must leave you here, Hester Snow. But I wish you good fortune at Seven Chimneys."

"Thank you. And again my thanks for your kindness tonight to a stranger, Mr. LeGrand."

He took my outstretched hand and held it within his warm, firm grasp. "I almost wish—" he began, then halted. Silently he stood there a moment, his hand enclosing mine. Then suddenly his mood changed. He freed my hand and shrugged. "Perhaps you will make out here, after all. It is easy to see that you have courage."

"And does it take courage to 'make out' at Seven Chimneys?"

He did not answer, for now Vene came up the path, my box on his shoulder. With a low "Good night," Roi LeGrand went swiftly toward the landing. Vene, saying "Follow me, ma'am," led the way up the steps to the porch. Opening the front door, he waited for me to step across the sill.

I stood in a large hall which held a fine stairway and which opened on both sides to wide, high-ceilinged rooms. In one danced the open fire which I had glimpsed through the windows, and in the other I saw a table set with crystal and silver. And as I followed Vene up the stairs, which at the half-way point crooked like an elbow, reassurance flowed back into me. For even in my brief glance at the rooms below I had seen thick carpets and fine bric-a-brac. This, I told myself, must be the home of gentlefolk.

On the second floor Vene led me down a broad passage-way to a door at the rear. Since both his arms were occupied with my box, he pushed the door open with his foot.

"This is yo' room, ma'am. Where you want yo' box?"

When the door had closed behind him I took off my hat and dolman and looked about me. The room was small and plain, exactly the sort of room that a governess might expect. But it was saved from utter cheerlessness by the fire on the hearth, and I foresaw that with my few personal possessions properly arranged it would be comfortable enough.

Going to the washstand I poured water into a china bowl decorated with pink roses and bathed my face and hands and made my hair neat again. As I thrust the last hairpin into the coil on my neck there came a discreet tap on my door, and I opened it to find a deep-bosomed mulatto woman whose black eyes inspected me boldly.

"Good evenin', ma'am. Madame LeGrand asks you to come down to the drawin' room."

I glanced swiftly into the mirror and was pleased with what I saw. My gray traveling dress was neat, my hair trim, my countenance serene. I looked exactly what I was—a governess.

I followed the mulatto woman back down the stairs into the large room on the left where the fire burned on the hearth. Now an elderly woman sat in a wheelchair beside the fire. I went forward to her.

"Good evening, madame."

"Good evening, Mademoiselle Snow."

She regarded me through large eyes just the color of gray moss. "I regret that I was unable to greet you on your arrival, mademoiselle. I am—as you can see—a prisoner." Her tiny childlike hands fluttered aimlessly.

"Indeed, madame, I understand."

She gestured toward a small sofa. "Sit down, mademoiselle. Margot"—to the mulatto who still hovered in the doorway—"bring mademoiselle a glass of wine."

While we were waiting for the wine she sat staring into the fire, her face blank and impassive. Covertly I studied the massive mound of flesh which made her small finlike hands seem all the more grotesque. From her black dress and the real lace cap and the velvet band about her throat I guessed that she fancied herself a *grande dame*. But I was not impressed, for in her face—as pasty as though it had been kneaded from dough—and in the noncommittal eyes I found greed and even cruelty.

Margot brought my wine and I sipped it gratefully while madame watched me. Not until I had replaced my glass on the small silver tray did she speak.

"Mademoiselle Snow," she said.

"Yes, madame?"

"My son will return soon and you will meet him. Before he returns I want a word with you."

"Yes, madame."

The small hands clutched, unclutched.

"My son is not an ordinary man, mademoiselle. Nor is this an ordinary house to which you've come."

I murmured politely and waited.

The mound of flesh straightened. "The LeGrands are a proud old family, mademoiselle. They built this house nearly a hundred years ago."

My gasp was a pretense of interest, but inwardly I sighed. Was I, I asked myself wearily, to hear a recital on the blue blood of the LeGrands—the vain boasting of "family" which I had heard was too often a characteristic of southerners? But the old woman was not so stupid that she failed to sense my thought. "I will not bore you, mademoiselle," her voice was as dry and cold as a herring, "but this I must say. In your charge we are placing my grandson Rupert, the last of the LeGrands. But one thing you must understand, mademoiselle."

"Yes, madame?" I interposed and waited.

The mound of flesh leaned forward tensely. "You are to keep him away from his mother, mademoiselle, as much as possible."

"I do not understand—"

The tiny hands fluttered, then folded tranquilly on her stomach. "I cannot say more, mademoiselle—except this: my son's wife is not well."

A log fell in the fireplace and a shower of sparks fluttered up the chimney. But I hardly saw them. I was too much engrossed with the emotion which had leapt from the hitherto impassive face of the old woman. I did not understand it, but it was there—something ugly had entered the room and fouled it.

Before I could give a suitable reply or even frame one, she turned a listening ear toward the long windows that ran across the front of the room. I, listening too, caught the tread of feet on the veranda. She clapped her small hands. "Margot!" Her voice was shrill. "Mr. Saint Clair is home."

Margot vanished from her post in the doorway and I heard her voice in the rear of the house, repeating "Mr. Saint's home!" Other voices caught up the phrase, and the result was a flurry of feet. Vene came up the hall with a small tray that held a bottle and a single glass, and sped up the stairs with it. Another Negro brought an armful of logs for the fire, and Margot, moving silently, returned to hold tapers to the huge double-branched candelabra on the mantel until they burst into a bloom of flame. Old Madame watched and ordered.

"The candles on the piano, Margot."

"Yassum."

"Has the wine been brought up for dinner?"

"Yassum."

I was both amazed and amused. I had heard stories of how much the southern gentleman demanded, of wives who waited hand and foot upon their lords and masters, of households run to suit their convenience. Now for the first time I saw it all in reality. And more than ever I was curious about Saint Clair LeGrand, master of Seven Chimneys.

But my curiosity was not to be gratified, at least for a while. True, the front door opened and my eyes turned toward it expectantly, but all I saw was a man, taller than ordinary, in a long dark coat, who without looking right or left ascended the stairs in leisurely fashion, even languidly.

My amusement grew. All these preparations, and then the hero goes upstairs without so much as speaking! Yet for all my amusement I could not but wonder about the man. And as Old Madame and I sat beside the newly stoked fire, I remembered what Mrs. McCrackin had said of him: "He walks like he thinks he is God A'mighty hisself." The little woman had not been so stupid after all.

Now I forced myself to attend Old Madame's conversation as she babbled on in a monotonous voice. I assumed the air of polite listening which is always proof of boredom. But this time she would not be denied. Did I know, she asked, then rushed on without waiting to learn if I did or no, that these sea islands of Georgia were the most illustrious part of the whole South? Did I know that only in these sea islands was there any real "aristocracy?" She spread her gesturing hands. The South consisted of hoi polloi, debtors, fleeing criminals. She laughed without mirth. Except for these sea islands there was no southern aristocracy.

But ah—these sea islands! Did I know that Pierre LeGrand had built this house in 1786, that the big gold-framed mirror on the wall was brought from France, that the clock on the mantel had belonged to Marie Antoinette? And did I know that Marquis de Lafayette on his visit to Savannah in 1825 had slipped away from the magnificent celebration that city had tendered him and come to Seven Chimneys to visit with his dear friend, Pierre LeGrand?

As I appeared to listen and made what I hoped were suitable replies, my eyes went roaming about the rooms. In the brighter, more revealing light I saw much which at first had escaped me. I saw that the carpet of faded rose and cream, which no doubt had cost a pretty penny, was dirty and even threadbare. The furniture showed need of repair and nothing in the room was well kept or even clean. Above the oil portraits cobwebs drifted and the long windows were blurred. Here, I perceived, was such slovenliness as a northern woman would not tolerate for a moment. Even Madame was smirched by it, for the real lace of her cap was soiled and the sleeves of her black silk dress needed darning.

Suddenly, Old Madame's voice stopped midway in a sentence and at the same time I heard footsteps along the upper hall. Simultaneously, Margot appeared in the dining room bearing great platters of food, and Vene circled the table pouring a ruby liquid into slender glasses.

Old Madame looked at me as triumphantly as though this moment was a victory for which she alone was responsible. "Mademoiselle," her voice was arrogant with pride, "now you will meet my son." And her eyes turned toward the stairs—as did mine—to watch the tall, elegant man who descended them.

Chapter Two

MY first meal in the house of the LeGrands was the most uncomfortable of which I have ever partaken. There were but three at the table, Old Madame, the master of Seven Chimneys, and myself. Of the wife and the young son whom I was to teach there was no sight and no word. And Old Madame's polite questions regarding my journey, requiring but a "yes" or a "no" in answer, were as small pebbles dropped into the well of silence.

For all my brave efforts I could eat but little. The food was over rich and too highly seasoned for my taste: a pulpy mass called gumbo, wild turkeys roasted with strong herbs, a giant pink ham encrusted with unrefined sugar; and besides these, vegetables swimming in the grease of fat pork, a sweet confection for dessert—pears cooked in spun sugar, heavy with cream. Even had the food appealed to me, my enjoyment would have been spoiled by Old Madame, sitting at the foot of the table gorging greedily with ugly sucking noises, her minute fingers fishing choice morsels from her plate.

I schooled myself to patience and in the long silences covertly studied the figure of Saint Clair LeGrand, who lounged at the head of the table as though possessed by a boredom too great to bear, his white hand lifting his wine glass languidly.

To this day I do not know whether it was his great height, his finely shaped head, the hooded eyes or the sum of all of these that made Saint Clair LeGrand appear so extraordinary. Certainly, he did not strike me as a handsome man though I admit there might be some who would disagree on that point. For my liking his face was too lifeless, his eyes too expressionless—yet it was a most impressive face with its tapering

elegance of contour disguising the strength of jaw, and its un-fathomable eyes; and about the whole man there was an air of pride and superiority that conveyed the idea of supreme indifference and indolence. And I sensed at that first sight of him that he would draw women as the candles on the table drew the miller-moths. And then and there I determined that never would Hester Snow pay homage at the shrine of Saint Clair LeGrand.

Except for the vaguest of nods in my direction when Old Madame presented me, for him I appeared not to exist. But I did not let this embarrass me. I sat and ate my dinner as calmly as though this silent meal were an everyday occurrence. I answered Old Madame's questions—where was I born?—how old was I?—did I find the South different?—how was it different?—and in turn asked no questions myself except one. I inquired about the boy Rupert whom I was to teach.

Old Madame's fingers in the act of conveying a bit of turkey to her mouth paused in mid-air while she answered. "Rupert was put to bed early tonight, mademoiselle," she said and plopped the turkey between her greedy lips.

Saint Clair LeGrand drawled in a voice that had not the slightest trace of interest, "Perhaps you'd better be prepar Miss Snow. Rupert was punished because of you."

"Because of me?"

"Rupert does not like Yankees. He believes that the horns and tails like the devil himself."

"I must teach him differently, sir."

He shrugged. "You will have to teach him a gr things," he said idly and fell into silence again.

For this I had no answer, so I continued to though I did not feel half so placid as I pret Surely—as Old Madame had said—this was no o The conversation was of too heavy a mood, th weighted with significance greater than or Even the Negress Margot moved about the too often for comfort I found her bold eye thought—if this dinner was a sample, life would be a dour business indeed.

But at last the long meal ended. Ol fingers for the last time and cleaned

Margot, her body making huge shadows on the walls, went to the back of Old Madame's chair and with the deftness that comes from practice wheeled it toward the drawing room.

I folded my napkin leisurely and with a polite "Excuse me" in Saint Clair's direction, arose and followed Old Madame's chair. In the hallway which lay between the two rooms she waited for me to come up with her.

"Good night, Mademoiselle Snow."

"Good night."

Her dead gray eyes went to her son who still sat at table drinking his wine. "Good night, my son."

He answered without turning his head, "Good night."

Her eyes slipped back to me. "My son will speak with you presently about my grandson, mademoiselle. If you will just wait in the drawing room—"

"Certainly."

She fluttered her tiny hands. "We go, Margot," she ordered. The mulatto woman, who was waiting, one hand resting on the chair, now turned it sharply and directed it down the hall. And I went into the drawing room toward the fire which, I saw, had been recently replenished.

But someone was there before me. The big chair at the corner of the hearth held a woman, and immediately I knew her to be Mrs. LeGrand. When I stood at the door hesitating, she leaned forward and beckoned to me. I saw in her eyes the strangeness of which the storekeeper's wife had spoken.

I advanced to her side. "Do you want me, Mrs. LeGrand?"

Warningly, her empty brown eyes holding mine, she laid her finger on her lips implying silence. "Miss Snow?" Her voice was almost a whisper.

"Yes."

"I haven't time to say all the things I want to say," she went on hurriedly, "but don't let him hate me."

"I'm sorry—" I began.

"Wait," she ordered and listened for a moment, her ear turned toward the dining room, then reassured she went on. "They want him to hate me. Don't let him."

What I would have said to this extraordinary plea I do not know, for now I heard the scrape of Saint Clair's chair as he rose from the table. With some impulse to protect this

woman—though I realized perfectly her plea might be only
the figment of a diseased mind—I moved away, and when
Saint Clair LeGrand entered the room I stood by the piano
inspecting some songs that stood on its rack. But though I saw
the cold narrowing of his eyes at sight of his wife, his impassive face changed not a whit as he went to lounge at the
hearth, one elbow resting on the handsome marble mantelpiece. When he spoke his voice was as lifeless as before.

"Do sit down, Miss Snow."

A little embarrassed, I sat on a low chair not too close
to the fireplace nor Saint Clair LeGrand. However, I was
somewhat annoyed. I could not help but be aware of the
undercurrents which were sweeping through the room, and I
deplored the manners of this family—who seemed to care
not a whit what opinion a stranger might gain of them. And
I was becoming conscious of another fact. If Saint Clair
LeGrand had ignored me heretofore, he did so no longer.
Now his unfathomable eyes were fastened on me, and I
suspected that his mind was prying into mine and that behind
the expressionless face a keen brain was weighing my faults
and pigeonholing them.

A small tapping noise intruded itself upon the silence. I
saw that it was Mrs. LeGrand's little foot beating restlessly.

"Shall I have Vene fetch the brandy, Saint?" she asked.
"Then we can discuss Rupert with Miss Snow—"

He continued to lounge at the mantel, his heavy lids almost
concealing his eyes.

"If you will go to your room, Lorelie—"

Her head turned toward him as though pulled on wires.

"But, Rupert—" she faltered.

His voice slid across her words and cut them smoothly,
"Good night, Lorelie."

She sat so straight and motionless that for a moment I believed she would rebel. Defiance was written in every line of
her body—her vacant brown eyes stared into space. But suddenly, whether because she did not care to win, or had no
hope of winning, she yielded, and rising she swept past me to
the door.

"Good night, Miss Snow."

"Good night, Mrs. LeGrand."

She went up the stairway, her train trailing behind, one thin hand tracing the path of the balustrade. At the curve she turned and looked back, and if ever I saw despair in a woman's face, I saw it then.

"Good night, Saint," she called, and I fancied I caught a beseeching note in her voice. He answered only with a tiny shrug of his shoulders. The last we saw of her as she ascended the stairs was the little snake of train that hissed over the worn carpet behind her.

Saint Clair LeGrand waited unspeaking while her footsteps died along the upper hall and the sharp closing of a door told us that she had entered her room. Even then he continued to loll at the fireplace in silence. And since I had nothing to say I was as silent as he.

Finally he drawled. "You are quiet, Miss Snow."

"I have nothing to say, sir."

He lifted his eyebrows. "What? No professions as to your capabilities as a governess, no promises as to the excellent instruction you will give my son?"

"I stated my qualifications plainly in my letter, sir."

"Meaning that you will live up to those qualifications and do no more?"

"I shall do my best, sir."

"But no virtues to enumerate? No examples to cite of what you did for Mrs. So and So's children, Mr. This and That's son?"

"No, sir."

"Then what am I to expect? I employ a Yankee schoolmarm as governess to my son, and she sits in my parlor calmly and promises nothing!"

"Yankee schoolmarms, as you call us, sir, are the same as southern schoolmarms, I imagine."

"God forbid. A southern woman is exceptional if she can add two and two."

"You are joking, sir."

"A southern girl is educated but for one purpose from the time she cries in the cradle—"

"And that is?"

"To catch a man and inveigle him into marrying her. Now

you," he lifted his lids and looked at me, "you were educated in a harsher school, were you not?"

"I was educated in an orphanage, sir."

"So I learned. And were 'let out' to earn your board and keep—"

"Yes. That is true."

"To cook and clean and wash dishes in return for bed and board—"

"Yes."

"And a good share of cuffs and blows, I expect."

"On the contrary, I was kindly treated."

"Kindly treated? By Yankees?"

"Do you, sir, believe as your son does, that Yankees have horns and tails? For the past two years I was in the home of a minister of the gospel where I knew only kindness and consideration."

"Then why did you leave?"

"Dr. Prentiss' wife died."

"And he was left a widower?"

"Yes, sir. With three small children."

"And you deserted him?" Again the eyebrows lifted cynically. "Was this Dr. Prentiss an old man?"

"No, sir. He is quite young."

"And did he not ask you to remain and care for his motherless children and console his lonely heart?"

"No, sir."

"Why not? You are not bad looking."

"You misunderstand—"

"Misunderstand? A young minister recently wifeless has in his household a cool, quiet, capable girl. And he allows her to escape."

I was growing angry at these bantering words drawled in the lazy voice.

"I would rather not discuss my personal affairs, sir. If you will just give me instructions about your son."

His heavy lids dropped over his eyes. His face, if such a thing were possible, was more lifeless than before.

"Very few," he drawled. "He is a spoiled brat. Give him some good Yankee discipline and common sense."

"I shall do my best."

"His mother has damned near ruined him." His face turned dark. "That is why I have hired you. To act as a wall between him and—" He paused and stared across at me bleakly. "You are quiet and cool. Try and teach him to be so."

"I will try, sir."

"Yes." His voice was cold and aloof once more. "I believe that you will try. Good night, Hester Snow."

I went up the stairs feeling that his insolent eyes followed me, but when I turned at the curve he was reaching with a languid hand to take the bottle which Vene had fetched on a tray. The neck of the bottle shone gold in the firelight.

Weary though I was, I could not sleep. I was in that state of exhaustion when the body aches for rest but cannot find it, for the mind shuttles back and forth, weaving with weary repetition the events of the day. And I lay in my bed (which was comfortable enough) examining with curious intent the pictures which flashed across my mind.

Coolly I tried to analyze what I had seen and heard, but this I could not do. Easy enough it was to tell myself that I had come to a broken-down southern family to tutor a spoiled child, and that in this family (I was being logical and reasonable) there was a master, his old mother, a young wife, and the boy whom I was yet to see. Yet as I sorted these facts and laid them in a row, as when a child I had culled seeds from my apple and counted them, I knew that none of these cold hard facts was important. The important things were those not seen by eyes nor heard by ears—the shuttered look on the steamer captain's face, the storekeeper's wife and her words: "They say the mistress is strange." And there was the mistress herself.

Some time after midnight I slept, though I was unaware at which moment consciousness became unconsciousness, when reality merged with dreams. For in my dreams the same faces continued to flash before me and I was weighed down by the same depression which the marsh, the hoot owl's doleful cry, and this dark house had induced on my arrival.

I do not know what startled me to wakefulness. I found

myself sitting straight and tense in my bed, my eyes boring the dark, my ears straining to hear, my whole body taut with listening. Yet I heard nothing except the thousand-throated night chant of the frogs and the sibilant whisper of pine trees. But it was not these which had roused me to tense wakefulness, I knew. These I had heard before I slept. Something else had penetrated my dreams, had brought my consciousness to attention.

Groping, I found the night candle and this I lighted, waiting while the flame flickered and steadied. Then donning my dressing robe and felt slippers, I moved quietly to my door, opened it and listened.

Standing there I could hear no definite sound, yet I knew that somewhere in this house there was movement and carefully guarded voices. And I, who ordinarily am not a nervous woman, suddenly felt that I must know what or who it was that made disturbance in this gloomy house.

Slowly and with utmost quiet I went along the void of black which was the upper hallway, my hand using the wall for guidance as I went. And as I neared the stairs I saw that a strand of light flowed up them from below. At their top I stopped. But I could see nothing, for the lower floor was hidden from my view by the curving steps. Yet I could hear voices and one I recognized. It was Saint Clair LeGrand's, listless and drawling, yet—though I could not understand what he said—with menace running beneath the sound of his words. However, I knew it had not been his voice that had waked me. It was another sound, a flicking sound rising and falling (where had I heard that sound before?) with rhythmical precision.

Almost silently I crept down the stairs one step at a time until I reached the point where they curved. Leaning over the balustrade, I peered below.

At the front door, now open, stood Saint Clair. His figure barred the way against a man who leaned nonchalantly against the door jamb, a smile of contempt on his face. And I was not surprised to recognize Roi—he who had brought me from Darien. Quickly I drew back—they must not see me, I thought. But I was not quick enough. Attracted no doubt by my movement, Roi's eyes flashed up the stairs and for a brief

instant met mine. Then his glance swung back to Saint Clair
and he laughed lightly.

"All right, Saint," he spoke clearly, almost as if he wished
that I might hear, "I'll go. But don't forget why I came."

"And you remember that I can do without your interference."

Relentlessly he closed the door in Roi's face but not before
Roi's eyes had flashed my way again for a second, nor before
I heard his taunting laugh defying both the closed door and
his brother.

Swiftly, before Saint Clair should turn and see me, I drew
back up the stairs and sped down the hallway to my room.
And suddenly I knew what sound had awakened me and
whence it came. I thought of the leather-thonged whip which
Saint Clair had held in his hand as he stood in the door,
cutting it against the air with the ease and familiarity with
which another man, engaged in casual conversation, might toy
with his watch chain.

But for me, inexplicably, that whip held horror. Recalling
the relentless up and down sweep of the leather thongs,
terrible things I had heard of this land came back to me. I
had visions of prostrate beaten bodies, merciless arms that
wielded the whip without pity. The scenes of Mrs. Stowe's
book passed before my eyes. Even when I crept back to bed
and lay staring again at the dark, I could not close out my
imaginings. And though finally I slept again, it was troubled
sleep. In my dreams I heard the flicking thongs of the whip
again, saw again Saint Clair's white hand curved about its
handle.

It is unusual fear or grief that can withstand the morning
sun. And when I awoke next morning to find it streaming
through my window, to hear the staccato of birds and chickens
and geese, and to catch the tempting odor of broiling ham and
boiling coffee, my imaginings of the night before lost their
nightmarish quality. As I washed and dressed I bestowed upon
Hester Snow literally a sound scolding.

My business, I reminded myself, was the tutoring of a small
boy. This boy must be my only concern if I was to remain at
Seven Chimneys. And in the saner mood of day I knew I

wished to remain. Even now, possessing all the dark knowledge which was to come to me, I do not call myself a fool because of that wish, though I know well enough there may be those who would.

My self-discipline was put to an end by Margot who tapped on my door and informed me with her bold insolence that my breakfast was ready and that Rupert was already at table. I followed her down the stairs and along the lower hall to a door which opened on a span of back porch connecting the major part of the house with the kitchen. In the kitchen at a small table beside a low window young Rupert was eating his breakfast. I saw that another place had been laid for me.

"Mister Rupert," Margot laid her dark hand on his shoulder, "here yo' new teacher, Miz' Snow."

The boy scowled at me without speaking and so, after wishing him a good morning, I sat down and unfolded my napkin, waiting while the skinny old Negress at the hearth dished up a bowl of cornmeal mush and brought it to me.

I looked around the enormous kitchen, delighted with what I saw. The vast fireplace, in which cranes swung pot-bellied kettles over the fire, was flanked by Dutch ovens for baking. Against the walls copper pans gleamed ruddily and from the rafters which braced the ceiling long strings of red peppers twirled. Already in the pots something bubbled and hissed, and a young shoat turned on the spit over the flame, its delicious aroma mixed with herbs and spices filling the room.

Maum Lucie, the cook, brought me my plate with its thick slice of ham, pink and curly brown at the edges, with generous helpings of hominy grits and fried potatoes as well. I viewed it with alarm. I wished for but a slice of loaf bread and a cup of hot tea. But it was not my place to make trouble about food, I knew, and so I nibbled at the ham and at Maum Lucie's insistence ate a hot biscuit.

As I ate I watched Rupert, careful you may be sure that he did not detect it. I found him an unusual child in appearance, small for his nine or ten years but with a lithe, delicately made body. His eyes were alert and intelligent under a mop of smoky hair.

He ate his mush swiftly, darting thunderous glances at me as though he dared me to address him. Here was a child, I perceived, who needed discipline sorely. His manners at table were uncouth, and I suspected that he was accustomed to ride roughshod over all that stood between him and his will. Yet he was not stupid. Already he sensed in me an antagonist who would defy him, and every line of his body was belligerent.

My task loomed suddenly large before me. I knew I could not sacrifice one whit of authority, yet gain his friendship I must, for I realized that this was a sensitive boy whose friendship would be hardly won and lost as easily.

I watched him as he finished his breakfast, sopped his last piece of biscuit in the gravy, then dropped his knife and fork with a clatter, and throwing his napkin on the floor, pushed his chair back noisily and started from the kitchen.

Before he reached the door I called to him.

"Rupert."

He wheeled, his thin shoulders hunched. "What do you want?"

"Come back, please, and pick up your napkin and ask to be excused."

He faced me, his eyes cold and narrowed, not unlike his father's. I saw his small chest rising and falling with the intensity of his anger.

Then he spoke, and never had I seen such contempt in young eyes, heard such contempt in a young voice.

"I don't like you, you dam' old Yankee you!"

I took a sip of my coffee with studied deliberateness. "I don't like you either," I told him matter-of-factly, "but that doesn't matter. I expect you to act like a gentleman."

I felt I had made no dent on the wall of his dislike, so I continued to drink my coffee tranquilly, meantime casting about in my mind for the word which would win the boy.

"Even if we are enemies, Rupert, we can do as the knights of old did when they declared a truce—"

He went on glaring at me, but I thought I saw a flicker of interest. Presently he spoke and the words came as though drawn against his will.

"What did the knights of old do?"

"Would you like to hear the story?"

He was tempted and almost yielded. Then his face

hardened. "You're a damned old Yankee. And Yankees are dirty bastards."

At the hearth Maum Lucie gasped, "Lawd help us!" and Margot dropped a pan and ran to Rupert's shoulder. "Mister Rupert!" she expostulated, "be shamed yo'self."

I interrupted her curtly. "Never mind, if you please, Margot. Rupert does not mean what he says."

"I do." He fairly spat the words.

"No, you don't, Rupert," I told him coolly, "for only a stupid person would believe such a thing. And you do not look like a stupid boy."

He continued to glare at me, his small fists clenched.

With my knife I drew a line on the table cloth before me. "Come here, Rupert. I want to show you something."

He hesitated, then curiosity won, and still swaggering he came to my side unwillingly. "What?" he asked.

"Do you see this line?"

"Of course I do. I'm not blind." The tone of his voice was as impatient as though I were the child, he the adult. And already I realized that in this nine-year-old there was maturity and thoughtfulness, badly directed no doubt but capable of much if disciplined and controlled. I realized too that never could he be ruled by threat but only by appeal to reason.

I etched the line deeper with my knife. "Rupert," I said, "if you live on this side of this line, and another boy lives here on this other side, does that make you a good boy and this one bad?"

"That's too silly to answer."

"Yes. Isn't it? But a line is all the difference there is between you and me. Yet you call me a Yankee, and yourself a southerner."

"The Yankees took papa's money and burned our cotton on the wharf at Darien."

"But that was war. In war men must do as they are ordered to do."

He considered this. "You mean," he asked, "that they *had* to do it?"

"Certainly, just as your southern soldiers were ordered to kill our men."

His eyes narrowed thoughtfully. "Do you hate southerners?"

"Of course not. I know the southerners did what they believed to be right just as the North did."

"But both couldn't be right."

"No, but each thought they were right. So you see neither should be blamed more than the other."

I folded my napkin. "Now I want to go out and look about Seven Chimneys." I spoke casually. "Will you come and show me around?"

I sauntered toward the door, knowing (as he probably knew too) that Maum Lucie and Margot watched to see what he would do. For a minute he stood without moving, but as I put my hand on the doorknob I was rewarded by seeing him stoop—somewhat shamefaced—to pick up his napkin. And after he had placed it on the table, he swaggered after me, his hands thrust into his pantaloon pockets.

Elated as I was that I was over the first hurdle toward winning the boy, I did not flatter myself that it was a complete victory. Indeed, I realized that it might be impossible ever to win him wholly. With his frail body and his dark eyes he reminded me of a young deer ready to take flight at the most quiet approach; and so, as we walked about the plantation, I was careful to say nothing that would jeopardize the advantage I had won. I talked to him as I would to one of my own age. And when I asked him questions regarding the plantation I was pleased that he answered them quickly and intelligently and I saw that he was flattered by the manner in which I listened. Here was a boy, I perceived, who had wished for someone with whom he could talk, as so many times happens with an only child surrounded by adults.

There was much I wanted to know about the place, for the daylight but confirmed the impression I had received the night before. The house was stifled by too many trees—live-oak, cypress and bay—rising thickly, their great trunks tortured as if they had escaped with agony from the rank undergrowth that choked their roots. Once, in the sickly glimmer of sunlight that thrust itself through a gap in the foliage, I saw a snake basking on a rotting log, ominously still.

Curiously I looked at the house and saw that it too was a part of the strangeness. Rising high and turreted, with narrow windows set deep in the brick walls, it might have served as a fortress. Again I could not but wonder what had caused the first LeGrand to flee and secrete himself in this dark place in this dark house. Now, like all else in this sad country, it suggested solitude and decay. The veranda was near to falling in, across its floor the leaves of many days drifted unswept, and in one corner touched now by a fugitive ray of sun, a lizard with bright oblique eyes sunned himself without fear of being disturbed.

In the front in a tangled mat of undergrowth and parasitical vines the garden stretched down toward the sound a quarter of a mile away. At the end was the water wall which Rupert informed me guarded Seven Chimneys against high tides. And he told me that the strip of black spongy land that lay between wall and water was quagmire. The Negroes called it "Mary-de-Wander Lane" and said that on dark nights a woman in white walked along it moaning and wringing her hands.

Beyond the Mary-de-Wander, upon the breast of the water, lay the marshes, couched low and like all else about the place oversated with beauty. As Rupert and I stood looking out at the scene, black and white birds, which Rupert called skimmers, trumpeted their way over the marsh, their plumage startling against the water where they settled to feed. Behind them crept a flock of wood ibis, their powerful curved bills making a great clatter, and then I breathed an "oh" of delight. A bird of delicate pink plumage floated down to feed alone in the shallows, its long bill skimming small fish from the water, its exquisite color jeweled against the green of the marsh. And Rupert, scornful of my admiration, said it was just an old spoonbill and not near as pretty as the blue herons.

Now we left the front garden and turned toward the rear, and I saw that the land stretched as far as eye could follow. Surely there must be many acres at Seven Chimneys, for the back gardens gave way to cotton fields which in turn stretched to the wall of forest on the horizon, and against the horizon on the river side I saw rice bottoms cut with many channels and surrounded by banks. But they were dry and caked now and grown up with reeds and undergrowth.

Signs of decay and neglect lay upon everything. The gardens

were rank with weeds, the cotton stalks were skeletons of many seasons past, and the rice bottoms looked as though it was many a year since they were sprouted. And when I peeped into the rice mill, I found the machinery rusted and fallen apart, and the great barn stood empty and unused.

Rupert plucked at my arm. "These are the slave cabins," he said. "My father owned enough Negroes to live in all of them before the dam' Yankees—" He broke off.

I ignored his allusion to Yankees and turned my attention to the slave cabins. They were the first I had ever seen, and my only knowledge of such had been gained through Mrs. Stowe's estimable book and various northern periodicals. Yet they were not unlike my mental picture. They formed a shabby colony at the rear of the plantation, made up of rude one- and two-room huts built of what Rupert called "tabby" and held to the ground with rock chimneys. All were empty now except for one occupied, said Rupert, by Vene and two Negro bucks named Sey and Boy.

A little farther on we approached another house standing apart as though it considered itself superior to the shabby shanties, and considerably better constructed than the others. Rupert said before the war it had been the overseer's house and that now Tawn lived in it. When we came up to it, I saw two small brown boys playing at the doorstep, and in the doorway a brown woman leaned, her wide dark eyes fixed steadily on me.

I bade her good morning pleasantly and would have paused to chat with her, for I saw that she was of different stripe from the other Negroes. Her skin was the color of a new minted penny, her body entirely free of clumsiness and finely formed. Leaning there against the jamb of the door she might have been some voluptuous figure cast in burnished copper.

But while she answered my good morning civilly enough, her manner did not encourage conversation, and I walked on.

"Who is that woman?" I asked Rupert.

"That's Tawn."

"Does she work in the house too?"

"Tawn never works," he answered, then added coolly, "Tawn is a brown bitch."

As much as I disapproved of his language, I could not sup-

press a smile. Perhaps, I thought, this self-willed young jacka-
napes had used Tawn's children illy and had known Tawn's
anger. The very arch of her insolent body told more plainly
than words that here was one who would not be put upon.
But as we walked back toward the house I pondered Rupert's
words. I knew that children only repeat what they have heard
from elders, and as we ascended the steps I wondered who else
at Seven Chimneys called Tawn a brown bitch.

But now the sun was high and it was time that we busied
ourselves about lessons. I found myself looking forward to
them with more interest than I had dreamed possible. For
Rupert during our walk had vouchsafed bits of information
about birds and animals and plants which proved he possessed not only an observing mind but a retentive one. Un-
doubtedly, with proper training he would develop well.

Old Madame sat at breakfast in the dining room when we
entered the house, but was too intent upon her food to notice
us. Of Saint Clair or his wife I saw nothing—but then it was
but nine o'clock. Perhaps they lay abed late. I had heard this
was a custom of southerners.

Rupert led me to the schoolroom, a dusty, disordered place
at the rear of the house containing a derelict desk and two
chairs. Over these and the floor as well, the dust lay thickly
coated. Even the papers on the desk were grimy to the touch,
and spiders had spun great cobwebs in the corners.

I could not work in such disorder. Bidding Rupert wait, I
went kitchenward to seek a broom, a pail of water, and dust
rags. Margot, when I asked for them, looked at me almost
with contempt, as though my intention to work lowered me
in her estimation. Nevertheless she supplied me, and thus
armed I returned to the schoolroom and went about sweeping the place vigorously, first pinning my skirt up about my
waist to guard it against the dust that rose in heavy swirls.

Rupert, leaning against the desk, watched me as I tied a
rag about my broom and dampened it in the water.

"What are you going to do now?"

"I am going to mop the floor with this wet cloth and wipe
down the baseboards."

I saw in his eyes an expression not unlike that which I had

seen in Margot's, as if he too held me in contempt. And when I suggested that he take another rag and dust the desk, he refused flatly. "It's nigger's work. Let Margot do it."

"Perhaps Margot is busy elsewhere."

But he was firm. "It's nigger's work. You're doing nigger's work."

"I'd rather do it than live in dirt."

"Would you really?" His surprise was genuine. "Then you are not a lady, are you? Ladies don't do nigger's work."

"Stuff and nonsense, Rupert." I spoke sharply for I was provoked by his attitude.

"That's what makes your hands funny, isn't it?"

I stopped and looked at my hands. "Are my hands funny?"

"Yes, my father's are much whiter and softer."

I looked at my hands self-consciously and saw that what he said was true. My hands did bear evidence of the hard work they had known in my lifetime. But well-shaped enough they were, and at least they were not ineffectual like Old Madame's. And I thought how almost since I could remember my hands had been busy earning what livelihood I had possessed.

I leaned against my broomstick and spoke with seriousness to Rupert, for I thought it a shame that this young boy should scorn honest labor.

"Do you not know, Rupert, that it is commendable to work? To be able to *do* for yourself?"

"Why is it? That's what you have niggers for. My grandmother has never put on her own stockings in her whole life."

I considered it a poor thing of which to boast, but this I kept to myself. Instead I reminded him that unless we work we do not justify living; that everyone is created to accomplish, and that only the parasite is content to live on the industry of others.

He listened attentively enough but was unconvinced. "Maybe some people are meant to work like you," he reasoned, "and some meant not to work—like papa."

"And doesn't your father work, then?"

He drew his small figure up proudly. "Papa is a gentleman."

"But not everyone has money, Rupert. Some, like me, must work for a living."

He shrugged. "But papa doesn't have money either. It's

mama's money. And we have some fine rows I can tell you—
last week mama screamed and screamed—"

This I could not discuss, so I tacked my sail in another
direction. "Look at the room, Rupert. Is it not a pleasanter
place?"

He looked at the damp dustless floor, the ordered desk, its
neat pile of papers. "Yes," he said, "I like it. I never saw it
clean before."

I heard the door behind me open and turned to find Saint
Clair LeGrand in the doorway. Rupert ran forward. "Look,
papa," he cried, "the schoolroom is clean!"

His father's eyes traveled about the room lazily while one
white hand played with the massive watch chain that lay
across his fawn-colored vest.

"We are not accustomed to so much cleanliness, Miss Snow."
His voice was as ever drawling, and not knowing whether he
was pleased or displeased, I answered somewhat tartly: "I can
see that, sir. In all my life I have never seen so much dirt. And
Negroes thick underfoot too."

"Negroes, Miss Snow, are the most no-account creatures
alive."

"I only wish I had the ordering of—" I began, then stopped,
afraid that I had overstepped.

But he ignored my words. "I'll be away for a day or so,"
he drawled. "You will proceed with Rupert as you think best."

"Mrs. LeGrand is going with you, sir?"

His lids whipped up and I saw how pale and cold his eyes
could be. "Mrs. LeGrand?" he repeated. "Mrs. LeGrand is not
well enough to travel."

Without further word, he left, closing the door quietly,
leaving Rupert and me to reading and writing and arithmetic.
But as we read and totted up sums I was remembering the
tall figure of Saint Clair LeGrand lounging in the doorway,
bored and contemptuous. And when I happened to look
down and realized that I had talked to him with my skirt
still pinned up about my waist and with my petticoat showing, I felt the blood rush to my face. And I shamed myself
for being glad that I had worn my best petticoat, the one with
the little embroidery ruffle.

Chapter Three

LIFE is meaningless—or so it has ever seemed to me
—unless it has form and pattern, yet at Seven Chimneys I
found no order and no plan. The days unwound and rolled
one into another, like a drab ribbon, each one as colorless as
the day before and the one to come. There were no yesterdays
worth remembering, no tomorrows worth anticipating.

Old Madame, fusty in worn silk, sat in her chair by the fire
babbling of past grandeur whenever by chance she could waylay me. She was forever nibbling on some tidbit fetched by
Margot from the kitchen. When she was not eating (which
was seldom) her futile hands fluttered and gesticulated, but
never once did I find them busy with a bit of fancywork or
darning, or with a useful task of any sort. And indeed in all
the house I saw but little industry. In the morning Margot
and Maum Lucie would murmur on the backsteps, their
shoulders hunched, while all the work within went undone,
and I noticed that directly after breakfast Vene would vanish
and not a trace of him would be seen until near to mealtime.
And there was no one to ask the Negroes why they idled nor
to chide them that thus it was.

For I perceived (and within a very few days) that the wife
of Saint Clair LeGrand concerned herself not at all with such
matters. She rarely appeared below stairs until noon, and
then she crept down, still wearing her nightgown beneath her
wrapper, to sit in the drawing room like a pale wraith, staring
into space a while before she crept up the stairs again. At
supper time she was apt not to appear at all; and if she did
her eyes would be overbright and her cheeks flushed from
brandy, as I learned, and she would sit at table smiling
foolishly into the shadowy corners of the dining room, eating

scarce at all, her thin hand shaking when she lifted the brandy glass to her lips.

A shame it seemed to me that this young and beautiful woman (for she still carried traces of a great beauty) should destroy herself with intemperance. But there was no one to try to help her. Indeed it seemed to me they abetted her in her indulgence. I knew Margot carried brandy to her room just as Vene carried it to Saint Clair's. And when Saint Clair was away, which was often, and Lorelie dined at table with us, Old Madame would see that Margot kept her wine glass filled; and when at last she arose and with faltering steps made her way up the stairs, Old Madame's eyes would follow her, gloating with something close to triumph.

But in this house of disordered rooms and lack of routine Rupert and I followed the pattern which I had laid down, for long ago the habits of order and regularity had been instilled into me. And sometimes it seemed that only the child and I moved forward in a path of action among other lives so inactive that they bordered on death. I saw much which disgusted me: beds unmade, great piles of soiled linens lying on closet floors, the closet shelves in the greatest confusion. There was slovenliness and waste in the kitchen, the butts of sweet pink hams left to spoil, the piles of leftover breads allowed to turn green with mold! And because my instinct for thrift and cleanliness was offended I spoke to Maum Lucie sharply.

"What are you going to do with this?"

The birdlike eyes in the shriveled face turned hostile.

"Ma'am?"

"This butt of ham. Surely you are not throwing it away?"

"T'aint enuf to bother 'bout."

"There are many ways it could be used." I took it from the pile of leftovers. "Put it in a covered dish in the safe." I followed her to the safe and peered over her shoulder.

"Those shelves are filthy. They need scrubbing down."

She mumbled sullenly as I went out, but next morning I saw that her kitchen was cleaner, the safe shelves scrubbed white.

I did not stop with the kitchen. Briskly, I called Margot's attention to the swirls of dust that lurked in corners and beneath beds, to the furniture that had not been rubbed for many a day, to closets and cupboards that needed ordering. And I named Monday morning as wash day and told her on that day she was to wash in the big cypress tubs that stood in the wash shed and boil in the three-legged iron pot in the back yard. Though her black eyes went hot with resentment she did my bidding.

Nor did my interference stop here. With sharp tongue I prodded Vene to rake the garden and clear away the weeds and undergrowth. He worked but surlily at first and with indifference, but finally he came to take an interest in his well-ordered paths and weedless flower beds and sometimes I would hear him singing at his work.

All this was but a feeble beginning, for on every hand I saw signs of shiftlessness. In the gin house I found what must have been the best part of a crop of cotton lying in dirty heaps and when I inspected it I found it literally alive with moths. It seemed a sin to me that those who had the ordering of affairs at Seven Chimneys should tolerate such waste. Yet Saint Clair cared or seemed to care not at all. I reminded myself it was but natural that the Negroes worked as much or as little as they pleased with such a master, and that it was small wonder there was waste on every hand—the cotton rotting in the gin house, the rice swamps lying unplanted and the big barn empty.

But even with these assumed duties added to Rupert's lessons my days were dull and monotonous, so dull and monotonous that I sought for trifling errands which might carry me to Darien. A bit of muslin for a collar, new stockings, hairpins—none was urgently needed but they served as the reason by which I might for a little while escape the somber house and the meaningless life there.

Always on these trips I stopped to visit with the store-keeper's wife, Flora McCrackin. While her dour husband received me ungraciously, the little woman gave me such cordial welcome that I knew she too had longed for companionship. Drying her hands on her apron she would lead me to her clean kitchen and together we would drink her strong tea and eat of her fresh-baked loaf spread with golden butter; and though at first we might talk of the weather and clothes and

the Loyal League, which had descended upon the South and
Darien, our conversation in the end invariably led around to
Seven Chimneys. I discovered that to Flora McCrackin—and
indeed to the whole community—the house was regarded with
the same superstitious wonder with which a child reading a
fairy tale regards the ogre's castle; and I, curious, deliberately
drew from Flora McCrackin the story of Seven Chimneys.

She didn't talk easily, for she was not one for fluent phrase;
indeed she was almost inarticulate. But gradually and at my
persistent prodding the story was unfolded. She told of the
first LeGrand, already an old man with a grown son when he
built the house on the marsh. He had brought its brick from
England and the gewgaws that furnished it from all over the
world. He had laughed (Flora McCrackin's eyes marveled at
his temerity) when they warned him that the house stood on
an Indian worship ground and that a curse would fall on the
man who defiled it. When it was finished he had fetched home
his greatest treasure—his young French bride. Just a girl,
she was no more than sixteen—or so folks told it—and he
had hidden her away from all eyes except his own jealous
jaded ones. Alone she had paced the boxwood paths hour
after hour while the old husband watched from the windows
of the house. On the day when he caught her in his young
overseer's arms, he put them both in a boat and turned them
out on the sound though a great storm raged. And they had
never been seen or heard of again. But still the wife walked
in the garden before a big storm, wringing her hands, they
said. (Flora McCrackin shook her head in wonder.) And less
than a year later the old husband had died. It had all worked
out just as folks said. The house lay under a curse.

Though I was tempted to point out that aged jealous
husbands and unfaithful young wives were not restricted to
houses that lay under a curse, I withheld comment and instead
prodded her again, with "And what happened then?" And she
told of Philippe, son of the first LeGrand, who came from
France to take over Seven Chimneys. And as she talked I could
not deny that inarticulate as she was, she did not entirely lack
expressiveness. The picture she drew of Philippe in her simple
words was as clear as that of Pierre. Pierre she had made a
wizened old dandy, cruel and suspicious; but Philippe was a

fine fellow, what with his deer hunts and regattas, his gambling and his women. But the curse had fallen on him too, she said, and soon. His second-born had been found smothered in its crib (here the little woman's eyes widened with horror) and it was *coal black,* folks said. And as if that wasn't curse enough Philippe himself had been killed soon after—shot in the back on a hunt, and by his best friend. The morning after he was buried in the grave lot they had found his body dug up and the right hand cut off and taken away. Voodoo, the family had called it, but folks had known it was the curse again. Philippe's wife had lived on at Seven Chimneys and had sent her eldest son to Europe for schooling. When he came home to take over, he too had brought back a French bride—she who was Old Madame.

"The present Old Madame?" I interposed.

Yes—Marie something-or-other, her name had been. That was Old Madame. And didn't she give herself the fine airs, like she was a queen? Why, they said she never turned her hand—not even to put on her own stockings! Slaves to do everything! Her boat in which she went to Darien and visiting on the islands was painted gold and with satin cushions and with eight slaves in livery whose only task was to row the mistress when she went out.

Listening I received the impression of great wealth, of almost voluptuous luxury and ease; and I said as much to Mrs. McCrackin.

Yes, she said nodding, there was plenty of money. For the second Pierre was an able man, for all (here she pursed her lips) his hard drinking and evil reputation about women. She had heard her mother tell of the great crops of cotton, and about the Seven Chimney flats floating down the sound with their loads of rice. He had owned almost a thousand slaves, had Pierre LeGrand.

"And," I asked, "he had how many children?"

"Only two. Saint Clair—him that lives there now—and a daughter."

"A daughter? And isn't there another son? Roi, I think his name is?"

"Yes, ma'am, but he warn't a proper child you see—"

"What do you mean—not a proper child?"

"She—Old Madame, I mean—is not his mother. He was born out of wedlock. His father took him to Seven Chimneys when he was just a child though, and gave him what he gave the others. Some said that Roi was his father's favorite. But when he died he cut Roi off without a cent. But then he was a wild one, Roi was."

So now, I mused, I knew the explanation of Roi. No son of a rich father, but the illegitimate black sheep of an illustrious family. Small wonder his name was never mentioned at the house, that he never came there.

I prodded the little woman again. "And did you say there was a daughter?"

"Yes, ma'am. Cecile. But she is dead. She died—oh, three or four years ago. The first year of the war, it was. I remember because—"

I broke in upon her, remembering. "The curse again, I suppose," and I could not hold the irony from my voice.

She gazed at me gravely. "Yes, ma'am. The curse."

She told me about Cecile then. A pretty little thing, she said—like a young deer, somehow. She had been to France, had been presented at the court of Napoleon III. It was all written up in the Savannah papers. But she came home still unmarried though folks said Saint Clair (he was the head of the family since his father died) had wanted her to marry a French nobleman.

"But she wouldn't marry him?"

"No, ma'am. You see she loved young Bob Kingston, who was just a poor boy, a soldier. And one night when young Bob was at Seven Chimneys a dreadful thing happened—"

"Yes?"

"He fell down the stairs. His neck was broken." Her candid eyes met mine squarely and her lips curled. "They said it was an accident, but some said it warn't—that he was thrown down the stairs—"

"Thrown?" I was incredulous.

"Yes, ma'am. And before three months Cecile died. A broken heart," her voice dropped to a whisper, "they said."

So earnest and credulous was the little puckered face that I could hardly hold back my smile. Nevertheless I held it, for

I knew nothing I or anyone else could say would ever convince Flora McCrackin that young Bob Kingston (in his cups, no doubt) had probably tripped and fallen down the curving stairway. Nor, I saw, did she wish to be convinced. So I held my tongue. Why, I asked myself, strip her ogre's castle of its mystery.

"What happened to the land itself? The war, I suppose, changed things—" I interrupted as she sat staring into space as if unable to return to humdrum reality.

Yes, she said, the war had stopped everything. The Le-Grands' money was worthless—the Yankees had burned their cotton on the Darien wharf. The freed slaves had left; gradually the place had gone down. The cotton land lay unploughed and slowly but surely the marsh began to reclaim the rice bottoms. "It was a shame," Flora McCrackin said. "A crying shame." She shook her head regretfully as she poured me another cup of tea.

After such talk I would return to Seven Chimneys with the scenes Flora McCrackin had described limned against my brain and would be struck anew with the inertia which held the place in thrall, the once productive land which lay as under a blight. And almost idly I began to speculate on what it would need to bring it back to productiveness and prosperity again.

Negro hands, I knew. But I knew too that now these could probably be had by applying at the Freedmen's Bureau in Darien, for I had heard how the onetime slaves after their first taste of freedom were now drifting back to the plantations, willing to hire out to their old masters as freed men, or seeking new masters. Money it would cost; that I knew too. For added to the monthly wage of each hand would be the cost of "carrying" them until time of settlement. Five thousand dollars was the least possible sum with which it could be managed. But perhaps if I talked to Saint Clair LeGrand, convinced him that I had the knowledge and experience to manage the project, he could arrange to get the money for the purpose.

As the idea, which had grown from idle thinking, took form and crystallized into a definite plan, I began to figure and calculate in earnest. And as I did, it dawned upon me that perhaps here, on this down-at-heel plantation, lay the opportunity which back home I had dreamed of finding.

Now with my plan in mind I began to take long walks about the land, going first to the cotton fields, then on to the rice bottoms. I looked with calculating eyes at the upland which stretched away from the shore. It was, this upland, the perfect place for vegetable fields, for when I dug beneath the surface with a sharp stick the ground, resting after all these years, was rich and black. Here I told myself lay the foundation for crops that would pull Seven Chimneys from its slough of laziness and poverty.

One day when I had taken such a tour about the land, planning in my mind what I would plant as earnestly as if already the actual work was upon me, I went on past the fields and entered the forest beyond which walled them. Here was dimness and shadowy coolness and quiet. No birds chattered here; no frisky squirrels peeped at you with bright questioning eyes; only the pines had the temerity to speak and their voice was but a whisper that trembled to quiet. And suddenly I realized that this square bordered with boxwood and shadowed by great trees was the family grave lot. The tombstones centered on a decrepit sundial on which little sun could now ever shine. Taking a twig I brushed the leaves from its surface and read the inscription blurred by the time it had told for so long. "Time runs fast," it read, and standing there in the dim quiet, broken only by the whisper of the pines, I had a sense of the years going on relentlessly. And as I went to walk among the graves, I shivered.

Here was the grave of the first LeGrand, its stone lurching drunkenly. PIERRE DUVAL LEGRAND—*1716–1788*. Philippe too lay here and beside him one Angelica, wife of Philippe. Then another Pierre (that would be Saint Clair's father, I reasoned) and beside him the newest grave of all: and on its stone the single name CECILE—*1846–1862*. Standing there I remembered what Flora McCrackin had told me of Cecile.

So few graves, I thought, to account for the passage of almost two hundred years. Indeed, except for a few pitiful graves of children, these were all. The LeGrands had been no great burgeoning family, I saw, but had produced charily—as if they had held themselves aloof even from life itself.

It was after this visit to the grave lot that I went to the lower rooms and lighting a candle that I might better see, inspected the portraits which hung there and which heretofore had held but slight interest for me. There were Pierre, beak-nosed old dandy, his mouth a cruel line; Philippe, resplendent in white satin, his cap of dark hair and the mocking narrowed glance not unlike Roi's; and in the features of the young woman in hoop skirts who simpered from the canvas I traced a likeness to Old Madame; but even youth had been unable to conceal the craftiness in the myopic eyes. In the hall a younger Saint Clair stared down at me in the elegance of fawn broadcloth, and finally I came to Cecile. Cecile in her pale blue gown, her eyes like a startled doe's, standing forever against a marble balustrade. Cecile who had lived only sixteen years.

Chapter Four

ON a cloudless October day when the first few yellow leaves were drifting from the trees and the mockingbird roused from the inertia of summer, I stopped beside Vene as he worked in the flower beds. When I had praised him (and he was the pick of the lot for work), I asked him flatly what his wages were.

He dropped his eyes to the flower bed again.

"Wages?" he repeated. "We doan' get no wages, ma'am."

"You mean that you get only bed and food?" I asked incredulously.

"Yassum. Dat's de way it's always been."

"But things are different now—you can demand wages."

He continued to pull weeds, and I couldn't see his face.

"Didn't you know that?" I insisted sharply.

He stood then, rubbing the black earth from his hands. "Yassum. We know 'bout dat."

"Then why do you go on working for nothing?"

"We'se Seven Chimney fokes—" he said slowly.

"Still, you are entitled to pay."

"Mister Saint Clair ain't got no money," he spoke defensively, "and we'se Seven Chimney fokes."

I thought of all the rich food that heaped the table every day, the cases of fine wines and brandies that came from Savannah on the boat, and then I thought of these Negroes bound by their stupid loyalty to a master who gave them no more than he would give a dog, a roof over their heads and food for their bellies.

But I said nothing of this to Vene. I passed on into the house mulling over the matter. And yet I could not blame Saint Clair, for he—it seemed to me—was caught in a mon-

49

strous trap. All these mouths to feed, all of these dependents unable to fend for themselves, and no money with which to provide. Too well I knew how the lack of money could bring a sapping, sucking despair that pulled one down for good and all. Small wonder, I thought wryly, that he allowed the Negroes to do much as they pleased. It is no easy task to force today's work from those you could not pay yesterday.

It seemed to me the more I thought upon it that Seven Chimneys was a giant yoke laid across the shoulders of its master, a yoke which at times must weigh unbearably heavy. And then and there I made up my mind that at the first opportunity I would have a talk with Saint Clair LeGrand.

But my opportunity was to be deferred, for that very afternoon I heard him order Vene to have the longboat in readiness to take him to Darien within the hour. Very fine he looked as he strolled down the path to the landing. And I could not help but ponder upon the business that took him on these trips to Savannah. What did he do when he reached the town which, Old Madame had told me, was a gay and lively place?

It was not until three nights had passed that he returned, and then he came at dusk and barely answered the civil greeting that I gave him in the hall before he went on up the stairs to his room in the turret. A little later I saw Vene following with the tray and bottle. Old Madame, Rupert, and I went in to supper without him.

But I was not to be forestalled in my determination to have a talk with him. And so after supper I left Rupert in the drawing room with Old Madame and climbed the narrow stairs which led from the second floor to the turret room. I knocked briskly on the door. And when he called "Come," thinking, I am sure, that it was Vene or Margot, I opened the door and went in.

"Could I speak with you a moment, sir?"

He sat at a card table beside the fire in a patched purple dressing gown, a bottle of brandy at his elbow. His fingers did not pause in their task of dealing the cards. Indeed he hardly glanced up. I waited for him to signify that he was ready to hear me, and while I waited my eyes were busy; for never before had I dared penetrate this, the sanctuary of Saint Clair

LeGrand. Now I saw a vast square room with high cell-like windows on all sides flanking even the fireplace, a room that served as both bed and sitting room. It was furnished with almost sybaritic luxury. The rug felt deep and soft to my feet, the chairs were wide and cushioned, the bed a picture of voluptuous comfort. But here as everywhere else within the house I saw dirt and disorder. The fine old highboy was cluttered with miscellaneous objects among which I recognized the whip with the carved and jeweled handle. I wondered how many slaves had felt it coil around their bodies.

I was recalled to my mission by Saint Clair's drawling voice. "Do you want something, Miss Snow?"

"Yes, sir. I would like to talk to you about Seven Chimneys."

"What about Seven Chimneys?"

With my hands clasped behind my back I faced him, pretending a bravado I was far from feeling. Indeed, so bored and lifeless he seemed, I wondered if he would even trouble to hear what I had to say. Nevertheless I hurled my questions at him. Why had the cotton been allowed to rot in the gin house? Why did the rice bottoms lie unplanted and idle? Why did we have to buy corn and tomatoes and other vegetables in Darien with rich land at hand, needing only the seed and a little tending? Didn't he know that Seven Chimneys could be a productive and prosperous plantation? Did he know of the waste and the sloth that spread through his house and over his land like some dreadful blight?

He heard me to the end without speaking, sipping the brandy, his long white fingers cupping the glass delicately. When I had done, he drank the last drops and patted his lips with his fine handkerchief.

"So this is an example of the famous Yankee get-up-and-get," he mocked. "You come to my house and hardly get your hat off before you want to run it."

"It is two months since I came to Seven Chimneys," I pointed out tartly. "Time enough to see what I have seen."

He studied his empty brandy glass, then placed it on the card table with a shrug. "It takes Negroes to produce cotton and rice."

"There are Negroes to be hired in Darien."

His eyebrows lifted. "At the price your Freedmen's Bureau

sets up? Twelve dollars a month—half to be paid monthly, half in crop? Where would I find money to pay them?"

"Then send these you have packing. They do not even earn their food."

"I can't send them packing. They are Seven Chimneys Negroes. Oh, they left once after your 'emancipation.' But they came back. You see, for twelve dollars a month they had for once to work."

"But don't you see," I cried, "that you are like a man caught in the quagmire of the marsh? You are being drawn down and down. All these mouths to feed—"

"Shall I let them starve?"

"Force them to work! Don't sit there just waiting to die!"

His pale eyes met mine unblinking. Not the least shade of expression touched them. "Don't you realize," I demanded, "that it is men like you who must rebuild the South?"

"Rebuild the South?" he mocked. "Do you know, Hester Snow, that for all the platitudes your Mister Lincoln has mouthed the South today is a subjected colony? That—as you just said—we can only sit and wait to die?"

"But that is ridiculous. The South is not defeated in spirit."

"In spirit?" he repeated. "Do you use the word by any chance in connection with the war?"

"But they say—"

"They say—they say! They say 'the soul of the South,' 'the lost cause.' Useful enough slogans in their day when you were trying to persuade a dirt farmer to fight for you. But wars are fought for only one thing, Hester. Dollars and cents."

"The war was fought for states' rights and tariffs."

"States' rights—tariffs! Let me tell you this, Hester. No state in the South would have fought for them alone. When Andrew Jackson was president, South Carolina wanted to fight about tariffs. But no other state abetted her." He shrugged again. "So the matter was dropped. But why discuss it? The question between North and South was slavery—Negroes, merchandise—dollars and cents."

I struck the mantelshelf with my fist in exasperation.

"Why talk about the war?" I cried. "It is over. Now you must learn to live another way."

"And just what is the other way?"

"Hard work! Why, if Seven Chimneys were mine I'd follow the plough till I dropped."

Something fluttered in his eyes and then stilled. "Yes, I believe you would. You were not reared to despise work."

"It is nothing of which to boast," I told him hotly, "to despise honest labor. The man who works at least pays his debts and walks a free man."

He stifled a yawn with languid fingers. "Still you do not understand. We of the South are not free. We too are slaves, Hester. Slaves of an antiquated mode of life, known throughout the rest of the world as serfdom. However, we have given it another name. We prefer to call it, 'living like gentlemen.'"

"I don't believe it."

"It is true." He paused, then suddenly leaned forward and held out his hands. "Let me see your hands."

I thrust my hands behind my back. "What do my hands have to do with it?"

"Rupert says they are not like a lady's."

"Rupert is unaccustomed to hands that have done work. My hands have worked."

"Soothing your parson's brow, I suppose?"

Suddenly I was angry, as one is angry when earnestness is met with amused banter.

"What is the matter with you?" I cried.

"Matter?" His eyebrows quirked. "You surprise me. I am a southern gentleman, capable I hope of winning favor even in your eyes."

"Perhaps that is it."

"It." Again that cynical eyebrow. "You speak in riddles, What do you mean by 'it'?"

"That you are a southern gentleman. You see, I have never known one before."

"You have known only northern gentlemen, I take it?"

"I have known men."

"And they are not as I?"

"No."

"In what way are they different? Do they have the horns and tails with which we were ready enough to credit them?"

"They work."

"Ah, they work."

"They till their fields and make their goods—"

"And sell them to the South at a fine profit. And underpay the southerner for his crops."

"I know nothing of that. But I do know that you must work to justify your existence."

"Hester Snow! Hester Snow!" Suddenly he stood and came to assume his habitual position at the hearth, elbow crooked on the mantel. "Do you think," he drawled, "that I do not see"—his hand gestured lazily—"all of this—the ragged rugs, the dirt, the shiftlessness?"

"But you do nothing to change it?"

"How can I? Without Negro labor, enough Negro labor, I am helpless."

"Will you let me help?"

His pale eyes looked at me oddly. "Help? How can you help?"

"Let me have the ordering of the place, direct the Negroes."

"What do you know about crops and the handling of Negroes?"

"Enough to hire a good headsman," I retorted. "And I lived six years on a farm with farm people."

He sighed in utter boredom. "Do as you like with the place."

"The rice mill will need repairing, and the plough mending. We will have to have a stout mule."

His face was impassive. "There is no money."

"I will make a bargain with you. I have a small savings laid by. I will lend you enough to repair the mill, mend the plough, and buy the mule. I am willing to advance it at six per cent interest."

I thought I read contempt in the glance he gave me. But he only said, "Very well. Do as you will."

"When it comes time to plough and sow we will have to hire more Negroes. Can you raise the money to pay them?"

His pale eyes stared at me steadily for a space, then he said quietly, almost too quietly: "I will get the money."

Slowly I told him, "It will take a great deal more money."

His eyes met mine unchanging. "I have said I will get the money."

"Very well. But understand, I shall want complete authority over the Negroes."

"I hope you may get it."

"I shall want absolute supervision over Seven Chimneys, the kitchen, the house, the servants."

"Everything shall be to your ordering."

I pushed my advantage home. "Beginning tomorrow?"

"Beginning tomorrow."

I stooped and picked up the tray of dirty supper dishes that still stood on the floor. When I rose I found his eyes upon me, but ignoring them I coolly turned to the door. "Good night, sir."

"Hester Snow." His voice stopped me.

"Yes, sir?"

"Why do you do this?"

Holding the tray, I faced him, but for the life of me I could find no words with which to answer him; nor did I know the answer, in truth. Perhaps it was my loathing for waste; perhaps it was a vague idea that some day Seven Chimneys would be Rupert's, of whom I daily grew more fond; perhaps I hoped that in rebuilding Seven Chimneys I might build a different life for myself; and perhaps (I say it now, but never had I dreamed it then) it sprang from a desire to lighten the burden of the tall, bored man who looked at me so steadily. But even as I groped for words with which to answer him, he spoke again.

"They say," he said sarcastically, "that Yankee schoolmarms come South to be ministering angels, martyrs, or to find husbands. For which of these reasons did you come, Hester Snow?"

I could not answer for the indignation that swept me. I wheeled and with his supper tray in my hands went out. And as I went out I slammed the door.

Chapter Five

BUT little rest did I take that night, and long after Seven Chimneys slept, I sat beside my candle with paper and pen, planning the work that lay before me. Tomorrow I must go to Darien and arrange for the repairing of the rice mill and mending of the plough, and must look about for a stout mule. And I would stop at the Freedmen's Bureau as well to discuss the possibility of hiring good Negroes for the ploughing and seeding. Until that time came Vene and Sey and Boy would have to start to ready the land. The cotton fields must be burned off and the palmetto scrub and reeds dug from the swamps. There was the moth-eaten cotton to be burned too . . . we would be hard put to have all in readiness by ploughing time.

It was still but daybreak when I dressed and descended to the kitchen. I told Maum Lucie, who was raking the ashes from the glowing bed of her banked fire, to ring the big bell which stood in the back yard. I had learned it was used to summon the Negroes.

They ambled from the cabins after a bit and clustered in the back yard, yawning and sleepy-eyed. In the gray dawn I stood on the backsteps and faced them. Quickly I counted them, Vene and Margot, Sey and Boy, Maum Lucie. But I saw that there was one who had not heeded the sound of the bell.

"Tawn. Where is Tawn?"

No one answered, but a film closed over Margot's hostile eyes, and Maum Lucie stared at me parrot-wise.

Standing there I deliberated if I should send Vene to rouse Tawn, or should I deal with her later? I decided in favor of the latter course. And so in simple, straightforward words I told the others that now I was in charge of Seven Chimneys, that in the future they would take orders from me and no one else. I told them also that each one must work, that it was my job to see they worked—and they could be assured I would attend to my job.

They heard me in silence, eyes fastened upon mine. I could not guess whether they were displeased or not, so blank were their faces. But when I told them that on Saturday nights each would receive two dollars in cash money, I saw a little stir of interest grow in their faces. They would, I pointed out, get house and food as well, and when we had put Seven Chimneys on a paying basis they would get even more.

Then briskly I gave each his stint of work for the day. Maum Lucie was to redd up the kitchen and pantries. Margot was to start within the house and room by room clean it thoroughly. Sey and Boy were to order the rice mill and make it ready against the time the engines would be repaired. Vene today would row me to Darien, but tomorrow he must clean the barn and burn the useless cotton. And—at the last—I told them that each morning I would meet with them at dawn and give them their day's work.

I shall never forget their eyes as I talked to them in the early gray of morning. Margot's black and cold as ice, Maum Lucie's narrowed like a lizard's and as unrevealing, Vene's slipping away from mine furtively. I might have been, I thought, in darkest Africa, and for me the house and cabins vanished. I was aware only of the jungle-like undergrowth that rose behind their dark bodies, of their dusky faces below me, still and guarded. And I remembered what Saint Clair had said when I had insisted upon complete authority: "I hope you may get it."

Dismissing them curtly I went down the backsteps and found my way through the sweetness of pale-tinted morning-glories rioting over trees and paths to the overseer's house. It was quiet now, its door and windows closed, and this angered me. Why should this Negro wench lie idle when all others were up and about their tasks? Did she not receive the bounty of Saint Clair even as they?

Imperatively I rapped on the door.

I waited impatiently, hearing the soft stirring within, and then the door was half opened and Tawn, her eyes velvety with sleep, looked out at me.

"Yassum. What you wantin'?"

Crisply I told her that there was work for her to do. It was time she was up and about. She looked at me steadily and I saw the same hostility which often glazed Margot's eyes.

"Yo' want me to wuk, Miz' Snow?"

"Yes. You are to help Margot about the house."

She surveyed me for an instant. "Did Marse Saint Clair say for me to wuk?" she queried softly.

I told her that now I was in authority here. She, and all the rest, were to do my bidding.

She listened, her wide eyes on mine. When I had finished she smiled at me as she would smile at a demanding child.

"Yo' ask Marse Saint Clair if he wants I should wuk," she said softly. "If he say I wuk—I wuk."

Gently she closed the door in my face, and I heard the bolt drop into place. I was left standing there, defeated by a brown wench who had smiled.

But this matter I would attend to later. Now I must have breakfast and tell Rupert he and I would go to Darien. He was as excited about the trip as though it were a holiday jaunt and fell into an anxious discussion of which pantaloons he must wear, that lasted all through our breakfast.

We were ready to leave by the time Margot rolled Old Madame to the dining room for breakfast, and as I donned my dolman I heard Saint Clair descend the stairs. Quickly I put on my hat and followed him, a paper in my hand. (In the light of my candle the night before I had prepared it.) It stated in what legal phrases I could bring to bear that one Saint Clair LeGrand did owe to one Hester Snow the sum of three hundred dollars which he would repay at the rate of six per cent interest.

When I called to him in the lower hall he came back to lounge against the stair post in his patched purple dressing gown. Patches or no, he looked the fine gentleman just the same.

I handed him the paper, and he glanced at it contemptuously. "You want me to sign this?"

"Please."

Leisurely he crossed to the desk and with the quill pen

wrote his name in the curious handwriting which had so struck me when I first saw it in his letter. Then without speaking he returned the paper to me. Coolly I glanced at the signature to see that all was in proper form and thrust it into my reticule.

"Rupert and I are going to Darien," I told him, "to see about a mule and someone to repair the rice mill."

"I can attend to those things."

"I prefer to do it myself. I intend to get a good mule not too dearly, and the rice mill should not cost much."

"Then you think I can't drive a good bargain?"

"I do not say that. But I know I can."

He looked at me strangely. "I believe you there easily. I am beginning to think you are a hard woman, Hester Snow."

"I do not consider it hardness to insist on fair value for money spent."

He continued to stare at me with a light in his eyes which I neither understood nor liked. "Yet there are some, no doubt, who could thaw that hardness."

Angry, as always I was angry at his way of turning the conversation to the personal, I drew my dolman about me and called to Rupert that it was time to go. As I did so, I gave one of those unconscious glances which women resort to, at the big gilt-framed mirror which hung on the wall.

Behind me he spoke. "So you are a woman after all—and with the usual set of vanities, I'll be bound."

I did not like his taunting voice and so I gave him no answer to this, but held out my hand to Rupert. "Come, Rupert," I said, and with the boy's hand in mine went out the front door and down the path to the landing where Vene waited in the longboat to row us to Darien.

Darien, I found, was a vastly different Darien from the one I had seen on that first afternoon when I waited for the longboat to meet me. Then it had been almost deserted, but now the Negroes milled along the sandy streets dressed in their gaudy best, and the doors of the ramshackle shops stood wide, in hopes that the cheap wares—overpriced I noticed—might attract the wages in their pockets.

Few whites were to be seen except shopkeepers and their helpers and a sprinkling of "crackers". The men wore faded patched overalls, the women cheap calico, their sallow faces shaded with sunbonnets. And even these went about their business quickly, as if they disliked mingling with the Negroes.

As for me, I found the sight of so many Negroes reassuring. I foresaw that when time came for ploughing and planting there would be labor aplenty to be had, and so as Rupert and I made our way to the Freedmen's Bureau, I was in a sanguine frame of mind. Here, right in Darien, I saw there was enough and to spare of the help we needed for the work at Seven Chimneys. And doubts as to the blackamoors' ability to work did not once enter my mind, so strong-muscled and cheerful they seemed as they jaunted along Darien's square, jostling and happy as children on a holiday.

But once inside the Freedmen's Bureau my confidence was somewhat dampened. Not at first, for Captain Peake, the rabbity little man in charge, was all courtesy and anxious to be helpful and I was careful to defer to him with respect, realizing that on this ordinary little man so puffed up with self-importance, the success or failure of my venture depended. I spoke about engaging some fifty-odd Negroes for the ploughing and planting, explaining I could not pay the usual monthly wage but I would carry them until crops were made, and then would settle with them in full. He pointed out with the greatest show of regret that this was against the rules of the bureau. Each Negro must have a contract not only for housing himself and his family, but for wages as well. When I persisted, not forgetting to mention casually that I was from New England, I saw he began to weaken somewhat. But it was not until I had taken a greenback from my reticule and slipped it across the desk surreptitiously that I knew I had won. For after a swift glance about the little office to see if he was observed, he quickly concealed the money beneath a pile of papers and pulled a blank form toward him. He began to pepper me with questions. Did I, he asked, have adequate place to house the Negroes?

I told him I had houses aplenty and they would be put in good order.

His rabbit's nose twitched again. And did I understand that the contract must include a plot of ground where the Negro could raise his vegetables and that they must be fed as well as housed?

I signified to Mr. Peake that this was understood. He took up his pencil.

"And where is your place, miss?"

"It is the plantation known as Seven Chimneys."

His pencil poised in mid-air.

"Seven Chimneys, you say, miss? Down where the river runs into the sound?"

"Yes."

He chewed his straggly mustache nervously and then in a halting voice began a garbled explanation of why it might be difficult to obtain the Negroes when I needed them.

"But there are so many hereabouts. Surely there can be no difficulty," I remonstrated.

He hemmed and hawed and went into another tiresome preamble. The Leighs over on Butler Island had the best of the Negro labor contracted; Major Meade over on Canon's Point was going to use a hundred Negroes at ploughing time. If I would drop back later—in the meantime he would see what he could do. . . .

I was somewhat puzzled as Rupert and I left the place, and I remembered some of my earlier misgivings about Seven Chimneys. The shuttered look on the face of the captain of the steamboat, the wondering eyes of the storekeeper's wife, when they learned I was Seven Chimneys-bound. Now, I found the same withdrawal in Mr. Peake's rabbity, twitching countenance, and my common sense told me that this could not be caused solely by the strangeness of Saint Clair LeGrand's wife. However, I was not discouraged. Too well I knew that when one agrees to pay, there are but few difficulties that cannot be overcome.

Now Rupert and I turned toward the other side of Darien where, I had learned, I would find the slovenly abode of one Tom Gribble who might be hired to repair the rice machine. After my bargain with this shifty-eyed "pore white," he told me of a neighbor farther on who had a mule for sale. He was even accommodating enough to clap his torn straw hat over his bleached hair and conduct me there, where I dickered successfully for the animal.

Busy with my plans for beginning work on Monday, I had retraced our path toward Darien hardly conscious of where I went; but now my thoughts were interrupted by Rupert, who suddenly stopped dead in his tracks. "There's Uncle Roi," he said. I saw the brown-clad figure approaching on the dancing Sans Foix. When he caught sight of us he straightway reined the mare and came toward us.

I looked down at Rupert who still stood motionless in his tracks, his face revealing conflicting emotions. It was as if he exerted his young will to hold back from a pleasure he would welcome.

"Come, Rupert," I chided, "are you not going to say good day to your Uncle Roi?"

"Papa said that I was not to speak to him."

"Your father has given me no such instructions," I reminded him. "Go—say good day to your Uncle Roi."

His face lighted and dropping my hand he ran forward to meet the figure in brown buckskin.

"Uncle Roi!" he cried.

Roi LeGrand gave me a hail with an outflung hand and with the other caught Rupert to him and tousled his hair. "Hello, Rupert boy!"

I came up with them. "Good day, sir."

"Hello, Hester Snow. And what do you two do in Darien? Have you come to the carnival?"

"Carnival?"

"Didn't you know? There is a carnival in Darien. With a spinning jinny."

Rupert clutched my hand. "Oh, Hester! Let's go to the carnival," he pleaded.

"Where is this carnival?" I asked.

"In a cleared spot in the woods, other side of town."

"And what is it like?"

"Dull enough unless one has little amusement." He looked at me significantly.

"There are animals, I suppose."

"A moth-eaten monkey and a bear. And a couple of piney rooters—"

"And a—what did you call it—a spinning jinny?"

"Yes. There is a spinning jinny."

Rupert danced up and down in his eagerness. "What is a spinning jinny, Uncle Roi?"

"A contraption that goes round and round like this," he demonstrated with his hand, "while music plays."

Rupert was ecstatic. "Hester, please, let's go."

I laid a calming hand on his shoulder. "Tell me, sir, is this place you speak of in walking distance?"

"It is a longish walk, but there is Sans Foix."

"Three on one horse?"

"You and Rupert together weigh no more than one. Sans Foix will not know," he smiled.

I considered the matter while Rupert tugged my hand. Looking into his eager face, I thought it was true, what Roi had said. Rupert had too little of amusement. I decided we would go to the carnival.

Roi swung me up on Sans Foix's back easily, explaining how I could use the horn of the saddle, and it became almost like a lady's sidesaddle. Rupert was in front of me, and the boy straddled the horse, his face beaming with the excitement of adventure. Then, getting up behind me, Roi reached around and gathered the reins in his hand. To do so his arm must encircle me, but I considered it would be overprudish to notice it. And so we rode off toward the forest.

It was pleasant, that ride through the woods. The autumn leaves crisped beneath Sans Foix's feet and the air was sweet and cool. Partridges whistled and larks rose, singing as they went. And I thought that never had I seen such primeval woods as these woods of Georgia— cypress, live-oak and sweet-smelling bay, all matted together with smilax that swung from one tree to another and then swung back again.

Yet with all there was for me to see, I must admit I was more keenly aware of the lean brown hand that held the reins, of the scent of tobacco that came from the shoulder pressing mine. At once I was impelled—by what I do not know—to turn my head and look into the tanned face at my shoulder. Roi's eyes smiled down into mine and his left arm pressed me close.

What possessed me I do not know, for certainly I was never one to yield to idling flirtation or to man's flattery. Indeed, I held in contempt those loose women who did. But now I felt the blood mount to my cheeks like any silly schoolgirl's. And it was more anger at myself than at him that made me draw my body straight so that it escaped the touch of his arms.

But he said nothing, and so after a while we came to the carnival, which was set up in a small clearing. There we dismounted and while Roi tethered Sans Foix to a tree, Rupert and I went toward it. It was, as Roi had said, a dull affair, a circle of tawdry painted tents, their center dominated by the famous spinning jinny, which was nothing but two wide planks centered on a revolving base, with rude chairs at the planks' ends. But the Darien folk had flocked to enjoy themselves. Each trip the spinning jinny made its seats were filled, and before one tent as many as fifteen people laughed boisterously at the antics of two black-face men who sang and danced and sold cough syrup between songs.

Rupert was enchanted. Indeed, it was hard to resist the laughter and fine holiday feeling. Even I was swept into it, and as eagerly as Rupert I let Roi take us inside the tents for the minstrel show and the wild man. Between shows we drank pink lemonade and ate gingersnaps. At the shooting gallery where for ten cents you had three chances to shoot at a villainously painted picture of General Sherman, I felt a tug of shame when Roi's bullet pierced that brave soldier squarely in the wild blue eye the artist had given him.

But the crowd roared its approval. "Give it to him," they yelled, "the dam' Yankee."

Roi held out the prize to me, a tiny paper fan gay with flowers and birds. I thrust it into my reticule while his eyes looked into mine, gay with teasing laughter because I had seen him shoot General Sherman in the eye.

Dusk was filtering into the clearing and blurring the outline of the matted growth of forest that enclosed it when on Sans Foix we turned toward Darien again. Rupert, tired but happy, leaned his head against my breast as we rode, and suddenly I realized that I had come to lean against Roi. Instantly I stirred and straightened, but his arm drew me back gently and his lips touched my ear.

"You are a darling, Hester Snow," he said softly.

I did not speak, I could not rebuke him. Something strange

yet sweet swept through me. And it seemed to me that never had the world seemed so fair a place before. Even Darien was no longer the dull bleached town of white sand but a magic city whose lights beckoned to high adventure.

But no sooner had he lifted me from Sans Foix at the wharf and my feet were firm on the ground once more than the enchantment passed. Darien was Darien again, and I was a Yankee schoolmarm who had been embraced on a country road like a common serving girl.

I could not meet his eyes for shame as he slid the sleepy Rupert down into my waiting arms. He dismounted himself and stood, his arm cupped carelessly about the mare's neck.

"Good night," I said, still not lifting my eyes from Rupert who drooped against my skirts.

But he did not say good night just yet. Instead he asked, "How do you get along at Seven Chimneys?"

I forgot my recent shame, knowing his surprise when he heard what I had to say.

"Not badly. I now have the ordering of the house, the land, and the Negroes. Today I have purchased a mule and hired Tom Gribble to repair the rice mill."

He looked at me as though he did not believe me. "Ordering?" he repeated doubtfully.

"Yes. I am in charge of the planting and harvest. In all things I am to do as I think best." I paused, and when I spoke again I could not hold the triumph from my voice. "That, sir, is how I am getting along at Seven Chimneys."

He continued to look at me with a little smile—a strange smile, bold and mocking, yet with gentleness in it too.

"Hester Snow! So you have turned overseer?"

I could not help but laugh, so puzzled was his face. Yet I said stubbornly, "Seven Chimneys will be a profitable place again. You will see."

"And will you wear overalls?"

"Marsh lands rich as cream—"

"And boots? And a whip in your belt?"

"And plenty of Negro labor to be had—"

"Will you whip them when they loaf on their jobs?"

"It only needs a bit of money spent. A new plough, the rice mill fixed—"

He laughed then, and his laugh was less merry.

"There'll be no money for such things, Hester Snow. Not when there is wine to be bought and the table loaded with fancy foods. It's a way we southerners have. We are great on the luxuries, but the necessities we can do without."

I exclaimed impatiently, but his upraised hand stopped me. "But I believe that you'll make out, Hester. You have set your mind on improving things. And it's many and many a day since anyone did that."

"Yet many with a home like Seven Chimneys would work their fingers to the bone—"

He stared at me steadily in the gathering dusk. At last he said, "All weakness starts at the top, Hester. Remember that."

At first I did not gather his meaning, and when I did I was annoyed that he who took no responsibility whatsoever should criticize his brother who was so heavy-burdened. Flatly I told him so.

He laughed at me, dark, bitter laughter. "Saint heavy-burdened?" His mouth twisted wryly. "That's something new to hear at least!"

"And no help for him from you or anyone," I retorted, "His wife but another irresponsible child—"

For a moment he stood there unspeaking. Then he got upon Sans Foix and from the saddle looked down at me.

"I remember her when she first came to Seven Chimneys," he said slowly. "She was the sweetest thing I ever saw." He picked up the reins. "Be kind to her, Hester. In all that house she has no friend."

"No friend?" I exclaimed. "With her husband, her child, her mother-in-law—and aren't you her friend?"

He stared off toward the marsh where a mauve band of light lay on the horizon. "Yes," he said, "I would walk barefooted through hell for her." Then, suddenly, swiftly, he swung Sans Foix's head toward the forest and was gone. I was left standing there in the gathering night with Rupert whimpering sleepily at my skirts. And as we went toward the wharf where Vene waited in the boat, I thought upon what Roi had meant.

Chapter Six

As autumn wheeled into winter and the cool days came, those words of Roi's were in my mind many times and at each remembrance of them I resolved that when I could find the time I would be kind to Lorelie LeGrand. But before such an opportunity arrived, I became aware that Lorelie was not as oblivious to my presence as I had heretofore believed. One day, turning from a drawer of linens, I found her in the doorway of the room in which I worked, her wide eyes fixed upon me steadily. And when I explained that I sorted linens for Margot to mend, her mouth curved in a slow, scornful smile; and afterward, whatever I did or wherever I worked, I was conscious of her thin figure hovering.

Old Madame was another matter altogether, though I knew that she too was aware of the authority which I gradually assumed. But she constituted no problem; greedy old woman that she was, she only seemed to relax deeper into indolence, to take a sensual pleasure in the more comfortable life which was now hers. But if she was pleased because of the added comfort or because she knew it displeased her son's wife I could not decide, though I had come to know that she hated the younger woman and sought to harass her. Sometimes their enmity, for the most part held to slumbering malignant resentment, flared into the open. Often, seeing Rupert to bed, I would hear Lorelie's laughter (it was the laughter of madness) scream out in the drawing room below in response to something Old Madame had said; and at one such time when I went back down the stairs Lorelie's hurrying figure passed me, and she was panting like an animal in flight. But when I re-entered the drawing room Old Madame sat stolidly beside the fire, the picture of bland repose. "My son's wife is not well tonight, mademoiselle," she vouchsafed as I returned to my chair and picked up my embroidery. A little later she intoned meaningly, "My son has much to bear."

Such incidents did not disturb me. I was too keenly conscious of the emotional unbalance in Lorelie, the desire to persecute in the Old Madame. But I was concerned with their effect on Rupert, for I saw that he, lacking emotional balance himself, was caught in the storm seething between the two women and was constantly pulled in two directions. There were nights when Lorelie, pleasantly drunken, came down to pet and fondle him (and it was easy to see that she idolized the boy) and when Old Madame, who for the most part ignored the child, would maliciously and with promise of sweetmeats try to entice him from his mother's side. Then Lorelie, comprehending Old Madame's tactics, would clutch Rupert to her with fierce possessiveness. Old Madame, as if this was the victory for which she had battled, would spread her hands and say with ominous quiet, "Never mind, Rupert—your mother is not herself tonight," and Rupert, turning narrowed, questioning eyes up to the tortured face above him, would twist from her arms with, "Let me go, mama—let me go!"

At daybreak each day I was up and setting the Negroes about their tasks and when they had ambled off to cotton field and rice bottom, I followed to see that yesterday's work had not been slighted. And each morning—or so it seemed to me—I found signs of idling and laziness. The palmetto scrub dug up and left where it had fallen, the cotton land but half burned off, though Sey and Boy had taken enough time to do the job twice over. And what irked me most of all was the bland innocence with which they met my scolding.

I wearied too of their childish complaints of "de misery" that held them from their work, and I learned that each had his own particular misery which he used without conscience both as reason and alibi. Maum Lucie had a misery in "de back" and many days crept about the kitchen bent almost double. Margot had "de misery in de haid" and wore a wet white cloth to "hol de misery down," Vene had "de misery" in his feet. He "allus had trouble wid his feet," and Sey and Boy, big hulking Negroes though they were, would clasp their stomachs and with rolling eyes groan dismally whenever they preferred not to work. Yet on Saturdays when they came to the makeshift office I had set up for myself in the small pantry just off the kitchen, they expected their full pay regardless of the days the "misery" had kept them idle.

But, though they idled and spent twice the time on each task that it required, the work did go forward, and when December came—mild and warm it was, and more like April—the cotton land lay burned and cleared and Boy and Sey had started on the clearing and cleaning of the rice channels. In the wood-lot the logs were stacked high against the fence, and around the stone ledge of the spring house I had had Margot store wild honey in piggins. Maum Lucie's apple jelly and black-berry jam, conserved with much grumbling you may be sure, stood jeweled row on row in the big pantry, and Margot's sweet-smelling bayberry candles were wrapped in neat piles beside the cakes of lye soap which we had boiled in the iron kettles in the yard.

Even their superstitions, whether truth or sham, proved another obstacle. "De moon ain' right" interfered with the simplest duty. The hoot owl's shuddering cry meant death if shrilled too near the house at dusk; and when Maum Lucie burned her bread it was not her carelessness she blamed, but some unknown enemy who "conjur" her.

I knew this to be a part of the voodooism brought to America long ago by the African natives. Yet if I dismissed lightly the dark tales Maum Lucie told me, I knew she and the other Negroes believed them. And when I found her brewing mysterious potions over the kitchen fire and asked her tartly "whom she planned to conjure now," her birdlike eyes would meet mine, as cold as ice, and she would tell me they were her medicines, made from herbs and plants, with which she kept the house supplied. This one, she said, pointing her skinny forefinger, was the cure for fevers, a mixture of wartroot and sassafras; and this stopped nosebleed, and this powdery mix-ture if worn about your neck kept off the bloody flux.

From Vene I learned that the redheaded scorpion, which lay in the swampy undergrowth and surveyed you with sharp bright eyes, barked like a dog. (Though he admitted when I pressed him that never had he heard one bark.) And he told me too that the lizards which slid through the garden lived in the stumps of trees. He named them for me—the race nag and orange tail and the various ground species. And he called me to see the chameleon in leaf-green coat and white waistcoat and related how in mating season he advanced to his lady, bowed solemnly and expanded to full glory his throat fan of brilliant pink. "He sho' is a braggin' man," he finished.

And it was from Vene I learned of "mornglowm"—that eerie hour of daybreak when the hants came out. It was then, he added, that the woman in white walked along the Mary-de-Wander wringing her ghostly hands. And when I asked him who the woman was and why she was foolish enough to walk on quicksand, he looked at me with eyes that marveled at my audacity and told how she had been "de young mist'is" and how her old husband had put her out during the big storm. And ever since when she walked along the Mary-de-Wander wringing her hands, it meant that somebody would be "drownded."

I do not know if it was the story of this unfortunate woman that made me think of Lorelie LeGrand, but I recalled again Roi's request that I be kind to her. And so on a night when Saint Clair was away, I stopped at her door after I had seen Rupert to bed, and rapped.

When I entered she was sitting before the fire—which was all but out—gazing into its graying embers desolately. Her wide brown eyes turned toward me. "Yes, Miss Snow?"

"If you are not sleepy, I thought I would sit and chat a while, Mrs. LeGrand."

She stirred restlessly in her chair. "Yes, do. Sit down, Miss Snow. This—this is a surprise."

"I have often wished to come, but I didn't know if you'd like—" I hesitated.

She broke in hastily. "Yes. You're quite right. Quite right." Her eyes wavered away from mine, her mouth grimaced. "You understand, often—often I am not—not well."

I saw that the effort of her subterfuge excited her, and so I directed the conversation into calmer channels. I spoke of Rupert, of how quickly he learned, confident that discussion of her son would please and interest her, but as I talked she only stared at the wall behind my head, and when I finished, somewhat lamely I must admit, she sat silent and continued to stare into space.

I sought about in my mind for another topic of conversation, for I realized that I must bear its weight. This woman was either too ill (or too drink-befuddled) to talk coherently. And so in as soothing a manner as I could muster up, I began to speak of Seven Chimneys, of how its strangeness and weird beauty had first impressed me.

She came to life then. "Yes, yes, I thought it strange too at first," she assented feverishly.

"Where was your home before you came, Mrs. LeGrand?"

"In Savannah. My home was there—in Savannah. I had such a beautiful home, Miss Snow. Just Tante Marie and the servants and me. At night when I am trying to sleep, I remember the cape jessamines in the garden. They were so cool —so sweet. . . ." Her voice trailed, died.

"Do you go back often?"

Again that dreadful grimace. "Often? Oh, no. Not since Tante Marie died. Just think, Miss Snow, other people live in my home now. Other people that I don't know. I always dream that Rupert and I are back there." She turned her ravaged eyes imploringly on me, "Now we can never go—"

She sat staring into space disconsolately then suddenly rose and, crossing to a table, brought me a small gold-framed miniature which she put in my hand. "Look," she said, "that is I on the day of my marriage to Saint. Do you not think me pretty?"

I looked at the young girl in the picture, dimpling up at me, and knew a great pity for the haggard woman who waited for my answer. "You were lovely," I told her, and indeed she had been if the little painted miniature spoke truly.

She almost snatched it from my hand, and holding it tightly, she looked at it hungrily, then began to talk in her light, hurrying voice. "I was the prettiest girl in Savannah, and I know now that I was the happiest. But I didn't know it then. You see I had never known unkindness, never even an unkind word. I didn't know there could be unkindness in the world. There were just Tante Marie and the servants and me, and in the morning old Benbow brought me my chocolate and

I could lie in bed and look out in the garden where the cape jessamines bloomed." She raised her eyes and looked steadily. "When Rupert and I go back I'll be happy again like that, won't I?"

I assured her as I would have assured an unhappy child, and in an effort to turn her mind from the past I spoke of other things. How about Christmas, I asked. Should I plan a tree for the Negroes—provide gifts for Tawn's two boys? She must advise me, I told her, for in all such matters I found they managed differently here.

Again I saw she didn't even hear me. And I knew a tug of discomfort at the light that had come into her eyes as she stared at me. It was an overcunning so near to madness that quickly I rose to go. But her thin outstretched hand caught my skirt. "Miss Snow—"

"Yes, Mrs. LeGrand—"

"Why don't you go away—"

"Go away—?" I echoed.

"Yes."

"But—" I began but her hurrying voice cut across mine.

"You know things are bad here. You know that since you came they are worse. You said yourself that the place is strange. Then why don't you go—go quickly before it is too late?"

As I looked down into the overbright eyes turned up to mine I could not repress the shudder of disgust which the normal always feels for that which is abnormal. Yet I felt pity too, and as kindly as possible I spoke to her.

"You are tired, Mrs. LeGrand. Another time we will talk of this. Now you should go to bed and rest."

Not by an inch did she alter her position nor the hold of her hand on my skirt. "Don't speak to me as if you think I am mad," she said slowly, a smile curving her lips. "Or as if you don't understand. You do understand, don't you—and you don't believe I'm mad, do you?"

"Another time—" I began and moved as if to go, but still she did not release my dress.

"Once I was young," she spoke monotonously, "and I came to this house, and there was no one to do me the kindness I try to do you—no one to tell me to go. And so I stayed. I was sucked down into all the ugly horrid things—and now I cannot escape. And now I am one of the ugly things, too." Her hand tightened its grasp. "Will you go?" Suddenly her voice softened and cajoled.

"You are ill—you should see a physician," I said.

Before I could add more, she released my skirt and, throwing her head back, said in a voice I could scarcely hear, "See a physician so that Saint can swear I am mad?" Swiftly she rose and sweeping to the door opened it and held it wide. "You are like the others, I see. You are strong, but not strong enough to escape the evil Seven Chimneys holds. Good night, Miss Snow."

Back in my room, try as I would, I could not erase her wasted figure from my mind. I resolved that the next time I saw Roi I would tell him that according to his wish I had been kind to his sister-in-law; and I would tell him also that she had passed beyond the place where kindness mattered.

But it was not Roi to whom I spoke of Lorelie. It was many a day before I saw him again. Instead, it was to her husband.

A day or two later, as I raked the leaves with which autumn had blanketed the path between landing and house I saw the longboat, paddled by Vene, coming up the channel. And though I continued my raking I watched Saint Clair as he stepped onto the landing and in his customary leisurely manner sauntered up the path. When he came to where I stood, he paused and surveyed me with the cynical amusement which he always conferred on my "tasks." That look, coupled with his impeccable elegance, immediately made me conscious of the dust on my shoes—and my unkempt appearance.

"Do you never stop your infernal working?"

"The paths must be cleared," I retorted, then felt myself flushing as I realized how pedantic the words were.

"They went without clearing many years."

I stifled the impulse to tell him that for years the whole place had been slovenly but I said nothing. Instead, I leaned on the rake, waiting for him to go on.

"And," he continued, "if it is necessary to your soul's good that they be cleared, why not let Vene do it?"

"Vene had to go to Darien today to meet you."

"If I interfere with your passion for housekeeping," the indolent voice was tinged with sarcasm, "I am sorry."

"It is of no importance."

Leaning on my rake I watched him go, then on sudden impulse called to him. "Mr. LeGrand—wait, please."

He halted and waited until I, carrying the rake, came up with him. "Yes?" he said.

"I wish to speak to you—about your—your wife."

"What about my wife?"

For a moment I stood there seeking for the proper words with which I might say what I wished to say, knowing that human nature can accept any affliction more easily than madness in those they love. But before I could shape my thoughts his voice prodded impatiently. "Well, Miss Snow?"

"I think your wife should see a physician."

"Is Mrs. LeGrand ill?" he drawled.

"Isn't she?" I asked gravely.

"If you are speaking of—" he paused, "her usual ailment, no physician can cure her of that."

I knew he referred to her drinking. "Perhaps that is the cause, but has it occurred to you that her mind—?"

"Her mind?" Something flickered in his eyes and vanished and for a breath he stood there motionless. Then he asked slowly, "You mean you think her mad?"

"I certainly do not think she is sane."

"You have noticed instances?"

I remembered Lorelie's thin hand clutching my dress, heard her voice cajoling. But these I would not mention, though Saint Clair's voice prodded again. "You *have* noticed something?"

"I think she needs medical care—there are institutions where they help such illnesses." Quietly I added, "There is Rupert to think of."

He continued to stand there, his eyes looking across at me without the least shadow of expression. Finally he said, "Perhaps you are right. Tonight I will speak to Mrs. LeGrand about consulting a doctor." Seemingly no more perturbed than when he stepped from the longboat, he continued his way to the house and I went back to my raking. But as I raked, my thoughts were upon Lorelie LeGrand and I was asking myself if I had been right to suggest madness to her husband; or had I judged her emotional unbalance (which might be due to some real physical disability) too harshly?

But that night when again I heard her weeping I decided I had acted wisely. No doubt she wept because her husband advised her to see a doctor; surely only a mad woman would weep so desolately for so small a cause.

Whatever Saint Clair said to his wife it bore immediate results. For the very next day, accompanied by Margot, she went to Savannah. She came down to midday dinner dressed for her journey, a poignant figure not entirely stripped of beauty despite her emaciation and despairing eyes. And as I refilled Rupert's plate, I caught her watching me intently; and suddenly her voice broke across Rupert's chatter.

"Rupert is not so thin. He eats well—do you not think so, Miss Snow?"

"Rupert is much better, Mrs. LeGrand," I spoke calmly, "since he follows regular routine."

She agreed feverishly. "Yes, yes—routine." Her smile twisted. "Sometimes mothers are bad for their own children—aren't they, Miss Snow?"

"I wouldn't say that, Mrs. LeGrand. But it is true that mothers can be so fond of their children that it is not for the child's best interest."

She covered her face with her hand. "Yes, yes." The words were almost whispered. "I am a bad mother, but I cannot help it—I cannot help it."

Old Madame at the end of the table observed the distraught woman, her eyes bright with malicious triumph. "Control yourself, Lorelie," she advised in the same voice she would have used for a peevish child. "You should not let Rupert see you in this condition."

The week after Thanksgiving I went to Darien to learn from the rabbity Captain Peake at the Freedmen's Bureau how it stood regarding the Negro hands I must have. For now the time drew near when the cotton land must be turned and allowed to lie fallow before planting, when the rice bottoms must be ploughed and ditched, the drains and quarter drains put in, the banks thrown higher and made secure against the alligators that sometimes tore them down. Oh! there was work aplenty to be done if all was to be ready for the planting.

In Darien, I found that Captain Peake had contrived well for me. He had—with what work and cleverness he was at great pains to inform me—arranged for fifty good, sound Negroes, half made up of families, the other half of Negro bucks. These, he pointed out again, must have housing on the place until after harvest, a small patch for garden stuff, and a pigpen if I'd allow it. This last, he explained, was not compulsory. And he seemed elated that for headsman he had procured one Shem. He had good sense, did Shem, and a way of handling the gang which would save me a mort of trouble, the captain pointed out.

On a bit of paper he figured out the weekly cost of this, and when I looked at it I was staggered by the sum. I could not help but wonder, though he had said he would obtain the money, where Saint Clair would lay hands on it. But this I did not betray to Peake. Instead I folded the slip and thrust it into my reticule and assured him coolly that on the fifteenth of January everything would be in readiness for the Negroes at Seven Chimneys. Meantime I told myself I must speak to Saint Clair and remind him that the money must be forthcoming as he had promised.

The very next day I set the Seven Chimney Negroes, even Margot and Maum Lucie, busy redding up the Negro cabins. The mattresses must be stuffed with fresh straw, the walls white-washed and the floors scrubbed clean. I even dipped further into my little hoard of money to buy gay calico for the windows. In the cleared spot before the cabins where the ground was worn satin-smooth, I had Sey and Boy repair the brick oven where the gang cook would prepare the food, and I laid in a great supply of dried field peas, salt pork, corn meal, and molasses. These, Captain Peake had told me, constituted the main diet of the Negroes.

But as I directed and watched to see that directions were followed, I had my mind upon Saint Clair and the money, and I anxiously awaited his return from Savannah. I had some vague idea that he would procure it from a bank.

Captain Peake had informed me that many planters were doing so to make a fresh start, and I knew that such transactions take time. It would be an end to all my hopes if something went amiss and the money was not forthcoming after all. Not only would my own money have been wasted, but all my planning and effort as well. More important still, Seven Chimneys would lie idle and unproductive for another year.

But the days passed and Saint Clair did not return. Each morning when I waked (so anxious I was for assurance) the first thought that flashed into my mind was, "Perhaps he will come today," and each night my last waking one, "Perhaps he will come tomorrow." But the days dragged on, one into another, and still he did not come.

On Friday the weather changed. When I went down at five, my usual time for rising, Maum Lucie, raking the ashes from her banked fire, said "De curlews is flying inwards— dat mean de big stawm on de way." And when I asked her what she meant she told me how when the big storm rolled in from the outward sea, the birds fled into the forests for safety. I took this for more of her foolish superstition and paid but scant attention to her, but when I went into the back yard to ring up the other Negroes, I saw that surely enough the birds were flying inland in great flocks. The sun which had lasted since Thanksgiving had given way to leaden racing clouds; the Sound was no longer a smooth sheet of saffron but coiled and rolled like some huge reptile.

At breakfast Rupert chattered of the storm. When it broke it rained and rained, he said, and the water rose and we couldn't even get to Darien. Sometimes the waves were so high that it looked as if they would sweep over the water-wall. And papa had said that sooner or later the water would take Seven Chimneys. And always, during the storm, somebody was drowned; they were silly enough to go out in a boat and, pouf! the boat went over.

The day wore on without any lifting of the darkness. At noon Margot had to light the candles which gave but a drear half twilight. Old Madame sitting by the fire stopped me at every opportunity, and I found that she too wanted to talk of the big storm, and recall, for my benefit, the year when the

Pulaski foundered in it. Finally, I could bear it no more, and throwing my shawl about my shoulders I left the house and plunged across the land to the rice mill to see that it was safe against the coming rain. It would be a cruel trick indeed if the newly mended machinery should be rusted and put out of order before we had as much as used it.

It was while I was closing the windows of the rice mill that the rain began to fall, huge pattering drops at first, but mounting to a torrent soon. It pelted the earth with tremendous force. And standing in the doorway of the mill I watched it, watched too the Sound being whipped into greater and greater fury as the wind swept over it to the land, where it seized the branches of trees and bent them groundward as though it would tear them to pieces.

But there was no fear within me. On the other hand I was stimulated by the wind and the rain. Too many times had I seen the gales roar on my New England coast, felt the cold salt spray against my face. And when the downpour showed no signs of slackening but rather increased in force, I decided there was nothing for me to do but make my way through it to the house. After bolting the door with care I started across the land, blurred and strange now under its mantle of water.

Lowering my head that I might better buffet the driving wall of water I ploughed over the land with difficulty, for the wind whipped my skirts about my ankles and impeded my progress. Already I was drenched to the skin. So I was not displeased when suddenly Sans Foix reined up beside me and Roi LeGrand held out his hand.

"Get up," he said and thrust out his booted foot that I might use it for stirrup.

He swung me into the saddle before him and reaching about me guided Sans Foix over the stubbled fields. But I saw that we were not headed for Seven Chimneys. Instead we went in the opposite direction. I turned and faced him.

"Seven Chimneys lies that way," I pointed out.

He laughed and suddenly he leaned forward and kissed me impudently on the mouth. I gasped and turned so he would not see the flush on my cheeks.

"Where are we going?" I demanded.

"To my place. You have never seen my place, have you?"

"I thought you lived in the dens with the foxes. And you owe me an apology, sir."

"For what?"

"I am not the sort of woman who lets any man kiss her," I said stiffly.

"I am not any man and I do not apologize. It was a sweet kiss if a moist one."

For me to have said more would have made me ridiculous in his eyes. I, who could talk boldly to Saint Clair and command the Negroes to service, had been rendered speechless by one kiss!

We had left the cleared land and plunged into the forest which was Seven Chimneys' horizon. Always I had wondered what lay beyond that wall of forest, and now I saw that it was a dark and gloomy place of sighing pines tortured by the wind, and that the narrow path along which Sans Foix picked her way so carefully was bound on either side by banks of ooze as black as tar.

A memory tinkled in my brain. "Are these the Black Banks?" I asked.

"Yes."

"Where the alligators live?"

He told me that the alligators did not live here but the place served as a sort of crossroads for them as they came up the creek on their way to the river. And as we crossed the now turbulent creek on a makeshift bridge of logs, he recalled a battle he had witnessed between two bull 'gators and how they had slashed the mud for fifty yards with their tails and their bellowing had shaken the earth for miles.

"And do you live here with the alligators?" I asked tartly.

"Soon you will see where I live," he told me.

And soon we came to it, an old building of tabby which had once served as a carriage house. It stood in a few cleared acres that had once been cultivated, but it was walled in on all sides by forest. And when we had alighted I looked around, conscious of more interest in the place than I would have him know.

"Is this your land?" I asked.

His face darkened. "I have no land," he replied shortly. "This is on the Contineau plantation. No one lives on the place now," he laughed, "except the ghosts the Negroes claim they see."

"Not the same ghost that walks on the Mary-de-Wander?"

He threw me a level glance. "Who told you that story?"

"Vene told me. That and others. I never heard of so many unfaithful wives—do you think it was the climate?" I asked in pretended innocence.

Stooping, he picked up a stone and hurled it across the field. "The southern husband has always been a tyrant," he said casually. "He must be waited on hand and foot. He allows his wife no opinions except his own. No wonder the wives rebel. But come, Hester, let's not stand in the rain. There is a good fire on my hearth."

Opening the door that stood flush with the ground he led me up the narrow steps that rose to the floor above the stables, empty now of carriage or horse but retaining nevertheless their smell of leather and hay. At the top of the stairs he opened another door and I found myself in a long, low room with a gabled roof. On the hearth a log fire burned.

He took my dripping shawl and spread it on a chair near the blaze. "Isn't this better than Seven Chimneys, Hester?"

I did not answer, but I found the place agreeable. From the rafters that braced the roof he had hung his hunting trophies —fox tails, deer antlers, and even the fierce head of a black bear. There were, I saw, but scant furnishings—a narrow cot, a chair or two, and at the hearth a hand-hewn settle. But all was clean, and corner shelves held cooking and eating gear.

"Do you cook for yourself?" I asked surprised.

Lightly he said that he did. "Sit here, Hester," he ordered, "and I will brew you such a cup of coffee as you've never tasted. At least not in Georgia."

I sat down on the settle. With deftness he prepared the coffee and put it on the fire, then fetched cups and saucers from the shelf and placed them on the stone hearth for warming.

"You would be surprised to know the good suppers I can manage in one frying pan," he laughed. And yet, remembering the vast unused rooms at Seven Chimneys, the table with its never-lessening load of rich foods, I could not help but wonder why he chose this rude way of living when there was the other.

"Why do you live here, like this, Roi?"

He poured the coffee into the cups and added hot milk from a saucepan. "Because I prefer it. Here, Hester—drink this. And I will tell you the secret of good coffee."

"But it isn't natural that you choose this when you could have Seven Chimneys," I persisted.

He stirred his coffee thoughtfully. "I do not like Seven Chimneys. I would not live there."

"But you did live there once, Rupert says."

"Yes."

"Then why did you leave?"

He continued to stir his coffee and gave me no answer.

"Did you quarrel with your brother?"

He laughed shortly. "Did I ever do anything else but quarrel with him?"

"And that is why you live here?"

He drank his coffee quickly, then rising put his cup on the mantelshelf. "Hester—"

"Yes?"

"Don't you know that Saint and I are not—true brothers? We are only half-brothers. We had the same father, but different mothers. My mother was the daughter of a dirt farmer. She died when I was born."

Slowly I said, "But you did live at Seven Chimneys, didn't you, Roi?"

"Yes," he spoke quickly. "My grandmother cared for me until I was half grown, and when she died, my father took me there. I was raised to have all that Saint had. As long as my father lived it was my home."

I stared at him without speaking, thinking that at least on this point Flora McCrackin was correctly informed. Roi was the bastard son of Pierre LeGrand. And yet as he sat across the hearth from me, son of farmer's daughter or no, he carried the stamp of breeding upon him as much as ever his brother did.

Now, suddenly, he cast seriousness from his face and voice

as he might throw off a cape and crossing sat on the settle beside me. "Is it because you are such a prying woman that I like you?" he asked impudently.

But I would not be diverted. "Tell me, why did you leave Seven Chimneys?"

He lounged beside me, his boots stretched toward the blaze, and answered grudgingly. "After the surrender, when I came home, things were changed—"

"You mean there was less money, and no slaves?"

He looked at me steadily, his eyes ashine with mockery. Then he laughed as if vastly entertained, but immediately turned grave again. "Very well, Hester. Let's say there was less money and no slaves. And now for heaven's sake let's forget business. And talk about . . . your mouth for instance. Has anyone ever told you how sweet your mouth is?"

"Don't be ridiculous!" I drew up stiffly.

"Or how your brows lift like wings?"

"This is utter nonsense—" I began, but halted, for his arms were around me. He pulled me close, so close I could feel his hard frame pressed to mine. With my hands I pushed against his chest and tried to free myself, but he caught my hands in the vise of one of his. Suddenly I lost the desire to free myself. Roi's mouth was on mine, hard and cruel. I was drowned in a wave of feeling that swept the world away. I thought of nothing, wanted nothing except the nearness of his body and his mouth that held such sweetness even in its hurt. In all my life I had not dreamed that this could be, or realized that buried deep within me lay this magic which transcended the world and time and space.

Only when his hands began to fumble at the buttons on my bodice and his warm fingers cupped my breast did reason clear and cold cut the sweet daze which held me. Then with all my strength I pushed him from me. "No, no!" I cried.

He released me so quickly that I was near to falling, and springing to his feet crossed swiftly to the chair which held my shawl. "Come," he said roughly and laid the shawl about my shoulders. "I will ride you to the clearing."

I followed him down the steps and let him lift me to the saddle but when he sprang up behind me and held me close I stiffened, for I was shamed beyond telling when I remembered how, in that shabby room, I had been swept almost beyond prudence by the bastard son of a dirt-farmer's daughter.

Now I sat rigid and kept my eyes upon the path ahead.

But he only laughed softly and drew me closer. Then his whispering voice went on close to my ear. "I've waited for you such a long time."

His voice angered me anew. Such love had no place in my plans—that I must make him understand.

"I shall never forget," I said, and hardly knew my own voice, hateful and cold, "that the only time I was under your roof—you took advantage of me."

"You mean because I kissed you?"

"Yes."

He did not speak for a space and we rode on through the rain. When he finally spoke his voice was as hateful as ever mine had been. "So you are a 'good' woman—eh, Hester?"

I stared ahead in the rain, my eyes searching for the clearing where he must put me down. He spoke again, this time coolly. "I do not think I like you, Hester, since you see wrong where no wrong was intended."

"Here is the clearing." I could hardly speak, for it came over me that I wanted nothing so much in all the world as to turn back to his arms—his lips.

He reined Sans Foix and I slid to the ground, then turned and looked up into his face.

"Whether you like me or no," I threw the words at him, "is of no import to me. But understand this once and for all: I am a decent woman."

He laughed down into my eyes. "I wish you joy in your decency, Hester—though I've heard it makes a cold bedfellow. And remember, Hester, I said I do not like you, but I said nothing of love. I love you—mean as you are!" Before I could frame a retort he wheeled Sans Foix around and galloped off toward the wall of forest. And I, holding my shawl close about me, plodded through the rain and mud Seven Chimney-way.

Chapter Seven

As I entered the house by the back door I heard the front door, driven by the wind, slam to. Peering through the half-dark of the hall I saw Saint Clair ascending the stairs. At last he had come home. Now I could speak to him about the money. Determined to waste no time about it, I turned back toward the kitchen. I would give him time enough to reach the turret room, then follow him with the bottle of brandy which I knew would win a welcome, even for me.

Crossing the back porch into which the rain swept in wind-hurtled gusts I entered the kitchen. Vene, who had brought Saint Clair from Darien in the boat, stood at the hearth, soaking wet, beating his hands together to bring warmth to them. By his side crouched Maum Lucie and Margot, listening with wide, intent eyes to something that he whispered.

At my entrance Vene's eyes slid away guiltily. Hurriedly he began to speak of the difficult time he had had to bring the boat through the sound. "De water is bilin'," he said. "By night de boat couldn't a' live' in it."

I knew he but dissembled and I would not be sidetracked.

"Is that why you three look as if you'd seen a ghost?" I inquired sharply.

Margot's bold eyes flashed and Maum Lucie's withered mouth pursed in a way that meant she was displeased. She spoke up pertly. "We wuz talking 'bout ghosties all right."

"The woman in white again, I suppose?"

Maum Lucie's eyes were more than ever like an old bird's. She said slowly, "She walked agin las' night."

"On the Mary-de-Wander, of course?"

"Yassum."

I laughed—then stopped short and ordered Vene to fetch

the brandy from the cellar. "Then get yourself into some dry clothes," I told him, "or it will be *your* ghost walking the Mary-de-Wander."

I waited at the hearth for the brandy while Margot came and went between dining room and kitchen, setting the table. Her eyes were smoldering, her manner of moving revealed her displeasure. And Maum Lucie continued to crouch at the fire, her eyes staring into the flames vacantly, as if there were no supper to be prepared.

I scolded her. "Stop worrying about ghosts and get about the supper. Don't you know there are no such things as ghosts?"

She stood unmoving and her voice intoned, "A person sees whut dey sees." She was as ominous as if she chanted dire incantations.

"And you saw her, I suppose?"

"No'm—not dis time. I *has* seed her—but not dis time."

"Then who did see her—and when?"

"Tawn. Tawn seed her. Last nite— Tawn wuz bawn wid a caul—she is a conjur woman."

"Tawn!" My anger flared and I almost hissed the name of the lazy wench who had nothing better to do than stir up these ignorant darkies with her tales of ghosts and cauls. Then and there I resolved that when I spoke to Saint Clair about the money I would get the business of Tawn settled once and for all.

I found him, when I had ascended the stairs to the turret room, already in his patched dressing gown, sorting some papers that lay on the card table before him, his face, if possible, bleaker than usual. The headings on the papers were revealing: *Gene Poitiers—Table Delicacies—Nicholas—Choice Vintages.* This, I surmised, was reckoning day.

He did not so much as look up when I entered, and so without speaking I opened the brandy and poured it for him. He took it and sipped it leisurely, one hand still sorting the bills. Finally he looked up.

"Did you want something?"

"Yes."

"Well?"

"I have arranged at Darien for the extra Negroes we need.

They are to come the fifteenth of January. Will you have the money?"

His pale eyes met mine, stared into mine steadily, but he did not answer for a moment and I was shaken by irritation. "You understand I must know before I go further with my arrangements," I said flatly. "Have you been able to arrange about the money?"

Quietly he said, "I have the money."

"You have arranged then?"

Suddenly he stood and went to the fireplace, but he continued to stare at me. I noticed that the pupils of his eyes, so seldom revealed, were pale gray and ringed with black.

He said, still quietly, "I tell you I have the money. How much will it take?"

I explained, and I could not conceal my satisfaction at the bargain I had made with Captain Peake. "So you see," I finished, "I will only have to carry them, provide food and small moneys for incidentals, all of which will be deducted from their wages when we settle with them in full."

"When will that settlement be made?"

"When the crops are made and sold."

He stood there a moment, then went to stand before one of the high windows and stared out at the stormy night. Then suddenly as if he had reached some sort of decision he wheeled, and going to the carved chest unlocked and opened a drawer and withdrew a package of greenbacks. For a minute he stood looking down at them, his white fingers touching them almost affectionately as if he loved them. Then he came over to me.

"I have managed," his mouth twisted wryly, "by hook or crook to lay my hands on five thousand dollars. Do you think you can manage on that?"

Stifling the disappointment that flared through me because the sum was so small, I did a swift problem in mathematics. The Negroes must be carried. There were a half-hundred of them to be fed and clothed, a team of oxen and ploughs to be bought, along with the other implements necessary for the work—harrows, hoes, and such. And added to these were food and clothes, all the small incidentals which the running of a house demands. My mind for an instant wavered away from the huge problem all this would present, and I knew a half-resolved temptation to say it could not be done with so small a sum. But in the next instant I knew I would do it—I must do it. It would mean counting every bit of food that went into each mouth, making each dollar do the work of two, but the rewards would be worth the stinting and struggle.

While I stood there thinking furiously, I was conscious of his waiting figure, so still it might have lacked life. Now I raised my eyes to meet his.

"I can do it."

Without a word he held the sheaf of greenbacks toward me. When I had taken them I saw the habitual little yawn, and he said carelessly and as if it were of no importance, "Tomorrow you'd better get that to the Darien bank. Now, is that all?"

"That is all."

I started toward the door, then remembering the matter of Tawn yet to be settled, I came back. "No, there is one more thing."

He had reseated himself at the card table; already the un-paid bills were slipping noiselessly through his fingers.

"Well?"

"It is the Negress Tawn."

The hands sorting the bills stilled suddenly.

"What about Tawn?"

"She refuses to work unless you give her orders. You understand, of course, that such insubordination undermines my control of the other Negroes. So I want you to instruct her that I must be obeyed."

Slowly he said, "Tawn must be left alone."

"Why should she be idle when the others must work? She lives on your bounty—she and her children."

"There are some things at Seven Chimneys that you cannot change, Hester."

"—And Tawn is one of them?"

"Tawn is one of them."

"Then I must be told why."

His hooded eyes lifted and stared at me levelly.

"You know perhaps that I have a younger brother. He doesn't live here now, but once he did. He was young—he saw but few women. Tawn was here—"

And then I understood, understood Margot's bold glances, Maum Lucie's pursed lips, Vene's secret laughter.

Saint Clair was speaking again. "Now you know why Tawn must be left alone, why she and her brats must be fed and clothed."

I managed through stiff lips, "Yes, I understand."

I left him sitting there and went about my tasks with a cold knot within my breast that lay like a stone. The whole world had turned ugly and bitter with the knowledge that Tawn's lover—father no doubt of the two small brown boys— had held me close, had kissed me. As long as I lived I could never be cleansed of that shame, I thought.

At five I went upstairs to wash my face and change into my green watered silk for supper, but at Lorelie's door I was held by the sound of her desolate weeping. Despair ran like an ominous undercurrent beneath it. I knew only too well what had happened. All the dark, dull day Margot had traveled second-storyward with brandy and Lorelie's lunch had come back untasted. Now I thought—and I could not keep contempt from the thought—she had reached the crying stage.

But as the crying persisted, I suddenly remembered Rupert must pass this door on his way to supper, and I went forward quickly and opened the door.

I was unprepared for what I found and, embarrassed, I halted in the doorway. Lorelie lay on the bed a crumpled figure, sobbing with the automatic rhythm of a child worn to death with crying but still uncomforted; and at the hearth, looking his usual imperturbable self, stood Saint Clair.

I said quickly, "I'm sorry—I didn't intend to intrude. I thought Mrs. LeGrand might be ill." I was about to withdraw when Lorelie sat up suddenly, her thin body twisting on the bed until she faced me. "I am—am sorry I disturbed you, Miss Snow."

"Is there anything I can do, Mrs. LeGrand?"

Her wide unseeing eyes turned to her husband, then came back to me. "No—no," she faltered, "only"—she leaned forward and her voice sank to a near-whisper—"only I just want to be left alone, just be left alone. . . ."

I glanced at the tall impassive figure at the hearth. He continued to regard his wife scornfully, and realizing that this was a scene in which I had no part, I withdrew, and closed the door behind me; but almost immediately, he followed. His face as he left her room was not a pleasant thing to see.

Yet as Old Madame, Rupert and I went into supper I could not blame Saint Clair overmuch. To come home to a wife drunken and disheveled, to a scene which to a fastidious man could only be revolting—it would be a poor husband indeed who did not censure a wife for such behavior, though, I reasoned, it was somewhat late in the day to censure Lorelie.

She came to the table as Margot brought in the dessert, still wearing her wrapper, her beautiful hair awry. For Rupert's sake I felt a twinge of uneasiness at what she might do or say. But I was needlessly alarmed. She sat staring at the walls smiling foolishly to herself now and then, as if she might possess a secret the thought of which brought her pleasure, crumbling the food on her plate with shaking fingers.

Afterwards we sat in the drawing room while the candles guttered in the wind that shook the house and rattled at the blinds. Old Madame and I at least made a pretense at conversation in an effort to surmount the depression that hovered over us like some gloomy bird. Lorelie sipped the brandy which Margot brought, her hands trembling as they carried the glass to her lips, trembling even more when she saw that Old Madame was watching her with unblinking gaze.

Rupert, tired from the long dull day, half dozed beside me, and rising, I told him he must go to bed. Willingly enough he stumbled to his feet, his small hand groping for mine.

"Say good night to your grandmother."

"Good night, grandmother."

"And now your mother—"

"Good night, mama."

Lorelie smiled crookedly and attempted to place her brandy glass on the small taboret at her side, but her uncertain hand fumbled and the glass splintered on the floor at her feet. She did not so much as notice but held out a shaking hand toward Rupert.

"Come here, darling boy."

His small body stiffened and I could not blame him over-much, for the wine had glazed her eyes and the silly drunken smile persisted. When she wheedled, "Come to your mama, beautiful boy," her voice was thick. "My beautiful, beautiful boy!"

Rupert's eyes were scornful. "You're drunk, mama," he said coldly. Dropping my hand he marched out of the room, his shoulders squared.

I followed him but not before I had seen the horror that widened Lorelie's eyes. Glancing back at the turn of the stairs I saw that she had crumpled in her chair and covered her eyes with her thin hands. And I saw too that Old Madame sat watching, her eyes clinging to that desolate figure like gray leeches.

As Rupert undressed I scolded him. Not harshly, for it seemed but natural to me that a sensitive boy should recoil from such a scene. He was too young to realize the dark paths human beings can come to travel, the depths to which, pulled down by a power stronger than themselves, they can fall.

Telling him good night I turned down the lamp and went out. As I closed his door I heard the wheels of Old Madame's chair on the way to her room. Lorelie was alone in the drawing room when I re-entered. She sat with her face in her hands and for what seemed an interminable time I sat there watching the tears crawl through her fingers.

When I could stand it no longer I rose and dried her hands with my handkerchief. She paid no more attention to me than if I had not been there; and I saw when I took her hands from her face that her eyes were as empty as a sleepwalker's.

Quietly I persuaded her to her room, helping her up the stairs, going with her into the disordered bedroom, urging her to bed. Fetching a basin from the washstand, I sponged her thin body, found a fresh nightgown in the chest and slipped it over her head. When I had tied the blue ribbon at the throat I brought her hairbrush and smoothed the light brown hair until it gleamed golden on the pillow. Then quietly I straightened the disordered room and at the last opened a window so that the cold wet air might clear it of the fetid vinous odor.

For a minute I leaned on the sill looking out at the night. The storm had ceased for the time being but the bellied clouds still scurried across the sky, pregnant with the promise of more rain, and I saw that the wind still tortured the trees and lashed the waters of the Sound. As I watched, a dark shape swooped swiftly, soundlessly upon its unsuspecting prey, then, as silently as it had come, floated upward, a limp shape dangling in its claws.

I lowered the window and went back to look at Lorelie. She lay with her eyes closed, but something of quietude had crept into her face. I dimmed the lamp beside her bed and started to leave the room. When I reached the door she spoke.

"Miss Snow."

"Yes, Mrs. LeGrand?"

"You have been very kind."

"Do you think you can sleep now?"

"I will be all right—thank you."

I hesitated. In the dim light she looked so young. Like a girl, almost, with her sheaf of hair and the blue ribbon at her throat. I knew a great pity for her.

"Shall I sit with you a while Mrs. LeGrand?"

"No, please. I will be all right."

I left her there in the dim room to wrestle with whatever devils she must face in the long night, knowing there was no comfort that I or anyone else could bring. But as I undressed in the raw cold of my room I felt guilt that I who had been so concerned with the house and the land during these past months had felt no concern at all for the mistress.

I did not sleep well that night. Through my dreams the ominous wind sifted and toward daybreak I heard the rain begin again. And even in my dreams I was ridden by a dark depression which caused me to toss and turn; and when I awakened I found that though the day was dark, my clock stood at six.

Shivering, I lighted my lamp and dressed, eager for the warmth of Maum Lucie's fire and companionship. But when I had thrust the last pin into my hair I stopped at the window and looked out upon the desolation wrought by the storm. Flowers and shrubs, beaten earthward, lay supine. Great limbs of trees hung low as if in weariness they had surrendered to the elements, and the channel lay swollen and writhing on land to which it had no right.

It was then that I saw Saint Clair and Vene on the landing, Saint Clair swathed in a long coat, his head bared to the rain. Both knelt on the wet planks of the landing. I could not see what they were doing, for their bodies obstructed my view. But I was curious about the errand which had forced them out so early in such weather.

It was when I descended the stairs that I realized something out of the ordinary had happened. Already a fire crackled on the drawing-room hearth and Old Madame, who never rose till nine, sat beside it fully dressed. In the rear of the hall Margot and Maum Lucie whispered, their eyes frightened, and I stopped to speak to them, ordering them to get busy about breakfast. Then I went in to Old Madame.

"Good morning, madame."

"Good morning, mademoiselle." Her hands fluttered. "This is a dreadful thing, mademoiselle."

"What has happened?"

"You have not heard?"

"I have just come down."

"My daughter-in-law drowned herself in the night."

I stared at her, unbelieving. "Drowned herself?" I repeated with the stupidity that comes of shock.

"They have just found her body washed up on the quagmire."

I stood staring into her face but I did not see her. I saw the worn rug, the dead embers dropped upon it from the fire. "I can't believe it," I cried. "I put her to bed last night. She was quiet when I left her, more rational than I have ever seen her."

Old Madame's eyes met mine stonily. "It has happened, mademoiselle," she intoned without expression.

Wheeling, I left her and ran through the hall and out the front door. Now I knew why Saint Clair knelt on the landing, what it was he knelt beside. I stumbled down the soaked path not caring that the rain pelted my face and drenched my clothes. At last I came to the landing and Saint Clair's side.

And then I saw her. She lay on the wet pine planking in

her scarlet cape, her hair dank and matted. And I saw that she still wore the nightgown I had put on her, the one with the blue ribbon at the throat.

If Saint Clair knew that I had come to stand beside him he gave no sign, but continued to chafe her wrists as if it were not obvious that she was beyond recall. Vene's eyes slanted up at me but dropped instantly and I stood there and watched that futile chafing.

It was too much to bear—the dark sky—the wind that moaned through the pines—the rain that fell—and Saint Clair kneeling there rubbing her hands. And when he laid his fingers against her throat where in life a pulse would beat, I could stand it no longer. "Don't you see," I cried out, "that it's no use?"

He turned then and looked toward me, his face as lifeless as ever. Whatever feeling his eyes might contain was hidden beneath the hooded lids.

"You are right," he said. "It's no use." And turning back he wrapped the quiet figure in the gay red cape and lifting her in his arms went up the path to the house. Following, I watched one of Lorelie's thin white hands which, slipping free, hung downward and swung back and forth in the rain.

Chapter Eight

EVEN after Lorelie LeGrand lay in her grave in the family graveyard, the rain continued to fall and we at Seven Chimneys lived through the succession of dark cheerless days as best we might. Her death made but little difference, and I perceived that life moved on without change. Saint Clair came and went as usual, Old Madame sat in her chair and nibbled on tidbits, even Rupert never spoke of his mother or seemed to miss her. I realized that Lorelie LeGrand living had meant but little more to her family than when she lay dead. How sad it was that she whose life had been so pitiful and brief—but twenty-eight years—had left no one who would grieve her passing.

It was not until three days before Christmas that the weather cleared and the somber racing clouds gave way to a sky of serene and spotless blue. Putting on my workclothes and heavy boots, I called to Rupert that today we would go into the woods and select the Christmas tree which Vene would cut down for us. And once we had escaped the house my spirits began to lift, though evidence of the storm appeared on all sides. Great branches of trees still lay on the ground, shrubbery hung in tatters, the bushes of oleander, myrtle, and jessamine were whipped to shreds. Nevertheless the birds piped their calls with fluting sweetness and the sunlight that angled through the trees held such warmth that it was easy to believe spring was near. And when Rupert and I had chosen our slash-pine Christmas tree and had watched Vene cut it down, we went on to gather armfuls of cassena and holly for the house. Rupert writhed up a huge cypress tree like a monkey to get the great bunch of the parasitic mistletoe which grew in its top.

On Christmas Eve we set up the tree between the long windows in the drawing room and decorated it with our home-made trimmings, pine cones which had been dipped in Maum Lucie's herb dye, strings of popped corn, stars and moons cut from colored paper. When we had inserted the tiny candles into the tin holders and lighted them, the tree flared to true beauty. With an air of intrigue Rupert hung the gifts which we had contrived for it. For his father a fine-sewn handker-chief, for Old Madame a new cap; and at the last we brought the neatly wrapped gifts for the Negroes—tobacco, lengths of calico, and such; and for Tawn's two boys slingshots which Rupert had fashioned from bamboo and stout rubber bands, as well as glass aggies and a sack of stick candy; and these we laid on the floor beneath the tree.

On Christmas morning I was awakened by the voices of the Negroes calling "Christmas Gif'" to each other, their voices merry against the still dawn. But when, after we had break-fasted and Rupert had inspected his gifts (they made but a poor showing I knew, but I had been hard put to provide them), I had Margot bring all hands into the drawing room, their merriment had vanished. They were silent and morose as I gave each his present and even the drams which I had Margot serve did not cheer them up. The gifts I had provided for Tawn and her boys lay beneath the tree unclaimed, for they had not come with the rest.

When the Negroes had drifted out, I took these packages and made my way to Tawn's cabin determined that she should have no excuse to feel slighted. The door stood open, for the day was as warm as September. I saw that Christmas had preceded me. Lem and Willie sat on the floor with the con-tents of their just-emptied stockings around them, their liquid eyes bright with delight.

I said cheerfully, "Merry Christmas, Lem, Merry Christmas, Willie," and laid my gifts in their laps. They looked up at me with childish shyness.

"Well," I asked, "what do you say when you receive a pres-ent? Don't you know you must always say, 'Thank you'?"

But before they could obey me, Tawn who was in the back room, slipped to the doorway and leaned there.

"Good morning, Tawn. Here is a gift for you too."

She ignored my outstretched hand with the package and spoke to the boys.

"Willie, Lem, give 'em back to her."

Their eyes darted from me to their mother but they made no motion of resigning their gifts. And seeing the longing in their eyes I turned to Tawn.

"Aren't you being childish?" I asked her.

She smiled the soft, insinuating smile that I hated. "No'm"— her voice was gentle—"but we don' want yo' presents."

"Perhaps you don't understand," I explained, "all the Negroes received gifts."

Her wide eyes met mine without wavering. "Yes, ma'am, I understan'." She might have been talking to a person of but poor wit. "It's you who don' understan'. We don' want yo' presents, don' even want 'em in our house!" Then with her noiseless feline tread she moved to Lem and Willie, took the packages from them and held them out to me.

"Take 'em," she said. "We don' want 'em."

But now I was angry. Moreover, I wanted her to know it. "You are impudent," I told her. "If you are not careful I shall report your impudence to Mr. LeGrand."

She smiled pityingly and went past me to the front door, where she dropped the packages on the ground outside as if they were unclean. Then she turned back to me. "You better go now." Her voice was like velvet.

We stood there, our eyes locked across the two feet that lay between us, but hers did not yield. It was I who, realizing the ridiculousness of the scene, left the place abruptly; but I carried with me the picture of her bronze body and wide slumberous eyes; and for some reason I thought of a leopard I had once seen in a circus. A leopard pacing the narrow space of its cage, with a regal indifference that captivity could not lessen.

The week following Christmas was a tiresome span of time. The Negroes idled at their tasks with sullen faces and I learned from Maum Lucie that they expected a three-day holiday. When I spoke to them sharply about their indolence, they met me with the bland assurance that "Allus we hab t'ree day fur Christmas." As I realized that all were working as little as possible, even Margot and Maum Lucie, and that what work they did was done sullenly, I gave them their holiday; and when Rupert taking his cue from them rebelled against lessons, I gave him one also. As best I could I kept the house in order and saw that meals were properly served.

But once the holiday was over I set them to work, first telling them that now there was much to be done and I would countenance no idling. The Negroes from Darien would move onto the place the fifteenth of January and there remained but little more than two weeks to have everything in readiness for their arrival. All hands were put to finishing up the cabins. The morning that Sey came to the house and informed me they were ready, I went to look them over, to see if all that I had ordered for their comfort had been done.

Leaving the cabins, I crossed the cotton land and took the short cut back to the house. As I went along the path I saw Roi coming toward me, leading Sans Foix by her bridle. When I would have passed by him with my head high—for at sight of his lean brown-clad figure the pain which had eased somewhat in my heart came alive again—he called to me to wait.

I waited. He came close and without so much as a "Good day" said, "Tell me."

I knew well enough what he meant and so in a flat voice and without embellishment I told him that his sister-in-law had drowned herself in the waters of the channel. He heard me with narrowed eyes and when I had finished he stood a space twirling the whip which he held in his hand. Then he looked at me squarely.

"And will you be mistress of Seven Chimneys now, Hester, as well as overseer?"

I pride myself that I am not more stupid than most women, yet at first I did not grasp the import of his words. When I did it was difficult to speak because of the anger rising within me.

"How dare you say a thing like that to me?"

He laughed mockingly. "That's what they're saying in Darien."

" 'They'? Who are 'they'?"

"The tongues that have never been idle since you came.

Don't you know that they call you the Yankee woman who works like a nigger?"

"No," I managed to force through stiff lips.

"You know it now. And they're saying also it is devilish convenient when the unwanted wife dies—if there's a young woman to step into her shoes."

My anger near throttled me. "It's a lie," I blazed.

His eyes met mine unwavering. "So I thought, too, Hester." Suddenly he passed his hands over his eyes as though to clear a dulled vision. "I speak like a fool, Hester. Forgive me."

"Forgive you?" I knew my laugh was ugly, but I could not hold it back. "For the vile thoughts that could only come to a man like you? Forgive you? There can be no talk of forgiveness between you and me, Roi LeGrand. I despise you."

I saw the red blood mount his face. "Be careful, Hester."

"You are less than nothing. I shame my every instinct for honor and decency by standing here and speaking with you."

"I tell you—be careful," he warned, and his mouth was ugly. "You try a man too far."

But I was beyond prudence. I only knew that I must hurt this man as he had hurt me. "You call yourself a man? Living in the woods, squiring every slut you can find, leaving your burdens to your brother! Why, he is thrice the man you are!"

His hand fell flat and stinging across my cheek and the suddenness of the impact shocked me to silence. I saw his face close to mine, thin and white with rage. My own anger cooled, and it came over me how I stood and wrangled with this man whom I had sworn to hate. Without speaking, I turned deliberately and went toward the house, and not once did I look back.

That night I resolved to leave Seven Chimneys. Where I would go or what I would do I did not know. And yet much as I valued the first security I had ever known, I saw clearly that I must give it up. For it had come to me some time in the hours since I had left Roi in the cotton field that I was endangering the only possession I owned—my good name. Already, if Roi spoke truthfully, it was being bandied about in Darien and I could imagine the pursed mouths and the sly suggestive smiles as they whispered about the Yankee woman who "worked like a nigger." And my spirit was sore, for I realized I had been a fool to believe I could live at Seven Chimneys, where centered the gossip of the community, without being drawn into its net.

But I would be a fool no longer. I would tell Saint Clair LeGrand that I must go. True, all my plans would come to naught—there was no one to see them through if I left. Captain Peake at the Freedmen's Bureau must be notified that after all I would not use the Negroes; and I would lose the money which I had spent. But even this did not weaken my resolution. To stay would mean the loss of my good name. That loss would leave me poor indeed.

Rising, I took my pen and sitting beside my night candle I wrote a note to Saint Clair telling him briefly—and without stating a reason—that I wished to leave Seven Chimneys and that before he left for Savannah, which I knew was his intention, I would like to settle what money matters stood between us. This I slipped beneath the turret room door before I went down to the kitchen at five o'clock to start the Negroes about their work. When I had breakfasted with Rupert, I put on my cape and made my usual rounds of the land to see that all had gone forward on the day before as it should. I went to the cotton field and the rice mill and came back the long way on the edge of the marsh, my feet sinking into the uncertain ground of the fen, my skirt becoming muddy and draggled.

I thought I had never seen a sweeter, cleaner day. It seemed as fresh as though the long rains had washed away all pollution and the land lay black and rich beyond telling. Almost I could see the rich harvest which would spring from it; and my heart was heavy to think that only in my imagination would it ever come to fruition.

When I returned to the house I went in the back way calling Rupert as I went, who to tease me often hid when lesson time came. But today he came to meet me. "Papa says I needn't do lessons, Hester. And he wants you in the turret room. He's been looking all over for you."

Because I was overwrought I was suddenly angry. Saint

Clair without so much as consulting me had interfered with our routine. As I passed through the lower hall past the drawing room where Old Madame sat with a tray of food on her lap, I resolved to tell Saint Clair so. With my mind braced with anger, I rapped on the turret-room door. And when his lazy voice drawled "Come," I entered.

He sat at the card table, as always, in his patched dressing gown, his long fingers shuffling and reshuffling cards delicately. Within the door I stopped.

"Did you want me?"

"Yes."

I crossed to the card table and stood there uncaring that my skirt was mud-bedraggled, my hair disordered by the wind.

He looked up from the cards, his eyes expressing nothing but indifference. "You are pale."

"My want of color is no fault of my own."

"You are also stubborn."

"That is like my paleness. Constitutional."

"Why are you in such a shrewish temper?"

"Because without consulting me you have interfered with Rupert's lessons."

His hands shuffled and reshuffled the cards gently; otherwise he was unmoving. I thought it not possible for a living man—wide awake—to look less animated.

"If you are leaving Seven Chimneys, what difference does it make about Rupert's lessons?"

"Rupert knows nothing of my intention."

He continued to shuffle the cards gently, and I was shaken with irritation. Sharply I said, "What do you want with me? I have tasks to do."

"Perhaps you'll be less concerned with your tasks when I tell you why I've called you here."

"That depends."

The cards slithered through his fingers again. "What would you think if I asked you to be my wife?"

"I'd think you mad."

There was not the faintest smile on his face, not the least trace of self-consciousness nor anxiety in his bearing.

"Yet that is what I am doing. Will you marry me?"

Despite his gravity, I did not take him seriously.

"What game do you play at now?" I demanded.

"It is no game."

"You ask me to marry you?"

"Yes."

"Why?"

He shrugged. "Must I give the stereotyped reasons? I love you and so on and so on?"

"No. They would not be true."

"Shall I say then, that you fill a place here—and admirably, by the way—and that I wish you to continue to fill it?"

"The truth is you want a good overseer who cannot leave you."

Again the infinitesimal shrug. "What matters the reason? I make you the offer. Do you accept?"

"I—I don't know—"

"Please spare me 'This is so sudden.' " His voice held a note of mockery.

The look I threw him was hostile. Yet, little as I had expected such an offer, it opened up possibilities beyond my most sanguine dreams. Mrs. Saint Clair LeGrand, Mistress of Seven Chimneys! A home—security—safety! No woman buffeted about as I had been could dismiss such an offer easily.

And the sudden realization flashed over me that pride, which had been trampled by the laughter in Roi's eyes, could raise its head again. That realization was sweet indeed.

Saint Clair's voice recalled me. "I am not flattered by the way you receive my offer."

"You should not complain. It is being received in the spirit in which it was offered."

"Let us not dally. What have you to say?"

"Just what does the offer include?"

"Damn your Yankee shrewdness! You would bargain on the bridal bed. What do you want it to include? The usual thing —with all my worldly goods I thee endow?"

"You have not enough worldly goods to make that important."

Suddenly he was bored. "Damn it," he drawled, "I am not going to plead and cajole like a schoolboy. I've made the offer. Take it or no."

"I must have time to consider."

"Very well. And when you go downstairs, tell Margot to fetch my breakfast on a tray."

Downstairs, I sent Margot kitchenward for the tray and seeking Rupert out I led him to the schoolroom.

"But papa said I needn't do lessons today, Hester."

"We will do them just the same."

"Aw, pshaw! I hate lessons."

"You only hate them because you have to do them. If I told you you could never open another book I expect I'd catch you hiding in corners to read them."

I sat at the desk and reached for his slate.

"What's the matter with you, Hester?"

"Nothing. Why do you ask?"

"You're"—he sought for a word—"funny. Almost like you had been drinking brandy."

"I've had no brandy, you may be sure."

"Your eyes are bright, like mama's used to be. And foggled."

"You imagine things. Here," I said, swiftly setting down sums for him to do. I knew my eyes were bright even as he had said and probably as "foggled" as if I had drunk brandy. And indeed it was a heady wine that had sent blood rushing to my face and given my body the odd sense of lightness, a sensation I think every woman must know when an advantageous marriage is proposed.

And—I do not deny it—I was clearly aware of the material benefits which marriage to Saint Clair would incur. To know that Seven Chimneys was my home, to know that no wind of ill chance could wrest me from it and send me wandering homeless again, loomed large before me.

How I would treasure Seven Chimneys! I would work tirelessly to make it what it once was, what it could be again. As Rupert added and erased and added again, in my mind I was harvesting great crops and shipping rice and cotton to Savannah. When the laughing eyes of Roi LeGrand flashed before me, ruthlessly I shut them out. He could be no more to me from now on than any other village ne'er-do-well. And I determined that the brown wench Tawn should leave my plantation at once.

Chapter Nine

THAT day as I went about my work, the fact that I was to be mistress of Seven Chimneys surrounded me like an aura, consoling and comforting. That I might refuse Saint Clair's offer no longer entered my mind. In acceptance I found —or thought I would find—recompense for all the lonely bitterness life had brought me—a home where I had been homeless, instead of mediocrity, the position of which I had so often dreamed. And as for love? Love I had done without before—love I could continue to do without.

That night I roused to startled wakefulness from a violent dream and sat erect and listening in the dark. Footsteps in the hall just outside my door had awakened me. Now I heard them again and the guarded opening of a door.

For a moment I sat there tensely in the dark. Who could be prowling in the hall at this hour which intuitively I knew to be a late one—and why? Then—and the act dispelled fear —I lighted my lamp and slipping into my dressing gown and slippers went to the door and opened it.

"Who is there?" I asked sharply, peering into the darkness.

Immediately the tall figure of Saint Clair emerged as he came toward me. And I saw that he wore his dressing gown —and that he was his usual imperturbable self.

He drawled, "I need clean cloths for a bandage. There has been an accident."

I stopped to stare at him wonderingly a second before going to the linen closet where I groped for a clean worn sheet I had tucked away against the time when Margot would need dust rags. His voice came to me through the darkness. "I shall need hot water."

I gave him the sheet. "Maum Lucie's kettle hangs over the banked fire—it is always full."

"Thank you," he said, turning toward the stairs. His voice came back to me through the darkness in so lonely a fashion that almost without volition I called impulsively: "Do you need help? Shall I come with you?"

He had passed from within the range of my lamp's glow and so I could not see him, but I sensed that he had stopped and turned back.

"Come with me?" he repeated and with a quality of cynical amusement in his voice which I did not understand. "Yes. Come with me. I might need help."

I followed him down the stairs and out onto the back porch where I waited while he fetched Maum Lucie's kettle, then we went down the back steps into the rear yard. But all this I had done as a woman moving in a dream—indeed the mood of my dream still held me. I felt neither surprise nor alarm; I did not wonder where we went or why. It was only when I realized we were headed for the Negro cabins that some unquiet fear stirred within me. When we entered Tawn's house and I saw Roi lying on Tawn's bed, his right arm swathed in a blood-soaked towel and Tawn standing in the shadows beyond the circle of lamplight, I knew the reason for that fear.

Of what I saw or felt, however, I gave no sign. Like an automaton I did as Saint Clair ordered, pouring the steaming water into a tin basin, holding it when he took the bloody towel from Roi's arm and with dexterity cleansed the wound.

"It is not as serious as I thought. The bullet glanced," he said. "It will heal quickly."

The brown woman in the shadows stirred and her sigh floated through the room.

"Bandage."

Tearing the sheet into strips I handed them to him. As he wrapped the injured arm I knew that all the while Roi's eyes with their taunting laughter were upon me.

"You are a good doctor, Saint," he gibed, "and your assistant is as cool as a surgeon's lancet."

At his bantering—carried on I knew to annoy me—the blood rushed to my face but I stood silent, folding what was left of the sheet into a careful square. And when the bandag-

ing was done Roi sat up, swinging his booted feet to the floor.
I averted my eyes that I might not see the lean brown face,
which no matter what he did seemed not to lessen in its
charm for me.

"Careful," Saint Clair warned him, "you have lost blood.
Take a swig of this brandy."

He drank, then sat with his head in his hands waiting for
the brandy to bring him strength. I looked everywhere—anywhere—but at the figure of Roi LeGrand on the bed of Tawn.
I looked at the scrubbed floor, the tawdry calendar on the
wall, the blue and white shepherd boy on the mantel. I saw
the pistol half thrust into its fancy leather holster lying beside
the shepherd boy. And beside the pistol lay Saint Clair's
jeweled whip, its rubies winking in the lamplight like evil
eyes.

The color drained back to Roi's face and he stood, but so
unsure were his legs that he would have fallen had not Saint
Clair thrown out an arm to steady him.

"You had better sleep at the house tonight."

"No."

Saint Clair shrugged. "Where is Sans Foix?"

"Under the magnolia tree."

"You can't walk so far—the bleeding—"

"Sans Foix can be brought to the door."

Saint Clair turned to me. "Here, Hester, give him an arm
while I bring the horse."

But to touch Roi LeGrand now was more than I could
bring myself to do. Instead I said, "I will bring Sans Foix,"
and went out of the door quickly. But not before I saw Roi's
eyes green in his white face and mocking.

Outside in the cool safe dark I cupped my hands about
my hot face for a moment, then walked to the magnolia tree
to fetch the horse. She refused to come with me, however,
snapping and biting my hands, threshing her head about,
stamping and twisting, and only when Roi whistled to her
from the doorway of the cabin did she let me lead her.

Carefully Roi raised himself into the saddle and picked up
the reins with his uninjured arm. "Good night," he said
levelly.

Saint Clair watched him through narrowed eyes.

"You'd better go to Toittant tomorrow and let him have a look at that arm."

"It will do well enough." Roi's voice was careless. "Shall I thank you for your services, Saint?" he asked insolently and when his brother made no answer he laughed. "You would have made a good doctor, Saint, except for one thing—how does the Scripture go? 'Heal thyself, physician'?" He laughed again. "That you cannot do, can you, Saint? Perhaps the cool Miss Snow—"

He broke off. Then, throwing me a glance almost of questioning—or so it seemed to me—he dug his boots into the mare's side and galloped off toward the forest on the horizon. And I waited until Saint Clair had fetched Maum Lucie's kettle and his jeweled whip as well, and together he and I walked over the dew-drenched land toward the house. Neither of us spoke, but the sound of his whip as he cut at the weeds in the path cracked like pistol shots in the still dawn.

In the kitchen he replaced the kettle, then lighted the candle on the shelf over the fireplace and turning surveyed me through examining eyes. "Sit down, Hester." His voice was as lifeless as customary. "You look ill."

I sat in Maum Lucie's splint-bottomed chair and moving silently he brought me a glass of brandy which I accepted and sipped slowly, grateful for the warmth which began to creep along my icy veins. Leaning against the mantelshelf he watched me silently at first but finally spoke, "You have no questions to ask—about what you have seen tonight?"

I shook my head in negation, "No questions."

"Still," he drawled, "if you are going to be my wife you may as well learn of any skeletons that hang in my closet."

"Perhaps I am not going to be your wife," I told him slowly.

He smiled—and I am sure no smile ever held less of mirth or warmth. "I see. Then I am still the eager lover waiting his lady's answer?"

I sat there, the glass in my hand, and made no attempt to answer his badinage. And suddenly his mood changed. The half smile vanished—his face was bleak and aloof again. Yet the casualness of his voice stripped his next words of any importance.

"You must not judge Roi too harshly," he said. "He is no different from any other hot-blooded young man confronted with a dearth of available women. Perhaps"—his eyes met mine unwavering—"perhaps I am wrong to interfere."

He did not know, I thought as I stared back at him, that every word he spoke was like a rivet of pain driven into the very depth of me. That the mere sight of Roi tonight—the lean brown face, the mocking smile—had crumpled my resolution to hate him as a tidal wave crumples the flimsy sand castles a child builds on the seashore, and had stripped the thought of marriage to Saint Clair of every particle of illusory grandeur with which I had invested it.

He did not know, I say. So now he took the wine glass from my hand and told me quietly, "Go to bed, Hester. It is nearly daybreak. You'll get but little sleep this night."

I suppose there comes a time in every life when artifice and sham are stripped away, when for the first time you meet the secret self heretofore unknown to you.

The hours of that dawn were such a time for me. It was then that I met another Hester Snow. From some hidden place she crept to taunt the dullness of my virtue, to scoff at all I had believed good. And I found that there had lain within me all these years a Hester Snow ready—even eager—to cast aside all the precepts which had entrenched me round about with virtue—a Hester Snow who yearned for love.

I crouched ashamed beside my window, for my conscience told me that this desire for Roi's arms and lips could not be right. But I knew that, unworthy though love may be, it cannot be plucked out resolutely, as is a thorn from the flesh. Come what may, it remains to pierce and bite with bitter hurt.

But no better proof do I need that will can triumph over flesh than I had in those hours. Because as night was lightened by the merest whisper of day, from somewhere—I know not where—there came a strengthening of spirit sure and strong. And when the day broke over the marsh and a rim of flame tinted the east with orange and crimson, I lay my head upon the window sill, grateful for the fresh unsoiled air of dawn; and I had the strength to say that no matter the cost, I would conquer the heart, which was so eager to betray my will.

Chapter Ten

ON a morning three days later Saint Clair LeGrand and I traveled down the Sound to the island of St. Simon and were married by the priest there.

It was not such a marriage as I had dreamed of. We left the house with no one the wiser for why we went, and to Rupert, who was pleading to accompany us, Saint Clair said, "You would be a nuisance. We go to see about a mule."

"But Hester bought a mule in Darien—didn't you, Hester? The day that Roi took us to the carnival."

I felt Saint Clair's narrowed eyes turn toward me. "So Roi took you to the carnival?" he drawled.

Rupert answered for me. "Yes, and it was fun too. We all three rode Sans Foix and Roi shot General Sherman in the eye."

Calmly, I finished drawing on my gloves and took a glance in the mirror—an act which did not escape Rupert.

"Why do you wear your best dress to buy a mule, Hester?"

I patted his cheek. "I'll bring you some candy," I promised.

As Sey and Boy guided the longboat down the channel toward the sound, I looked from my seat in the stern of the boat at the man who would be my husband, and if I felt not the happiness which another figure might have evoked, neither was I displeased with what I saw. Saint Clair LeGrand was a man no woman need be ashamed to claim as husband. Indeed, in his best broadcloth he was an elegant figure and one bound to draw attention; and if the indolence and indifference which irked me were there unchanged, I reminded myself that no woman—unless she were stupid—could expect perfection. I considered the amiable acceptance of his faults as small payment for that which I expected to receive in return.

And certainly he had been most meticulous of conduct since the morning he had made the offer of marriage. When—two days later (which I had waited lest I seem overanxious) I had informed him the idea was agreeable to me, he had taken it coolly without so much as kissing my hand and had informed me as casually as he would ask for rice at the table: "We will be married Wednesday at St. Simon's."

While I welcomed this lack of demonstrativeness, I deplored what seemed to me unnecessary haste and I pointed out that on Thursday the Darien Negroes were moving onto the place—that I would prefer a later date for our marriage. But before I could get the words out, his white fingers tapped his stifled yawn. "One day is as good as another," he drawled. "Let's get it over with." And so I agreed, though somewhat chagrined, for this was like no courtship I had ever met even in fiction. His manner toward me remained exactly as before, despite his evident haste for marriage; and I could not help but wonder if he would always be so cold and reticent—if he, under any circumstances, would ever reveal himself.

None of this had the power to affect me this morning, however. Now I saw my marriage as a new possibility capable of dissolving the conditions which heretofore had marred my life; and if last night I had lain wide-eyed, staring into the dark against which was limned the mocking, laughing face of Roi LeGrand, daylight had dispelled that vision.

This morning I liked a great deal of what lay before me. I saw myself moving triumphantly as the wife of Saint Clair LeGrand—mistress of Seven Chimneys—with the strength of marriage and a fine old name behind me. I did not need to remind myself that if like some silly schoolgirl I should change my mind, there was nothing of value to which I might return; and if the man I was marrying appeared somewhat formidable, I believed confidently that after marriage I would be able to manage him thoroughly. He would go his way—I would go mine; and I could foresee no rock on which our amiability might break.

The sun was far past noon when we came out of the dilapidated little church and made our way to the pine landing where Sey and Boy waited in the longboat. This I perceived with regret. I would have liked to walk about the island which—if I was to believe Old Madame's babbling—possessed a colorful history and many fine old plantations, though it appeared to me to be but a wilderness of swamp and forest. I mentioned this to Saint Clair as he helped me into the boat, but he only stifled a yawn with his tapered hand. "So you want to go sightseeing," he drawled. "Truly, a Yankee schoolmarm's honeymoon!"

These were his only words as we made the return trip to Seven Chimneys. He lounged easily in the boat, the gray water making a becoming background for his pale well-cut features and the finely formed hand with which from time to time he stifled his discreet yawns. I thought that never before, perhaps, had there been a bridegroom so nonchalant, so bored. But I cared not a bit. I trailed my hand in the water and watching the sun reach out its vanishing rays to turn the marsh into a quivering expanse of gold, wondered in what manner Saint Clair would announce our marriage to his household. Did he foresee, as I did, the sly insinuations that he had taken a new wife before the old one was cold in her grave? As for myself, none of this mattered. Old Madame and the Negroes I could dismiss with a shrug. Only the moment when I must face Rupert disturbed me—somehow I knew that this marriage would not be to his liking.

I spoke of this to Saint Clair as we went up the path toward the house, but with this subject—as with all others—he was profoundly bored. "My mother can tell the niggers," he said. At the note of impatience in his voice I felt my anger rise, but I remained silent. Surely, I warned myself, I must not quarrel with him before I had so much as crossed the threshold as his wife.

In the drawing room we found Margot lighting the candles while Old Madame sat in her chair and Rupert sprawled on the hearth rug with a book. At our entrance he sprang up and ran to meet me. "You were the *longest* time, Hester," he scolded. "Did you bring my candy?"

I gave him the bag of stick candy which Sey had bought while we were in the church and he dropped to the floor again to explore its contents, not noticing his father who went to lean against the mantelpiece.

Old Madame asked politely, "Did you buy a mule, mademoiselle?"

Before I could answer Saint Clair's voice slid in lazily, "Miss Snow and I were married this afternoon."

The room turned suddenly quiet—so quiet that the crackling fire, unnoticed before, now dominated it. I saw Old Madame's futile hands flutter together, saw too that Margot froze in her place before the inlaid chest and stood motionless, her lighter lifted. Rupert, his bag of sweets forgotten, looked up at me with startled eyes.

Then Old Madame cleared her throat. "Is this true?" Her expressionless eyes turned upon her son.

He drawled, "I would hardly jest about such a matter."

Her eyes crept back to me and over me and I knew the thoughts that circled in the shallow pool of her mind. This plain woman in her plain clothes a LeGrand! Mistress of Seven Chimneys! I returned her stare coolly. I had no intention of being intimidated by this greedy old woman. So when her eyes were the first to fall and she said, "Welcome to our family, mademoiselle," I could not deny the small thrill of triumph that was mine.

I thanked her briefly and turned to Rupert who had risen to his feet and who stood clutching his bag of candy. I held out my hand to him. "Do you welcome me too, Rupert?"

He looked at me steadily, his eyes narrow and contemptuous, his face in anger so much like Roi's that I was thrust by a needle of pain. But he only said quietly, "I did not think you would treat me this way, Hester," and ignoring my outstretched hand went past me and out of the room.

Oh well!—I thought—I can win Rupert over later, and I turned to go to my room where I would lay aside my hat and dolman. Then it was that I perceived that Margot still stood motionless before the candelabra on the inlaid chest and remembrance of all her insolent hostility rushed over me. I stopped and spoke to her sharply.

"There is no need to stand staring, Margot. Finish the candles."

"Yes—Miss Snow."

"And remember, please—I am Mrs. LeGrand."

"Yes, madame."

"And not 'madame.' Plain Mrs. LeGrand."

"Yes, Mrs. LeGrand."

I placed my foot on the bottom stair, then turned again. "And when you go to the kitchen you will inform the other servants that I was married to Mr. LeGrand today."

I stood waiting until I heard her reluctant, "Yes—Mrs. LeGrand," then continued on my way, walking briskly and in a manner meant to convey to her—and Old Madame too—that I had not the slightest intention of assuming in this house any other position than that which was rightfully mine. And I must admit that as I traversed the broad upper hall I could not deny my satisfaction—for the first time in my life I was "somebody"—I was walking through my own span of corridor —I had my own servants who must obey my ordering; for a woman bred in poverty, who had indulged in the usual womanish dreams without hope of fulfillment, I now found fufillment almost incredible.

Yet I did not underrate the value of that which I brought the name of LeGrand in return. I brought stamina to a family soft with parasitical living, energy and willingness to work to an aristocracy unfit to work for itself; no—I told myself— the advantage was not all mine.

When I had laid aside my hat and dolman and had made my hair neat, I went to Rupert's room to make my peace with him. I found him seated at the window, his chin propped on his hand, staring out at the dusk. When I entered, he rose and faced me.

"What is it, Hester?"

"I've come to make friends with you."

His smile was the scornful smile of childhood. "I am not mad."

"But you do not like it, Rupert, because I—" I hesitated.

"Because you have married papa?"

"Yes. Why do you disapprove, Rupert?"

The worn toe of his shoe began to trace the pattern of the faded carpet, and he dropped his eyes as if to watch that tracing. Thus we stood a moment. Then he burst out, "Papa takes everything. He leaves nothing—for anybody else."

"But that is silly. He married me to keep me at Seven Chimneys—for you."

His laugh held some ugly knowledge, fantastic in so young a boy. "Do you believe that, Hester? Well, it isn't true. He wants you for himself—he'll spoil you like he spoils everything; you won't ever be the same."

He was afraid that my marriage might alter my affection for him, and so crossing to his side I laid my arm about his shoulders and with all seriousness assured him nothing could alter that. He stood beside me, his body braced with defiance at first, but as I talked of the plans I had for Seven Chimneys —of how I would make it a home of which he would be proud—I felt the tension in the slight body ease, and after a little he somewhat shamefacedly laid his cheek against mine and said, "Don't change, for me, Hester. I wouldn't have anybody then." As I waited for him to wash his hands for supper I pondered this remark. It was strange, I thought, that Rupert too should feel alone.

There was nothing to differentiate my first meal as mistress of Seven Chimneys from the dull pattern of all the suppers I had eaten there. With vulgar noises Old Madame sat gorging herself, her enormous greed transcending the less important fact of a new daughter-in-law. And my new husband? He lounged in his chair as disinterested as though a first meal with a new wife were an everyday occurrence. Only Margot, sullen and bold-eyed, paid me the slightest attention; and it was of such surly caliber that had I been a shrinking bride I might have been intimidated.

Yet toward the last, one incident did break the monotonous pattern. It was as Margot served dessert that from the backyard, which lay just outside the dining room, there came a burst of laughter, a woman's shrieking, raucous laughter, that rang out on the night until it became as annoying as the too-near clacking of a hen. I inquired of Margot who it was that laughed.

Deliberately, she placed Old Madame's dessert on the table before answering. Her bold eyes looked across at me steadily and when at last her "I don't know, ma'am" came, I felt that other words would come on her lips if she chose to let them.

The laughter shrilled on and I spoke sharply. "Order whoever it is to find some other place for her amusement." Before she could do my bidding Saint Clair pushed back his chair and moving with his noiseless tread went down the hall toward the back porch. No sooner had the back door closed behind him than the laughter broke mid-air and was silenced. I would ask him who it was, I thought idly, when he came back to table; but he did not return and it was not until we had long left the table and gone to the drawing room that I saw him pass through the hall and up the stairs.

And so the early hours of my bridal night were spent in the drawing room with the old woman and boy, listening to Old Madame's braggart boasting. Tonight her conversational harp had gained another string, one on which she strummed with maddening persistence. Did I know——? she asked calculatingly, that always the LeGrands had married beautiful women, women of great families? There was Cecile de Montalet, the wife of the first Pierre LeGrand—he who had built Seven Chimneys! Ah—she had been a famous beauty of the French court—her father had been the confidante of the king; and as for her *own* family (here she simpered with false modesty) did I know that she had dined with the emperor? It was then that she had met her future husband, had heard of his vast estate in the Americas.

I realized clearly that this was the manner which she used to convey to me that in her opinion the present LeGrand had shamed these other LeGrands by marriage to an unknown Yankee schoolmarm. When I had heard all I could amiably endure, I somewhat curtly bade her good night and Rupert and I went upstairs.

As we neared his door he looked up at me.

"Where will you sleep now, Hester?"

I was so taken back by his question that my voice was tart without intention. "Where would I sleep but in my own bed in my own room?"

"Will papa sleep in your room too?"

I felt the red burn my cheek, but with what self-possession

I could muster I told him his papa would sleep in the turret room as usual. But his questions set to fluttering all the mingling of half-understood facts and images which had disturbed me since I had told Saint Clair I would be his wife. Heretofore I had ignored them ruthlessly as one who, visioning a great purpose, refuses to let minor purposes obstruct his view. Now at Rupert's questions the doubts which had assailed me rose like ominous cawing birds that would not be denied.

I had made a bargain, I told myself, and now I must pay, though as yet I had no knowledge of the price. Certainly Saint Clair had not intimated by the slightest word or gesture if our marriage would be one of convenience only or if the bargain included the privilege of my bed. And so indifferent and uncaring he seemed that it was with difficulty that I could imagine him in a rôle in which passion played a part. But I know now—and I think that I knew then—I but tried to delude myself.

So it was with conflicting emotions that I saw Rupert to bed and told him good night. When I reached my own room, which was neat and prim and exactly as always, assurance and common sense returned. After all, I reminded myself, I was no timid bride to tremble at the approach of a new husband to my bed; and if the image of Roi rose before me with such vividness that I could almost catch the tang of tobacco, I told myself that Saint Clair and not Roi was my husband and that no doubt I was neither the first woman nor the last to lie with one man while she hungered for another. I was a woman who by managing circumstance had evaded a losing destiny.

I was ready for bed and was laying out my clothes for next morning when the door opened and Saint Clair, wearing his purple dressing gown, came in. He closed the door behind him and his narrow gaze traveled around the room.

"Tomorrow Margot will move you to the big room."

I continued to lay out my clothes. "Oh, please not," I exclaimed lightly. "I prefer this one."

"You can't stay here." His arrogance was not lessened because his voice was quiet or because the hand that toyed with the tassel of his dressing gown was languid. "Why do you dislike occupying the other room?" he asked with eyes fixed upon me.

I pondered on the answer I should give. Should I tell him that the other room held horror for me because his first wife so lately dead—too lately dead—had wrestled with her devils there? Or should I tell him what was nearer the truth; that nothing, not even *that,* could annoy me half so much as submission to his will?

I caught myself up sharply. Of what use was this rebellion within me? This man was my husband and I had known that for marriage a price would be demanded. Was I going to grumble like a veritable Shylock at the first installment?

Yet I persisted. "If I find this room more comfortable why do you object?" I asked.

He gestured indolently. "My wife can't occupy the governess's room."

"Your wife is no whit better than Hester Snow."

He yawned and tapped his lips with his fingers—his way, I was to learn, of announcing that he was finished with a subject. "Margot will make the other room ready for you tomorrow."

I looked at him wonderingly. Was I to discover another side of him? Was what I had taken for languor and indifference an indolent strength which would persist relentlessly until what it pressured must in time yield? The idea startled and displeased me, for I had not the slightest intention of yielding my will to any pressure—however gentle. So now I turned and faced him.

"Let us understand each other," my voice was harsh and grating even to my ears. "You have called me your wife. Just what does the title include?"

His lids concealed his eyes and I thought an acid smile touched his mouth, but when he raised them and looked at me with his strange birdlike gaze, the smile had died.

"Shall we draw up a contract," he drawled, "stating that for bed and board one Hester Snow—spinster—takes Saint Clair LeGrand and accords him all husbandly rights?"

"Then you intend to claim those rights?"

The pale, black-ringed eyes stared into mine.

"Do you think me celibate, Hester? That I married you

because you know a good stand of cotton—or a good mule?"

He came toward me—one might be tempted to strike him, I thought, for the sake of forcing some trace of passion in his face and speech. "I could hire a nigger with that knowledge, Hester."

He towered over me, and I waited while his left arm encircled my body and his right reached languidly to snuff out the candle on the night table.

Chapter Eleven

NEXT morning when the first lifting of night—hardly less dark than night itself—foretold of day, I was up and dressed, my mind turning to the work before me eagerly. Only the impression of Saint Clair's head on the pillow remained as evidence that the night—which for me had been one long waking—had been anything but a harsh tense dream.

But as I went kitchenward I was buoyed with the excitement that can often come with pain, and briskly I ordered Maum Lucie, who puttered at the freshly raked fire, to ring the big bell and arouse the Negroes. For there was much work ahead of us. Today the Negroes found by Captain Peake in Darien were to move into the cabins; Sey and Boy must fetch them in the boat; there were the contracts to be signed, the iron pots in the clearing before the cabins to be brought to boil so that the midday meal of black-eyed peas and hogback might be ready for them.

It was nine o'clock when the first boatload of Negroes scraped the landing. A sorry-looking crew of tatterdemalions they were with their gear slung over their shoulders and so dirty and odorous that Maum Lucie and Margot lifted their noses delicately and muttered of "field hands" with withering contempt.

All morning I sat in my little office with Shem, the headsman, and endured the ordeal of getting each Negro to sign the contract which I had ready for him. It was a tiresome business. I had to read and reread the contract, then wait until the Negro in question deliberated—perhaps went out to consult with his friends. Each, it appeared, was half convinced that the signing of the contract bound him into slavery again. One old Negro wearing a battered silk hat and carrying an umbrella (for no reason—the sky was a quiet pool of blue) returned time after time to demand that "Missy read 'um contrac'" once more, popping in and out of the office all morning like a cadaverous blackbird and apparently unable to bring himself to putting his name on the line; but in the end he signed with a doleful face and ambled off toward the cabins.

Only once did I lose my temper or my patience. That was when one young buck by the name of John Eaton, whose sloe-black eyes were evil in his pointed face, told me insolently when I had explained the terms of the contract, "All right—you sign my contrac' mist'is—den I'll sign yours." Angrily, I ordered him off the place; but five minutes later I looked up to find him in the doorway, a devilish grin on his face. "I'se back again, mist'is," he said with perfect good nature, and without further ado placed his mark on the paper.

Back in the office I went over with Shem the work that must be got under way at once. First the cotton field and rice bottoms must be burned and cleared of dead cane and scrub, the cotton land ploughed and then the rice bottoms ditched, the drains and quarter drains put in, the dykes repaired and made safe against the alligators; and the rice seed must be sowed (they must be clayed I pointed out) in time for the high tides of March.

Shem, broad and so black that even his gums and eyeballs took on a purplish tinge, nodded. "Yassum—sprout flo'—hits gotta be timed for de high tides ob March. Hits easy to see we'se got wuk ter do."

But this was not all, I continued. The high land must be ploughed and planted. Here we would grow green stuff, corn, peas and cabbages, potatoes and beans—foodstuff for the house; once they were planted, I explained, Vene and Sey and Boy could tend them. He would need all the other hands for the rice and cotton; and he must watch, I pointed out, that he used the strongest Negroes in the rice swamps—the less strong and younger ones in the cotton field.

He nodded again. "Yassum—de rice swamps is pow'ful onhealthy. Las' year a passel of colored folks die wid swamp feber."

Here I interrupted him sharply, for I had no desire to hear

this sort of talk. Too well I knew the shamming illnesses by which the Negroes evaded work. "And remember, Shem," I told him sternly, "I will have no idling or loafing on the job. Make that clear to each and every hand. Tell them that if one bushel of rice is lost through laziness or carelessness they shall pay for it, according to the contract."

Despite my weariness from the morning's work, I had a definite sense of success. Fifty-two names were signed to the contract; the first step of my plan was accomplished. I knew the problems that lay ahead, the unceasing effort it would require to hold them to the work, the constant vigilance I must exert lest their childish wills get the upper hand of mine. But even now as I circled the field toward the house I could see the rich dark soil ploughed and seeded; the seed sprouting, growing; the cotton ripening, opening; and suddenly, I knew that I would win over the Negroes and the land; I must win; here I must not fail.

At midday dinner I must listen to Rupert's chatter. He had been everywhere during the morning—at the cabins, in the office, watching with avid interest as the Negroes ate under the trees; now he had a fund of what he considered interesting information to impart. John Eaton could play the jew's-harp, Uncle Early wore his kinky forelock tied with a hair from a horse's tail to keep the witches off.

Of Saint Clair there was no sign, but Margot informed me that he had dined in his room. Her scorn did not escape me and I was irritated to think that while I had worked since daybreak he had dawdled in his room—no doubt in his dressing gown—without interest in what went on. But I shrugged my irritation away. What difference did it make, I asked myself, if he was interested or not? I still had work to do—I must spend the afternoon with Shem completing plans for the work which tomorrow must go forward on schedule. So for another two hours I sat in the little office, the laughter of the Negroes drifting back to us as they sprawled with full bellies in the cleared space before the cabins and made a holiday. When at last I felt that Shem had a clear understanding of how the work must go, I told him to go and rest with the other Negroes, and I went to bathe and change.

But when I opened the door of my bedroom I stopped. The room had been stripped of my possessions, the bureau was bare, the open closet door revealed its emptiness. While I had worked, Margot had moved me to the big room; and turning I went up the hall swiftly and jerked Lorelie's door open.

Saint Clair leaned against the mantel perfectly at ease. When I hesitated in the doorway, he spoke.

"Is it as you like it?"

Glancing around the room I saw my belongings were arranged on Lorelie's dressing table. My scant wardrobe hung in her spacious closet. I shrugged. Why not, I asked myself, what mattered it where I slept?

"It is all right. But I preferred the other room."

"Preference, as you call it, has nothing to do with it."

"So it seems." I held my voice to lightness. "Do you always have your way?"

The pale, black-ringed eyes stared into mine and there was no answering lightness in his voice. "There are things on which I know best."

"And where I sleep is one of them, I suppose."

"Yes."

I shrugged again. "It is not of the least importance. Now—will you please go? I want to change for supper."

When the door had closed behind him, I bathed and dressed, admitting as I did—at least to myself—that the room reserved for the mistress of Seven Chimneys, with its four-poster bed, its deep chairs and pier-glass mirror, was far more comfortable than the one allowed the governess. Most of all I was pleased with the small lady's desk with its ivory fittings, as I planned how I would escape Old Madame's after-supper conversation and come here to do accounts.

Suddenly I could bear neither the room nor the house and quietly, lest Rupert waylay me and wish to go, I went down the stairs and out of the back and made my way to the Negro cabins. Here, I found a scene of peaceful domesticity that might have confounded those who shed tears over the Negroes' plight. The women, singing softly, padded in and out of the cabins, and on the doorsteps the men lounged as contentedly as though they held a charm against disaster. John

Eaton, propped against a tree in the clearing, played his jew's-harp, his black eyes darting here and there as his weird rhythm, not unlike a bird's thrumming wings, beat against the dusk.

Shem, mending the mule harness, rose at my approach and touched his forehead in respectful greeting. He handed me the "pass books" which I had provided for each Negro and in which would be entered the supplies and money advanced against the time when settlement would be made. I took the pass books for checking after supper and turned back toward the house, going along the narrow path that circled close to the river and the marsh that lay quiet past imagining now. Even the birds' staccato voices were stilled and the wild duck feasted in the marsh grasses undisturbed. The dusk like a silent, veiled woman slipped across the motionless landscape.

It was not until I came to the short cut that I saw Sans Foix tethered close by and Roi leaning against a tree that grew athwart my path. Averting my eyes, I would have passed, but his outflung arm barred my way. "Wait," he commanded.

I stopped and faced him.

"Is it true—this thing I hear?"

"What do you hear?"

"—that you have married Saint?"

"Yes. It is true."

He had continued to hold my wrist, but now he threw it from him, and his laugh was ugly.

"So you've turned strumpet," he said.

"Your words cannot hurt me." And I started to pass him, but he stepped in my path.

"But what I say is true. You've sold yourself as surely as any common prostitute." He laughed again. "I did not know you held yourself so cheaply. I would have put in my bid."

"I make no bargain with you or with anyone else."

His face was taut with anger, and coming close he lifted my chin with his finger. "You fool."

Again I tried to move away, but he followed me. "But I am an even bigger fool. I did not dream that he could touch you. Even when Tawn warned me, I did not heed her.

'She is too cool—too fine,' I said. And you end up in Saint's bed. Jesus!"

"And if I love my husband?"

The same light, mocking, maddening laugh. "Love Saint? Oh, no, Hester. I have it in mind that you love me."

He came closer and seizing me in his arms kissed me hurtfully on the mouth. I knew then that what he said was true. Words could deny, but now my lips answered his with truth. I loved him.

Lifting his head, he looked down into my eyes. "Hester, Hester, why did you do it?"

I stared up into his eyes without answering, feeling guilty that I should love him, never for a moment forgetting that he was father to Tawn's boys.

I slipped from within the circle of his arms and faced him in the dusk. Now once and for all I must settle matters between Roi and me.

"I want you to understand this, Roi. I shall never be unfaithful to my husband."

His eyebrows quirked. "Have I asked you to be unfaithful, Hester? As I recall," he said smoothly, "we were talking about something quite different—your marriage."

"You know nothing of the reasons for my marriage, and so you despise me—"

He interrupted, a strange little smile on his face. "Know nothing of your reasons, Hester? Oh, I know your reasons all right. You wanted to be mistress of Seven Chimneys—a great lady with lands and servants and money. It's what all the carpetbaggers want when they come South."

Slowly I said, "You can't understand that, can you, Roi?"

"I would lie in the fields with the animals before I would lie with a woman I didn't love, even if it meant sacrificing something I had hoped to gain."

I thought of Tawn and could hardly hold the contempt from my voice. "You are young and romantic, Roi."

"I was not aware they were shameful qualities."

I was silent.

"Besides—with me you could have had a home." He flung the words at me.

Now it was I who laughed. "With you? Living in the woods! Waiting for you to come home from your sluts! That is not a life I would choose, even if it were offered. And you never spoke of marriage to me."

He crossed to Sans Foix and swung into the saddle. "You are right," he said. "I never did. I had some foolish idea—after that day at my place—that you must be won slowly, that I must walk with care, lest I affront your sweet virginity. I did not know that you were an overripe plum ready to fall into any man's hand."

Rage such as I had never before felt enveloped me. "I never want to hear your voice again," I said with a low and deadly fury in my voice. And then my control broke. "Leave me," I screamed. "Leave me this instant!"

At my voice Sans Foix reared and with an oath Roi swung him sharply toward the wall of forest which bound the horizon; I stood there, my eyes following horse and rider until they vanished beneath the trees; and I felt the shock of Sans Foix's hoofs on my heart.

As I passed through the lower hall a few minutes later, Old Madame called to me from the drawing room, and I paused at the door. She sat before the fire with one of the numberless trays on her lap, and when I said "Yes," she waited until she had licked her buttery fingers before she answered. Her myopic eyes surveying me calculatingly, she said, "My son has been asking for you. Where on earth were you? He wants you to come to the turret room."

When I opened the turret-room door and entered, Saint Clair sat at the card table in his dressing gown and did not so much as look my way until I demanded, "What do you want?" Then deliberately he laid the cards down and looked at me. Not by the quiver of an eyelash did his lifeless face change.

"I only wish to let you know"—his voice was as casual as if he made polite conversation in a drawing room—"that I will not be made a fool of."

I could only stand and stare at him. I had not the least idea of what he meant, yet the significance in his voice did not escape me.

"Has anyone tried to make a fool of you?" I asked lightly.
"Yes. You have."

"To make a fool of you is the farthest thing from my thoughts. Will you explain?"

"You may as well understand that I know of the pretty scene which just transpired between you and Roi."

"You know?" I began—then remembering how Roi had held me in his arms, had kissed me, I fell into silence, a silence that no doubt admitted guilt to the man before me.

Our glances met and measured before he drawled, "I have always known there was something between you and Roi."

"How could you know what did not exist?"

He ignored my words and let his slide across them. "But I find it hard to believe that a woman who prides herself on her 'good sense' would waste time on Roi, who chases every harlot that comes his way."

"You are exaggerating the incident." I forced myself to calm matter-of-factness. "There is nothing to believe—or disbelieve."

Again he continued as if I had not spoken. "Roi has caused me no end of trouble of one sort or another. I have not the slightest intention of letting him cause more through you."

I could deny the reasonableness of this no more than I could deny his right to disapprove. There was Tawn and probably much more of which I had no knowledge; yet looking at him sitting there so lifeless, so superior—at least in his own opinion—I resented the fact that he had justice on his side; and I had to force myself to assure him his disapproval was unnecessary.

"You need not worry about trouble from Roi—as far as I am concerned," I told him.

"I do not intend to worry about it. But I won't have it."

"Are you going to be a jealous husband?" I made my voice light in an effort to bring levity to a scene which I found distasteful.

There was no responsive levity in him. "Jealousy has nothing to do with it. I won't be made a fool of."

He deliberately turned back to his card table. I swung on my heels and left the room. His voice followed me down the twisted turret stairs. "Have Margot fetch my supper," he called, "and a bottle of brandy."

As I retraced my path to the lower floor I wondered who had witnessed the scene between Roi and me. Who had hastened to impart that information to Saint Clair? I wondered too if every act of mine was to be spied upon and reported and if Saint Clair would consider it his right to judge my every action and on any matter however small try to force his will upon mine. If such were the case, I thought wryly, he would learn that I was not one to yield— as Lorelie had yielded.

I went through the lower hall toward the kitchen to give Margot orders about the supper tray. As I did so the big clock which stood there struck six. It dawned upon me suddenly that only twenty-four hours had passed since I had stood in the drawing room and heard Saint Clair drawl, "Miss Snow and I were married this afternoon." Only twenty-four hours.

Chapter Twelve

DAYBREAK next morning found me up and dressed and on my way to the cotton land that I had told Shem must be cleared at once and made ready for ploughing. I was anxious to see how capable he was of handling the Negroes, for although Captain Peake had spoken highly of him—as if I should consider myself fortunate to get him— I had to be convinced in my own mind that I could leave the work to his ordering. After all, Captain Peake's opinion of him might have been overrated.

But when I reached the field I found I need not have worried. The Negroes who only yesterday had seemed so stupid and childish, who had roistered before the cabins after supper with such abandon that you doubted if they would ever take work seriously, now stood quietly as Shem apportioned each one's task. When he had finished they picked up hoes and pitchforks and talking among themselves cheerfully, set to at the cane and scrub as docilely as good children.

As I watched them they broke from what had been before a solid blot of indistinguishable humanity and became individuals. Uncle Early, his grizzled hair gray with age but his wizened body spry as a cricket's—John Eaton with his black eyes wicked in the narrow face (I would never trust him, I decided)—Clarence, built like a monstrous gorilla, his splayed black hand powerful enough to kill with a blow but with infantile good humor beaming from his flat-nosed face—and Big Lou, swinging her elephantine buttocks as she walked, her pendulous breasts quivering as the bursts of rich laughter poured from her throat in a constant stream.

Rupert was already at our little table by the kitchen window when I took my place, eating rapidly without regard for the manners which I had tried to teach him. He was quick to inform me that after breakfast he was going to the cotton field to watch the Negroes. "Shem says I can tote water to them," he announced proudly. And when calmly, I told him that he must do lessons first he threw himself back in his chair and scowled at me across the table.

"Aw, Hester! I don't want to do lessons today."

"But we've missed three days already, Rupert."

"I don't care. Maum Lucie said you and papa would be bridegrooming for the longest time—that you wouldn't be thinking about lessons."

I threw a sharp glance at the old woman who suddenly with a great clatter of pans became very busy at the hearth. What nonsense had she put into the boy's head?

"We will do lessons today just the same."

He hunched deeper in his chair and continued to glower at me. "I wanted to watch 'em in the field," he grumbled.

"The word is 'them,'" I corrected. "Come, Rupert—you are acting like a baby. Sit up properly and eat your breakfast."

His face narrowed at the word "baby," but he straightened and began to eat once more and I considered the episode finished. Not until he spoke did I see that he was still angry. His voice was cool and drawling and edged with polite irony.

"Are you feeling well this morning, Hester?"

His manner was such a perfect imitation of his father's that I looked at him with amused amazement.

"I feel very well, thank you. But why this sudden interest in my health?"

He buttered his biscuit with elegant daintiness. "Oh, I just wondered. Margot says that Tawn is conjurin' you—like she conjured mama and that you'll be drowned like mama was."

"*Je fais—tu fais—il fait*," Rupert's voice droned on as monotonously as the bluebottle fly that struggled at the window and with almost as little progress. "Can't I go now?"

"Once more. Then you may go."

He yawned and sighed and cast a yearning glance through

the window but willingly enough began to stumble through the verbs again. I had to compel myself to patience for I too wished to be outdoors, to be in the fields, to see how the work progressed; I had no liking for the schoolroom and the dullness of French verbs.

But suddenly both of us were released from boredom. The door opened and looking up from the French grammar I saw that Saint Clair stood in the doorway, a letter in his hand.

"Yes?" I inquired politely.

"It is necessary that we go to Savannah on the afternoon boat," he drawled. "Will you have Margot pack bags? We may be there for a few days."

"But I can't go to Savannah. There is the work—the Negroes."

"Your headsman can see to it—probably better than you."

"But I don't wish to go—there is no reason why I should go."

The hand that held the letter gestured with the slightest of motions. "There happens to be a reason. My first wife's attorney requests our presence in his office. And at our earliest convenience."

"What does your wife's attorney have to do with me?"

The birdlike eyes met mine steadily. "That we will learn tomorrow."

Rupert who had stood by quietly ran forward. "Papa—let me go with you and Hester. Please, papa." In his eagerness he caught hold of his father's dressing gown; but Saint Clair, without looking down into the boy's upturned face, deliberately loosened the small fingers.

"Why not take him?" I intercepted the refusal which I saw coming. "I would enjoy having him along."

"I am sure you would"—the slight smile was knowing—"but I have not the slightest intention of being bothered with him." Without waiting to hear further pleadings he went his indolent way up the hall.

Rupert stood with clenched fists, his elfin face passionate with feeling. "I hate papa—I hate him. I wish I could stomp on his face till it bled."

Try as I might I could find no words with which to scold him.

Except for the memory of the small lonely figure of Rupert left standing on the landing as the longboat receded down the channel, I might have taken pleasure in the stir and bustle which we found on board the *Captain Flint* that afternoon. There was a large party of ladies and gentlemen on board—bound for some affair in Savannah, I learned. They were gay and lively, the gentlemen drinking in the ship's bar while their ladies, wearing the huge new bustles which heretofore I had seen only in pictures, clustered like gigantic butterflies in the large salon and on the deck.

Saint Clair and I, however, were excluded from this gaiety though I saw, as we passed among them, that several of the gentlemen spoke to my husband. But they spoke with a sort of guarded civility which told more plainly than words that they did not wish the chance meeting to develop beyond this point. Even Captain Pellet—the same with whom I had traveled to Darien—was somewhat stiff in his greeting. I noticed that the ladies turned their heads so that their eyes might follow the tall, elegant figure of my husband who appeared—as always—oblivious to his surroundings. Once he was past they whispered to each other behind their dainty hands.

That night as I stood alone on deck I was so intent upon my thoughts that I was unaware of the two men who had come to lean at the rail near by, until their voices, wafted clearly across the scant space between us, arrested my attention. Then I saw it was Captain Pellet and a ponderous man made faceless by the night; with surprise I realized they spoke of me.

"I brought her down early last fall," Captain Pellet was saying. "Going to be governess to LeGrand's boy, she said. And now by God she's married him. I never woulda believed it."

"She's a likely-looking filly," the faceless man laughed coarsely, "but not the stripe I'd think he'd hanker for. And there's a lot of talk going round. His first wife you know was drowned." He laughed again and I could almost see the lewd wink that accompanied his next words, "Suicide—they said."

"And she married him right off?" the captain asked.

"Afore the first one was cold."

The captain spat in the water disgustedly. "I never woulda thought it," he repeated, "she looked such a lady. And touchy? Good God! I was mighty nigh afraid to speak to her."

"And she's hiring Darien niggers"—the faceless man's voice turned mincing—"going to plant rice and sea island cotton. Oh, she's going to do great things"—now he was suddenly angry—"like the rest of the damned buzzards that come down here to pick our bones clean. Well—we know how to take care of the likes of her and the rest of 'em. And the damned Loyal Leaguers too."

They moved away still talking and I stood pondering on what I had heard. It was clear that already my marriage was the subject of gossip, and it did not tax my imagination to envision the tight lips and suspicious eyes as the news went from mouth to mouth throughout the community. No doubt they mistrusted and scorned me—thought of me only as an avaricious woman who had managed to acquire a desirable position. But I saw their scorn as that of the beggar who was too indolent to win for himself but who despised those who by industry did manage to succeed. Only a fool, I told myself, would be swayed by the opinion of others when the others were slaves of ignorance and prejudice.

So, when I returned to the cabin and must pass among the bedecked ladies, I returned their stares coolly and lifted my chin.

Chapter Thirteen

NEXT morning amid the shrill whistles of tugboats and the throaty cries of foghorns we went ashore in Savannah and were driven over the cobbled streets to the new Pulaski House, a modern and comfortable hotel which even had the new gas lighting. Savannah was like an old-world seaport, with narrow houses standing close to the streets, with grilled gateways and half-concealed gardens. The soft but insistent undertone of the past created as definite an aura as the tang of salt winds and the heavy sweetness of magnolias.

We no sooner reached our room at the Pulaski House, which was large and high-ceilinged and cool, than Saint Clair informed me we would go to the lawyer's immediately; so I took time only to wash my face and hands and redo my hair, conscious as I did, of the figure of my husband sunk in the deep chair. He appeared to take no cognizance of what I did, but I became self-conscious as a woman will when eyes watch her too closely at her toilette; and I must do the coil of hair on my neck a second time before it pleased me.

As I thrust in the shell pins he spoke. "If you cared about it, you might be a handsome woman."

His words confirmed my belief that he had not been so disinterested as he had feigned and so my voice was tart. "I am not concerned with whether I am 'handsome' or not."

"Does it please you to make yourself deliberately plain?"

"I have never aspired to be a beauty. And since I am a plain woman—it is proper that I wear plain clothes."

"That applied when you were only a governess. It does not apply now."

"Perhaps you would like for me to wear one of the new bustles—like the ladies on the boat?" I suggested saucily.

"I would like for you to look less like a damned Quaker woman."

I stifled the impulse to tell him I had always dressed as I pleased and would continue to do so. Instead, I shrugged and putting on my hat again announced I was ready to go to the lawyer's.

With one fluid motion he lifted himself from the chair and crossed to where I stood beside the bureau; and I saw something in his eyes which caused discomfort to stir within me.

"Shall we go now?" I spoke quickly and reached for my reticule which lay on the bureau with the intention of forestalling—I knew not what.

Quietly, he laid his hand upon mine and held it prisoner. "Hester—"

"Yes?" I raised my eyes to his.

The cold smile touched his lips briefly.

"You hate me, don't you?"

At first I did not answer. I only stood staring at him until his fingers tightened on my hand demandingly. Then I said slowly, "There can be no question of hate between you and me. You are my husband."

"Nor of love, I presume?"

"Nor of love."

Again the bleak, hateful smile. "Yet you accept my connubial caresses willingly enough."

I felt the color rush to my face—so baldly stated, my acceptance of that which I considered my duty was ugly and sordid; I could only stand there silent, unable to meet his eyes. Then my will asserting itself I faced him squarely.

"If I have willingly accepted your 'connubial caresses,' as you call them, it is because I consider them part of our bargain."

He took his hand from mine. "Yet I would swear they were not entirely unwelcome"—it was amazing how his voice, lacking all expression, could express so much—"or did you close your eyes and imagine I was Roi?"

I had no answer for this resurrection of my secret thoughts —I was powerless to command words that might have served for truth; and for a moment so we stood, he perfectly at ease, smiling the little smile which only seemed to intensify the bleakness of his face. Then he drawled, "Now—we will go to the lawyer's."

We drove to the lawyer's along the Savannah streets. Negro cooks swept off narrow stoops and haggled at the curb with hucksters. A Geechee man and woman, their baskets balanced perfectly on their kinky heads, chanted their ware: "Shrimp-crab-buya-shrimp-crab-buya." The carriage came to a stop at a series of old red brick buildings with iron railings. Bidding the driver wait, Saint Clair led me through a fan-lighted door-way into a high-ceilinged outer room where the sunshine flowing through high windows touched many bird cages holding tiny parakeets of brilliant hue. Here we waited while the old colored man in white coat announced us.

He returned before long to conduct us to another room, which was large and lofty with a fine carved ceiling and dom-inated in its center by a massive desk. At the far end of the room slatted blinds subdued the light and intensified the air of quiet seclusion of the place. At the desk Stephen Pearsall, a majestic figure, stood waiting as we entered.

Stephen Pearsall was not a young man. His age might have easily been reckoned over sixty, but there was in his face—as closely shaven and unlined as Roi's—the calm power that defies age; beneath the snow-white crest of hair his eyes were the clear eyes of a young man.

As Saint Clair introduced us, which he did with his usual irritating inertia, I perceived that the gaze Stephen Pearsall bent upon me was one of attentive interest, and when he spoke I heard in his southern voice the secret gentleness that no woman can resist. Once we were seated, he addressed him-self to me.

"I trust this visit to my office has not inconvenienced you, Mrs. LeGrand."

When I had told him it was of no inconvenience, he sat at his desk again and drew a sheaf of papers from the desk drawer. "I have requested you to come here, Mrs. LeGrand, because of certain facts regarding the first Mrs. LeGrand's last will and testament." He paused as if he expected me to speak, but I had no idea of what I was expected to say. Instinctively I turned toward my husband, but I received no help there.

He half sat, half lay in his chair, his eyes upon the gold watch chain with which his pale hand toyed.

"The first Mrs. LeGrand"—Stephen Pearsall's voice and manner were detached and dispassionate—"was a young lady of considerable fortune at the time of her marriage to"—here he hesitated as though he considered the proper word—"to your husband." His eyes lifted from the papers and rested upon mine searchingly, "You knew that, perhaps?"

Some quality in his eyes and voice brought me an inexplicable sense of discomfort and I sat in silent watchfulness, waiting to hear what it was he had to tell me.

"Much of that fortune," he continued, "has been"—he paused deliberately and his eyes turned to the figure of Saint Clair—"has been dissipated. At the time of Lorelie LeGrand's 'unfortunate' death, only a fraction of what was once a substantial fortune remained."

In his chair Saint Clair stifled a yawn. "How long will it take you to tell us what we already know, Pearsall?"

As far as Stephen Pearsall was concerned, he might not have spoken. Without so much as changing the direction of his glance, he continued, "Your husband knows of certain, unusual conditions specified in the first Mrs. LeGrand's will. Has he perhaps informed *you* of these conditions?"

I moved my head in denial, unable to choke off a strange feeling that some unforeseen complication was about to close about me.

Stephen Pearsall picked up the thread of narrative with exquisite ease. "Perhaps then I had better explain to you. At the time of the first Mrs. LeGrand's marriage to Saint Clair LeGrand, women had no property rights. You understand, do you not that until the passage of the Woman's Law in '66 a wife was entirely under the control of her guardian—in short, her husband?"

I moved my head again this time in assent and he went on. "Lorelie LeGrand's will was made shortly before her unfortunate death. In it"—he laid his palm on the papers beside him—"she bequeaths everything—*everything* to her son Rupert." He paused and the stillness pervaded the room. "And she names as guardian—in complete control of her son, his estate, and his welfare—Hester Snow. You, Mrs. LeGrand."

Blankly, I repeated, "Me?"

His clear eyes held mine as he touched the papers before him gently. "All is here in legal form and past controversy."

"But"—I gazed at him unbelieving—"I do not see—" I looked at Saint Clair questioningly. "What about Rupert's father?" I asked slowly. "He is the guardian according to law, is he not?"

Stephen Pearsall's eyes narrowed shrewdly. "I see you are not unfamiliar with legal matters, Mrs. LeGrand. You are right. A father is the legal guardian of his child—unless"—his pause was significant—"unless the father himself waives that right in favor of another. Saint Clair LeGrand did waive that right on a previous visit to my office—"

"But why? Still I do not understand," I stammered.

His fine hand tapped the polished desk gently. "Perhaps I should elucidate, Mrs. LeGrand. Less than two months ago Lorelie LeGrand came to this office in a state of great mental stress desiring to make her will. When she outlined the premise of that will, I—knowing her intentions would leave her will open to litigation on the part of her husband—frankly sought to dissuade her. It was then"—he looked squarely at Saint Clair—"that she informed me of 'certain' facts (and proof of those facts) with which to fight such litigation. When after her death I informed Saint Clair LeGrand of these facts, he agreed willingly to the conditions of the will."

Quiet invaded the room again until Saint Clair's drawling voice disturbed it. "May I see that will again, Pearsall?"

Stephen Pearsall's hand went unerringly to the document and placed it in Saint Clair's outstretched fingers, which received it as casually as if it were one of Gene Poiter's bills; and when he had leisurely, and without the least apparent interest, unfolded it and glanced at it, he returned it to the desk. "I see my brother Roi was one of the witnesses to this will. Just how did he figure in all this?"

Stephen Pearsall's hands formed a steeple before him and his finger tips touched and retouched with gentle rhythm. "He was of considerable assistance to your first wife, LeGrand—many times."

Saint Clair stifled his delicate yawn. "—And gave generously of his advice, I suppose."

"I do not think your wife needed advice, LeGrand." The lawyer's voice was now less dispassionate—its quiet was threaded with ominousness. "Your wife had sufficient reasons—you know them, I need not enumerate them here—for trying to safeguard the future of her son."

"The woman was mad," Saint Clair began, but before he could continue Stephen Pearsall interrupted him. "If you have any plans along that line, LeGrand, it may interest you to know that your first wife intercepted them. Two doctors have attested as to her sanity at the time she made her second will."

Presently his eyes came back to me. "I will be as brief as possible, Mrs. LeGrand, but there are certain provisions which I must outline to you."

I bowed politely.

For a moment he studied the papers before him—then resting his hand flat upon them he looked across the desk at me. "Lorelie LeGrand has instructed, Mrs. LeGrand, first: that all monies and properties—there is very little of the last, I will give you a list of them later—are directly under your control. Second: you will have complete control of the welfare of her son—his health, education, and future profession. . . ."

He paused and I nodded in understanding.

"Third: you will use what money you deem necessary for the improvement of Seven Chimneys and at the end of each year you will pay to Saint Clair LeGrand one third of the profits accruing from your management of the plantation, first deducting the yearly expenditures."

He paused again and when he spoke his voice had lost its gentleness; it was firm and registered each word so clearly that they might have been small pebbles dropped onto a hard surface.

"The provisions regarding Seven Chimneys will prevail so long as you control affairs thereon, Mrs. LeGrand." His calm, just eyes turned to Saint Clair. "You understand that, LeGrand?"

"I am not a complete fool," the insolent voice retorted.

"And"—Stephen Pearsall continued to emphasize his words as if to impress their importance upon me—"Saint Clair LeGrand is to receive no gifts of money from his son's estate other than specified above."

His voice sank to nothingness and we sat there in a quiet so intense that the gentle chattering of the birds in the next room penetrated the massive door. Finally the lawyer spoke again.

"There is one more condition by which you must abide, Mrs. LeGrand, in respect to the mulatto woman known as Tawn, and the two sons of Tawn. They are to be housed on Seven Chimneys and fed and clothed as long as they desire to remain there. And the two sons are to have any educational advantages possible to give them."

"The two sons of Tawn?" I echoed blankly.

"The two sons of Tawn," he repeated, his eyes looking into mine steadily. "You understand, do you, Mrs. LeGrand, why the first Mrs. LeGrand was concerned for the welfare of these boys?"

I might have cried out that I understood too well, that now as always when I thought of them I rebelled because the mere fact of their existence had power to wound me; but I gave utterance to none of this. Instead I nodded stiffly.

He sat silent for a moment, then in a more casual manner proceeded. "There are a few matters of lesser importance." His eyes ran down the page of the document swiftly. "You will continue to support Seven Chimneys and the family as Lorelie LeGrand has done for years—there are letters of administration to be signed—" He broke off and sat silent a moment; then he looked at me and his face was stern. "I shall not conceal from you, Mrs. LeGrand, that I did not wholly approve of this will of Lorelie LeGrand's, though I recognized the fact that some new arrangement regarding her son was necessary. Frankly, though she assured me such was not the case, I feared some undue influence had been brought to bear upon her."

I knew—his clear eyes told me—what he was thinking: that this upstart young schoolteacher had wangled herself first into the dead wife's confidence, then into her place; and I rebelled that this man should think me worse than I was. So before he could say more I arose and went to his desk.

"Mr. Pearsall, you seem to be laboring under some misapprehension as to my position in this matter. May I make it clear to you?"

He bowed ironically. "Certainly, Mrs. LeGrand."

"It occurs to me, sir, that perhaps you consider me some sort of an adventuress with sufficient shrewdness and little enough principle to inveigle myself into an advantageous position. You are wrong, sir. I came to Seven Chimneys as a governess totally unaware of the situation. And because I found the place lying idle and going to waste I did what I could to better it, even investing my own small savings to get the work started."

He asked gently, "And was this with the sanction of Lorelie LeGrand?"

"Whether she approved or disapproved I do not know, sir," I answered tartly. "I saw her on only one occasion when she was sufficiently sober to express an opinion. And she did not express one then."

"Ah," he interposed thoughtfully, "proceed, Mrs. LeGrand."

"What I have done, I have done because I dislike laziness and waste and shiftlessness. To see that land lying idle, the house dirty, the boy Rupert neglected—and no one to lift a finger—" I paused and quietly he inserted his next question.

"And that is why you married Saint Clair LeGrand, ma'am?"

I returned his speculative glance defiantly. "That sir—you nor anyone else should presume to ask."

He bowed gravely. "You are quite right, ma'am," he said. For a moment he continued to sit there with his eyes on the papers before him. Then, suddenly, he stood and for the first time since we entered the room smiled and I fancied there was warmth, even liking, in that smile. "Tomorrow, Mrs. LeGrand, if agreeable to you, I will call for you and escort you to the bank. You understand there are certain legal formalities to be gone through. Will eleven o'clock suit your convenience, ma'am?"

He waited for my nod of assent, then gave a stiff old-fashioned bow. "Then tomorrow at eleven," he said courteously, but with a finality that told me our interview was at an end.

Chapter Fourteen

Riding back to the hotel I stole a look at Saint Clair to see what effect the scene just past had had upon him. If it had affected him in the least there was no outward evidence to betray it. His face wore its same aloof arrogance. We might have just left a tea party where he had heard only the most casual conversation, and I wondered if what I had read somewhere could be true—that there are some in the world whose veins hold no blood but only a tepid fluid, incapable of warmth. Surely—if it were true—my husband belonged to the species.

As for my own feelings, they were of too mixed an order for analysis and I could not yet untangle the coil of circumstance which, moving in the subterranean channels of my life, had wrapped itself about me. But this much had been revealed to me. Lorelie LeGrand had thought to triumph over her husband by lifting the management of her son and her estate from his hand to mine. He on the other hand had tried to checkmate her by making me his wife. Now I knew the answer to the questions for which heretofore I had been unable to find an answer: Saint Clair's reason for marrying me and his haste for the ceremony. Yet he could sit beside me now knowing I at last realized his plan to use me, and still he remained undisturbed, even unconcerned. Perhaps, I thought, he would be less confident if he knew I had not the slightest intention of being used by him or any man.

When we reached our room at the Pulaski House, which was cool and dim and most welcome after the enervating midday heat of the town, I laid my hat and dolman aside with a sigh of relief. My husband, without speaking, changed his vest to one of finest brocade, taking greatest pains with the arrangement of his cravat. When he had accomplished this to his satisfaction (and he was fastidious in regard to his dress), he took his hat and moved toward the door.

"I shall have supper out," he drawled, "and probably return late. Do you mind?"

I knew his question to be one of politeness only, and whether I minded or not would have not the slightest influence upon him. So when I told him, "Not at all," I made my voice as casual as his.

"If you dislike eating supper alone, you can have it up here." He designated the room indolently.

"I have eaten supper alone too many times in my life to find it unpleasant," I retorted.

Without further comment he left—even his manner of closing a door conveyed lassitude—and I went to stand at the front windows which overlooked the hotel entrance and a minute later was rewarded by seeing his fashionable figure depart in a carriage. Then with a feeling of release I undressed and lay across the bed hoping I would sleep. But I did not sleep. Until the deeper shadowing of the room announced the setting of the sun, I lay there staring into space in that state of excitement in which a sense of shock is mingled with a feeling of triumph.

It was after five when I descended the stairs of the hotel with the intention of obtaining from the clerk information as to a place where I could have supper alone with propriety.

When I approached the desk I found him engaged in conversation with one whom, despite the fact that his back was toward me, I recognized. It was Roi and at a murmured word from the clerk he wheeled and came to meet me. "I was just asking for you," he said swiftly. "Where is Saint?"

"How did you know I was here?" I asked levelly.

The laughter rose in his eyes. "I learn things, Hester—"

"Then perhaps you know *why* we are here?"

"Yes, I know that too." He broke off then. "But we can't stand talking in a hotel lobby; there's gossip enough already. Where were you going?"

"To supper. Saint Clair is having supper out. He will not return until late."

He looked at me gravely a moment, then shrugged. "I will take you to supper. Come—let's find a carriage."

Once we were in the carriage which was musty and old with the smell of worn leather, his mood changed and as we started on our clopping way along the cobbled streets he said gaily, "I never thought you and I would ride through the streets of Savannah together, Hester." He leaned toward me and peered into my face. "Are you still mad with me?"

I did not answer. I was remembering how he had called me "strumpet"—how I had sworn to hate him—and I asked myself why it was Roi LeGrand's laughter could obliterate anything he said or did.

When I continued to sit beside him in stiff silence, he threw himself back against the leather cushions and crossed his arms. "Oh, I see! We have the schoolmarm with us. Very well, then, I shall take her on a sight-seeing tour. Over there, Miss Snow—pardon me, I mean Mrs. LeGrand"—his voice was taunting—"I call your attention to Savannah's first public building. John Wesley preached his first sermon on the site—please observe the carving. . . ."

I was in no mood for games and I interrupted him coldly. "What did you have to do with Lorelie's will?"

He turned serious again and when he spoke his voice was grave. "Nothing, Hester. That you must believe."

"Your name is upon it," I accused.

"Yes. I told her how the new Woman's Law made it possible for her to protect Rupert's rights—I was a witness. I met her in Savannah. Remember, Hester? The day she consulted a doctor? Poor thing, she hardly knew which way to turn; I went to Pearsall's office with her—"

I laughed, "A loyal brother you are, Roi."

His hand cut the air. "I owe him no loyalty," he cried. "I saw him destroy her—as he destroys everything he touches—"

"I suppose you think he will destroy me?" I asked scornfully.

"No," he spoke more slowly, "I think perhaps—" He paused. "But when I think that he has drawn you into the filthy mess—"

"He did not draw me. I went willingly. I knew what I was doing."

"You thought you knew. Christ, Hester!" He paused, then in

a quieter voice, "If you could know how I blame myself for not warning you."

"And of what would you have warned me, Roi? Would you have told me that he married me because he knew of Lorelie's will? It would not have changed me. I never thought he married me for love—do you think I was a silly girl who wanted love? Then you are wrong. I know that love is a soft, smiling thing, weak and selfish and disloyal. I want none of it. I knew what I was doing—what I wanted."

Suddenly he sighed and relaxed beside me, his brown hand touched my cheek in the briefest caress. "Hester—Hester— won't you ever learn that I never quarrel with you except for your own good?"

I felt the caress no more than if he had touched a stone. I stared ahead into the dusk that mingled with and became one with the gray moss which festooned the trees. "And when you called me evil names," I reminded him, "that was for my good?"

"No." The word came swift and whispered. "It was too late then to help you. You had married Saint. That—was jealousy, Hester."

I laughed. "And you think I didn't know it then?"

"I thought he could never hurt one I loved again. He'd hurt so many—Cecile—Lorelie—"

"You talk as if he were a monster—"

He spoke more slowly still. "A monster? Saint a monster? No. He's one of the damned, clinging to whatever he can get his hands upon, unable to face a world that lacks a hundred slaves and blooded horses and being a fine gentleman. He's evil, Hester, a greedy evil parasite who feeds upon others, who will cheat and steal—even kill—whatever stands between him and his greed."

I sighed wearily. "Oh, Roi—you speak so extravagantly—"

"Do I?" His voice was somber. "You don't know, do you, Hester, about the young soldier whom Cecile would have married? You don't know how Saint and his old mother between them made Lorelie's life a hell until she became—what she became—no woman could stand it—their hateful wills—poisoning Rupert's mind against her." His voice sank. "Poor Lorelie. And now you, Hester. I know I should have killed him long ago."

I shivered within my dolman at the dark brooding of his voice, but in an effort to bring matter-of-factness to the scene, I laughed lightly. "And that would be a fine solution, would it not? That you should kill him? And spend the rest of your life in prison?"

He sat unspeaking until I said, "But before you murder your brother, remember you promised to take me to supper. And I am hungry. I had no dinner."

We ate supper at Thunderbolt—named, Roi told me, by the Indians because a bolt of lightning struck the ground there and opened up a spring. While we ate, small boats bobbed up and down on the river and trawlers circled the wide bend, their nets glistening with the day's catch, the fishermen shouting and singing as they formed a line at the landing to unload. Above us branches of giant live-oaks draped with moss met like cathedral arches; beneath us the light of dusk was dim and shadowed.

At a clean-scrubbed pine table we ate the shrimp the Negro boy brought us. I watched Roi break the shells with his lean brown fingers and hold the morsels of sweet pink meat to my lips; but try as I might I could eat but little.

Suddenly his hand caught mine and cradled it. "Hester—sweetheart—"

"Yes—"

"Why don't you give it up? Leave Saint—and all the filthy mess. Come with me to Missouri. I know a man—Brad Busby—look." He reached into his pocket and brought out a crumpled letter. "Listen, Hester, he went to Missouri, this letter came to me just yesterday. There's land in Missouri, and Brad says fine land. Hester"—he leaned across the table in his eagerness—"we could stake our land and build our cabin—" Then he stopped at what he saw in my face. "But you wouldn't do that, would you?"

"No, Roi—I wouldn't do that." I could have told him that too well I knew the picture he would have drawn for me—the rude house in the clearing, the poverty and sordidness, all the namelessness and loneliness which I had escaped.

He dropped my hand as though it had the power to burn, and looked at me steadily. "You are a strange girl, Hester.

I know you love me. Why are you ashamed of loving me?"

I did not tell him why, and suddenly as a landscape is brought to life by angled lightning, it flashed before me that I could never tell him. Never could I confess to him the hunger I knew for him; it was a weakness to which I must not yield lest disaster engulf me.

I rose quickly. "I must go. It is late. See, they are lighting the lanterns." Without looking back or waiting for him I made my way to the road where the old Negro driver nodded on his box seat. When Roi leapt in beside me I was sitting stiff and cold again looking ahead, into the night.

He sat beside me quietly, his eyes upon the road ahead. After a while he spoke, his voice cadenced, close to whispering. "I knew you would come someday Hester, but little did I dream that you would be like you are. I don't know what I pictured but I knew you would not be too gentle or too loving. I'm sick of loving women who cling and tear. When I saw you that first time in McCrackin's store with your coil of brown hair and your steady eyes I said, 'It is she.' You were cool and straight, like the young trees I see growing in the woods. I thought nothing ugly could ever touch you," he paused, then went on thoughtfully. "That's what hurts most of all—like a young tree—and belonging to Saint."

Suddenly he came close and I felt his warm lips against my throat. "Hester—Hester," he murmured, "do you think I'm giving you up?" He laughed with soft triumph. "Never for a moment—remember, I am a LeGrand too. Nothing shall hold from me what is mine."

I sat straight beside him with cold, tight-clenched hands and tried to close my ears against his voice—my heart against the touch of his lips; but all at once the world seemed dark and desolate; the distant singing of Negro voices might have been a dirge—even the slim young moon took on a baleful air.

"Please tell the driver to hurry, Roi," I ordered coldly. "It is growing late. I must return to the hotel."

He waited for a moment and I knew he was angry again and when finally he spoke his voice came as light and cool as water trickling in a glen. "As you wish, Mrs. LeGrand," he cried with mock gallantry. "I will take you back to your hotel and your husband. May you be as happy as two thieves."

Chapter Fifteen

RUPERT waited on the landing when two days later Saint Clair and I returned to Seven Chimneys, his face eager, his hands reaching for presents before I had stepped from the long-boat. As we went up the path toward the house he could not conceal his delight but must walk beside me, holding my hand tightly as if he feared I might escape again. As we walked he was telling me in his swift, hurrying voice of events that had transpired in my absence: He had found a cooter terrapin; Shem had killed a big diamondback and was making a snakeskin belt to ward off rheumatism; Big Lou had cut her husband about Stella, the tall yellow girl.

In the living room I gave him the toy boat and glass aggies I had brought him and then while he sat on the floor to inspect them, I turned to greet Old Madame who, though it was only mid-morning, was having a "little something to stay her stomach" until dinner time. She greeted me with her customary ironic politeness, but it occurred to me that her eyes were less impassive than ordinary; that they were—as she lifted them to mine—wary and guarded as if the woman behind them were tensed to hear something beside the usual polite inanities. But she only inquired suavely, "And was your trip an agreeable one, mademoiselle?"

I murmured the expected response and quickly, before she could engage me in tiresome conversation, went upstairs to change, my eyes inspecting corners as I went to see if Margot had kept the house in good order. But subconsciously I was remembering Old Madame's eyes and speculating on what she knew of my trip to Savannah; some intuition told me she was thoroughly informed—had been thoroughly informed by Saint Clair. For long ago I had come to realize that while these two never by the least word or the slightest action betrayed fondness or intimacy, there existed between them a perfect understanding; what the son believed or desired found echo in the old woman.

What she knew—or did not know—however, gave me no concern, for since the day Stephen Pearsall had accompanied me to the bank to explain in complete detail the affairs of Lorelie LeGrand, I knew I had nothing to fear from Old Madame or her fine son. And then and there I had decided upon my own course of action and on the attitude I intended to assume. I had learned that within Lorelie LeGrand, whom I had considered a poor weak thing, there had existed sagacity, even cunning shrewdness. She had arranged money enough to insure the welfare of Seven Chimneys, to buy what was needed to assure my plans success; as if, I thought as I changed into my workaday dress, she reached back from the grave to do what she had never been allowed to do in life, control the destinies of Rupert and the plantation which would someday be his; and I did not deceive myself—to control the destiny of Hester Snow as well.

Though it was now nearly noon and the sun blazed high in the sky, I went at once toward the fields, anxious to see how the work had gone forward in my absence. As I neared them I experienced a thrill of surprised elation. Already the Negroes were ploughing the cotton land! In the distance I saw the team of oxen pulling the ploughs. The upturned earth lay like a huge black patch on the green land. I saw the furrows lengthening; I could almost smell the rich damp earth as it turned its carved face skyward, and I realized how Shem must have forced the Negroes to unflagging industry to ready the land for breaking. Surely, I told myself, he was capable and trustworthy—it would be ill of me to interfere; and so stopping short I turned and retraced my way to the house.

Within it I found signs of no such industry. Maum Lucie, I perceived at once, had let her kitchen lapse into its former disorder, and I spent some minutes pointing out the slovenliness and wastefulness, standing over her while she started to restore order. As I went about the lower rooms pointing out this and that which had not been done, Margot watched me warily as if she realized, in my manner, some new and firmer authority, as indeed there was. I was assuming the complete control which I knew I must. This I knew would impose more work upon me, for there must be no detail that did not pass under my supervision—but I had no misgivings. On the other hand I was buoyed by the added responsibility and by the thought that while there was so much to be done, there was money with which to do. Already I could imagine the results of success—could see Seven Chimneys rising to grandeur once again, yielding its fruitful harvests, with fine horses in its stables, with chickens and pigs and cows in its barnyard, bales of cotton being shipped to Savannah, flats loaded with rice floating down the river.

And as I planned I did not stop to realize that in these plans, fashioned to my own desire, the figure of my husband did not move; unconsciously, I had thrust him from my life.

It was these plans that buoyed me in the days that followed, that gave zest to my work—filled hours and robbed them of their drudgery. Now I was never idle. It seemed there welled within me springs of energy that were inexhaustible. As the days rolled into weeks and the cold snaps of February yielded to the gentle sun of March I was never at rest—how could I be? For now that the cotton field was ploughed and planted, the Negroes were busy in the rice bottoms, putting in the quarter drains, building up the dykes, making the flood gate which controlled the water sturdy.

Often I stood and watched the work and after a time I came to marvel at the ease with which Shem kept his eyes upon all things. Each day my respect for his knowledge and wisdom increased. Here was a man of intelligence and ability, I saw— only the accident of birth and color had condemned him to menial labor. He handled the other Negroes—many of them older than he—with paternal wisdom. Even John Eaton, most troublesome of all, responded to Shem's quiet ordering as a restive stallion gentles to a soothing hand.

So many of them fell ill, victim to this or that ailment, that at last, more in desperation than mercy, I set up an infirmary in one of the unused cabins where—when they were really ill —they could be tended with dispatch. This imposed still another task on me, for now every hand was needed in the fields and it fell out I must render many strange services.

As I worked in the hospital I came to know the small children who were left, while their parents toiled, in the care of Tib, a sad-eyed girl of twelve or thirteen whose scrawny shoulders seemed too frail to bear the bouncing weight of the fat babies she must watch. Sometimes as I passed her sitting desolately in the clearing, a wriggling infant on her lap, I would stop and try to talk with her, but beyond a quiet "yassum" or "no'm" she would say nothing; and I would pass on, carrying with me the hopelessness of her wizened face and melancholy eyes.

But I did not forget her, and one night when Shem came to my office to make the day's report I spoke to him of the child. He must arrange to keep one of the women at the cabins each day, I told him, and free Tib from her bondage. I would use her in the house for light work; and so it came about. Tib was taught to clean silver and set table and I had Margot make some plain dark dresses for her; the first time I went to Darien I brought her her first pair of shoes. And though she never took them from their box, each night before she went to bed in the little room off mine, she would look at them reverently.

As time went on and I perceived with what earnestness she applied herself, something not unlike affection sprang up within me for the child. It was then that I conceived the idea of teaching her in the schoolroom each morning after Rupert's lessons were done; and on the heels of that idea came the thought of Tawn's two boys and the responsibility which Lorelie's will had imposed upon me. They should have schooling too. Thus one morning as I circled back toward the house from the fields, I stopped at the overseer's house to speak with Tawn regarding the matter.

I found her lying—though it was all of nine o'clock—on the bed, that same bed where Roi had lain when Saint Clair dressed his wound—curled as luxuriously as a pampered cat. When I paused in the doorway, she sat up, stretching and yawning with animal grace. "Yassum," she queried softly, "is yo' wantin' me?"

"Yes. I wish to speak to you about Lem and Willie."

The soft inquiry in her face changed to cold wariness. "Yassum, what about 'em?"

I told her briefly of my plan for teaching them along with Tib and as I talked she sat on the edge of the bed, her wide liquid eyes upon my face, her hands—they were small and beautifully shaped—hanging loosely clasped before her. When I finished she asked still softly, "Do Mister Saint say it all right if you teach my boys?"

I informed her shortly that I did not consider it necessary to mention the matter to Mr. LeGrand—it was I who decided such things now; and when she had considered this gravely she said (and in the manner of one bestowing a great favor), "I got no reason to say no—if it's what you want." I told her then she must send the boys to the schoolroom each morning at ten— and when I added she must see they were neat and clean, her chin lifted proudly. "I keeps my chillun clean."

I had to admit that usually this was true. I had observed that her house was usually spotless, the calico dresses that sheathed the voluptuous body which so repelled me, fresh and crisp; but now as I stood in the center of the room I perceived (and it was a surprising discovery) that it was otherwise. The place was in the sort of disorder which comes from days of neglect— soiled clothes flung in piles on the floor—the beds unmade, even unclean—and Tawn herself, with her uncombed hair and dirty dress, as slovenly as any field Negro. It was the abode of a woman without interest or stamina. I could not help but wonder what had worked the change in her.

My eyes came back to her to find her watching me intently and sharply. I asked her why she didn't clean the place—occupy her time with something worth while instead of lazing on the bed; she smiled—some secret meaning behind the smile. "I'll be cleanin' it good one of these days."

I disliked her seeming passive gentleness as much as I disliked the smile, but determined not to reveal to this woman her power to annoy me, I turned to leave the place; halfway to the door I stopped—my eyes arrested by a minute figure on the chest of drawers, a crude clumsy thing of clay but one which I recognized with amusement, not unmixed with anger, as a tiny replica of myself. There was the hair coiled in a knot on the neck even as mine was coiled; even the miniature dress was identical with the dark work dresses that I wore each day. And

I saw that here and there a huge thorn had been thrust into the small body.

I knew it for what it was immediately, the voodoo charm with which Tawn hoped to exert her conjuring power upon me. I was seized by the sudden impulse to snatch the tiny figure and tear it into pieces. But I controlled myself and at least with outward calm I left and went on toward the house. As I went I was hot with resentment because Lorelie LeGrand had laid upon me the obligation of keeping Tawn on the plantation. Surely, I told myself, there must be some manner in which I could rid myself of her; for each time I saw her and her soft body with its insolent uplifted breasts, it was as fuel to the shame that never ceased to sear when I remembered—and when did I forget?—that I too loved Roi.

Chapter Sixteen

TAWN and everything else sank into unimportance as spring advanced and the sun beat down implacably on us who toiled. Now the work was a demanding master who allowed no rest from sunup to sundown. As for me, my tasks were like an endless sea. Keeping the account books required, or so it seemed to me, continuous toil. Each pound of seed, each side of bacon, the infinite small wares which the Negroes constantly besought must first be entered in my purchase ledger and again in the sales ledger as I set the item down against the Negroes' account. There was my planting plan to be discussed with Shem, for everything planted was marked on the rude plot of Seven Chimneys which I had made and hung on the wall of the little office. Then there was the house: bedrooms to be kept in order, meals to be planned, checking of chests and linens, constant counting of wash. And there were my keys. Keys to drawers, to chests, to food closets, to china and glass. Keys of various sizes and designs—and yet after a week of locking and unlocking, coming to be so familiar that in the dark my fingers went unerringly to the one I sought.

From five in the morning until sundown I labored. And even evening won no release for me. After supper I must go to the office and check the pass books with Shem, hear his report of the day's work, discuss tomorrow's work with him. Like as not I must return to the hospital for a last look at the sick. There were, it seemed, always tasks enough to keep me busy until from sheer fatigue I would go to my room and fall into bed.

Yet the work I did not begrudge. For each day tangible results of the labor were visible and on early mornings when I walked over the land, first to the cotton fields, then on to the rice swamps, swinging back by the upland where Sey and Boy weeded, I could hear the mingled sounds of industry, creaking of ploughs, clacking of hoes, and the voices of the Negroes as they worked, and I remembered Seven Chimneys as it had been when I first came—idle, inanimate, dead. The day that Shem and I discovered patterned row on row of tiny leaves along the cotton furrows, my triumph was not unlike that of the sculptor who watches the form, existing heretofore only in his mind, take shape in the clay.

Within the house too, results of my labor were evident. Now the rooms lay ordered and shiningly clean. Every closet was prim, every shelf spotless. Each week the clean sun-dried laundry was laid away in its rightful place by Margot, the silver kept to twinkling brightness by Tib's diligent hands, and for the first time—in no one could say how many years—no dust was allowed to intrude across the aquiline faces that looked down from the LeGrand portraits in the hall.

Yet I could not take wholehearted satisfaction in what success I had won. Gradually it had been borne upon me that with the inmates of the house I had not succeeded. Margot's eyes continued to be as hostile as ever. Maum Lucie's mouth pursed just as often, and Old Madame continued to sit like a fat spider, imprisoned in the web of her indolence, gorging on the unceasing flow of food that Margot brought, her manner toward me that of the lady of the house toward a poor relation.

As for my husband—I might still have been the governess. The fact that I was his wife had occasioned not the slightest change in his manner. He came and went to Savannah at will, telling neither me nor anyone else when he left or when he would return; and his attitude, at least toward me, was so casual, so aloof, that I found it hard to believe that this man was my husband.

Yet I did not try to deceive myself, knowing perfectly he was not so indifferent as he feigned and that his eyes, which had a habit of seeming to observe nothing, observed me steadily. But there were times when my resolution to resist him wavered, when I found worthless all my effort and my struggle. It was on those nights when I lay dreading the opening of my bedroom door and in those dawns when I left that bedroom feeling bruised and shaken, knowing a shame that negated all accomplishment.

But the work—and time as well—went forward. It was on a night the first week of March that Rupert and I walked after supper to the barn to watch the claying of the rice seed—an event, Shem had informed me, which the Negroes anticipated eagerly and one for which I was expected to furnish supper and a dram.

We found the hands gathered under the trees around the barn, their strident voices and glistening eyes attesting that they already had drunk freely from the keg of whiskey I had provided; and on one side suckling pigs roasted over red embers and sent their smoky fragrance out into the spring dusk.

When Rupert and I approached, the Negroes broke into a fervent welcome. Big Lou cried, "Dere our mist'is and de young gennamun," and Stella, the tall yellow girl, usually sullen and ready to fight at the drop of a hat, now cackled, "Dere she, our little lily-white mist'is," and there ensued a general bowing and scraping which had I known them less well I might have mistaken for genuine devotion. But I was not deceived. Too well I knew their childish ability at play acting. So bidding them "Good evening" with pleasant detachment, I went into the barn.

Here I found much to interest me, for I had never seen a rice claying. In the rafters huge flatwood flares cast their orange light, transforming the figures of the Negroes into huge monsters that slipped along the walls. In the corner two barrels filled with clay and water were being stirred to the consistency of molasses. Later, Shem explained, the clay water would be poured over the rice seed spread now on the barn floor. Then the claying would begin.

But it was not until they had eaten their supper, had drunk the last of the whiskey, that Shem called out, "cum on now— les' git de claying done a'fore yo' licker die out." The good-natured crowd pushed its way into the barn, standing against the wall as two bucks dipped the clay water in piggens and poured it over the rice seed, calling out helpful information, "Here now—more clay ober here. Don' git it too gummy, Sam. . . ."

When this had been accomplished to Shem's satisfaction, John Eaton, lithe as a cat, vaulted to an upturned barrel and pulling his jew's-harp from his pocket cupped it to his lips and began to play; and no sooner had the first bar of weird rhythm fallen on the night than the Negro girls and women like puppets controlled by one string began to dance upon the clay and rice, weaving in and out while the men stood against the wall egging them on with much clapping of hands. Both men and women sang, their voices picking up the melody, chanting the cadence of John Eaton's music in a melody at once haunting and impressive.

With amazement I saw with what dexterity the nimble brown and black feet shuffled the grain in the wet clay until each separate grain wore its coat of brown. Even after the rice was sufficiently clayed, they danced on. Now as John Eaton's music increased its pace, they danced with wildest abandon. Uncle Early suddenly deserting his place as onlooker joined in the dance, pirouetting up and down like a black crow on a limb; Big Lou's flesh jellied into a quivering mass of motion. Faster and faster they whirled beneath the guttering lights! Swifter and swifter their voices chanted! It was as if the wild, beating rhythm had stripped them of the last veneer of civilization.

Suddenly I was tired of it. I found myself being unpleasantly affected by the noise, the dust, the odor of unwashed bodies mingling with that of greasy pork. So beckoning to Rupert— a fascinated onlooker—I stepped outside and paused to breathe the fresh, untainted air.

Tib, who had been standing apart watching, crossed to me and I told her she must go to bed; but even as I spoke such a dizziness swept over me I must grasp her thin shoulder for support. I hung onto her while the world blurred and retreated, fighting off the blackness which flowed down, thinking with a sort of wonder, "but I never fainted in all my life. . . ."

I came back from a boundless void to find myself lying on the ground, my head pillowed on Big Lou's lap. For a minute I lay there reaching for reality—conscious of many bodies hovering, of voices coming as from a great distance.

"Not too close now—gib her air"—that was Shem protesting—"hits just a faint—"

"Faint?" This was Stella's voice strident and contemptuous. "Hits dat Tawn and her conjurin'—didn't she conjur me and mek me cause trouble 'tween Big Lou and Lonnie—ain't she talkin' 'bout what she gonna do ter de mist'is?"

I pushed my way back through swirls of darkness and sat up.

Big Lou crooned, "Not too fas', honey—res' here on Big Lou," and Tib's anxious voice followed: "Miz Hester—is you sick, Miz Hester?"

"I'm—I'm all right, Tib," I managed to assure in a shaky voice. "I must go into the house."

Unseen hands helped me to rise and Tib linked her skinny arm in mine protectingly. "You lean on me, Miz Hester— you'se sick fer sho'. You'se white as a hant."

Followed by commiserating voices we went toward the house. And as the noise and odor of pork receded, the feeling of nausea lessened; but another came to take its place—a sort of startled wonder which left me numb and cold. For now I knew that what I had suspected for many days past was true: I was going to bear Saint Clair LeGrand's child.

Chapter Seventeen

THE knowledge that I was to bear a child, a possibility which I had often considered—and with distaste—now that it was a fact altered the very face of life. That night as I lay awake this and many other things dawned upon me. Heretofore I had striven to progress with but little regard for the man I had married, seeing him only as a tool which I might use in order to attain my goal. Now he assumed a more important rôle—he held it within his power to affect the future of my child; and for the first time I was able within my own mind to justify the fact that I had married him for the sake of personal achievement. My child would bear a proud name; Seven Chimneys would be his home; he would never know the lonely destiny that had been mine.

Sometimes in the long night—and I heard the clock in the lower hall strike every hour—it was borne in upon me that consciousness of the child gave deeper meaning to my struggle. Where before I had wished only for my own security—my own escape from mediocrity—now I must win my child's whole future.

Crossing the back porch the next morning, I entered the dark kitchen, thinking to eat a bite before I started for the rice bottoms (for today we were to start seeding the rice fields). Before I had reached the safe, Shem's voice called guardedly from the yard, "Miz Hester—Miz Hester," and I went out to meet him as he came up the back steps.

He said quietly, "Got a leetle trouble dis mornin', Miz Hester. De hands say dey ain't goin' to der swamp. Looky here."

He handed me a square of paper. It looked to be a placard of some sort, unreadable in the dark.

"What is it, Shem?"

"Hits one of dem things de Loyal League is putting up all round. Hit order all us colored folks to Darien to register today."

"Where did this come from, Shem?"

"Hits dat John Eaton. He brought hit from Darien las' Sat'day—been talkin' to de others too—stirrin' up all de trouble he can. Whut it mean, Miz Hester?"

"It's the politicians, Shem—they want the Negroes to register so they can vote at election time. But you've got three days in which to register. Tell the hands that they can't go today. The rice must be planted."

He scratched his head dubiously. "I'se talked to 'em—hits dat John Eaton, eggin' 'em on."

"Where are they now?"

"At de cabins—makin' ready to go."

For a moment I stood considering how I should handle this situation, for I knew that it presented a sort of crisis: the manner in which I handled it would influence the outcome of all future crises. I had heard too much of the trouble experienced on surrounding plantations to hope others would not arise. The privilege of voting which had just been bestowed by Congress and the descent of the Loyal League upon the South to round up freed Negroes for the elections had not helped matters, I thought wryly. Yet I could not blame the Negroes either, free for the first time and now offered the initial fruits of their liberty by the politicians.

When a minute later I walked with Shem toward the cabins in the dawn, I had decided upon the attitude I would assume. I knew they were like children, yet I must not treat them as children. They were too conscious that now they were citizens with rights equal to mine; I must use reason and logic as I would with any other human beings.

Yet when we approached the cabins my resolution weakened. I saw we were none too early. Already they were gathered in the clearing and I knew in another moment they would have been headed along the trail which led by Black Banks toward Darien. As we approached they huddled together, their eyes watching Shem and me warily. John Eaton's evil smile with its quality of triumph did not escape me.

Nevertheless I walked up to them so close that I caught the collective odor of their bodies. Halting, I smiled at them. "Good morning." I was casually pleasant. "Shem tells me you want to go to Darien and register today."

As I looked from one to another, their eyes, still wary, slipped away from mine furtively and I could not help but think how these were the selfsame Negroes who had welcomed me so effusively last night at the claying. There was no welcome now. Murmuring movement ran through them like a faint wind, though no one spoke outright. But I saw that tall Stella tossed her head like a skittish horse and cut her eyes around to meet John Eaton's derisively.

Calmly I said, "Let me explain to you why it is good neither for you nor for me that you go to Darien today. You *can* go, of course—you are free men and women. But if you go, all your work and all my money will be wasted. If you stay and plant the rice it means money for you and for me. At the end of the year you will feel good money in your hands—money that will buy new clothes and food and whiskey."

I paused a moment, heard the murmured movement run among them again, watched their eyes shifting. Quickly I pushed my advantage. "You are free, you tell yourselves. And that is true. If you march off now, neither I nor anyone else can stop you. But only children run away from their job. You are citizens now and good citizens stay and finish the job and have good money at the end of the year."

Almost I could see the lessening of their defiance. It lessened even more when Big Lou said, "She right—our little mist'is is right," and Uncle Early (resplendent in his silk hat) echoed "Amen," but John Eaton was not so quickly convinced. Like a lizard he slipped from his place at the rear of the crowd to my side, his pointed face twisted and twitching.

"Don' you lissen to her," he lashed out. "Don' you let her out-talk you out ob yo' rights. You know what Tawn say—she am wicked—dat she make de odder wife die so she kin marry de marster. If you don' go to Darien and sign yo' name yo' kaint vote—don' you let 'er talk yo' out ob yo' vote."

Already I could see the Negroes' emotional reaction to the shaking voice—the frenzied gestures; I knew they must be stopped lest I lose control; and seizing the oxen leather that lay across Shem's arm I raised it and brought it down across John Eaton's back. Time and time again I raised it and let it fall and then suddenly I was done. Throwing the leather on the ground, I turned on the huddled open-mouthed onlookers. "Get to the field," I commanded, "and let me hear no more of this. To-morrow I will give you a holiday and let you go to Darien to register. But today you plant the rice field. As for you"—I swung to John Eaton who stood hunched, his eyes darting in his face—"get off the place and stay off. I'll have no trouble-makers here."

As brave as I sounded, however, within I was frightened. Suppose they refused to return to work—suppose they followed John Eaton. I had a merciless vision of the rice unplanted, the young cotton unweeded, Seven Chimneys returning to idleness and unproductiveness again. But even as I feared, the tension broke. Big Lou sang out, "John Eaton be shame yo'self—causin' all dis ruckus. We'se got a good place here." And a chorus of assents followed. Uncle Early scampered into his cabin taking his moth-eaten silk hat off as he went, and suddenly the band broke and dissolved. Only Shem, John Eaton and I were left.

Shem said, "I spec John Eaton done sorry, Miz Hester—and he's a good worker."

But I was adamant. John Eaton must go. Moreover he would forfeit any wages due him and his share of crop, according to contract; and I saw him a few minutes later come from his cabin, his belongings in a bundle, and his eyes met mine hot with hatred.

But the rice planting got done, and that afternoon I stood beside Shem in the rice swamp and watched "sprout flow," heard Shem call to the men who handled the guard gate, "Not too fas' now, less she wash de seed," and saw the sallow coil of river spread its sinuous length along the bottoms where the rice seed had been dropped until field and water intermingled and became one—a wide smooth lake of mystery.

Overhead the rice birds circled greedily and Shem cast a baleful eye in their direction. "Dey is de ornriest critters," he grumbled, "hab to fight 'em day and night." And then as we stood watching, he told me of other enemies which menaced every rice crop. Sometimes freshets from the hills came down and drove the sea water through the dykes, not only ruining the crop but rendering the land useless until it was "leached." And sometimes the full-moon tides left devastation in their path—sometimes he wondered if rice was worth the trouble. And when, surprised, I asked him what other crop would pay so well he answered, "garden truck, Miz Hester—garden truck to ship east. Dis fine truckin' lan'—but dey hangs onto rice and cotton." He spat disgustedly into the yellow water that swirled below us. "Garden truck—dats de ticket."

He drifted away, intent on the flow, and I was surprised to find Vene at my elbow, for he should have been weeding the vegetable plot.

"Dere's a gennamun at de house axing fer you, Miz Hester."

Thoughtfully I asked, "A gentleman? Did you tell him that Mr. LeGrand is in Savannah?"

He shook his head. "Hits you he's wantin'—not Mister Saint."

I swung around the cotton field to the short cut and a few minutes later entered the house by the back door, pausing in the rear hall long enough to give my hair a hasty scrutiny. Vene's "gennamun" would have but a poor impression of the mistress of Seven Chimneys, I thought, for my hair was blown and the work dress I had worn to the swamps was far from neat. But it would have to do, I decided, and I entered the drawing room to find the visitor seated gingerly on one of the Louis Sixteenth chairs listening politely to Old Madame's chatter—such a cherub of a man that stripped of his foppish black, he might have hung on the top of a Christmas tree. His face wore a fixed smile, his short fat arms ended in dimpled babyish hands, his tiny ladylike feet, which reached futilely for the floor, seemed forever poised for dancing. But as he rose on my entrance, I saw that the blue eyes turned my way were as round and cold as marbles.

Old Madame said, "My daughter-in-law, Mr. Hibbard."

Instinctively I did not like the man and my nod was cool.

The hard blue eyes above the fixed smile stared into mine. "Please believe, Mrs. LeGrand, that I am sorry to—shall I say—intrude. But I am here on confidential business"—he cleared his throat significantly—"which I must state to you alone."

Without answering I stepped into the hall and called Margot, then went to stand at the hearth until after a flurry of inconse-

quential politeness between Old Madame and the little man—
she had wheeled Old Madame's chair down the hall.

Then Mr. Hibbard sat forward on his chair. His minute feet
now barely touched the floor, and he cleared his throat again.

"Please believe, Mrs. LeGrand, that I would not—shall I say
—presume to annoy you except that I find myself in—shall we
say—an uncomfortable situation."

I waited for him to proceed, certain that he was some trades-
man's emissary come to demand payment on the growing stack
of bills on Saint Clair's secretary. No doubt, I thought wryly,
I would be visited by many such who would descend upon me
like a flock of vultures.

The hard blue eyes glued themselves to mine, bright with
expectancy. "Shortly before your marriage, Mrs. LeGrand, I was
persuaded"—he paused as if he desired to force the importance
of what he was about to say upon me—"persuaded to lend your
husband a considerable sum of money."

If the pretentious little man expected to surprise me with
this statement which, judging by his intonation, might have
pronounced the sentence of death, he failed of his purpose. The
only element of surprise it held for me was that Saint Clair had
been reduced to borrowing from the unpleasant person who
stared across at me with the unwavering smile. "Did you know
of this loan, Mrs. LeGrand?"

"I knew Mr. LeGrand obtained a loan—yes."

He edged still farther forward on his chair. "And did you
know also, Mrs. LeGrand"—his voice held a sort of metallic
brightness—"of the—shall I say—unusual arrangement under
which I was persuaded to advance your husband this money?"

"I only know Mr. LeGrand found it necessary to borrow for
the growing of rice and cotton." Neither my eyes nor my voice
were free of contempt. "That, I believe, is not 'unusual' in the
South."

He continued to stare at me through his smirking smile like
some grotesque caricature of mirth. "Not at all unusual, Mrs.
LeGrand. It was your husband's—shall we say—'arrangement'
regarding the payment of that loan which was 'unusual.' "

"And what was that arrangement?"

"That the money would be repaid immediately on the death

of the first Mrs. LeGrand," he paused, and the round eyes held some unclean brightness. "Does it strike you as unusual, Mrs. LeGrand, that within a week after your husband made this—shall we say—extraordinary arrangement, the first Mrs. LeGrand should die?"

I was about to retort, "And what has that to do with me?" when the significance of his calculated words struck me and I was swept by a wave of feeling. The world in which I seemed so secure started to crumple and fall away, leaving me hanging over a dark chasm which might reveal—if I looked too closely—things more terrible than I had dreamed could ever be. But the cold blue eyes watching me served as a warning; not by the least word or action must I allow this little man to suspect how I felt or what I thought.

"I cannot believe my husband borrowed on any such arrangement. It was unnecessary. There were banks—"

"Banks, Mrs. LeGrand, consider 'character' and 'reputation' when making a loan."

Slowly I asked, "And just what do you mean to imply by that?"

"That your husband could not have borrowed so much as a dime anywhere in this community—except from me."

I stared at him disdainfully. "Are you a moneylender, then?"

The blue eyes blazed above the smile and he cleared his throat deprecatingly. "I am not a moneylender, Mrs. LeGrand. I am—shall I say—an associate of your husband's."

"In what way?" I asked flatly.

"In"—he hesitated a space, then continued—"shall I say in various ways."

"And why do you come to me?"

He spread his babyish hands. "You control the money, do you not?"

"Do you mean you are asking me to repay this loan?"

"You would not have me lose money which I advanced on good faith?"

"I am afraid you misunderstand. What money I control belongs to the son of Mr. LeGrand. Naturally, I cannot repay his father's debts with it."

His ridiculous little body stiffened, then as suddenly relaxed, and for a moment he sat quietly, with his eyes cast down. When he looked up at me again, the smile was still there; when he spoke his voice was still gentle.

"Do you fully realize, Mrs. LeGrand, that I might use—shall I say—this unpleasant implication to force payment from you?"

"I am aware of no unpleasant implication. As for your forcing me to pay—please remember that at the time the loan was made, I was only the hired governess. So I am not affected one way or another by the affair."

Staring at me (and by now I loathed his unfailing smile) he said softly, "You were only the hired governess. Yet Mr. LeGrand gave me to understand he borrowed the money at your suggestion."

I was so irritated by the crafty, smirking face I now made no effort to conceal it. "Just what are you implying?" I demanded.

"I am implying, Mrs. LeGrand, that Saint Clair LeGrand borrowed money from me which he promised—and in writing, mind you—to repay on the death of his wife. And I am implying also that within a week his wife died—shall we say—under peculiar circumstances. Furthermore, I imply that you possessed full knowledge of that loan and Mr. LeGrand's arrangement, though you were only the hired governess, and that within a short time—a very short time—the 'hired governess' (the words are yours, not mine) became the wife of Saint Clair LeGrand!"

I stood and stared at him, my mind rebelling because this evil little man had it within his power to say such things to me. Yet as he said them I saw the whole thing slip into pattern so smoothly that I was seized by the conviction that it was true and that even if it were not true the world would believe it; I felt that I stood on quicksand which might—unless I moved with care—engulf me. I summoned what control I could bring to bear in an effort to address the little man with cool politeness.

"I am afraid, Mr. Hibbard, I must ask you to excuse me. I am very busy. If you wish further discussion of this I advise you to see my lawyer—Stephen Pearsall. He's on Bay Street in Savannah."

He slid to his dancing-teacher's feet and stood staring at me through the bright hard eyes. "I need not tell you, Mrs. LeGrand, I have not—shall I say—the slightest intention of discussing this with your lawyer. I know that you'll pay before you'll let this—shall we say—extraordinary affair come to light." His pirouetting feet carried him to the door, where he stopped and looked back at me, the vacuous smile unchanged.

As the door closed behind him I heard Old Madame's chair come up the hall.

"Mademoiselle—" Old Madame called.

"Yes, madame."

"What did the man Hibbard wish to speak to you about?"

I looked down into her upturned eyes. Surely they held something beside curiosity, some urgency not unakin to fear.

"Mr. Hibbard's business did not concern me, madame. I told him he must see your son."

A hardly discernible relief, more movement than expression, flickered across the blank face and when finally she spoke it was with majestic calm.

"You were quite right, mademoiselle. My son will know how to deal with him."

Before she could say more I turned and made my way up the stairs. But I said to myself wryly, "So she knew about *that* too."

Chapter Eighteen

THROUGH all the hours of the day suspicion festered in my mind, but it was not until Old Madame had finally said good night and Rupert had gone to bed that I was able to escape to my room and turn the key in the door. For a long time I sat staring into my fireless hearth.

That the man Hibbard's accusation was true I could hardly believe, and yet I knew for all my attempt to reason that I did believe. And I marveled at my blindness which had refused to perceive the truth before, though incident after incident had thrust itself up before me; Lorelie's appeal that I leave, Roi's warnings, Saint Clair's haste for our marriage—now these coiled themselves about me like an evil enchantment and with a new consciousness I relived the time that had led me unsuspecting to the hour which now confronted me.

But, I asked myself, what if the accusation were false? My mind grasped at various channels by which I might verify truth or falsity: I could go to Saint Clair and charge him with it, or better still, perhaps, lay the whole ugly thing before Stephen Pearsall; but even as I pondered I knew I would do neither. However hateful uncertain knowledge was, certainty (if the thing were true) would be unbearable. And I told myself that I must move cautiously. I was like a child who continues to cling to a toy she values, refusing to believe it has been smashed.

During the days that followed I was as a woman caught in some monstrous web, who holds herself carefully while she considers this and that manner of extricating herself, not daring to make the least move lest she tear the structure in which she is enmeshed and plunge into irrevocable disaster—and that I had no intention of doing. For—after my first impulse of horror— my determination to remain at Seven Chimneys, to wrest some sort of victory from the chaos which now surrounded me, remained unaltered. In my consciousness this willingness to continue on as the wife of a man who outraged both my emotions and my principles stared at me like an accusing phantom. I knew the world would consider me wicked because of this willingness; and at this thought I knew a startled rebellion, but I resisted even more passionately the idea of leaving Seven Chimneys. This was the home I had won for myself and for my child. I would not relinquish it.

The days passed, taking with them the March breezes that tempered the crescendo of the heat of the sun, and I, working as hard and as long hours as before, gave no outward evidence of the questions that fermented within me like some unquiet yeast; nor did I allow the morning sickness which now assailed me to deter me from my work, though often I felt so ill that control slipped its leash and I would find myself berating and nagging the Negroes in the frenzy of frustration. They would turn sullen and obstinate as I plunged into the task at which they seemed to work so stupidly, goading and accusing them because the world revolved sickeningly about me. One evening when I had forced myself to change into a flowered lawn and go down for supper, I sat before my plate revolted by the odor of the food. Rupert's observing eyes watched me. He asked, "Why are you so white, Hester? Are you going to faint again?"

"No—no, Rupert," I managed hastily, "the candlelight makes me look white."

Saint Clair turned his eyes my way deliberately. "And when did Hester faint?"

Glibly Rupert told him. "The night of the rice claying, papa. And Stella said Tawn is conjuring Hester like she did mama. Did Tawn make mama die, papa?"

Sudden stillness engulfed the room and hung unbroken for a moment. Then Old Madame leaned over and rapped Rupert's knuckles with her fork.

"Be quiet, boy," she commanded. Then with fawning solicitude she turned to me. "You have been unwell, mademoiselle?"

"I am quite well," I told her shortly, for I saw that from the head of the table Saint Clair continued to regard me steadily and I thought—though I may have imagined this—that a sardonic smile hovered at his lips; but he only shrugged as he rose from the table. "If you will persist in working like a nigger—" he threw over his shoulder as he sauntered away.

But Old Madame was suspiciously concerned. "My son is right, mademoiselle—you must not overdo. The weather! The heat! The swamp fever!" Perhaps I had better instruct Margot to put up the mosquito canopies earlier this season, she told me. Vene said a Negro had died over on Butler's Island with (she leaned forward and her voice sank to an awed whisper) *Yellow fever.* . . . Had I ever seen Pierce Butler's daughter? She and her father were trying to work the Butler plantation with freed Negroes. Did I know that her mother was that notorious woman Fanny Kemble—such a silly emotional woman —but her daughter now, she had heard, was of another stripe— plain practical. . . .

To escape her tiresome monologue which did not falter even after we left the table and sat in the drawing room, I took Rupert to bed early. Then going to my own room, I undressed and sponged my body in cold water and put on the thin nightgown Tib had laid out for me. Braiding my hair demanded more energy than I could command, so I removed the shell pins that held it and let it hang free and almost eagerly got into bed. When I had relaxed on the smooth sheets the claw of nausea loosened and fled.

Tib came through the door quietly and stood regarding me with her monkey-like eyes. "You sick, Miz Hester?"

"Just tired, Tib."

As noiselessly as a cat, for all her clumsiness, she went about the room snuffing each candle except those on the night table, bringing the room to shadowed quiet. Then she came toward me, the hairbrush in her hand.

"You just lay there and res', Miz Hester. I brush yo' hair."

I closed my eyes while she brushed, soothed by the rhythmical sweep of her thin arm, remembering that once Lorelie had lain on this bed while I brushed her hair. It had looked like a sheath of gold on the pillow that night—but next morning it had clung dankly to her thin face.

Tib said quietly, "You'se got pritty hair, Miz Hester, when it like this—how come you wear it so plain-like?"

As if Tib's "how come" had the power to turn back time and distance, I was back at the orphanage in the bare little chapel in the gray dawn . . . I saw the headmistress (a heavy black-browed woman with a mustache on her lip), heard her cold voice as it warned that beauty was evil, self-adornment the instrument of Satan . . . her eyes like black ice traveling over us as we shivered in our seats before her in our homespun dresses and heavy boots, our hair pulled back from our scrubbed chapped faces. Now, remembering, I sighed. Her lesson had fallen on fertile ground; never had I been able to bring myself to tie a ribbon on my hair without a sense of guilt; yet lying here relaxed and soothed to the point of luxuriousness I wondered if Roi would think my unbound hair "pritty"?

Abruptly I said, "That will do, Tib. You must go to bed now."

She was gone noiselessly and I lay there staring at the shadows the night candle made on the ceiling, reveling in the quiet, thinking drowsily "Tonight I will sleep."

But the thought was stillborn. Suddenly I sat erect, weariness dropping over me again like a cloak. I had heard the door of the turret room open and close, and almost immediately my own door opened to admit Saint Clair in his dressing gown. From the doorway he surveyed me through narrow, examining eyes.

"You are ill, then?"

I reached for my wrapper which lay at the foot of the bed and pulled it about my shoulders. "I am perfectly well."

He came toward the bed, his white hand outstretched. "Why have I never been allowed to see your hair like this?" he asked, and the quietness of his voice did not deceive me. Suddenly his hand buried itself in the hair that hung about my shoulders.

Swiftly I caught it up with both hands and divided it for braiding. "My head ached." I looked up at the still face defiantly. "And I am tired."

His eyes stared down at me and for a moment he did not speak. Then he said in the low, inward voice which always meant he was angry, "I have no idea how long you think I will put up with this."

"Put up with what?" I asked flatly.

"With being treated like a lecherous schoolboy when I approach you."

I continued to stare up at him.

"After all," he went on, "you are my wife. I expect certain things and I expect you to accept them amiably."

I finished braiding my hair and slipping my arms into the sleeves of my wrapper, got up. "Even if I am your wife," I spoke lightly, "your most devoted wife, there will be times when your 'approaches,' as you call them, will be less welcome than at other times." I tried to speak more pleasantly. "Did you wish to see me about something?" I asked.

"Yes."

I motioned toward the chair opposite mine. "Then why not be comfortable?" He sat down as languidly as usual.

"We must come to some understanding about money. I can't go on living like a confounded beggar, you know."

I returned the steady look in his birdlike eyes coolly. "Well—"

"Let us understand each other." His voice was unchanged—was its usual polite conversational self. "If you suppose that I am going to 'ask' money of you, dismiss the notion."

"I entertain no such notion."

"Whether you do or not does not signify. But you may as well know that I must have money—and at once. And I'd like to remind you that not so long ago I borrowed money which you for the most part used."

"I have used it to improve your property."

He gestured away the unimportance of this. "I had a devilish hard time getting the money. I had to promise to repay it immediately."

Instantly I realized here was confirmation of the man Hibbard's accusation, for how and on what premise could Saint Clair have hoped to repay except by gain from Lorelie's death? But on the heels of this realization came another; I must never let him know that I knew. If I was to win over this man—and I must win—my advantage lay in concealment.

Still I could not resist applying the whip. "How could you promise to repay?"—my voice was as ingenuous as Rupert's might have been—"when you had no prospect of paying?"

He stared across at me, his face as impassive as before, but he only drawled (and with no less arrogance than he would use toward a servant), "I must have the money—and at once. You understand, do you not? I must have the money at once."

"Certainly I understand—but what do you expect of me? I have no money."

"You control a considerable sum."

Now my surprise was genuine. "But that belongs to Rupert."

"If you are clever you will arrange something."

I stifled the impulse to tell him I did not "arrange" things with other people's money and resented inwardly that this man, who had no scruples himself, should believe me equally unscrupulous; but I gave no hint of my resentment; instead, pretending to misunderstand his meaning, I asked thoughtfully, "You mean, don't you, that you would like for me to arrange a loan from your son's estate?"

That this was far from his intention was evidenced by the dislike that flashed into his eyes before he concealed them beneath his lids. But I cared nothing for his dislike; for even as I spoke it dawned upon me that here was the way in which I might win over this man—a way which heretofore I had not considered, but now that it presented itself to me was so obvious that I was impatient that I had not thought of it before. And so before I spoke again—and motionless and silent he waited for me to continue—I considered carefully means by which I could persuade him to this plan.

"Please"—I made my voice placating, almost anxious, as though I too were genuinely concerned with his problem—"do not think me indifferent to your financial worries. I have seen the stacks of bills—"

"Unfortunately that doesn't get them paid."

"No, but after all—why shouldn't you borrow from your son's estate?"

"With that old watchdog Pearsall to get by?" He was frankly contemptuous.

"I believe he would agree to the arrangement that occurs to me."

"And what is that arrangement?"

"That you give Seven Chimneys as security."

"Doesn't it occur to you that I could borrow anywhere with Seven Chimneys as security?"

I doubted this. I knew how many plantations lay idle because there was not money forthcoming for their revival. Then too, I recalled Hibbard's insinuations regarding Saint Clair's credit and reputation. As if I possessed none of this knowledge, however, I asked innocently, "Why should you go elsewhere? Why not let your son's estate benefit from the interest? If you like I will go to Savannah and lay the proposal before Mr. Pearsall."

Almost before I had concluded my sentence he uncoiled himself from the chair and was on his way to the door. "You will arrange the matter—and as quickly as possible." He was as indifferent as if he had no further interest in it.

I waited until he reached the door, then spoke. "Wait, please," I said coolly.

He turned without taking his hand from the doorknob and looked back without speaking.

"I do not know if it is of the slightest interest to you"—I knew my voice sounded hard and flat, but for the life of me I could not force warmth or feeling into it—"but you may as well know now: I am going to have a child."

The pale eyes met mine across the space that lay between us and the hateful smile flitted across his face.

"A child?"

"Yes."

He stood silent for a moment before he drawled, "Why do you think I am not interested?"

"Because you are interested in nothing except yourself," rose to my lips but I did not say it, and before I could frame a speech less liable to annoy he spoke again, turning the knob of the door as he spoke: "On the other hand I am most interested."

Angered by the quality of his voice I said sarcastically, "I find that hard to believe."

He opened the door but continued to stand in the doorway looking back at me. "But I am interested," he repeated, "most interested—in knowing whether the child is mine—or Roi's."

Chapter Nineteen

PERHAPS a more timid woman might have been deterred by the insinuations (and that they were threatening insinuations I did not doubt) of Saint Clair LeGrand, but they did not discourage me. They only intensified my resolution to place myself outside the realm where this man could affect me or the life I was determined to have, and at once I began to calculate the means by which to gain Stephen Pearsall's approval of the loan. Considering the matter I decided that my plan, which now appeared as the way I could secure a future for myself and for my child, would be expedited if instead of my going to Savannah, Stephen Pearsall came to Seven Chimneys. Here he could see for himself the results of my management and labor. Accordingly I dispatched a letter to Savannah inviting him to be my guest at Seven Chimneys at any time he named; and promptly he wrote back naming Thursday of the week to come.

The days that lay between the receipt of his letter and arrival were busy days for Seven Chimneys, for determined that he see the plantation at its best I set Margot and Vene to work immediately ordering the house from top to bottom—Sey and Boy to the task of trimming garden and paths and while Tib's hands rubbed silver to brightness, mahogany to satin luster, I was everywhere.

But at last the house was in readiness for Stephen Pearsall. Rupert's pantaloons and jacket sponged and pressed! Margot ordered into fresh gingham! Old Madame polished and groomed to a nearer semblance of the *grande dame* she thought herself to be! And finally came Thursday morning when Vene moved away in the freshly painted longboat toward Darien to fetch the visitor.

It was on a warm April day that drowsed beneath a sky of clearest blue that Stephen Pearsall, impressive in white linen, stepped upon the Seven Chimneys landing and I, who had been watching the channel from the west windows, went down the path to welcome him. When I had apologized for Saint Clair's absence (he had been called to Savannah, I said, though the truth was that he had taken himself off deliberately the afternoon before to avoid "that old ninny Pearsall"), I led the way to the house.

After midday dinner he and I got into the buckboard which Shem brought to the door and were driven around the plantation, I with a feeling of elation. For never had I seen the land so fair. The dark limbs of trees wore a mist of tenderest green, the golden jessamine sprayed everywhere, thickets of wild plum banked snowdrifts against the green of shrubbery; and already the mingled fragrance of bay blossoms and myrtle was stirred into perfume by the fresh wind from the river where the marshes, turning from russet to green, quivered delicately.

I knew from the moment Stephen Pearsall had stepped upon the landing nothing escaped his eyes—either the orderly gardens or the spotless house. And seeing it through his eyes, comparing the Seven Chimneys of today with the one which I had first seen, I knew a half-startled wonder that so much had been accomplished—as a woman laboring over the making of a dress, when she dons the finished garment and views herself in a mirror, is struck by wonder at her success.

But Stephen Pearsall made no comment. The buckboard drew up at the vegetable field and I watched him as his eyes traveled over the vines which were heavy with promise of bounty. Then we went on to the cotton field and though I was proud of that cotton, and with reason, still there was no word from him; and it was not until we had arrived at the rice swamps and, leaving the buckboard, stood on the spongy banks and looked out over the bottoms carpeted with thousands of young green shoots that he turned to me and said, "You have done well, Mrs. LeGrand." At his praise I felt myself flushing like a schoolgirl.

Later in my little office I went over accounts and pass books with him, explaining to the last cent what money had been spent and why. And though at first he spoke no praise of my management I knew that he approved when he said slowly, "Thrift and work can overcome many obstacles, can they not, Mrs. LeGrand? I am thinking of the many fine plantations down here that are returning to swampland—of the families sinking into deeper poverty and despair . . ." He shook his head sadly. "I wish they could see Seven Chimneys."

But it was not until we had eaten Maum Lucie's supper of delicious roasted ricebirds served with crab-apple jelly that I spoke to him of the purpose that lay behind this visit. Before I did so I set my stage—saw that Rupert was in bed, Old Madame safe in her room, one of Saint Clair's gold-necked bottles at Stephen Pearsall's elbow. Then sitting across from him in the drawing room, whose wide-opened windows admitted the frog's chant and the muted call of whippoorwills, I laid my proposal before him.

"You realize, do you not, Mrs. LeGrand, the risk you run in lending this money to—er—your husband?" he said after a long while.

"You mean?"

"He will not repay it," his voice was harsh with contempt. "Saint Clair LeGrand never paid an honest debt in his life except with his wife's money."

"Then," I paused deliberately so that the significance contained in my next words would sink in, "then Seven Chimneys would belong to Rupert."

Surprise flickered in his eyes and was instantly controlled. "I see," he said softly. "I see. You are banking on that? That he does *not* repay?"

"Wouldn't it be the best possible solution for Rupert and for Seven Chimneys?"

He stared down into his wineglass then looked across at me. "Yes," he spoke slowly, "you are right. I have feared that Seven Chimneys would be dissipated as Lorelie's fortune was—to pay his gambling debts. I know that the idea made her miserable many times." He paused, and when he continued his voice was dispassionate again. "Still, there is much to be considered before you take this step. First, to lend this money will deplete the sum in the bank considerably. You would not have enough to finance the plantation another year—I am taking your present expense as the base of my calculation, you understand. Had you thought of that, Mrs. LeGrand?"

"Yes, sir. I expect to clear enough on my rice and cotton to finance my next year's crops."

"I see." He turned thoughtful again. "But there is still this to consider. Your rice and cotton are flourishing now, but that does not necessarily imply a profitable year. Particularly with rice. A sea tide—a big storm—your rice would be worthless. Have you thought of that?"

"I cannot stand to think of it," I told him simply. "It is the one thing that must not happen."

"Still it might happen—it has happened many times. Nature, I fear, does not take our small plans into consideration."

"Then"—my voice was unnecessarily defiant, but the pictures his words projected into my mind appalled me,—"then I would sell the timber on the left acres. It is indeed a splendid stand."

He looked at me a moment then shook his head in mock bewilderment. "A lawyer is supposed to be beyond surprise"— his smile took the sting from his words—"but I am constantly amazed at the calculating brains that often hide in pretty women's heads. Yes," he spoke seriously again, "you could sell the timber. Any number of lumber enterprises are in the air right now—only last week a Mr. Cram was in our office making inquiries about timber stands, for what purpose I do not know since he isn't the stripe of client we prefer." He fell into silence and sat musing. "I wonder why your—er—husband, if he is so pressed for money, has not thought of the timber?"

I was about to tell him that Saint Clair had probably never seen the timber, that his knowledge of the land began and ended with the pathway that led to the landing, but before I could voice the thought, he spoke again.

"Just what is it you want of me in regard to this—er—plan, Mrs. LeGrand?"

"Your approval, sir."

"I do approve—moreover I know that this is as Lorelie Le-Grand would wish it, and I do not mind telling you that she had this very plan in her own mind at one time but was never able to persuade her husband to agree to it—" He broke off, and there was speculation in the glance he gave me. "I am wondering by what means *you* persuaded him, Mrs. LeGrand."

But I had no intention of revealing to Stephen Pearsall (or anyone else) the unsavory knowledge which had made my success possible, and evidently, perhaps from some expression in my face or manner, he divined this; for when he continued it was in another direction.

"Perhaps," he said, "this is what Lorelie LeGrand intended when she left her affairs in your hands—perhaps she foresaw that you would have a strength which she herself did not have. And there is justice in this solution. Saint Clair bled the poor woman unmercifully—stripped her not only of her material possessions but more important still, her child's love—her self-respect. Yes, it is justice that Seven Chimneys be saved for her son."

"Then Mr. LeGrand and I may come to your office next week and arrange the matter, sir?"

"On any day you name, ma'am."

We sat there a moment, neither speaking, then suddenly he discarded the legal manner for the courtly grace of a southern gentleman and stood. "But come, Mrs. LeGrand, we have talked enough of business—let me pour you some wine." He poured a glass and gave it to me with an old-fashioned bow. "Tell me, ma'am—how are the freed Negroes working out? I hear complaints on every side."

As we drank our wine I told him of Shem who kept my hands in line despite the northern politicians—despite their own opposition to labor and responsibility; and as we talked the night deepened, the frog orchestra crescendoed to a maddening symphony, and through the windows we could glimpse the staccato dance of the fireflies above the gardens.

Later at the foot of the stairs I gave him a lighted candle and told him good night. But he did not go immediately. Instead he stood on the bottom step looking down at me, and I saw that his face, which had lightened during our conversation until it was friendly and charming past believing, was grave again.

"I feel that I would be neglectful of my duty, Mrs. LeGrand, if I failed to say what I am about to say." His eyes searched my face and his hand ran through the plume of white hair. "It concerns your husband."

I looked up at him and waited for him to proceed.

Gently he struck the newel post with his palm. "It is this. Do you realize the character of—er—your husband?"

"I think I do, sir."

"Do you know him as I know him? Know that he is not one to yield? That he gets what he wants by hook or crook?" He smiled and spread his hands. "You see I am trying to say that I question his willingness to mortgage Seven Chimneys to his son's estate? It is not like him."

Slowly I told him, "The only reason that he does, sir"—I could not hold the grimness from my voice—"is because he cannot help himself."

He regarded me thoughtfully for a moment, half smiling, half serious. "It is not a pleasant thing to feel impelled to warn a lady about her husband—"

"It is unnecessary, sir," I assured him.

Still he did not go. "Nor," he continued gently, "to warn a lady of herself."

Surprised I repeated, "Myself?"

"Some day, Mrs. LeGrand, medical science will find a name for those like your husband, who believe themselves beyond man's law or God's—to whom money and material gain supersede all human obligations. It is a thing that works quietly and in unexpected places."

I had not the least idea what he was driving at so I waited for him to continue.

"Sometimes our fancied need for 'security'—our desire for freedom from want—can give rise to strange and terrible impulses," he said. Suddenly he laid his free hand on my shoulder and his eyes looked down into mine steadily. "Be careful, my dear, be careful."

He stood there for a second more, then removing his hand said, "Good night, Mrs. LeGrand," and turning went up the stairs. As I moved about the lower rooms snuffing the candles I was thinking of his last words and finding myself amused by them. As little as I agreed with Saint Clair on most matters regarding Stephen Pearsall I did have to agree: he was something of an old ninny.

Chapter Twenty

ON Thursday of the next week Saint Clair and I went to Savannah and in Stephen Pearsall's office the affair of the loan was consummated. Saint Clair signed the papers, and Stephen Pearsall in turn gave him a check for five thousand dollars which my husband received with such contemptuous arrogance that to an onlooker he might have been the bestower of a great favor, and Stephen Pearsall and I but humble recipients. I marveled anew that nothing—not even the obvious dislike in Stephen Pearsall's eyes—had the power to pierce the man's confidence in his own superiority.

In silence we rode back to the hotel through the Savannah heat that seemed to melt all energy and drenched our clothes with clinging dampness. It was not until we approached the Pulaski House that Saint Clair spoke. Then he said idly, "I will drop you at the hotel and keep the carriage, if you don't mind. I have business to attend to."

I wondered if his "business" had to do with Mr. Hibbard—if beneath his icy exterior he was experiencing a warm rush of relief because now he could repay the loathsome little man and get his neck from under the tiny foot which despite its pirouetting would be, I knew, a merciless one. Certainly nothing in his manner led me to think this. He leaned back against the carriage cushions, his white hand dawdling with the heavy watch chain, the very picture of a gentleman enjoying a leisurely airing.

We drew up before the hotel entrance. Without the least gesture of assistance from him, I stepped down to the curb and would have gone directly into the hotel, but his voice stopped me.

"Are you staying overnight in Savannah?" he drawled.

I turned back surprised. "Overnight? Oh, no. I must get back. I will take the afternoon boat."

He smiled unpleasantly. "No doubt, now you will work more like a nigger than ever."

I retorted, "I have always worked," and abruptly turned toward the hotel. Yet I knew as I ascended the stairs to my room that what he said was true. In the bank there now remained only enough money to see me through the year. On the success of the crops hung the whole future of Seven Chimneys. And Stephen Pearsall's talk of sea tides and storms still hung too unpleasantly in my ears for comfort. I was, I thought, not unlike the gambler who against heavy odds risks everything on one throw of the dice. And I did not need Saint Clair to point out to me the vulnerable position in which I had placed myself.

Back at Seven Chimneys next morning I could hardly wait to change into my work dress before I was off to the fields, half fearful that during my absence some untoward happening had made futile both my plans and my labor. But when I gained them I was reassured. The hands worked industriously in the cotton rows, and the clack-clack rhythm of their hoes was as music to my ears. And when I went on to the rice swamps that lay like huge checkerboards—their green cut by drains and quarter drains—I was even more encouraged. I told myself again that I was lucky to have Shem for headsman.

As spring advanced from April toward May, the heat descended and all but engulfed us, beating down so near and hot that sometimes I fancied I could, by lifting my hand, touch the brassy sun. With the heat came mosquitoes and sand flies; the last were minute insects that swarmed in hordes, stinging where they settled, defying even the net canopies which Margot had erected over the beds. Across the garden paths the snakes, lured hence by the sun, slithered back to safety at approach. Once I almost trod on a huge rattler which lay athwart my path and when I had crushed the flat evil head with a dead limb—and it did not die easily—I leaned against the nearest tree, violently ill.

But uncomfortable as I was both day and night (the airless nights beneath mosquito nets brought scant relief), I gloried in the weather which was working near miracles with my crops. When my vegetable fields began to yield and the pearly corn, the rosy tomatoes, the crisp sweet garden greens poured like a

vast colorful stream into the big gathering baskets, I forgot the
heat altogether. Even after the hands received their share no
dent was made in the bounteous supply, so I set Maum Lucie
and Margot to canning and preserving, and for days the house
was redolent with piccalilli and tomato catsup. Next year, I
resolved, I would grow garden truck to ship North for I had not
forgotten Shem's words "garden truck to ship North—that's
our ticket."

The long hot days that followed failed to bring the
sense of relief that I had imagined would be mine once the crops
were up and thriving. They were hazardous days—so hazardous
with their alternate hope and fear that I was reminded of the
time when as a small girl I had been sent to the woods adjoining
the orphanage to gather deadwood and had had to cross the
angry creek on the unsure log that spanned it. Now, it seemed,
I was faced with a balancing feat equally perilous. My rice and
cotton—on which hung success or failure—turned out to be
far more desperate struggles than I even in my moments of
greatest doubt had dreamed. In the cotton field weeds and army
worms were relentless enemies which must be fought unceas-
ingly—the weeds lest they gain the upper hand, the army worms
lest they devastate my cotton overnight. Even the long dry spell
of heat which lasted through May and went on into June proved
to be a mixed blessing; it was fine for cotton-growing but as a
builder of storm pressure it proved a constant menace to my
rice. And a sudden gale the first week of June indicated to me
past doubting the slender thread of chance on which the rice
crop hung. The sudden swift wind swept the river over the
dykes, overflowing the fields in an hour and causing no less than
five breaks in the banks. Only when the wind died and the
water had receded so Shem could mend the banks did I breathe
easily again; and after that a mass of thunderheads or a sudden
wind had the power to throw me into a state of anxiety border-
ing on panic.

As the heat persisted and the long hot days wound one
into another, life at least for me became more leisurely. The
crops were all up and flourishing; there remained but the tasks
of keeping the cotton clear of weeds, the swamps wetted and
drained. These Shem could see to without my help. So it fell

out that I was in the fields less often—and to tell the truth I was less and less inclined to trudge over the land beneath the withering sun as I had done before. And this was only natural; for I had felt the first movement within my body that meant life in the child. I contented myself with a daily trip to the fields in the buckboard and an interview with Shem in my office after supper. And beyond seeing that the house was kept in order and as comfortable as the heat would permit, my days were free of tasks.

For long hours I would sit idle in my shadowed room letting Tib fetch and carry for me, possessed by some terrible inertia, and though I would become impatient with myself, feeling I must check the linen closet—must go over Rupert's clothes, I would continue to sit there, unable to force my body to obey the ordering of my will. Sometimes I would look down at my hands and feel that even to lift them required more effort than I could summon.

Sitting there my mind would turn over this or that question— the advisability of planting rice another year—the possibilities which might lie in the raising of garden truck—but always my thoughts had to do with impersonal affairs; never with the personal. Even thoughts of the child I held at bay and but rarely did I stop to realize that my thickening body and pinched face were caused by a human being which lay coiled, already perfectly formed, within my body. Even the sick distaste I suffered when I remembered that the child was Saint Clair's seemed to lessen; it was as if nature, determined to protect the child, created a mental vacuum where troubled thoughts could not enter. Even remembrance of Roi was a vague formless thing, no matter how hard I tried to bring it alive.

But it was during these days of heavy inertia that I became aware of a change in Rupert.

He had grown, I discovered with surprise as I examined him closely for the first time in weeks and had left baby boyhood forever. His body had lengthened and thinned, his face had lost its childish contours, and with a start I realized that no longer did he run to me to prattle of his games—indeed he no longer played at those games. Now he moved about the house as quietly as ever his father did and I saw with amusement that his youthful eagerness had been supplanted by a blasé, grown-up manner. And when it dawned upon me that his manner toward me had changed, that he answered roughly when I spoke to him and met any suggestion of mine with a shrug, I smiled in what I considered understanding. Rupert, I told myself, was experiencing growing pains; it was only natural that he should pull away from too much feminine supervision.

But no sooner did I arrive at this conclusion than I had reason to discard it. Rupert, I discovered, was not aways blasé and grown up. Entering the drawing room unexpectedly, I would find him buried in a chair staring into space and by the half-frightened eyes I knew that some inner turmoil gripped the boy. Often as we sat in the drawing room after supper I would look up from whatever work engaged my hands to find his eyes upon me with an expression close to dislike. Although I would smile across at him as usual, he would send back no answering smile but would only stare through eyes that were frankly hostile.

Bending over my sewing I cast about in my mind for an explanation. Had he learned of the child? Did jealousy lie at the root of the matter? Had the gossiping Negroes distilled some poison into his young mind? Well, whatever it was, I must clear it up. I had labored too valiantly to win his friendship to watch it slip away uncaring. I would have a talk with Rupert.

Before the opportunity for that talk presented itself I realized another fact, one which I—heretofore engrossed with plantation affairs—had let escape me. It was the change in Saint Clair's attitude toward his son. I saw that where before he had more or less ignored the boy, addressing him only when he considered a reprimand was needed, he now made deliberate efforts to win him. I would find them in the drawing room after supper, Rupert standing at his father's chair while Saint Clair fashioned paper boats or adjusted the bands on a slingshot, the drawling voice relating as he worked, the sport he had known as a boy. And on his next trip to Savannah he returned loaded with presents for Rupert. A new jacket and pantaloons, a riding crop with twisted silver handle, and supreme gift—a small gun; and I saw Rupert respond to his father's attentions as a small plant withered by the heat lifts its leaves to the first drop of rain.

Now, though the heat persisted, the aspect of the weather changed. The sun disappeared behind a leaden sky and the monotonous gray was reflected in the waters of the Sound. The whole landscape—sky and water and land—seemed to be enclosed in a smothering blanket of heat and stillness. Not the smallest ripple fluttered the water, not the stirring of a single leaf robbed the trees of their immobility. The depressing gray and heat penetrated the house, seeping into closets and leaving ugly gray mold on clothes and shoes, its domination challenged only by the mosquitoes and sand flies which descended in hordes to add to the intense discomfort; and Maum Lucie, going about her kitchen listlessly, said it was "de miasma" and that it bred sickness and death.

If I found it easy to disregard her dire predictions, I was less inclined to shrug when Shem reported two of the hands down with chills and fever. "Hits de drought"—he shook his head—"allus when you kin see de bottom ob de crick hit means sickness. Whut wurries me—dere's likely to be more."

With an unpleasant picture of all hands ill and to be cared for, I dispatched Vene to Darien for quantities of quinine and Dover's powder, and instructed Shem to take Big Lou from the fields to tend the sick. "Above all, Shem—keep the well away from those in the infirmary," I warned.

He looked at me doubtfully. "But chills and fever ain't ketchin', ma'am—leastways not dat I eber hear."

I did not tell him there was talk of yellow fever on the islands, that Savannah—according to the Savannah *Morning News* which now and then Saint Clair purchased and which I perused eagerly—had warned that the city had more than the usual number of plague cases. While chills and fever lacked the horror of plague, it too, I knew, could cost me dearly if not stamped out.

It was with the sum of the day's worry pressing upon me that I went to the supper table that night. Thus when Rupert announced that after supper he was going to the rice swamps with his new gun to shoot ricebirds with the bird-minders, I told him at once and in no uncertain tones that he would do no such thing. "If you wish to practice shooting," I finished, "put up a target in the garden. It will be just as good practice and will not jeopardize your health."

His eyes as he looked at me across the table were bright with animosity. "But I *am* going, Hester. Papa said I could go." He turned to Saint Clair. "Didn't you, papa?"

Saint Clair's glance slid down the table toward me, though his answer was directed toward Rupert. "There is no reason why you shouldn't go," he drawled.

"No reason?" I threw at him. "Well, there is reason. Already we have two cases of fever in the infirmary—and both of them worked in the swamps."

He interrupted dryly—"Niggers don't have swamp fever."

Now I interrupted him. "So I have heard"—I spoke sarcastically—"so your mother told me. Nevertheless they are ill, if not with swamp fever then from some other fever generated by the swamps."

As if irritated beyond eating he suddenly shoved his plate back and stared down the table at me. "You can't keep the boy tied to your apron strings the rest of his life."

I turned to Old Madame, who actually had found enough interest in the scene to cease eating. "But you, Madame," I said urgently, "it was you who told me how dangerous the rice swamps are—how white people dare not go near them in hot weather—"

She looked at me with the false benevolence which so often I had seen her bestow on Lorelie. "You are needlessly upset, mademoiselle," she soothed. "Rupert will come to no harm. And it is unwise for you to upset yourself now."

With effort I desisted and held back the angry words which fought for release, for even as she spoke I saw the glance she threw Saint Clair—the one which he had sent her in return; and though it was as brief as the flickering of a serpent's tongue, it reminded me that on this subject, as on all others, these two acted and spoke in perfect accord—an accord against which an outsider was powerless. So when after supper Rupert, swaggering in high boots (another of his father's gifts), went off to the rice fields with Vene, his gun held under his arm, I, without a backward glance at Old Madame or Saint Clair, left the drawing room and went upstairs.

After hours of anxious waiting for Rupert's return, I was aroused by the sound of his voice in the hall below and rising swiftly I went down the stairs, relief flowing through me like a warming stream. He sprawled in a chair while Vene kneeled before him and pulled at the muddy boots, telling his father of the ricebirds he had shot. "Thirty-eight," he boasted, then for the first time deigned to notice me. "I'll keep you in ricebirds from now on, Hester," he offered patronizingly.

"That will be fine," I told him, my voice dry with disbelief. "I didn't know you could shoot so well. But come now—it is late; I will see you to bed."

The boots at last off, he stood, his shoulders squared, his hands thrust debonairly into his pockets. "I don't want you to see me to bed, Hester," he said arrogantly, "ever again."

"I will see you to bed just the same," I retorted. "And stop giving yourself airs."

Deliberately he turned to his father who lounged at the mantelpiece, watching us with eyes in which there was a certain sardonic amusement. "I am too old to be put to bed by Hester, papa. Please may I go by myself?"

"Why not?" Saint Clair shrugged. "It is time you learned to look after yourself."

Realizing that I was vanquished for the time anyway, I dropped the matter. But when Rupert a second later left the room it was with an obvious swagger and he could not refrain from gloating; and though he said, "Good night, Hester," with utmost politeness, he deliberately grimaced as he passed me and thrust out his tongue.

The heat-laden days crawled on. I, going about my household tasks, could not shake off the heavy oppressiveness which weighed upon me. Nor could the light of out-of-doors dispel it. For often I went into the garden hoping that the normality of sunlight would free me from it; instead it seemed to gather strength until it became reality and I, the woman whom it pursued, became the shadow.

Impatiently I would assure myself that the matter of Rupert merited no such importance. Rupert was only a boy—and how changeable and impressionable a one I knew better than most. Surely that which I would clear up at the first opportunity could not be the reason for my heavy mood. Yet even as I re-assured myself, I would turn restless and wander from room to room trying to escape the somber thing that kept me company —yet never able to put in words what it was from which I craved escape.

But a week later it all crystallized for me—a week in which Rupert went nightly to the swamps and returned so elated with success that each day saw him grow more impudent. During that week I made several overtures toward a "clearing up" of whatever stood between us. But I met with little success. He ignored the friendly gestures I proffered and managed on some pretext or other to leave the room; and I would stand amazed at the adroitness with which he had evaded me. But on Thursday there occurred the incident that gave me clearer insight into the situation.

I was in the kitchen that morning doling out Maum Lucie's supplies for the day when he entered the room and crossing, stood at the table beside me as I worked. "Hester," he said.

"Yes?"

"I want some seed rice."

"What for?"

Impatiently he explained. The rice was under water and the number of birds had lessened—he was able to catch fewer each night. The bird-minders said if he would scatter seed rice they would flock back to feed again.

I did not relish giving up the precious hand-milled seed rice which was so hard to come by; I was saving it for the planting of the July fields. On the other hand I greatly desired to placate Rupert; and so I took the seed-room key from my pocket and handed it to him.

"You may get a cupful," I told him.

He had stretched out his hand to receive the key, but now he withdrew it quickly.

"A cupful?" he echoed. "I want more than a cupful—I want lots."

"That is all we can spare, Rupert."

He stood stiff and straight and his eyes narrowed with anger —for a brief shocked moment I thought he would strike me. But he didn't. He stared at me, his eyes full of dislike. Then he burst out, "It's not your rice—it's mine—you give it to me."

"No."

His body tensed with anger and frustration and he stood motionless, his contemptuous young eyes staring into mine. Then suddenly he turned to go—and I sighed with relief. I thought the thing was done with, but I was wrong. At the door he turned back—his anger-bright eyes upon me: "Papa is right, Hester—you are a mean, greedy woman—you're trying to take everything papa and I have. I think I hate you."

When he had gone I leaned sick and shaken against the table. So this was how it was. I had blamed the Negroes for poisoning the boy's mind—had even suspected jealousy of my unborn child. Now I knew that the change in Rupert was caused by none of these. Rupert's mind had been poisoned—yes. But it was Saint Clair who slowly but surely was weaning the child's affection from me—who distilled evil into the young mind; and while I leaned there, something close to fear raised its cautious head within me—as an animal in the forest stops to listen at the sound of danger.

Wearily I pushed the damp hair back from my face. What, I asked myself, was fermenting in Saint Clair's brain now?

Chapter Twenty-one

FROM that day on I was never free of that small, inward claw of fear. And now as I watched Rupert with his father, I was painfully divided by the dread of seeing evidence that justified this fear, and of failing to see anything which might spell harm for the child—harm that I might have arrested. It was as if I must observe a transforming process which changed him from the lovable boy I knew to one impudent and unlikable; but when I tried with every guile of which I was capable to pass beyond the wall now reared between us, Rupert's eyes would meet mine cold and hateful and almost before I realized he would slip away with an air of unpremeditated ease.

I told myself repeatedly that nothing had happened to justify my presentiment. Surely the fact that a careless father had suddenly turned attentive—had begun to lavish expensive gifts upon his son—was neither the unusual nor suspicious matter I would make it. I reminded myself that often fathers are indifferent to their sons until they see their own masculinity beginning to be reflected in the boy. Yet even as I brought what rationalization I could to allay the fear that worked within me, each day deepened my conviction that behind Saint Clair's actions lay some secret scheme; every morning the gray dawn peering into my window seemed to symbolize that conviction's returning. And as I got up and dressed and went about my tasks, it accompanied me.

On the Fourth of July—a day of general jubilation for the Negroes—Seven Chimneys was almost deserted. All the Negroes, even Margot and Maum Lucie, had yielded to the lure of the grand picnic staged for the freed men in the woods beyond Darien by wily northern politicians, and I with Tib's help had to manage. But this I did not mind. Saint Clair was in Savannah and the sight of Rupert cleaning his gun contentedly inspired a like content in me.

By sundown a slight breeze swept in from the sound, tempering the still enervating heat. After our early supper I left Tib to do the dishes and went outdoors. The sun dying behind the gray clouds touched the landscape with a sinister green-gold— a gold which would be swiftly vanquished by the mist that hung like swirls of smoke over the marshes and muffled the world beyond, and which later would roll inland and submerge the countryside.

But it was more pleasant than indoors, and relishing the absence of Old Madame's futile talk, I strolled along the path that led to the short cut and the little cove. I had gone only a little ways when suddenly I stopped, and fright ran through my veins like a chill fluid. A man had just slithered from the undergrowth that bordered the path, and I recognized John Eaton—he whom I had driven from the place. He crouched against the wall of brush like a hunted thing, but as I watched my fright passed. This, I perceived, was no Negro bent on evil as I at first had feared, but a man desperately ill. The body under the filthy rags was scarecrow-thin and shivered violently as with ague, and the eyes were sick and vacant in the gaunt face. Quickly I went to him.

"John Eaton—you are sick?"

His eyes turned toward me but no light of recognition relieved their glassiness. "Water," he mumbled, "fur Jesus' sake —water. . . ."

For a minute I stood there considering what I should do. Obviously the man was too ill to reach the cabins and the infirmary. Yet I could not leave him to lie in the woods all night —which my common sense told me he would do if left alone. Even now he had sunk to the ground and lay with closed eyes as if beyond knowing or caring what became of him.

In the end I persuaded him to follow me to an outhouse that had stood unused for many years. Now it was near to falling in, but once it had housed the young colts, and I recalled that straw still littered its dirt floor. Preceding John Eaton, who lurched after me like a drunken man, I entered the place and working swiftly piled the straw into a sort of pallet. Then I bade him come and lie upon it. Tottering, he obeyed, mumbling in delirium, the ghost of the old derisive smile on his face, and sinking upon the straw he curled his emaciated body upon it; he might have been a dead man lying there.

With what haste I could force from my heavy, clumsy body, I made my way back to the house and calling Tib I bade her fetch quilts from the press in the upper hall while I brought a crock of water from Maum Lucie's big bucket. Then Tib and I returned to the outhouse.

But when I re-entered I knew at once that John Eaton was beyond the warmth of the cover or the refreshment of the water. He lay as he had when I left him, curled like a thin cat, the glassy eyes seeming to peer derisively from beneath the half-closed lids as if he had died without so much as stirring since he sank upon the straw.

Yet I was to learn, he had moved. For Tib, standing in the door holding the cover, whispered—and there was some dreadful urgency in that whisper—"Miz Hester! Look!" I saw that she stared at the ground beside the straw and that fright rode like a terrible banner in her eyes. I followed the direction of her knuckly, pointing finger, and terror as great as hers—perhaps greater—rose within me. Then it was I realized that John Eaton had moved; that sometime between my leaving and returning he had retched; and the pool of spew that lay on the ground was flecked with black blood.

On panic-clumsy feet I stumbled toward the door, my outstretched hands pushing Tib backward with such suddenness she was near to falling. And in the brief moment it took us to gain the out-of-doors, thought had risen and burst like a giant wave. I had seen Seven Chimneys deserted and devastated —the Negroes fleeing in terror at the words "yellow fever"; I had seen my crops perishing, the plantation sinking to decay—thrust there by the horror of pestilence.

But this, I told myself, this yielding to panic would not do. Standing there I pressed my palms against my eyes to close out the pictures I had just glimpsed—to still the roaring in my ears. Then suddenly I was aware of Tib beside me and opening my eyes I saw that hers were piteous with fright. I gripped her trembling arm, not caring when she winced with hurt.

"Tib."

"Yassum."

"You are to tell no one. Hear me?"

She gazed at me mournfully. "Will I cotch hit, Miz Hester?"

"No—no," I lied hastily. "You have to touch them."

"I didn't tech 'im," she whispered.

"But you're not to tell a living soul. Understand?"

"Yassum—I ain' goin' tell. Whut yo' goin' do wid 'im, Miz Hester?"

But that I would not tell her, though already I knew what I must do. Instead I bade her go back to the house to wash in strong lye water. I watched her turn like a good child (had I told her to thrust her hand in fire she would have obeyed as docilely, I thought) and plod off carrying her load of cover. Then I closed the door of the outhouse carefully and finding a stick, thrust it through the faulty lock. As I did so, the horror returned—I felt as if some foul impurity emanated from the dead man within and seeping like a mist through cracks of the shanty polluted the very air of Seven Chimneys.

Even as I sat in my room and waited for the house to settle to quiet, the croaking of the frogs was an omen of the horror I must yet endure. It seeped up from the night outside, peering into the windows, lurking in the dim corners of my room; and its presence rolled away the world that had been into a timeless void, as if the mind found unbelievable a life free of pestilence and death.

And yet I viewed the thing I was about to do—the thing I knew I must do—with a curious detachment. My mind turning on ways and means—considering this, discarding that—was cold, passionless, deliberate. And if something stirred in my thoughts—a horror because I was not horrified—I was like a woman who looks into a mirror and sees a strange and loathsome shape she knows to be herself yet is neither surprised nor frightened by the ugly vision.

It was ten o'clock before I dared venture on my dreadful errand. Just as I would believe that at last Old Madame slept, noises from her room—her phlegmy cough—the rattle of her glass—would warn me. Only when listening from the top of the stairs I heard her chortling snores, did I feel secure. Then thrusting a length of dark veil into my bosom and wrapping my long black shawl about me, I stealthily made my way through the house to the kitchen where I found the can of coal oil Maum Lucie kept against the time of wet firewood. Taking it, I went down the back steps and along the path that led to the outhouse.

It was a night of strange heavy warmth, windless and—I was thankful for this—thick with a mist that submerged both land and water in which familiar landmarks took on unfamiliarity. As the circling path neared the water its suck and hiss among the grasses intensified the pulsing quiet. When I approached the outhouse, dread came to walk with me again—a dread that wrapped me round and swept clean through me, that stayed with me as I pulled the stick from the broken lock of the door. But it did not sway me from my purpose. When I had swathed the veil about my face to keep out pestilence I pushed the door of the outhouse, and when it slowly swung open I entered.

A sickening stench from the corpse assailed me—the foulness of blood, and sour spew and stronger than these the stench of pollution and decay. I felt nausea mount to my throat and controlled a swift terrified impulse to turn and flee. But I knew I could not flee. Only by remaining and destroying the thing that menaced could I free myself and Seven Chimneys of it. Deliberately I pulled the cork from the can of coal oil and raised it.

Outside again I rolled my length of veil and my shawl into a bundle and tossed them back into the hut where already the fire had begun to lick its tiny tongues along the straw. I had a swift, sickening vision of John Eaton curled like a cat in their greedy center. . . .

Standing at a distance I watched the flames leap high to change the mist that hung above into swirls of crimson bloom and I pressed my sleeve against my face to hold out the sweetish sickening odor of burning flesh. I told myself it would be quickly over—that the old wood of the outhouse burned like paper—in but a little time only a pile of gray ashes would remain.

As if the fire had the power to propel me back into the past, suddenly as I stood there I was a child again—a child standing beside another fire in another wood—the wood which adjoined the orphanage. It was dusk and there were three of us, all children, though counted old enough for heavy work. All the gray afternoon we had dragged firewood to feed the big stoves and now we clustered about the flame we had started to warm our blue-cold hands. The snow, feathery and soft, fell quietly . . . tiny stilettos of ice hung to the bare limbs of the trees. The little flame we had nourished so carefully grew and grew and we stood there motionless—Janey, spare-boned and stolid—Alberta with her wizened monkey's visage—I, youngest of all, my eyes big in my pointed face as though drugged by the warmth; and as if the flames had thawed some ice within my childish breast, the face of all of life to come was warmed and lightened. Oh, I knew that day that life held only wondrous things for me. Now, standing by the burning outhouse I fell to bitter weeping and it was as if I would never again cease to weep.

Chapter Twenty-two

NEXT morning, however, when I arose at five, my languor and inertia had vanished and by seven I had breakfasted and was toiling over the land toward the cabins and the infirmary, unmindful of the heat, already almost overpowering, and of the heaviness of my body, which heretofore had seemed to weigh me down. It was as if apprehension released some powerful stimulant into my blood which defied the hottest sun, the most laborious effort.

At the infirmary I inspected the sick, closely searching for the symptoms I dreaded to find, but I did not find them. Indeed, I found nothing more serious than the usual minor summer ailments—intestinal upsets, chills and fever, a case of "dew-poison" feet. And as I left, after listening to a seemingly endless series of complainings and groans, my spirits lightened.

Nevertheless my vigilance did not relax. Each day I went my rounds at the infirmary, heard the same childish complainings, was subjected to their effusive gratitude for the gifts I carried —calf's-foot jelly, beef tea and such, and in the house I was equally watchful. Each inmate—Saint Clair, Old Madame, Rupert, and above all Tib—came in for careful and constant scrutiny. Yet when Rupert did fall sick—it was on Monday a week later—I knew no panic. Too many times in the days just passed I had faced such a contingency to be caught unprepared, and with calm inspired by determination, I isolated him in my room and gave orders that no one except myself was to enter. And for a day and night I sat beside him while he burned with fever or shivered with ague, my caution on guard as I sponged his lips with vinegar water or thrust hot bricks to his feet.

But after twenty-four hours my anxiety eased. There were no signs of purpling skin, no blood-flecked spew. I told myself Rupert's illness was nothing more serious than one of the obscure fevers that emanated from the swamps, and I plied him with quinine, the traditional remedy for such. In the days that followed my assurance lessened and I came to know a dread almost as great as dread of plague, for Rupert's fever did not yield to quinine. Instead it soared to new heights each day until when it stood at its peak he babbled in delirium. And this would be followed by the fever's swift descent, plunging him into chills which would shake him as a vicious dog shakes a rat. When this passed, he would collapse into utter exhaustion. Seeing the sunken face, the body from which the flesh seemed to fall away, I feared that he would die.

Now I knew no life outside his sickroom. Night and day lost their identity; time had no meaning of its own but became a matter only of cold vinegar cloths and hot bricks, alternated as the fever waxed and waned. Wearily, I thought, I did not know which I dreaded most: the fever's rise and his frightened babbling or its drop and his hands clutching me as he begged piteously, "Don't let me get cold again, Hester—don't let me get cold!"

Sometimes as I sat beside him in the dim room Saint Clair would come to stand in the doorway and inquire about Rupert, but so casual and detached was his manner I could not really believe he felt the least genuine concern. Old Madame too was equally disinterested. If I passed through the lower hall on one of my frequent trips to the kitchen, she would look up from her tray. "And how is my grandson this morning, mademoiselle?"

"He is worse, madame. Already his fever is higher than yesterday."

She would "Tch tch" and gaze at me with apparent commiseration; then her fingers, which had been stilled for a moment, would begin to prowl stealthily like white mice about the plate in her lap. "The fever will run its course, mademoiselle. Then my grandson will be better." Already her fingers had grasped some tempting morsel of food. As I continued on my way to the kitchen, I knew that to Old Madame neither the illness of Rupert nor anything else was of importance so long as Margot brought her trays.

But one day (it was the tenth day of his illness) I was seized by the conviction that Rupert was about to die. His fever had rocketed to new heights, the chills, increasingly vicious, had plunged him into a stupor like death itself, and I knew a swift and sudden panic. Though it was late afternoon I sent Tib scurrying for Vene and when at last he came I dispatched him to Darien to bring Dr. Toittant. While I waited for their return, I paced restlessly, going from Rupert's side to the front door where I would search the channel for the longboat thus back to the dim room again, to stand above Rupert despairingly. Once as I stood thus I became aware that Saint Clair stood in the doorway.

"My mother tells me you have sent for Toittant at last."

Quickly, lest our voices disturb Rupert, I crossed to stand facing him in the doorway. "And what do you mean—at last?" I asked coldly.

"I mean you should have had him days ago. Why didn't you? What were you afraid of?"

I did not deign to answer. Nevertheless, doubt flashed into my mind. What did he know—how could he know I had feared yellow fever? Or did the question spring from his constant desire to punish, even when no punishment was deserved?

"Is that all you wish to say?" I asked.

"No. I wish you to know that you've made me miss the boat to Savannah. Vene was to row me to Darien. A fact, I presume, which is of no importance to you."

"It is not of the slightest importance. That Rupert have a doctor is important."

"It is devilish inconvenient—my missing the boat—just the same."

Going still nearer I thrust my face close to his. "Don't you know that Rupert is desperately ill? Desperately! And it is all your fault."

A wintry smile touched his lips. "So now I am to be vested with providential powers. Just how am I to blame?"

"You sent him to the rice swamps. If you had wished to murder him you could have chosen no surer way—"

I had uttered the words thoughtlessly, as one will under stress, and without serious intent so I was unprepared for the consequence. His white hand whipped out and struck me swiftly and cruelly across the mouth. I heard his voice, omi-

nously quiet, saying, "Be careful what you say, you fool," and
stunned with surprise I could only stand and stare at him, my
hand nursing my bruised lips. The eyes that stared back at me
were so malignant, so evil, I would not have been surprised to
feel his hands on my throat.

But before I could speak, before I could even encompass
the meaning behind the blow or the words which had invited
it, I saw Vene's face at Saint Clair's shoulder, his eyes sliding
from Saint Clair to me, heard Vene saying, "Here de doctah,
Miz Hester." The ponderous figure of Dr. Toittant loomed
behind Vene.

Still I could not speak. Like a stone I stood there while Saint
Clair drawled, "Oh it's you, Toittant. Have a look at my son.
Come, Hester, you must meet Dr. Toittant. My wife, doctor—
she'll be needing you herself before long." And perfectly at
ease, he passed me and led the way into the room. "Here's the
boy, doctor."

I stood at the foot of the bed while the doctor leaning over
the bed examined Rupert, his not too clean hands pressing the
small abdomen here, shifting to press there, moving to grasp
the lifeless wrist—but I was hardly aware of what he did. For
Saint Clair, coming to stand beside me, had laid his white hand
against the polished wood of the bed and I stared at that hand
with fascinated horror. I felt again its flickering blow across
my mouth, heard again the ominous voice warning me to quiet;
and suddenly the hateful scene—not understood before—was
lit up for me as a corner cupboard of Stygian darkness is flooded
with brilliant light. I knew when I had cried out my unwitting
words of accusation he had feared that Vene and Dr. Toittant
coming up the hall might hear, and that if heard, the words like
pebbles thrown into a pool might start a series of circling
dangers which, looked into too closely, might mean disaster for
him. For some reason, though spoken thoughtlessly, my words
had held menace for him. Now I knew that reason. I had spoken
truly. *He had meant Rupert to die.*

But Rupert did not die. There came the days—years, it
seemed, though it was only weeks—when the fever's peak was
less high than for many days, when the succeeding ague appeared to have spent its force and the period of rest between

them lengthened as if the body, at last rebelling against the punishment it had taken, rested and gathered strength. In the dusk of a late August afternoon I roused from a half doze in my chair beside his bed to find his eyes upon me; they were clear and sane.

"Hester," the weak voice said.

"Yes, Rupert."

"I have been sick, haven't I?"

"Very sick, but you are better now."

He lay motionless but continued to regard me steadily from wide clear eyes. Then he spoke again, "Hester—"

"Yes, Rupert."

"It wasn't true—what I said that day. . . ."

I sat quiet, anxious for a moment—was his mind really clear? —but when he went on I realized of what he spoke. "I don't hate you. I didn't ever hate you like I said."

I put my hand on his. "I knew you didn't hate me. I understood."

He said slowly, "I saw papa hit you there in the door—"

"Hit me?" I laughed lightly. "Oh no, Rupert. You had a bad dream."

But steadily he said, "I saw him. The day the doctor came."

I lied to pacify. "You were so ill. Your papa was worried and upset."

He moved his head in denial. "No. I saw papa hit you—I heard what you said to papa."

"You heard?"

"You are right, Hester—it is papa's fault I am sick—he wanted me to be sick."

In his eyes, dark and wide, I saw a great wondering and I was suddenly afraid of what his next question might be, and so to divert him from his dark wonder quickly and casually I spoke of the beef tea which Maum Lucie had simmering in the glass jar each day for him; I was glad when his eyes brightened a little with hunger. But as I went toward the kitchen to fetch it I dwelled upon his words; thinking them over I could not be altogether sorry Rupert had been ill. It was as if the fever had burned away all the doubt and ugliness which Saint Clair had reared between us—had sent him back to me and, moreover, stripped Saint Clair of the chance of ever taking him again.

No, I could not truly regret Rupert's illness. In this at least I had won over Saint Clair.

August, with no diminishing of its heat, was turning toward September before the fever finally loosed its febrile hold, before the ague was robbed entirely of its force. But even in defeat it won a dubious victory. For it left Rupert but a shadow of his former self and so weak and listless that I wondered if ever the ravaged body, the bird-claw hands, the ribs that arched like knives above the hollowed chest could be brought to robustness again. But even in my concern I did not dream months were to elapse before the disease which had crept upon him from the malarial swamps would loose him wholly. Time and time again he was to be without warning plunged back into high fever and its accompanying ague, as if the disease could not bear to let him go.

In the early days no hint of this occurred, and with the aid of Maum Lucie and Tib I plied him with nourishing food and cool drinks, alternated the hours of games and books with periods of rest and sleep. Gradually the body lost its gruesomeness. The hollows in the chest filled out; the bird claws became Rupert's agile, clever hands again, which could fashion paper boats and sail them on the sea of counterpane.

It was in the first week of September when he was allowed to slide from the bed to the big rocking chair to eat his breakfast and when, leaving Tib to watch him, I went down the front steps and with Shem's help climbed slowly and awkwardly into the buckboard. For the first time since Rupert's illness I was going to the fields. Indeed, I felt that I must go, for this morning cotton-picking had started. As Shem took the reins and clucked to the hard-tailed mule, I was as excited as a girl going to keep tryst with a lover long unseen.

Sitting beside Shem I breathed in the matchless beauty of the day, my eyes traveling from garden to water, reaching on toward the big fields and past them to the rice swamps just visible against the horizon. Already I saw September had laid her sweet brown hands on summer. Here and there a gold or scarlet leaf glowed among the green, and the sumach bushes were like fagots of fire in the underbrush.

As the mule ambled across the land Shem spoke of the way the picking was going. Stella would pick her ninety pounds today. He chuckled when he spoke of Linette who, not to be outdone by Stella—cause of marital infelicity between Linette and her husband Tobe—was picking like a demon. But time it would take, he went on, to get the cotton in, even with the extra hands he had hired from Darien. And once it was in, rice harvest would start. All we had to worry 'bout now was the weather—this he said with a quick glance at the faultless sky.

When he stopped the mule at the big field, I sat gazing out over the snowy expanse of fully opened bolls, stretching as far as the eye could follow, and at the sight I was so deeply stirred that had I been a more emotional woman tears would have drenched my eyes. This was the realization of a dream, a dream won with so much effort that the dream itself had been submerged by the winning. I wondered if it was ever so—that in the struggle for attainment the magic of the dream is lost.

Sitting in the buckboard beside Shem I watched the Negroes weaving up and down between the rows, their hands plucking and dropping with almost lightning speed, some silent, some calling to each other as they worked or some humming softly to themselves. I saw Big Lou's buttocks swinging as she picked, Uncle Early's hands like darting blackbirds, Stella and Tobe managing to work in the same row while from the next one Linette, wizened and wrinkled, picked furiously and kept a suspicious eye on them at the same time.

Again Shem chuckled. "Dat Stella! She don' keer er rap fer Tobe. She jus' pull 'im long atter her lak a kite tail jes ter pester Linette. Linette oughter know dere ain' but one man Stella hanker fer. . . ."

Amused, I asked, "And who does Stella hanker for, Shem?"

"John Eaton. You 'members John Eaton, don' you, Miz Hester?"

My amusement was short-lived. Again I saw John Eaton's body curled on the straw like a sick cat with the greedy flames licking about it—I had not known that Stella was waiting for him.

With deliberate carelessness I asked, "What became of John Eaton?"

Shem shook his head doubtfully. "Nobuddy knows. Not eben

Stella. Some say he wen' ter Savannah—odders say he was in Darien just afore de celebration on de Fourth. An' Stella! Sometimes she near crazy wid worriment whut wid Ku Kluxes whipping and burning and John Eaton so brash."

He turned the mule toward the rice swamps but as we drove along the road I was less cheerful. It was not until we had left the buckboard and stood on the rice banks and I saw the stalks of grain glowing goldenly in the sunlight that my spirits were able to surmount thoughts of John Eaton and Stella. Then I forgot them, for Shem was speaking of the rice. He had counted as many as two hundred grains to the stalk; he said, it would weigh, he'd wager, forty-seven to the bushel instead of the standard forty-five. And pleased with his pride—it was the pride of the craftsman in work well done—I resolved that, once the harvest was all in, I would buy him one of the big silver watches which I had seen prosperous headsmen wear; no doubt I could purchase one right in Darien at not too dear a price.

With the help of the extra hands Shem had hired from Darien, by the end of the week the cotton was all picked and bagged and ready to be flatted to the factors in Savannah. Checking as Shem counted, I knew the triumph the gambler playing against heavy odds must feel when luck finally turns his way. The cotton would bring me three thousand dollars at the least and if all went well the rice would bring me that much again and more. That thought sweetened labor and even rid the stifling heat of the shed where we worked of some of its discomfort. As the number of bags mounted and I listened to Shem's comments—"it was first-rate long staple cotton," he said, "and would fetch a good price"—I could almost feel the winnings in my hand.

On Monday the rice harvest began, and six o'clock found me in the fields, despite a sleepless night when my back had ached like a bad tooth. At rising I had feared I could not go. The room had whirled dizzily around me and the face I inspected in the mirror had been pinched and pallid. But I had thrust down my ill feelings. Nothing should keep me from the rice fields.

During the days that followed I spent every minute in the fields marveling at the way Shem drove the Negroes—marveling equally at their willingness to be driven. They worked steadily and swiftly these days for over all—the hands and Shem and me—hung the threat of rain and the damage it could wreck on the new-cut rice. Sometimes, watching Shem, hearing his "How much you cut, Clarence? Cut another quarter fore dinnertime" —"Hop to hit, Tobe, we'se got lot ter do," I had the feeling that we were racing with nature, though the sky was of a spotless blue, with no speck of cloud; only the heat that hung in a glimmering haze warned of pressure building toward storm for the faultless sky persisted through cutting and drying, and each day found me in more sanguine mood.

But when the time of toting came I felt less so. True, the sky still arched clear and blue when I reached the fields that morning, but fluffy white clouds drifting idly, as if without purpose, were nevertheless banking in the west. I perceived that Shem cast an unhappy eye their way time and time again as the Negroes, working almost feverishly now, lifted the bundles of rice to their heads—bundles so big that the upper halves of their bodies were hidden—and toted them to the flats anchored in the river, stepping with the greatest ease over the quarter drains from one bog to another.

So well they worked at Shem's persistent prodding that before the bank of clouds above had darkened, the last sheaf had been put on the flats and poled up the river and stowed under the flathouse. And when Shem had posted Clarence to stand guard against thieving vagrant Negroes he returned to fetch me. As we got into the buckboard and headed for home, he was in a fine humor. The piled-up clouds, which had darkened in the last half hour, now received but a contemptuous glance. He had worried lest the storm break all day, he admitted. Now let her break: the rice was safe.

I was hardly aware of the meaning in his words. The pain which for days had prodded at the small of my back had become torture and I sat stiffly on the edge of the hard seat, my hands gripping its edge, my lips clenched. Vaguely I realized the sky was suddenly black, that the trees tossed their heads like wild horses, that arrows of orange zigzagged across the sky; but I was conscious only of the pain in my back which had spread to catch and hold my thighs in an agonizing vise.

From a great distance I heard Shem's voice, "Jes hol' stiddy,

Miz Hester. I'se goin' ter get you hum"—but the words had nothing to do with me. A thunderbolt crashed close overhead —I saw a giant oak riven from top to base and that riven tree was part of the pain that shattered me—like that tree I was being disemboweled—a woman screamed and screamed again, but not until Shem lifted me in his arms to carry me into the house did I know it was I who had screamed.

I was in bed—not my bed—Rupert lay in my bed—this was the governess' bed. The pain rose and ebbed—it was not pain but Rupert's fever rising falling, rising falling. I floated on the edge of consciousness, now slipping to the dark side of oblivion, pulled back by the pain to awareness—awareness of hurrying feet, of Maum Lucie's "Dis chile comin' afore hits time," of Margot's voice cold and suggestive "Mebbe not afore hits time."

Mingled with the pain was the sound of wind, of rain slashing at the windows, of lightning that seared its way across the room, of the sonorous roll of thunder. But the rice was safe— and just in time. Then the rice was a faraway thing—only the pain was close. I was a tree standing in the woods. "Like a young tree," Roi had said. I was a tree and each time the thunder broke it was the pain closing in again. Why must that woman scream and scream?

I heard the name Dr. Toittant. And sometime later—it had the semblance of eternity—I felt rather than saw Saint Clair's figure towering beside me. "She is doing well enough," he drawled. "No need to bring Toittant out in all this storm." Then I laughed. I was remembering Roi's voice saying, "You would have made a good doctor, Saint—but heal thyself, physician," and I wondered if Saint Clair knew why I laughed. Then the thunder came again and with it the pain—and that woman's screams drowned out my laughing. Why did that woman scream and scream?

I awakened to the sound of gentle rain, to firelight that danced on the walls of the dark room, and there was only me and the rain and the firelight and the release from pain. I tasted that release avidly yet cautiously as one famishing might taste the first clear cold water. Somehow I knew my baby had been born, but how—whether dead or alive—I did not know or even care. I only wanted to lie in the dark room unmoving, fearing movement would bring someone to my side, and I wanted no one. I only desired to lie without pain and without thought, sensing that thought would again confront me with the problems which pain had let me escape.

But after a little my dormant consciousness began to function, became aware at first of a noise—a small *creak, creak* somewhere in the room, rhythmical and persistent, connected somehow and moving in unison with a grotesque shadow on wall and ceiling; and emerging to clarity I knew someone sat in the low chair by the fire and rocked. In the shadow on the ceiling I recognized Tib's plait-studded head.

"Tib," I said, and I was startled by my thread of voice.

The rocking stopped abruptly and she came to my bed, her arms cradling a white bundle, her eyes peering. "Did you call me, Miz Hester?" her voice was reverent.

"Yes. Is that the baby?"

Even in the dark I knew she grinned, but she did not answer. Instead she placed the bundle beside me. "Hits a boy, Miz Hester."

"Turn up the lamp, Tib."

When she had done so I leaned on my elbow and turned the blanket back from the baby's face and looked at him. This, I told myself, was my son. Yet even as I shaped the words they had no kinship with reality, nor did I feel any kinship with this tiny wrinkled figure. Conceived without love, planted within my body against my will by one whom I abhorred, I had carried him with a feeling close to rebellion—the rebellion one might feel for a parasite which, attaching itself, would have the power to fasten itself permanently. I had felt so about my unborn child; not wanting it, yet sensing I would never be free of it— that it would never let me go.

Now, leaning there on my elbow looking into the remote eyes I became aware of a shadow which moved between me and the light and turning I found Saint Clair standing beside the bed in his purple dressing gown.

"Are you all right?"

At the inquiry, though it was delivered with utmost disinterestedness, weakness sent a rush of tears to my eyes. But he must not see them, I told myself; and to conceal them I looked back toward the tiny form beside me. He, believing no doubt that the action was the usual maternal devotion, asked—and his voice was as careless as before—"What are you going to call him?"

Annoyed by his disinterest I looked back up at him. "You speak as if it is of no importance—what I name my son."

"It is only important that you do not give him my name."

"Why?" I spoke flatly. "You think he is not worthy the name?"

He smiled his mirthless smile. "I think that Roi would be more appropriate. . . ."

I knew what he wished to imply but I knew too that he had no faith in his own accusation—that he only voiced it because it offered another means by which he might make me wince— and so I ignored it and told him coolly, fighting the weakness which made me feel inclined to tears again—"I shall call him David."

"David?" His brows lifted cynically. "Why David? Or was that the name of your Dr. Prentiss whom you deserted so suddenly and so ruthlessly?"

I stared at him defiantly. "I shall call him David because it sounds like the name of a good man. We could use some goodness in this family."

He glanced down at the small quiet face beside me. Then he drawled, "He is puny enough. He looks as if he has little enough chance of ever being a man."

Anger rose like a bitter brew and choked me. But I would not give him the satisfaction of seeing. I sat rigid and unmoving until he had noiselessly withdrawn down the hall. And the taste of hate rose like a gorge in my mouth

The baby stirred—it was the slightest of motions—and I looked down at him again. As I looked, I saw how helpless he was, and how his sad blue eyes now seemed to look up at me, wearily, as if he had found no joy in entering a world that held no welcome for him.

Suddenly I took him close, feeling the small helplessness of him, conscious of the tiny curled fingers, conscious above all of the sad remote eyes. My feeling, pitying, all-encompassing, crescendoed to positive pain—the pulling pain of birth. Fiercely I told myself—he is mine—no one but me loves him or wants him. With all my love, all my strength I would stand between him and whatever hurt might threaten him. At the thought that he would ever know hurt and suffering, it was as if the blood in my heart stood still and ceased to flow.

Chapter Twenty-three

EVEN during the days following David's birth when I must lie in bed I could not rest. How could I rest? There was the rice and cotton lying at shed and rice mill waiting to be sold—the "settling up" with the Negro hands for the season's work to be faced. Then there were plans for next year's crop to be laid out with Shem, and besides all these, the procuring of new hands to work it, for—so Shem had informed me—a number of the present gang would not contract with me another year. Some were hiring out to other plantations, others planning with their earnings to buy their own patch of land and independence. Although Shem assured me new hands would be easily found (after a year of freedom and loss of faith in the promises of northern politicians many Negroes were anxious to work again, he said), I knew that we must act at once lest the best labor escape us. And so on the fourth day of my lying-in, when I began to feel less languid, I called Shem to my room and together we went over plans for the next year.

The very next day I wrote to Stephen Pearsall requesting that he find reputable factors for my rice and cotton so that when I was able to come to Savannah the sales would be expedited as quickly as possible. For now I had a sense of working against time. Lying there in bed, my mind considering every aspect of my life, it had dawned upon me that I was about to face some sort of crisis. Quietly, stealthily, the dark evil of Saint Clair's machinations was moving to work against me. Intuitively I had known it since the day I had felt the blow across my mouth when his pretense of politeness had been shattered like a house of cards.

On the first day I was up—and I stayed abed but little more than a week, for it seemed that my strength responded to my need for strength—I plunged into the work that confronted me. The first thing I did was to summon Vene and Sey and Boy and transform two rear rooms on the first floor into bedrooms for David, Rupert, and me. Heretofore the rooms had stood unused except as refuge for decrepit furniture, old trunks and such. Now they were transformed into pleasant uncluttered quarters almost as bare as the dormitory at the orphanage; but immediately I felt at home in them, as if I belonged there. Never— and I was willing to admit it now—had I been able to banish wholly the pale unhappy spirit which, at least for me, had hovered in Lorelie's room.

There were other more tangible reasons why my new quarters pleased me. I could give Rupert, who at night was often drenched with night sweats, the constant attention that he still needed. On mornings following the sweats he would be too spent to get up, and must be waited upon almost as much as when he was ill.

Then there was David. And David did not thrive as did the buxom babies of the farmers' wives. The cow's milk which I had substituted for my own lack agreed with him so poorly that despairingly I was often tempted to find a Negro wet nurse for him. But the thought of his feeding at heavy black breasts was so repugnant to me that the temptation passed swiftly. Yet he did not fret and whine as the puling children I had cared for had done. He lay for the most part motionless with the weary remote eyes of the very old as if he lacked strength to move, and I was frightened of that stillness—that remoteness. Time and time again I would hasten to his side to listen to his light breathing; seeing his eyes in the light of the candle staring up into mine with a sort of uncanny knowing clarity, I would think, "I did not want you," and taking him to my breast I would hold him fiercely as if I hoped to give my strength to him who had so little. Whenever I must be away from his side—conferring with Shem, directing the affairs of the house—anxiety hovered over me like a shadow. So slight a hold he seemed to have on life I dreaded lest at some moment when I was not watching he might slip away altogether.

There was still another reason why the two cool dim rooms on the first floor pleased me. They served as a barrier between Saint Clair and me, made impossible Saint Clair's nightly visits to my room—those visits which had ever held such dread and shame for me. These new quarters with both children present —with the door between always standing wide—solved that problem. And that Saint Clair realized my purpose was evidenced by his words the day after the move when, returning from Savannah and having been informed by Old Madame of what had transpired during his absence, he came to dawdle in the door.

His eyes took in the quiet room.

"Is there some reason for this?" His query appeared on the surface to be an idle one, his gesture designating the rooms almost imperceptible. "Or is it another of the mad whims to which you women are prey?"

I was sorting David's small clothes and putting them into drawers, but I stopped and turned toward him squarely. "Certainly there is reason," I said.

"And just what is that reason?"

"Neither David nor Rupert is well. This will make the care of them easier for me."

He fixed his unfathomable gray eyes upon me and I—as so many times before—suspected that his mind was prying into mine—that he divined perfectly my other reasons for appropriating these rooms. And his next words convinced me.

"If you think to 'deprive' me of anything, you could have saved yourself this trouble."

"I do not know what you mean. Depriving you did not enter my mind."

"—And do not try and hoodwink me as to your intentions." His voice slid across mine lazily. "I realize them perfectly. And if I failed to realize them, these rooms"—the white hand gestured again—"would be revealing. You have returned to the virginal purity of spinsterhood. Even your bed"—his acid smile was knowing—"is the bed of an old maid. I want none of it."

"Then," I told him slowly, "at last we understand each other."

A semblance of a smile touched his face. "If there has been misunderstanding"—his voice maintained its usual disinterested casualness—"it has been on your part, my dear." The endearment, uttered sardonically, might have been another blow in my face. "I have never failed to understand you. I understood you when you married me—I understand this now." For the third time the white hand gestured toward the rooms.

"You say you have never misunderstood me," I told him levelly. "But you have *always* misunderstood me. You misunderstood or you would never have asked me to be your wife—you would never have agreed that I be Rupert's guardian. You would have known that I had no intention of conniving with you to deprive your son of his inheritance." I lifted my head arrogantly. "And that is what you intended, isn't it?"

He only continued to stand there, his face unchanging like a giant bird of prey; and under his relentless gaze I began to feel not unlike the fluttering victim powerless to escape the hawk. But I would not let him perceive it. I faced him with the air of arrogance which I did not feel, and finally he spoke.

"If you think," he drawled, "that I mistook your willingness to be my wife for anything except Yankee avarice, then you are a fool. I knew why you married me, but it happened to fit in with my plans just as your acting as Rupert's guardian fitted my plans—for the time being. But I am not an utter fool, you know. And when I wish to resume the position as my son's guardian I shall do so."

"Yes?" I asked sarcastically. "Perhaps Stephen Pearsall will have something to say about that."

"What he will say or think is a matter of indifference if I specify that you are unfit to act as my son's guardian—"

"And just what do you mean by that?"

He looked across at me, his mouth shadowed by a sneer. "It will only be necessary for me to inform the proper authorities of your affair with my brother—and the fact that you have borne his child . . ." His pale cold eyes bored into mine across the space between us.

Scornfully I told him, "You wouldn't dare—"

"Wouldn't dare?" His brows lifted for a brief second. "Oh, yes, I would dare. I would only need to tell the truth. How you, a carpetbagger, came into my home, poisoned my mind against my wife, suggested that she was mad—you did suggest it, you know—inveigled me into marriage, and with 'sweet persuasion' had me put the guardianship of my son into your hands. It is not a pretty story, my dear." His voice and smile were insolent. "And the South right now is not fond of carpetbaggers."

"You know it is all a pack of lies—" I began, then stopped, for his eyes were on me and by the deadly evil of his smile, set and unwavering, I knew I but beat against a wall. I knew too that he would dare anything—*anything*—would even brand his son and mine as illegitimate to gain control of Lorelie's estate again; and with panoramic swiftness I glimpsed the events such an accusation would set in motion: the hearing before the ordinary, the testimony of witnesses . . . Old Madame and Margot, even now I could imagine their voices—Old Madame oily and sanctimonious, Margot deceptively humble as they told of the greedy, grasping Yankee woman—stating as truth what Saint Clair had instructed them to say. And though my reason told me Saint Clair—guilty of so much himself—would never dare try to fasten false guilt upon me and if he dared, would fail, nevertheless, I was sickened. I stood there silent until he had gone his horrible noiseless way up the hall.

That night—a hot airless night it was—after David and Rupert slept, I went down the back steps to the garden and for a long time stood looking out over the marsh. Distant and aloof, the sky was peppered with stars, the harvest moon arching its way up over the horizon a thing of glory. Near me a mockingbird spilled its rapture skyward, but for me the night, the rising moon, the mockingbird's song held no power to dissolve the dark forebodings which came upon me like a wave flowing over and submerging me.

For now—and I had known it since this afternoon—I faced a new contingency. Heretofore when I had contemplated leaving Seven Chimneys—and I had contemplated it many times— I had seen my departure as a voluntary action. It had never occurred to me I might be banished. But this afternoon Saint Clair had revealed to me his determination to thrust me away and to brand me as a lewd woman. And I was sickened anew when I foresaw what my life would be following such banishment. My almost hopeless search for work, burdened as I would be with a child—perhaps in the end forced to place David in an orphanage so I might earn my way. But almost before my weary mind could suggest these possibilities to me I dismissed them. This I would never allow to happen, though how I would prevent it I did not know.

Quietly I began to pace the garden path, trying to form some sort of plan which would fortify me against the struggle which I knew was about to confront me. As the first step I told myself I must go without delay to Savannah to sell the rice and cotton and get what moneys were forthcoming from them in my hands. Perhaps if I did this and Saint Clair received the portion which Lorelie had specified, it might divert him from whatever step he was about to take and give me time in which to rear my defenses.

Pacing there in the garden I was vaguely aware of the passing of time, yet hardly conscious of time. Only when I realized how far the moon had traveled up the sky did I realize how late it must be. As one napping is startled to learn when he is roused that he has slept at all, I turned back toward the house.

But suddenly I stopped and listened. I had heard not so much a noise but movement, stealthy and guarded, like the shadow of a noise on the back porch. Instantly I was alert. Who, I asked myself, could be on the back porch at this hour?

The noise lost its shadow-like character and grew into the definite sound of footsteps which came down the back steps and along the path that circled—the path which I had taken so many times on my way to the cabins. Instinctively I stepped into the inky shadow thrown by a group of trees and there I waited, not moving until the advancing figure came into view.

I do not know what I thought when I recognized Saint Clair —Saint Clair wearing his purple dressing gown—but immediately I knew there was strangeness in his going along that path with his noiseless almost furtive tread—strangeness most of all in the whip he carried, with its leather thongs swinging out behind his body, twisting and writhing like snakes as he walked. Strangeness I say (for when had he ever walked this path before?) but as yet no awareness.

I was both curious and suspicious watching him circle, pass close to where I stood, and continue on. Did he go to the shed to count my cotton—to the rice mill to check my rice? Did there live in his conniving brain some plan by which he hoped to further thwart me? Whatever it was I must know.

Hardly breathing I stood waiting for the distance to widen between us; then clinging to the undergrowth I followed, moving as silently as he, pausing if I gained too swiftly, proceeding only when I deemed it safe. He neither accelerated nor slowed his pace and by this I knew he did not dream of my presence but went on as leisurely as though he strolled for pleasure in the night. Sometimes when the branches of the trees converged above the path and there was blackness below, I lost him; only when the tall figure emerged into moonlight did I breathe freely again.

But now as I slipped forward my eyes were caught by light that shone straight ahead, such a light as might creep through half-closed shutters from a lamp-lighted room. From whose room did it gleam? In whose house did it burn? What connection, if any, did it have with the tall figure that seemed to move toward it?

At first I believed it to come from the Negro cabins, but my sense of direction told me it was too far to the right. Then it struck me—and with the force of a blow—that it burned in Tawn's house; it was to Tawn's house Saint Clair went.

At this realization I stopped again, dark wonderings moving under the surface of my consciousness like sluggish fish in a pool. Why did he go to Tawn's house? Did he hope to surprise Roi again—as he had surprised him that other time? Did he include Roi and his association with Tawn in whatever ugly plot he had evolved to rid himself of me? And why did he carry that evil twisting whip?

Whatever it was I must know. In a patch of shadow I waited while his tall figure went on until he reached Tawn's door and as one familiar with that door unerringly found the knob and entered.

Even after the closed door had swallowed his figure, I hung there in the sheltering darkness and made no attempt to follow. For now my circling thoughts were confused. I was at a loss how to proceed. Should I too enter the door—perhaps to find Roi there again? Should I wait until I saw Saint Clair leave and accost him, demanding to know why he came here at this hour?

Yet even as I stood pondering, a dark cognizance began to seep into me—one so dark, so horrible that it might have been the poisonous air of the marsh sweeping over and defiling me. Chaotically I remembered things read, things whispered—dark things which could not be brought forth into the wholesomeness of daylight; of souls twisted and distorted. I had read and heard but had pretended not to believe, as a woman conscious of a cesspool lifts her nose and turning away pretends it has no existence.

But now I did not turn away. Now I must know. For this— this thing which I suspected was a part of the life which I had reached out for and taken; part of the web which I had woven; and so moving furtively as an animal might move through the forest, crouching to listen, advancing again tentatively, I came to Tawn's half-shuttered window, through which the light flowed, and looked into the room.

Later I stumbled back the way I had come, telling myself, "I must not think—I must keep sane." But the words had no rescue in them, no power to banish those minutes I had just lived through. They continued to shuttle against my brain with the nightmarish quality of a sick dream. Tawn's naked supine body—the whip descending and rising, coiling and uncoiling. And more terrible than whip or Tawn the face of Saint Clair at ordinary times so lifeless and expressionless, now maniacally intense, with eyes that shone in the lamplight like those of a wild animal.

And now I knew at last the secret of Seven Chimneys—knew the reason for the pursed lips and leering eyes with which it was regarded—knew too the thing that had broken Lorelie, that hung over the house and all who lived within it like a noisome blight and separated them from normal life and living by an unbridgeable gulf. No wonder, the words cried out within me, people had talked when I willingly had made myself a part of it. This Roi had known. This was what he had meant when he said, "I should have warned you." This was what Lorelie had meant when she said "I have been pulled down into all the ugly things—now I am part of the ugliness." And now remembering, and remembering too my conceited smugness, I was sick with shame; even when I told myself, "I didn't know—how could I know?" the words only emphasized that I had played the dupe and brought no consolation.

But what of Roi? Had he too gone along the path to Tawn's cabin? Had it been brother against brother for Tawn? Or had Saint Clair lest suspicion on my part threaten his plans, coiled that guilt about Roi's neck knowing it would throttle the feeling I had for Roi? And if this were true (and already I believed it true), was Roi the father of Tawn's sons? Or had Saint Clair bestowed that guilt upon him too? If so, then I had despised Roi for that of which he had been guiltless, had scorned his love because I had thought it shameful!

Now while I stumbled along in the dark, the ominous future was pierced by a single ray of light. Even yet there might be rescue for me. For I must be free of Saint Clair and free of the ugliness with which marriage to him had encompassed me. To go on living as his wife knowing what I now knew would be to resign, myself to an evil as great as his. Lorelie had accepted it, but I could never do so. And as one in great pain visioning relief from pain I saw a life which might even yet be mine away from him. I saw David, Rupert, and me living together in the healing light of normality and laughter, and that vision was like meat to one who has long languished for food.

Yet even as I entered my room, I was swept by a feeling of hopelessness. To escape I must leave Seven Chimneys, and to Seven Chimneys I was bound—bound by the futures of David and Rupert, to whom some day Seven Chimneys would belong; bound by my rice and cotton; and bound besides by something stronger than myself which would not let me go out to wander with David homeless and unwanted.

But if Saint Clair could be made to leave? No sooner had this solution presented itself than my mind began to play with the idea of a Seven Chimneys freed of its master; yet that too was shattered by cold logic. By what means did I hope to rid the place of his presence? Did I believe that some aloof and distant god would hurl his thunderbolts and strike him from my life?

Braced there against the door I laughed and the sound hung bitter and ugly in the room. No, I did not believe it. God would not help me, I told myself. And why should He? This web I had spun myself. By myself I must escape from it.

Chapter Twenty-four

THAT night for me was a night to be long remembered. As I lay in my bed, or turning restless, rose to sit at the window gazing out into the night unseeing, I was reminded of an old woman who had lived down the road from the orphanage. Weak in the head she was, and all day she sat in her little yard, her lap filled with colorful quilt patches which she eternally tried to fit into a pattern without ever quite succeeding. So it was with me that night as I endeavored to form a pattern of action by which I might extricate myself without sacrificing that which I had worked so hard to gain.

But even as I tried to plan I was held by hopelessness. For who, I asked, as I placed one incident beside another, who would believe the accusations I might bring against Saint Clair? Who would regard as other than fantastic imaginings my own convictions regarding Lorelie's death, Saint Clair's too willing acceptance of her will, his obvious reasons for making me his wife? And even if my convictions should gain credence, by what means would I prove them? Even the man Hibbard, quick to accuse, would, I knew, never abet me.

But from all the tangled confusion one idea at least I reaped from that wakeful night. It was in regard to Tawn. As I sat by the window at dawn, watching the veil of night lift from the hidden face of the world, the wording of Lorelie LeGrand's will returned to me and suggested a way whereby I might rid myself and Seven Chimneys of Tawn.

Thoughtfully I repeated that wording to myself: ". . . shall remain on the plantation Seven Chimneys as long as they so desire and shall be housed, clothed, and fed." But what if Tawn no longer desired to stay on Seven Chimneys? What if of her own volition she left the place? Then I would in no part be

guilty of failing to carry out Lorelie's request, yet Seven
Chimneys and I would both be freed of her and all her presence
there implied.

Yes, I must see to it that Tawn of her own free will left Seven
Chimneys, and I would attend to it today as soon as Saint Clair
went to Savannah, where I knew he was to go, for I had heard
him tell Vene he must be ready to row him to Darien in the
longboat.

Rising as usual at six I went to the kitchen to give orders
about breakfast. Once it was over I plunged again into the task
of teaching Tib to care for David while I was gone. It was
laborious work—so stupid she seemed about the smallest
detail; but I persisted, though many times I was near to being
ashamed of the sharpness with which I repeated my instructions. But as the day advanced I was rewarded by seeing her
"catch on" and as I went to prepare a midday tray for Rupert
who had waked listless and spiritless again, I sighed with relief.
Surely in another day Tib could be trusted with David while
I went to Savannah.

I had just given a tray to Rupert, who sat in a chair by the
window looking out at the garden without interest, when
Margot came to the door of his room to tell me Saint Clair
wished to see me in the drawing room. When I had tucked
Rupert's napkin about his neck and lingered to urge him to eat
a good lunch (for his appetite was fickle these days), I went to
the drawing room where Saint Clair meticulously—indeed
almost foppishly—dressed waited before the fireplace; and in
the double doorway I stopped short and asked "You wish to
see me?"

"Yes."

I waited for him to speak and when he failed to do so I
said shortly, "Well?"

"I want to know when you are going to sell the rice and
cotton."

"As soon as I can go to Savannah."

"And that will be—?" he left the question unfinished.

"At the earliest day I can leave Rupert and David."

He shrugged this away. "Well, I wish you would make haste.
I'm devilishly hard up for money."

"I have told you I will go as soon as I can." I was fully aware, despite his quiet manner, of the pressure he was exerting upon me and I was irritated. "And when I do, you can rest assured you will get your share."

His contemptuous eyes slid across the room at me. "Do you have any idea, by the way, what my share will be?"

"How can I until I know what the rice and cotton will bring?"

He was silent for a moment, then drawled, "Well, I hope it is enough."

"And what do you consider enough?" I asked sarcastically.

"I mean I won't be satisfied with any niggardly sum. I have certain pressing obligations—"

"But you borrowed from Rupert's estate to pay them."

He shrugged again as if what I thought was of no importance, but I knew as well as if he had told me so in words that he had failed to pay off his debts with the borrowed money. He had squandered the money—on gambling no doubt—and now found himself in the same position as before. Had he failed to pay Hibbard too? I wondered.

But now he was touching his cravat and cuffs with elegant, indolent fingers and I perceived he was preparing to go. But as he strolled with imperturbable poise toward the front door I stopped him. "Just a minute," I said. "There is something that must be settled between us—and now."

Then he turned back. "Yes?"

"It is about Tawn."

Though not a muscle of his body or face changed outwardly, nevertheless I sensed the inward tensing which followed my words; but he only asked—and as if he was totally without interest in the subject—"Tawn again? Are you never going to get over your jealousy of Tawn?"

I looked at him in disbelieving amazement. "I—jealous of Tawn?"

His smile of knowing discounted my amazement. "You have always been jealous of Tawn."

At the brazen effrontery of his charge I was furiously angry and yet there was a certain horrible amusement in my anger. Standing there I laughed and laughed; and while I laughed he waited motionless, his eyes fixed upon me. When my laughter died, he drawled, "You are amused?"

"Yes, I am amused."

"And may I ask what amuses you?"

"Yes," I broke out, "and I will tell you—I am glad to tell you. I am amused because you think me fool enough to believe your insinuations against Roi—for you mean that I am jealous of Tawn and Roi, don't you?"

"The night you saw him on her bed"—his smile was evil and suggestive—"you were like a puling cat. . . ."

I rushed on. "Yes. Because you meant I should think Roi—" I broke off. "And for a time I did. But now I know better. Now I know it is and has always been *you* and Tawn!"

"Are you mad?" his voice held to an unbroken level was none the less ominous for the levelness.

"No, I am sane for the first time since I married you. You see, now I know everything."

"What has Roi told you?"

"He has told me nothing. There was no need for him to tell me—"

"Oh, I see! You are merely indulging in your usual dramatics."

I looked at him with level eyes.

"Last night I followed you when you went to Tawn's house. I saw—through the window."

He might have been a statue standing there unalive without life or breath, but I saw a deadly intentness veil his eyes; yet under the stimulus of anger it did not daunt me.

"And you," I went on, "dare threaten me and my son! Well, I warn you. Be careful before you try to harm us. For I'll brand your perverted shame throughout the land."

I sensed that a giant reptile coiled before me ready to spring would be no more dangerous than he, yet I divined he did not dare to spring then; and intuition told me I had won some advantage over this man. I pushed it home.

"And now—the matter of Tawn. Rupert's money has supported her and her boys long enough. Now she must work as the other Negroes work. And I will have no interference from you. Is that understood?"

I observed him, my eyes refusing to flinch beneath the gaze he bent upon me. As I looked I saw the animal intensity of his gaze grow to a terrible brightness; and aware of some terrific struggle that seethed within him, it was suddenly revealed to me that I dealt with madness. I would not have been surprised to hear him scream out with the unleashed scream of the insane.

But for the time at least he did not slip the bounds of control. After a minute in which we stood facing each other, each pair of eyes refusing to give one whit, he said, "I have told you Tawn must be left alone." His voice was as emotionless as ever.

"Tawn is going to work—"

". . . and if you molest her—"

"What will you do?" I asked slowly, scornfully.

At first he remained motionless, his eyes probing mine. And then for the first time in my knowledge of him, he laughed. It was not such laughter as I had ever imagined: it was horrible silent laughter that made no sound yet which, soundless, pervaded the room and filled it with evil. When he had ceased to laugh he turned and went his noiseless way out of the front door and down the path toward the landing. Swiftly I went down the hall to the back porch and descending the back steps followed the path that led to Tawn's house.

Suddenly, as if action motivated by anger had dissolved them, all my dark forebodings, all my fears for the future melted away. Suddenly I was not afraid.

Even as I neared Tawn's house I saw her. She leaned against the door much as she had leaned on that day—how long ago that day seemed now—when I had first come to Seven Chimneys. Now, recalling the steady regard she had bestowed upon me that other time, other recollections of her arrogance swept over me: her refusal to work; her scorn of the Christmas gifts; the tiny image of me thrust with thorns; and whenever I chanced to pass, her high-headed insolence! And with these recollections my determination that she leave Seven Chimneys hardened and stifled the pity which I had felt momentarily, remembering her as I had seen her last night when she had seemed a beaten dog worshipping a mad master still. Walking with resolute tread, I went on until I stood below her at the doorstep.

Her soft brown eyes, that were nevertheless wary, looked down at me.

"Yassum," she said and waited.

"I wish to speak with you."

"Yassum," she intoned gently and waited again.

"It is about your working." Though I spoke in the authoritative tone that implied I would give no quarter, yet I was careful to speak with utmost civility. "Tomorrow morning you will come with the other Negro hands and receive your stint of work for the day."

She listened, her face grave; then asked and with the complete simplicity of a child, "You mean I'se got ter wuk?"

"That's exactly what I mean."

"Is Marse Saint Clair say fur me ter wuk?"

"I am in charge here. You will take orders from me, and I am ordering you to work as the other Negroes work."

Even before I had finished speaking I saw the secret smile which I hated creep over her face. In it was a blending of pity and amusement such as one might bestow on a child's unreasonable demand. For a space she stood there with the smile persisting, then she queried softly:

"You knows I ain' gonna wuk, don' you?"

The frank avowal of her intention caught me unawares, yet I wondered what I had expected. Had I not seen her always go her arrogant, confident way as if she possessed some secret knowledge which held her secure against the world, against life itself? And something like shame twisted within me. She, the concubine, knew a security which I, the wife, did not know —had never known. And at that thought my pretense of civility crumpled.

"Who do you think you are?" I asked slowly, scornfully. "Why do you think you and your children should be fed and clothed when you do nothing to earn?"

Her wide dark eyes met mine steadily. "I'se belong ter him," she said proudly. "I'se done belong ter him a long time now. You cum down here"—the eyes turned sultry—"an' you think you tek him. But he don' wan' a skinny white thing like you."

"How dare you speak like this to me?" My voice cut across hers. She continued as if she had not heard.

"What kin' of love kin you give him? I give him kin' of love he want." Without warning she moved, and the brown face was thrust near mine. "You white women is all alike. You think a man oughter be happy 'cause you let him play wid you a little bit in yo' prissy beds."

I went rigid with hate of her, for the dark skin, for the smell of her woman's body that came to me. I was overwhelmed by the desire to hurt her, she who had always been beyond my power of hurting.

I said through anger-set lips, "You'd rather he slip in at night to beat you like a dog, wouldn't you?" My laugh was a harsh, rasping sound.

Proudly she said, "He kin do wid me what he wants ter do. That's why he's got ter have me. When you marry him he stay 'way." Again the slow pitying smile. "But he cum back." Suddenly she stepped back and said softly, "He allus cum back."

"Tomorrow"—now I spoke in the voice of cold unemotional authority—"you will report for work. You will be paid two dollars each week and receive house and food. And when you fail to work you will be docked." I paused, then asked insistently, "Is that clear?"

Her eyes searched mine gravely. "You ain' worryin' 'bout me wuking, is you? You wants me ter go 'way, don' you?"

"Whether you go or stay makes no difference to me. But if you stay you must work."

She moved her head in slow denial. "No'm, I ain' gonna wuk. He wouldn't want me ter wuk. Jes' me waitin' fer him—that's whut he want."

"And I tell you if you stay you'll work."

"I ain' gonna stay—I'se goin' away frum here. Dat's whut you wants, ain' it?"

I drew a deep breath—yes, this was what I wanted, that she should go quietly and without further trouble; but I concealed any outward signs of this. Instead I was able to bring my voice back to civility again.

"If you refuse to be governed by the rules which govern the other Negroes, perhaps it is better that you go."

She reiterated softly, "I say I'se goin'."

"Very well. When Vene returns with the boat I will have him take you back to Darien if you will be ready." Then at some light of uncertainty that moved in the wide eyes I added, "That is, if you *really* mean to go."

"Yassum." Her voice was almost a murmur. "I'se goin'."

Without further ado I turned and started to retrace my steps toward the house; but her voice—and it was not soft now—rang out proud and confident: "I'se goin'," she said, "but I'se comin' back. He'll bring me back."

Go she did. Late that afternoon I saw her and Lem and Willie on the landing, each carrying his bundle of gear, and at sight of them I knew a twinge of compunction, for Lem and Willie were like two frightened rabbits as they clustered at Tawn's skirts. Where would they sleep tonight? or eat? I wondered, and calling Tib I sent her hurrying down the path to the landing with two dollars, which I bade her hand to Tawn. From the window I watched as she did my bidding; but I need not have wasted my sympathy or my money, for when Tib offered it to her, with a swift fury, that even reached me in the window, she snatched the money and hurled it into the waters of the channel, then rubbed her hand as though it had held some unclean thing. A little later when she got into the longboat I knew from the insolent lift of her breasts her anger still burned, and as the boat receded down the channel she sat straight and proud. Her sultry eyes gazed back at Seven Chimneys with longing until the trees hid it from her view.

Chapter Twenty-five

TWO days later Vene rowed me to Darien where I would take the boat for Savannah, and no sooner had we started down the channel than my spirits rose. All morning I had worked at last-minute tasks occasioned by the prospective absence from home, with special numerous instructions to Tib as to the care of David and Rupert. So torn was I by the parting with my pale quiet David and by the wistfulness in Rupert's eyes that had my trip been of less urgency I would even at the moment of parting have remained with them; only the devil of necessity held me to my journey.

But as the longboat went down the channel and swung out into the Sound I knew a sudden lift of feeling. So long a time had it been since I had left the plantation that it lent interest even to dull Darien. And I recalled the talk I had heard mostly through Shem of what had happened in Darien during the months of my absence; how the Negroes, at last realizing that forty acres and a mule were not forthcoming, had turned sullen and restless and large-scale vagabondage had reached such a climax of lawless independence that talk of an uprising fermented, throwing the community into a general state of uneasiness. I had heard too how the Ku Klux Klan, terrible because it moved in darkness and secrecy, and bearing in itself the seeds of its own destruction, was riding nights to accomplish ends which could not be reached openly.

All this I had heard, I say, and so I was curious to see Darien again. Thus when I landed on the wharf and realized I had time to spare before the boat arrived, I crossed the square to visit with Flora McCrackin whom I had not seen this long while; and I saw but little difference in the town. True, knots of men clustered here and there, but perceiving they were comprised for the most part of "pore whites," I attributed no special significance to their presence, and passing among them I proceeded to Angus McCrackin's store.

It was empty when I entered and for a moment I stood within its dimness assailed by memory of my first entrance there. Here was the same counter of cheap tumbled goods, the same crockersacks of potatoes sifting earth onto the floor. Even the smell of the place—pickles and leather mingled with tobacco—was unchanged. Only I had changed, I thought, remembering Hester Snow of that other time in her gray dolman and with her faith in the unknown future.

But there was no profit in this sort of thing, I told myself sharply; I but wasted time; and going to the rear door which led to Flora McCrackin's kitchen I opened it and looked in.

Flora McCrackin, kneading dough at the flour table, looked up and on seeing me dropped the dough and rubbing it from her hands, came toward me; but there was no welcoming smile such as she had given me heretofore. Almost she looked like a frightened child, and before I could so much as say "Good day" she sent a quick searching glance into the store behind me and, passing me, closed the door, almost furtively. Then she turned back to me.

"Oh, miss!" she exclaimed anxiously. "Whatever did you come here for?"

I surveyed her in wonderment, for this was far different from the friendly chat I had anticipated.

"Mrs. McCrackin, what on earth?"

She wrung her floury hands. "It will only make trouble for you and for me too—"

I caught her hands, flour and all, in mine and held them firmly.

"You must tell me what this means," I told her quietly.

"You don't know?" the childlike eyes distressed and uneasy turned up to mine. And then Flora McCrackin told me what they were saying in Darien—those voices which whispered of my helping to get rid of Lorelie so that I could take her place. They even said I had failed to call the doctor when Rupert was sick, she blurted out. And with a shamefaced look she said, "They say your baby—is Roi's."

Gratefully I laid my hand on hers again. "Thank you, Flora McCrackin," I said softly, then fearing the dour Angus would return and find me here and I might be the unwitting cause of still more unpleasantness for her, I opened the door and walked swiftly through the empty store.

My good intentions availed me nothing, however, for as I stepped from the store to the street I almost collided with Angus McCrackin, and when I would have passed him, he planted himself squarely before me. "Just a minute," he ordered.

To be the center of a disagreeable scene—and I knew by the leering in his foxlike face it would be disagreeable—was the least of my desires; and so I stopped and waited politely as if his request had been a courteous one. Perhaps, I reasoned somewhat wearily, if I let him have his say the sooner it would be over.

But when he began to speak I despaired of avoiding unpleasantness, for his voice raised—and deliberately rose I knew —attracted the scattered knots of men. I saw them, as he ranted, separate and slide toward us like a rope drawn by an unseen hand, until at last Angus McCrackin and I were surrounded by a ring of faces as leering and suspicious as his own, and I stood pilloried before them.

I was hardly aware of what Angus McCrackin said. Vaguely, as if my mind refused to absorb that which would shame me, I heard the word "carpetbagger," the allusion to "nigger-lovers," the sly insinuations regarding Lorelie's death. I was conscious that he ordered me to stay away from his place and his wife, that he even resorted to scriptural quotations regarding a strange woman. And half hearing, yet trying not to hear, I recognized his tirade for what it was—a fanatical exhortation without reason or sense.

But if my mind refused to absorb, my eyes could not avoid seeing. And I saw the glances that passed among the circle of leering eyes, saw the shoulders, lazy and indolent before, now hunched with something not unakin to menace. But even then I was uncomprehending.

I did not know who threw the first stone or that it had been thrown at all until it struck my face. I remember touching my cheek and when my fingers came away bloody, being surprised. But none of the other stones touched me. They whipped my skirts and one knocked my hat awry. And uncaring that the blood ran down my cheek, I straightened my hat with careful hands.

Suddenly it was over. There was a thundering beating of hooves and suddenly the circle of men scattered like leaves before the wind. Sans Foix, racing like the wind, plunged into their midst.

Then Roi was beside me, his eyes dark in his white face. He cupped my chin with his hand while he wiped the blood from my cheek.

"Stop trembling, sweet," he counseled, and not till then did I know that every nerve in my body quivered.

"Are you going to Seven Chimneys?" he asked, turning my face that he might better clean it.

"I'm waiting for the boat to Savannah. I came to visit with Flora McCrackin. When I came out they—"

He laid his fingers lightly across my lips. "Hush, you need not tell me. I know. There! Your face is clean again." He bent close, his eyes examining it. "It will not leave a scar." He smiled, "If the whole damned bunch of mongrels weren't watching I'd kiss your hurt and make it well."

Such a healing draught was the tenderness in his smile that already it was closing over the hurt. Yet some part of it continued to throb.

"Roi, do you know what they say of me? They say my child is yours."

For that too he had healing, and when he said in a low quick voice, "If only it were true, darling," I was comforted. A minute later when we walked across the square together and I saw the furtive, curious eyes follow us, I knew the question that lay ambushed behind each pair of suspicious eyes, but just the same I walked with pride.

It was ten o'clock that night when the boat finally docked. She had, we learned on her arrival, been trapped by one of the numerous sand bars and had lain so for five hours before she could be freed.

But neither Roi nor I chafed at the delay. By seven the wharf was deserted with the exception of a Negro or two, and even these ambled off to supper but a little later. Only Roi and I remained, and obscured by a piling we sat on the edge of the wharf as alone as if we were on a desert island—but not lonely, for between us there breathed a pulsing, living thing that made even the touching of hands precious and ever to be remembered.

We sat on the edge of the wharf above the dark water and while the frogs and whippoorwills vied for domination of the dusk which floated down like a veil, we talked. And it was as if a stream long pent were freed at last. All each had withheld from the other could now be said, what I had believed of Roi and Tawn and how he, knowing what I believed, had allowed me to believe. He could not bear that I learn the truth, he said.

"I was a fool"—his hand slashed the dusk with the old impatient gesturing—"to think it could be kept from you. I have damned myself a thousand times for not telling you the truth myself before you married Saint. But then," he defended swiftly, "I didn't believe that you would marry him. Even when Tawn tried to warn me I wouldn't believe. You always seemed so cool, so sure. Even that night you were cool and sure."

I raised my head from his shoulder. "Which night do you mean, Roi?"

"The night she shot me."

Wonderingly I asked, "You mean Tawn shot you?"

He laughed grimly. "You've never known what happened that night in Tawn's cabin, have you, Hester?"

"I thought Saint Clair surprised you there," I spoke slowly, recalling that night which seemed so distant now it might have happened in another lifetime, "and that you two quarreled." My fingers touched his arm. "Tell me—why did Tawn shoot you?"

He did not comply at once, but continued to look across the water; then he told me.

"She sent for me that night. Vene came to my place, said she must see me, that it had to do with you. And so I went to her house. She told me Saint meant to marry you. And I laughed at her for thinking such a thing could ever happen, whatever Saint's intentions." He paused, and when he spoke again his voice was as shamed as a guilty schoolboy's. "You may be sure my face is red when I remember that I laughed, Hester."

"But surely she didn't shoot you because you laughed," I said unbelievingly.

"No. It was when Saint came, not knowing I was there. Came with that whip. When I saw it, the whip I mean, it rushed over me how many lives it had scourged. My father's, Cecile's, Lorelie's—and now he dared to think of you. I would have killed him then, and Tawn knew it. So she shot me."

I sat there held to speechlessness by the pictures his words evoked, but after a little I whispered, "You said your father, Roi. Has Saint Clair always been like that?"

"Not always the whip," he said. "But even as a small boy possessed of a lust for inflicting pain." And he told me how at the age of eight Saint had delighted to torture, how once his father had found him—

Sick with horror I cried out, "If your father knew this, why did he leave Saint in charge of Seven Chimneys?"

"But he didn't!" Roi said. "Share and share alike, he left everything—money, land, and the house—to Old Madame and Cecile and Saint. But Saint meant to get all the control into his own hands, and he didn't rest until he succeeded. He had no trouble getting Old Madame's—she has always pampered him; she couldn't refuse him anything he asked."

"What about Cecile?"

"Saint would have had to account to Cecile's husband for her share. Yet Bob Kingston's death was called an accident. Oh, yes, Saint managed that with his usual skill. No one but Old Madame and Cecile ever knew what happened, and Saint handled them all right, even Cecile.

"Saint has destroyed everything he's touched. My father died a broken man because of him and then Cecile. When he had squandered her money and his mother's too and the debts were about to sink him, he married Lorelie. I was only a boy then, eighteen or so. The first time I saw her I planned how we would ride and have gay times together. She was about my age, you see, and so pretty and gay." His voice sank somberly. "We never did any of the things I'd planned, though. After her wedding night Lorelie was never gay again."

"You mean—the whip?" I whispered.

"Yes."

"But why did she stay? No one could have forced her to stay; why didn't she leave?"

"She loved him, Hester. Oh, don't ask me to explain why, but she loved him till the day she died. Some women are like that."

"Some women are fools."

He ignored this and went on as though I had not spoken. "When I came home from the war, I saw what Saint had done to her. He'd paid his substitute, you see, and stayed at home. Three years I was away. When I came back I found Lorelie drunken and half crazed, and I found Tawn's boys."

"She knew that too?"

"By then she knew everything there was to know."

"And yet she stayed on," I pointed out.

Quickly he turned toward me and cupped his hand beneath my chin. "And are you better than she was?" he demanded. "You know all there is to know—the whip and Tawn's boys, Saint's madness. And yet you stay on."

He held my chin firmly and I could not but look into his eyes. Yet for the life of me I could find no answer for him. I could not tell him I had so much to lose by going; I could never make him realize why I quailed at the thought of giving up what I had gained; and so I faced him unspeaking. And suddenly he freed my chin and drawing me close into his arms, began to talk again. "You know that you must go, don't you, Hester? Take your boy and go? You can sue for divorce and when you win it we'll go West and stake our homestead claim." He smiled down into my eyes. "You'd be a good farmer's wife, Hester."

Farmer's wife! At his words I withdrew from the circle of his arms, for I saw the farmers' wives I had known pass before me, a terrible gray procession of women, broken, all of them, by hard work and child-bearing; and I knew I would never be a farmer's wife. But Roi, mistaking my silence for acceptance, talked on, his cheek against mine, his voice hurrying as if to speed the reality of his dream. And indeed it was a fair picture he painted—the cabin in the clearing, the long days of sun, the nights of love. So bright his dream, I thought, and so undoubting; yet hearing I was saddened, for I remembered the drought that parched, the biting frosts, the winters long and cold. And always the heartbreaking toil, the endless struggle to survive.

These I had known and the knowledge was a searing thing which scarred me till this day. But these I had escaped. I would not return to them.

And yet, I told myself, after Roi had put his mouth on mine and we had sat there murmuring in the language that only lovers know, why shouldn't I have love and security as well? Surely there was a law which would force Saint Clair to provide for David and me. When I saw Stephen Pearsall tomorrow I would consult him on the matter, learn just how much I stood to lose or gain. Surely only a fool would throw away for love all she had struggled to win and I was no such fool. But if I could have love and security as well. . . .

I said nothing of this to Roi, but while his fingers traced the widow's peak on my forehead and etched the shape of my mouth, my mind was busy with the idea of divorce. Even the swift vision of the only divorced woman I had ever seen did not deter me—though she was a grim figure, target for the towns-people's eyes, the phrase "grass widow" following her like an unclean shadow. But tonight she had no power to affect me, for tonight I had heard for the first time the delicious language of love, had felt for the first time the touch of a beloved hand upon my breast. And though I scolded Roi, I was not angry.

Yes. Tomorrow I would speak to Stephen Pearsall regarding the matter of divorce.

Chapter Twenty-six

Next morning when I entered Stephen Pearsall's outer office where the parakeets chattered on as unchanged as if time had hung motionless since my last visit, I was in a most sanguine mood and the desire to discuss divorce was uppermost in my mind, even taking precedence over the question of factors for my rice and cotton. But on being informed by the white-coated Negro that Mr. Pearsall was out of the city—that Mr. Sharpless, the other member of the firm would see me, the balloon of my buoyancy was punctured. While I had had no dealings with Mr. Sharpless—my acquaintance with him was limited to the coolest of nods if we chanced to meet—nevertheless, I did not like him. Furthermore, I knew instinctively that neither did Mr. Sharpless like me.

When I entered his office, his small stabbing eyes beneath the beetling brows inspected me boldly with a glint of cynical amusement, though I was at a loss as to why he was amused. And his response to my cool but courteous greeting was abrupt to the point of rudeness.

"Pearsall called away," he barked. "Important matter. Asked me to see you when you came in." He opened a desk drawer and his stubby hand ruffled through a pack of papers he found there. "Matter of factors, wasn't it?"

I replied that I had written Mr. Pearsall to contact reputable factors for my rice and cotton crops, but almost before I had completed the sentence he began to bark again, "Yes, yes, yes—understand." He thrust a memorandum toward me. "Barkley and Blakely. Ask for Jonas Blakely. He'll buy your crops—pay you top price." He grimaced. "Everybody talking about your crops. Yankee woman showed us, they're saying."

"I don't understand—"

233

"What's to understand? Said it couldn't be done. Rice a dead crop—free niggers wouldn't work. Well, you showed 'em. Now all of 'em wanting to start over again. Bring back the good old days—money and fine horses and sailing regattas." He grimaced again, his nearest approach to a smile, I imagined. "Never do it. Rice a dead crop. Dead as a dead Yankee."

I thrust the memorandum into my reticule and with a "Thank you" turned to go, but he barked at me again.

"Minute, please. Some information. Think you ought to know."

"Yes?" I waited.

His hand fidgeted with the pompous gold chain that hung across his stomach and the prying eyes bored into mine.

"Do you know LeGrand is planning to sell the place—lock, stock, and barrel?"

"Going to sell—?" I began fighting to keep at bay the sick, cold feeling that seeped through me.

"Sell. Seven Chimneys," he repeated, and I would have sworn with relish. "To a man named Cram. Cram here yesterday making inquiries. Knew all about your crops, the timber—"

It struck me that the ferrety eyes shone with malicious triumph and dazedly I wondered why this man should be pleased at my undoing. Had he, too, heard the ugly things they whispered about me? Was he, too, glad to see the grasping Yankee woman get her come-uppance?

Impulsively, I cried out, "But he can't sell Seven Chimneys."

"Can't?" His beetling brows quirked. "Why not? Belongs to him. And Cram will pay a pretty price."

With the calmness that comes with despair I asked, "Who is this man Cram?"

"Nobody." His grin was one of mockery. "A poor white that made money out of the war—God knows how. Now he wants to be an aristocrat. Will, too. Rich as Croesus. Oh, yes—got a daughter."

"A daughter?"

"Yes, a daughter. Apple of his eye. Thinks his money can buy what he couldn't give her—fine old plantation, background, place in society. The things"—no mistaking the significance in the leering smile now—"women sell their souls for."

For a moment we faced each other in absolute understanding. I knew he thought ill of me, that he wished me to know it. But neither of us spoke and when I saw the restless hand creep toward the gold chain again I bade him good morning and at least with outward equanimity left the office. He should not perceive, I told myself, remembering the triumph I had surprised in his ugly little eyes, the panic that was sweeping through me, that walked with me as I left his office, that entered the waiting carriage with me—that I knew would never leave me until Seven Chimneys was safe again.

Of what transpired in the offices of Barkley and Blakely in Factor's Row that morning I have but faint remembrance. But this I do remember. I drove a hard bargain, so hard that time and time again I found Jonas Blakely contemplating me with much the same expression he might bestow on a lady who, before his very eyes, had been transformed into a monster. But I was indifferent. Coldly I stated my prices and though he talked at length and with much persuasion not by one cent did I deviate. I watched him, not without amusement, as he mopped the sweat from his rubicund face time and time again, and I repeated my figures. At last—he was a worn man by this time—he agreed to meet my demands, and still perspiring profusely filled out two checks, one for the rice and another for the cotton. Before the ink was dry I was back in the carriage and on my way to the bank where I would deposit them and draw out enough for the Negroes' wages.

While I waited for this sum to be counted in the small bills which I had requested, I was aware of unusual stir in the ordinarily dignified bank, and after a bit it dawned upon me that I was the cause. Counting out money, the teller would murmur through his grated window and the customer would turn curious eyes my way. Mr. Telfair, the bank's portly president, came to shake my hand and congratulate me on my crops. "They're the talk, ma'am, not only of Savannah, but of all the sea islands." He bowed low over my hand. "We've had any number of planters in this past week to discuss financing next year's crops. You've given us hope again."

But instead of experiencing a natural elation at his felicitations, I was seized by a feeling of frustration. What availed it that my crops had been successful, that enough money to see me and Seven Chimneys through another year was in the bank? Saint Clair was going to sell Seven Chimneys. And with that danger so near and live a thing, I realized the truth. I wanted Seven Chimneys and the promises it held for my and David's future more than anything on earth.

Next morning when I stepped on deck I saw that the sun of yesterday had been vanquished. The sky instead was a limitless stretch of gray and the water on which we traveled ominously still. As I stood at the boat's rail I heard the captain, a huge ruffian of a man with a scar down his cheek which pulled his eye askew and gave him a piratical air, say that we were in for a storm. All morning as the boat groped her way around the treacherous sand bars, the atmosphere became more and more depressed until the whole scene settled into utter lifelessness and we might have been a paper boat riding a paper sea.

Aware of the pressure that lay beneath the uncanny quiet of sea and sky, I was thankful I had told Vene to meet today's boat, though at the time of telling I had not known if I would be able to return so soon. But when we nosed up to the Darien wharf I saw him waiting beside old Zabo's shrimp boat and I was glad. We could make Seven Chimneys before the storm broke and just in the nick of time.

I told Vene to put my bag in the boat quickly, for we must reach home before wind and water rose—and so well did he obey that his oars were pushing against the Darien wharf before the last passenger had left the steamer. In another minute we were going down the river. Then, feeling I had been away two weeks instead of two nights, I began to bombard Vene with questions. How were David and Rupert? How had things gone in my absence?

In his soft, almost unintelligible voice he answered, "Rupert was sassy enuf dis mawning. Tib say de baby don' eat his food, she worrit some about him."

I sighed in exasperation. Accustomed to Negro babies who apparently thrived on a diet of field peas and fat back, Tib expected my frail David to bring the same gusto to his food. To persuade him to consume his numerous small portions of diluted milk called for more understanding than she possessed. Would Tib, loving as she was, ever learn?

I was recalled from my thoughts by Vene's voice.

"I'm sorry, Vene. I didn't hear you."

His eyes slid to mine before he spoke again as if he wished to observe the effect his words might have upon me.

"I sez we'se got comp'ny at de house."

I sat erect. "Company? At the house?"

"Yassum. Dey cum yestiddy wid Mister Saint. On de boat frum Savannah. You-all mus'a pass each udder on de way."

"Who came with Mr. LeGrand, Vene?" My voice was sharp and with good reason, for before he answered, intuition told me what that answer would be.

"De gennamun and de young lady."

"What are their names?"

For a moment the undertow, which always made turning the boat into the channel difficult, demanded his whole attention and he could not answer. But I knew the name he would call. Mr. Sharpless had spoken it yesterday. "A Mr. Cram," he had said, "was making inquiries." And further back than yesterday Stephen Pearsall had spoken it in the drawing room at Seven Chimneys while the fireflies danced their staccato dance over the gardens. "A Mr. Cram, but not the stripe of client we prefer." Almost I could hear his gentle southern voice intone the words. How little had I dreamed that even as we sat there fashioning a plan for victory over Saint Clair, a man named Cram, unknown to me and never seen by me, would be the means by which my plans would be destroyed.

And now he was at Seven Chimneys, brought by Saint Clair for the purpose of showing Cram what his money would buy. Remembering the house I had set in order, the land I had with labor and struggle made valuable again, I was sick with the realization it was to go. Yet how could they take it from me? It was neither his house nor his land. They were mine. I had brought them forth from dirt and squalor as surely as I had brought David forth from my womb. Yet even as I said "They are mine," I was struck by the thought that even now they might be sold, might belong to Cram; and with this realization came near panic. Leaning forward, I ordered Vene to hurry,

hurry, and I sat cold and taut until the boat bumped against the landing.

When I entered the front door and stood for a moment, voices and the tinkling laughter of a woman came from the dining room. Saint Clair and his guests were at midday dinner. Walking quietly I went toward them and halted in the double doors, immediately aware of the best china and glassware, the extravagant food, the amber wine that danced in the glasses. Then my eyes traveled around the table, taking in my fine husband at the head, Old Madame smirking at the other end, and the two guests for whom this costly meal had been spread.

They were unaware of my presence, each too intent on his own affairs to dream I watched them. Old Madame's babbling voice held the attention of the man Cram, whose back was turned my way, and Saint Clair, his fingers twirling his wine glass with his customary elegant lassitude, listened with eyes down to the girl who sat at his right and who, her prominent blue eyes roguish, chattered in his ear in a manner which I knew to be her idea of a "society lady."

"I reckon you think I'm a case, Mr. LeGrand," she burbled, "but you mustn't blame little me. Papa spoils me something terrible. And when I told him I just wouldn't live in Charleston—I didn't care if the old house was more than two hundred years old—why, he just let me have my way. Not," she added quickly, "but what Charleston is nice in some ways. And it can be fun—the Saint Cecilia balls and all that—but the people are so uppity."

Suddenly she saw me, and her mouth opened with surprise. Then she laid her hand on Saint Clair's arm. "Mr. LeGrand, there is someone—"

All eyes turned my way, the man Cram twisting in his chair that he might observe too. Saint Clair without the least surprise or discomfiture drawled, "Oh, you're back"—then with a casual gesture toward me—"My wife, Mr. Cram—Hester, Miss Genevieve Cram."

I said "How do you do" with detached pleasantness, then refusing Old Madame's offer that Margot set a place for me, I turned to go to David and Rupert, but Saint Clair's voice deterred me. "Did you have a successful trip?" His question might have been that of a considerate husband but I was not deceived, for I saw the speculative gleam in his eyes which told me plainly his interest lay in the prices my crops had brought. But I determined not to satisfy his avidness. Shrugging, I answered in the lightest of tones as if the matter merited no attention, "So-so," and he did not even try to conceal the venomous dislike which shone in his eyes before he turned back to the girl beside him. "Mrs. LeGrand," he told her, "raises rice and cotton."

Mr. Cram twisted still further in his chair until he faced me, his small piglet eyes traveling over my figure. "I've heard about that cotton and rice, ma'am. If I buy Seven Chimneys, you'll have to give me some pointers—tell me how to get your kind of results."

Saint Clair's eyes slipped back to me, Old Madame's fork halted in mid-air and I knew both waited to learn what effect this speech would have upon me. But I remained unruffled and unsurprised. There was no need on my part for play acting, as Mr. Cram had said *if* I buy Seven Chimneys. So the sale had not been consummated. Perhaps it might even yet be left to me.

Now Saint Clair turned back to the girl, Genevieve. "Do you think you could work like a nigger and raise rice and cotton?" She struck him a playful blow with her fan. "I wouldn't even try. I'm a lazybones. Ask papa." Her protuberant eyes rolled from one to another, came to rest upon me, and I saw their babyish innocence had turned cool and hard. "I reckon you think I'm a case, don't you, Mrs. LeGrand?"

Lacking an answer for so inane a query, I murmured "Excuse me" and went to the children. For a time at least the strangers in my house and the reason for their presence slipped into the limbo of insignificance, for David smiled up at me from his crib and his thin hands reached for my face; Rupert, the picture of boredom when I opened the door, brightened at once, and Tib's grin of welcome warmed me through and through.

In the kitchen I found the hullabaloo I expected, with Margot rushing to and fro, Maum Lucie as busy at the hearth with her pots and kettles as an orchestra leader endeavoring to play all the instruments in turn, to the accompaniment of her chronic grumbling. "Marse Saint heself order de supper—on my feets all day—not er minute since daybreak to res' 'em."

Peeping into her pots and kettles I learned that the supper menu was both bounteous and extravagant, roasted wild turkeys and pigeon pie, crayfish with wine stuffing, creamed oysters, a huge shoulder of pork roasted with sweet potatoes, hot breads, jams, jellies, and condiments. Saint Clair, I perceived, had returned to his old-time lavishness which I had so drastically curtailed—and also to his old time indifference to cost, I noted as I watched Margot unpack the gold-necked bottles which, she informed me, had arrived by boat yesterday.

But I did not tarry long in the kitchen. I returned to the drawing room to learn from Vene, whom I met in the hall loaded with a tray of bottles and glasses, that Saint Clair and Mr. Cram had repaired to the turret room. With that information I turned so apprehensive I could not settle to the numerous tasks which so obviously needed doing. I wandered from room to room so engrossed in speculation as to what was happening upstairs I was hardly aware of the storm—which had broken at last—though it thundered about the house like a thousand fiery steeds; and the day was so dark that Margot had to light the candles though it was only four.

At last I brought my darning and sat in the drawing room where I might watch the stairs and wait anxiously for Saint Clair and Mr. Cram to appear, believing I would be able to read from their manner whether the sale had been settled or not. When near to five they finally descended the stairs, I searched their faces closely trying to find an answer to the question that tormented me.

They told me little, however, and if I fancied I saw a more dogged line to Mr. Cram's jaw and an "I'll be damned if I do" air which encouraged me, my first glance at Saint Clair's face dissipated it. Too well I knew that manner, calm and unruffled on the surface, but with a cold deadliness within. How long, I wondered, would the man Cram be able to withstand the pressure of that relentless will? That he was aware of it was obvious; he was like a quivering pig, but an obstinate one, before it. He sat before the fire, his fat hands twisting his kerchief into shreds, his piglet eyes bright with anger—the picture of a spoiled child denied a toy he was determined to possess. But even as I perceived his struggle to resist, I was sick with anxiety. Seven Chimneys was the toy he coveted and I did not delude myself. Have it he would, however dear the price.

Now into the quiet of the drawing room—both Saint Clair and Mr. Cram were unspeaking, only the battle of their wills made itself heard—burst the vision of Genevieve, a bewildering vision in pale blue velvet, monstrously draped and bustled, her shoulders rising plumply from cascading lace, a jeweled comb restraining the tossing curls. And such fluttering and preening! Such playful sallies thrown in the direction of Saint Clair who, lounging at the fireplace, regarded her with the tolerance a mastiff might bestow upon a frolicsome puppy.

I realized, of course, that the silly girl was enamoured of Saint Clair and, I grudgingly admitted, with some excuse. His figure, elegant and indolent at the hearth with the well-ordered drawing room as its background, might attract any woman, even one of more sense than Genevieve Cram; and to her no doubt he presented manifold attractions. An old name, wide lands, the background which her father was so obviously trying to buy for her and which I surmised he had been unable to buy in discriminating Charleston.

As we ate Maum Lucie's delicious food and drank the golden wine at the lavishly spread supper table, the wind and rain lashed at the windows and the candles trembled like pale frightened ghosts. I was reminded of another supper at this table when the wind had torn at blinds and doors, when the candles had guttered even as these. Lorelie had sat at that other table on the night before she was drowned—and suddenly she was before me again, with her wasted figure and ravished eyes, crumbling the bread on her plate with thin fingers and smiling into the shadowy corners as if she possessed some secret knowledge which brought her pleasure.

Was she at this table too? I asked myself. Had she, knowing her plans for Rupert were dangerously near to disaster, found peace impossible even in the quiet grave lot?

Chapter Twenty-seven

AFTER supper when we withdrew to the drawing room, I sat in the big chair beside the fire and pretended to give my undivided attention to my basket of darning. Nevertheless, for all my industry nothing escaped me—neither the angry eyes of Mr. Cram as he thumbed through the latest *Harper's Weekly*, nor Saint Clair who, lounging in a deep chair, pretended to listen to Genevieve's chatter, but did not fail to watch her father with his unblinking gaze.

It was neither of these, however, who after a while won my serious contemplation. It was Old Madame. It dawned upon me after an interim in which she started nervously at each onslaught of wind, glancing toward the front door apprehensively, that she was not her usual complacent self. Moreover, I discovered—and much to my surprise—she was making a definite effort to propitiate me. She inquired with a semblance of friendliness I had not deemed possible about my trip to Savannah. Had I found it tiring? Had I been able to sell my crops? And when I told her I had met with fair success, she surprised me still more. "You are a clever woman, mademoiselle," she said.

So well I knew her greedy calculating mind I was instantly suspicious of this sudden admiration she professed for me, and I replied to her obvious flattery tartly. "Clever?" I held my needle mid-air and looked across at her with raised brows. "I do not think of myself as being clever, madame."

"Yes, yes," she insisted hurriedly, "you *are* clever, mademoiselle; for you no situation would be too difficult. You would know how to handle it."

Her manner and words were such a total departure from her usual bland assumption of being my superior that I glanced at her nonplussed.

Even after Margot had wheeled the old woman to her room and I continued to darn, ignoring the peevish glances with which Genevieve tried to convey to me the idea that I was *de trop*, I could not forget the imploring eyes. So I was not surprised somewhat later when, glancing up from my work, I saw Margot in the hall who, now having caught my attention, beckoned to me. Thrusting my darning into my basket, I rose with casual good nights—which received good nights even more casual—left the room and followed her down the center hall to the narrow passage which, turning right, led to Old Madame's room. Preceding me down this passage, she opened Old Madame's door and when I had entered withdrew, closing the door softly.

At Old Madame's side I looked down at her. "You wished to see me, madame?"

She raised herself laboriously to lean upon her elbow and looked up at me. "Mademoiselle, we must speak quietly."

I lowered my voice. "Yes, madame."

Panting, she lifted her body still higher and her eyes implored. "Mademoiselle, you say you sold your rice, your cotton?"

"Yes, madame."

"And you brought the wages money with you?"

"Naturally. You know that I must settle with the Negroes. Already they've waited too long."

Her futile hand caught mine. "You must let my son have the money, mademoiselle."

"Your son?"

"He is in danger, mademoiselle, grave danger. That money can save him. You must give it to him tonight."

"But I can't do that, madame. The money belongs to the Negroes. It is not mine or your son's."

She dropped back on the pillows, turning her head as if in actual pain. Yet even as I stood looking down at her I saw her face change, saw craftiness grow upon it, and she sat up again.

"You are clever, mademoiselle. You will think of a way to save my son." The not overly clean fingers clung to mine again.

"What is he in danger of, madame?"

She beckoned me nearer and I sat on the bed beside her.

"He is in danger of prison, mademoiselle. Margot heard them in the drawing room. He married you when you were a nobody and made you a LeGrand. Now you must save him. He mustn't go to prison."

I cut in upon her frantic babbling. "Madame, if you will explain."

"Yes, yes." Her tiny flabby hands met and twisted together. "He came last night, mademoiselle, at suppertime. He stayed for supper. He was so polite, so charming. I did not realize then why he came."

I interrupted her. "Who came, madame?"

"That Mr. Hibbard. He came to see you once, mademoiselle?"

"Yes, yes, I remember. Go on."

"He was so polite, so charming, at first. Until Mr. Cram and Genevieve had retired and they were alone in the drawing room, he and my son. Margot carried brandy for them, and she listened in the hall." Her voice sank to a whisper. "He told my son he must have money. 'Thirty-six hours I give you,' he said, 'or you go to jail.'" Her eyes clung to mine. "Already twenty-four hours have passed, mademoiselle."

I sat beside her, silent, gathering up the threads of this night and weaving them into a pattern. Almost it was complete. Saint Clair rearing his plan of obtaining money by selling Seven Chimneys, on the verge of selling it; then the appearance of Hibbard, needing money himself, no doubt; threatening, if it was not forthcoming, to disclose what he knew about Lorelie's death, shrewd enough to realize that with the Crams in the house, Saint Clair was in a vulnerable position. And Saint Clair, forced before the Crams to play the courteous host with disaster hanging over him, yet had nowhere to turn for the money to pay off Hibbard. Almost I could laugh. His own scheming had defeated him.

But I did not laugh. For even as I felt the desire for laughter I was struck by a sudden thought which stifled it. The wages money! I had thrust it into a bureau drawer on my return. Perhaps even as I sat here he was in my room—

I stood suddenly. "Madame—"

"Yes, mademoiselle?"

"This man Hibbard. Where is he now? Did he return to Savannah?"

"No, no. I do not make myself clear."

I grasped her shoulder, shook it. "Where is he, madame?"

"He is waiting in Darien at the Magnolia House. Margot heard him tell my son—'In thirty-six hours I'll be back.' "

I turned to go and her voice followed me. "You will do something, mademoiselle?"

I answered without turning back.

"Yes, yes. I will do something."

Back in my room my first act was to go swiftly to the bureau drawer where I had put the money and when I touched it the fear which had gripped me—that Saint Clair had taken it even as I sat in Old Madame's room—was dissipated. For the present it was safe, but I knew that sooner or later Saint Clair would come to demand it. I must get it beyond his reach, I told myself. Not because I was afraid. My protection—and this gave me a sardonic satisfaction—lay in the presence of Cram and his daughter. I need only scream to bring Saint Clair's house toppling into the dust. No, it was not for reasons of safety that the money must be beyond his reach. Rather it was because I saw the money as the hinge on which success or failure of his plans hung. If Hibbard failed to receive the money so long due him, I did not doubt he would use the dark knowledge he possessed to punish the man he had aided and who refused to repay; almost I could picture the consequences of such a dénouement . . . the man Cram, purpled and apoplectic because he had been taken in . . . his silly daughter shrinking from the very man she had been so eager to enslave, and both fleeing the place which so short a time before had seemed so desirable; leaving it, with Saint Clair removed, to David, Rupert, and me.

But I must not stand here like a dolt, I reminded myself, fashioning pictures which mirrored my desire. I must prepare for the thing I must do, knowing almost without thinking how I must proceed. Moving quietly I awakened Tib, who slept on a pallet beside David's crib, and when she was sufficiently aroused to understand, I told her I must leave the house for a while. She must listen closely for David and Rupert.

She nodded obediently as always and lay down again and in a moment I knew from her quiet breathing that she slept. Then still moving with utmost quietness, I took my long black cape from the closet, and mindful of the storm which still raged, wrapped it closely about me. Then with the packet of money beneath my cape I went as silently as a phantom down the rear hall, crossed the back porch and descended the steps which led to the garden.

The storm assailed me but it did not dismay me; rather I enjoyed the rush of wind and rain and the sense of swift movement which was like a pent-up resolution set free at last. My fear that Saint Clair discover my absence, that I fail to get the money in the Darien bank before he catch up with me, was stronger by far than any fear of night or storm.

I followed the little winding path which led to the cabins and then on between the Black Banks to Roi's place, for it was toward Roi's I was headed. Roi would saddle Sans Foix and ride me to the river bank and when Joe poled his raft across from Darien at daybreak, I would make the return trip with him. At nine o'clock when the Darien bank opened I would deposit the wages money. Then and only then would I feel safe.

As I plodded toward Black Banks, tales I had heard of "hants" seethed through my mind, but my sanity rejected them. These were Negro superstition. No doubt seeing my figure crossing this cleared space tonight would evoke talk tomorrow of a ghost that walked the open. And it would be as true as all the other tales they whispered. So when I entered the forest again I was able to go at least without fear of the dead, though in truth I started at the limbs of trees which the storm had blown to the ground, and when I crossed the makeshift bridge which spanned the creek, I fancied I could make out huge scaly bodies and malignant eyes of the alligators on the banks. But I could see nothing except the night.

Once over the creek my courage returned. Now I had but a short way to go before I reached the carriage house. Another five minutes and it emerged from the night a blot, a shade darker than the night itself. And finally—and so battered was I by wind and rain I felt I had reached the end of human endurance—I reached the door and pushing it, found it unlocked.

Clinging to the wall for support, I ascended the narrow stairs toward the door at their top, but when I was but halfway up I heard the thud of feet above me, then the opening of the door. "Who is there?" Roi called sharply.

"Roi, it is I, Hester," I called back.

"Hester," his voice was filled with wonder, then suddenly sharpened. "What's wrong? Has Saint—"

His warm hand reaching from above found mine and drew me up into the room which was dark except for a bed of hot embers on the hearth. Roi went toward these swiftly and throwing fatwood into their midst, blew upon them until they burst into flame, then placed a log atop them.

"Come, Hester. Stand close to the fire. Then while I get into my clothes tell me."

Standing before the fire looking into the glowing flames, I related all that had happened since two nights ago when I had left him on the Darien wharf, and as I told I was struck with wonder that only two days had elapsed. As I talked, he dressed in the corner where his cot stood, a corner escaping the firelight, then came to lean against the mantelshelf and listen. In the firelight I saw that his eyes were a little mocking, a little challenging. And at the last when I drew the packet of money from beneath my dolman and told him I must prevent Saint Clair getting his hands on it, his brows lifted.

"I see," he said, and for the time I was deceived by the gentle thoughtfulness of his manner. "If Saint fails to pay Hibbard he gets thrown into jail."

"Yes," I supplied quickly, "and the sale of Seven Chimneys would fall through."

He looked at me across the firelight and laughed. It was soft laughter and yet it was ugly, too, as if with his laughter he spewed forth bitterness and defilement.

"Damn your conniving soul, Hester," he spoke levelly and somehow it imbued his words with greater contempt than anger, "for the greedy bitch you are." He laughed again. "Why don't you go the whole hog? You say Hibbard is at Darien— well, make a deal with him. Then you can be sure Saint goes to jail."

I regarded him, dumbfounded. Little had I expected this sarcasm, this criticism. "I take it then, Roi, you do not wish to see Saint in jail." Now it was I who laughed. "How is it you have turned suddenly sorry for Saint Clair?"

"Sorry for Saint?" He laughed. "He deserves anything he gets. But damn it, Hester, there is Rupert and your own boy to think of. Why don't you just leave Saint, let wiser hands than yours mete out his punishment?"

Suddenly I crossed and laid my hand on his arm. "But don't you see, Roi? Divorce would be a simple matter this way."

I felt the arm beneath my hand stiffen before he moved away. And I was surprised anew. This was a different Roi from the one I had known heretofore. A sterner, older Roi. His eyes, which so many times had looked into mine with laughing tenderness, surveyed me now narrow-lidded and cool, almost with hate, I thought; and I was suddenly aware that something precious was fleeing, lost.

Swiftly I followed him across the hearth to stand before him again. "Roi, don't you know why I do this? I want us to have Seven Chimneys—and each other."

His mouth curled with distaste. "You need not try to tell me that tale, Hester. I know why you do it." His voice dropped. "Too well I know. I am stupid not to have realized it before."

"Realized what?"

He crossed his arms and looked at me steadily. "That the Hester Snow I have loved does not exist. I built her up in my mind, because that night in McCrackin's store she looked as sweet and cool as a spring." His mouth twisted. "Now I know that spring water can be polluted."

I heard these quietly spoken words with a dismay that seemed almost more than I could bear. I looked at Roi, at his lean brown face, the eyes which held such appeal for me, and I wanted to cry out that I loved him, that I was not what I seemed to be. But I could not; there was not time. I must get to the river bank.

"Will you saddle Sans Foix and ride me to the river bank?" I asked.

Arms akimbo, he said quietly, "No, Hester."

"Very well. I shall walk."

I took my rain-soaked cape, pulled it about me and went to the door. But there I turned back and looked at him; I was torn with hesitation and doubt and a fearful sense of urgency. Was it worth the cost—this thing I was about to do? Would I lose Roi? But I could not let everything I had worked for be swept away. Roi *must* understand.

I put my hand on the doorknob and looked across at him.

"Roi?"

He did not answer but continued to stand there, his eyes mocking me across the firelit room. I went out and closed the door behind me.

Daybreak found me on the river bank, my eyes following Joe's raft which danced perilously upon the water. Time and time again it was deflected from its course and the lanky Joe was hard put to bring her back to tail again. His passengers— Negroes plantation-bound after a night in Darien—clung to its floor like black bugs on a wet plank, fearful, no doubt, that each swell would hurl them into the churning river.

I clung to the raft precariously while Joe poled back across the river, my eyes fixed upon the Darien shoreline toward which we seemed to inch so painfully. The rain had stopped for the time being. And clinging to the floor of the raft in the daybreak which was half night, I recalled another storm when for a space the rain had ceased, when bellied clouds had foretold of more rain just as these. It was on the night I had tied the little blue ribbon at Lorelie's throat and had leaned from the window. Now remembering, I remembered too the dark shape which had swooped from a tree and had risen with its soft dangling prey in its claws.

So sure and strong I had believed myself to be that night! Between it and this hour lay so many dark twistings and turnings. I had not dreamed where they led—even now I could not know. But this I did know: Saint Clair hated me and wished to be rid of me, Tawn wished me evil, and there was Roi. Roi once loving and trusting, now perhaps hating me, too. Suddenly I was seized by despair. I saw myself surrounded by currents as uncontrollable as the storm, capable as the storm of wreaking destruction. Confident as I had been heretofore that I would win over Saint Clair, I had on this dark morning no such assurance.

But this was emotional reaction, I told myself. Was I, just at the moment when I needed courage, going to turn coward? Did I not realize that fear itself engendered defeat? That victory lay in my power to overcome circumstance? But what more could I do than I had done, I asked? Should I go to the Magnolia House, as Roi had suggested, though with irony, and agree to pay Hibbard the money owed by Saint Clair on condition he reveal what he knew regarding Lorelie's death? Saint Clair, I knew, would never dare risk exposure now. It would give me the whip hand over him.

Yet even as the raft went its tortured way under the dreary sky, I think I knew, as I know now, that I could never hold the whip hand over Saint Clair. But I would not admit it then. And not admitting it, I resolved that I would call upon Mr. Hibbard at the Magnolia House. I would have plenty of time before the bank opened.

When the raft reached the Darien side, I gave Joe the coin he charged for passage and went along the side street toward the square. On all sides I saw evidence of the storm—great limbs of trees lying torn, the street strewn with sand and water and at the wharf the fishing smacks, usually out for the day's catch by this time, tied fast.

Though no rain was falling now, I knew it would fall again in even greater force than before, for the sky that hung above Darien was a remarkable sky. Never had I seen one like it. It was a dark confusion of flying clouds tossed up into heaps now but closing in swiftly and densely, overpowering the whole sky. And as it darkened, the wind, which had blown all night with a great thundering, died to stillness as ominous as death itself.

Now and then as I went along the sleeping street I would see a door opened furtively, see one of the townspeople hold the door carefully as if they feared the elements; but these were few. Darien might have been a city of sleeping dead as I, hugging my cape close about me and clutching my packet of wages money beneath it, made my way to the Magnolia House and pushing against its heavy door entered the lobby.

It was deserted except for a raw-boned young clerk who yawned behind the counter which served as desk and who, on my entrance, ceased to loll and fixed me with suspicious eyes as I advanced toward him. And I knew my appearance justified his suspicion. My cape, sodden and wrinkled, dripped water along his clean floor; my hair was dank. I knew I presented a haggard and disheveled appearance. But I was too tired to care.

"Can I help you?" he snapped as I came to lean against his counter.

"Yes. Is there a Mr. Hibbard staying here?"

He gave me a sharp glance, then with official pompousness consulted the ledger, his blunt forefinger sliding down the page. Then he looked up. "There is a Mr. Hibbard."

"I wish to see him."

His eyes traveled to the clock on the wall. "It is only seven o'clock. What do you want to see him about?"

His assumption that I was some common woman angered me. After all, he was but a country bumpkin swollen with self-importance. Sharply I slapped the counter with my hand.

"I don't need to explain to you, young man. Tell Mr. Hibbard that Mrs. Saint Clair LeGrand wishes to see him. And at once."

Whether it was my sharpness or my name that worked the change in his manner I do not know. But change it did. The officiousness was replaced by sullen curiosity. He looked me over again and with a muttered "I'll send a nigger," vanished through a rear door.

I sat in one of the three chairs which furnished the small lobby, my mind so oblivious to my surroundings that I am amazed I can still recall perfectly the anemic palm and the shining cuspidors. While I waited, I improved my appearance as well as I could, squeezing the water from my cape and with my fingertips smoothing my hair, sensing that Mr. Hibbard would use my appearance as he would use any weakness to his own advantage.

When he came I was glad I had taken these pains, for he was foppishly garbed and as neat as if he had popped from a bandbox; but the fatuous smile was unchanged and the eyes as blue and cold as my memory of them.

"Mrs. LeGrand." He bowed before me. "This is—shall I say—quite a surprise. To what do I owe this honor?"

I stood and returned his bow. "I wish to speak to you, sir, about a personal matter."

He looked at me steadily and it flashed through my mind that he might refuse me. But he did not. Instead he asked, "Is it regarding—shall I say—a certain financial matter, Mrs. LeGrand?"

"Yes."

He spread his fat dimpled hands. "Well?" he said softly, and
waited. But I had no intention of discussing my business here,
for I was aware that the clerk, pretending to be busy at the
counter, kept his ear cocked our way. I gestured in his direction. "I must speak to you privately," I told him.

He understood at once. "Of course, Mrs. LeGrand." He stood
considering, then bowed again. "I am about to breakfast. Will
you join me?"

Before I could voice the refusal which rose to my lips, he
intercepted me softly.

"The dining room is deserted at this hour. Did I understand
you to say 'privately,' Mrs. LeGrand?"

I followed him to the dining room, a pleasant place with
windows overlooking the water. White-covered tables and a
log fire gave a sense of cozy comfort. From the rear came Negro
voices and clattering pans, prelude to breakfast at the Magnolia
House. The savory fragrance of coffee and bacon floated en-
ticingly, and at our entrance, a white-coated Negro emerged
from the kitchen as if at a prearranged signal.

We sat at a table near the fire and Mr. Hibbard, ignoring
my protestations, ordered a bounteous breakfast for two. This
done, he folded his babyish hands and looked across at me.

"Yes, Mrs. LeGrand."

I leaned across the table. "Mr. Hibbard, some time ago
you called upon me regarding money you had loaned my
husband."

"Yes, Mrs. LeGrand. I recall that visit perfectly." He
smirked at me across the table, the smirk telling me plainer than
words that he recalled, and wished me to know he recalled,
the incivility with which I had met him.

I pretended not to notice. Instead I asked coolly, "Mr.
Hibbard, was that money repaid?"

"Repaid?" The eyes staring into mine turned even harder
than their wont. Then softly, very softly, he said, "Why do you
ask, Mrs. LeGrand?"

"Because I arranged a loan from his son's estate for Mr.
LeGrand for the purpose of repaying you."

He sat so still, his face so immobile, I knew a twinge of
uneasiness. Had I come on a futile errand? But looking at him,
though he continued to sit silent, I saw the angry red creep

slowly up from his neck to mottle his face, and the knuckles of his dimpled hands whiten. And I was reassured.

Finally he said slowly, "He did not pay me a dime. Moreover, he came to me with other—shall I say—plans whereby I was persuaded to lend him even more." His mouth thinned. "He's got into me for a pretty sum."

I leaned still further across the table. "He will never pay you."

"Oh, yes! He will pay me."

"How? He has no money."

"He will have money when you sell your crops. I know about those crops."

"And do you have any idea of the sum he will realize from them?"

"He gave me to understand it would be considerable."

"You were a fool to believe him."

The red drenched his face again. "Oh, no, I am not a fool. Sometimes it costs good money to collect bad, but I will collect."

His confidence disturbed me. If only I possessed it, if I could only persuade him to join forces with me. Perhaps if I assured him of repayment. . . .

"Mr. Hibbard, how much does my husband owe you?"

"Shall we say—about ten thousand dollars?"

I sat back in my chair in amazement. "Ten thousand!" I laughed. "After expenses are deducted, his share from the crops will be far less than that."

I knew from the tightening of his face he was angered anew and I could not blame him. Saint Clair had used him badly, had failed to repay him after obtaining the money which made it possible. Yet I figured this might work to my advantage. To even the score with Saint Clair he might be willing to align himself with me.

"Mr. Hibbard," now I spoke swiftly and earnestly, "you and I are in the same boat. Saint Clair LeGrand has used both of us badly. Why can't we—you and I—arrange something?"

His eyes narrowed a fraction. "Just what sort of arrangement would you suggest?"

"I will pay off my husband's indebtedness to you." As I said the words a thousand questions fluttered in my consciousness. How could I ever raise so much? It would take my year's profit, the timber—but somehow I must raise it. I looked across at him. His eyes had dropped to his babyish hands, almost I could see the calculating brain at work; yet what I saw encouraged me. At least he did not totally refuse the idea.

Then he looked up. "I am fully aware, Mrs. LeGrand, you would want something from me in return for this—shall we say—reimbursement of funds. Am I right?"

"You are right," I told him flatly.

"And what would you want from me?"

"Listen, Mr. Hibbard," I spoke slowly. "You and I understand each other," and as I uttered the words, I realized with surprise it was true; we did understand each other. "Saint Clair LeGrand has victimized both of us. From you he has taken a large sum of money which he had no way of repaying. And when a way was arranged he pocketed the money which was rightfully yours. He has treated me equally ill. With hard work I have redeemed Seven Chimneys, brought it back to the place where it is valuable property again. And now he plans to sell it."

Softly he inserted, "And you do not wish that to happen?"

"It must not happen. For my child's sake I must prevent it."

"And you think I can be of help in preventing it?"

"Yes. You possess certain knowledge."

We sat with eyes locked and I saw that his were bright with something akin to glee. Beyond him through the windows I was conscious of a weird yellowish light which had pervaded the earth to add ominousness to the stillness. Subconsciously I knew it foretold another gust of storm, but now it made but little impression upon me. I was interested only in what Mr. Hibbard would say.

When he said "Mrs. LeGrand," he still spoke quietly but I knew inwardly he had tensed.

"Yes, Mr. Hibbard."

"You mention some knowledge I have concerning your husband. Just what is this so-called knowledge?"

"That is what I want you to tell me."

"And in return for this so-called knowledge you will pay off LeGrand's debt to me?"

"You are correct."

He pursed his lips and his fat face was as sly as an evil boy's. "But suppose I tell you I have no such knowledge?"

"I would know it isn't true. You yourself spoke to me of it that day at Seven Chimneys. 'Extraordinary arrangement,' you called it. And two nights ago you went to Seven Chimneys and threatened my husband with prison."

The silly smirk faced me, the hard blue eyes were bright. "And yet I insist I have no such knowledge."

I could only look at him as if I distrusted my ears.

"And even if I had"—his words were so oily, so ingratiating I had to separate their meaning from their quality—"why do you presume to believe I would use it to help you?"

"Perhaps for money," I told him insolently.

He smirked at me openly. "I'll get my money. But I won't help you, Mrs. LeGrand. I would have once but you wanted none of it. Proud and mighty you were then. Well, you're not so proud now, are you?"

His hard blue eyes and the tight mouth told me he relished refusing me, that it satisfied the vanity I had offended on that day at Seven Chimneys, and I knew no appeal I could make would change him. My ingenuity was powerless. So I rose abruptly, but I could not deny myself a parting shot.

"Perhaps I shall have to appeal to the proper authorities. Let them extract the information which you refuse to give me."

He rose and leaned on the table before him. "You be careful before you go to the authorities, Mrs. LeGrand."

I surveyed him scornfully. "Careful? I have nothing to fear from you."

He leaned more heavily on the table and the hard blue eyes were those of a snarling cat. "And I tell you again, be careful. There's ugly talk aplenty about you. The authorities might have some questions to ask about your visit to me this morning. A decent woman ain't so ready to throw her husband in jail." He paused. "Not that you can do it. Saint Clair LeGrand has outsmarted smoother customers than you."

I waited to hear no more but went swiftly around the tables to the door which led to the lobby. I had failed and with the realization of failure, my fears were revived. Would any of my plans succeed? I wondered. At that thought my life at Seven Chimneys flashed before me. I knew again the labor and worry, the struggle. But I felt I had struggled with the shadow of Saint Clair dooming my efforts from the first, that never once had I grasped reality. And in my mind, those last words of Hibbard's tolled like a knell. "He's outsmarted smoother customers than you." Suddenly I knew them for the truth. I would never win over Saint Clair—and yet I must, I must.

Passing through the lobby, I glanced at the clock. It lacked a few minutes of eight. A whole hour must elapse before the bank opened. Yet where could I spend that hour? Once I could have gone to Flora McCrackin's but no more, and the idea of spending an hour in the Magnolia House lobby under the eyes of the curious clerk and with the possible added unpleasantness of encountering Hibbard again was not to be thought of. Yet I must wait somewhere.

Opening the door, I stepped into the street and halted, struck by the appearance of the world. The yellow light I had noticed through the dining-room windows had deepened to an unearthly glow and the stillness was almost unbearable. The scene before my eyes—the rainswept streets, the shuttered buildings—was totally devoid of life. Not a leaf quivered, not a human being moved along the square. In all this unearthly world wrapped in the ominous stillness of a fearful dream, I might have been the only living thing.

It was then, turning my head to look up and down the street for a possible shelter, that I saw Saint Clair. He leaned against the wall of the Magnolia House wrapped in his long coat, his eyes watching me with a terrible intentness.

I stood there like one turned to stone as he came toward me, and suddenly I was afraid. This was reality and reality was more terrible than any dream.

I crouched in the bow of the boat as we went down the Sound beneath that eerie saffron sky and watched him as he worked the oars, hating his pale face and the hands that looked so white against the wet cedar. Hated him and wished him dead, with all my soul wished him dead. He had taken the wages money from me easily, as if I had been a child, and I had had no will left to struggle. I had thought of a dozen things I might do. I thought of screaming, of bringing the Darien folk gaping to their doors; but then I remembered they believed ill of me and I had not screamed. I thought too of taking refuge in the Magnolia House but there was Hibbard. So I did nothing. I allowed him to take the wages money unresisting, allowed his pale hand on my arm to guide me to the boat. Now I sat like one half-witted as if my will, confronted by that which I could neither master nor endure, had receded in precipitate flight leaving only numbness in its wake.

But this was madness, I told myself, and now more than ever in my life I needed sanity, for the boat was an eggshell upon the heaving rolling water. Yet it was not the water that I feared. It was Saint Clair, who even as he swayed with the movement of the oars, watched me with that terrible intentness, and whose face by its deadly stillness suggested the power to destroy. I knew he need only to move abruptly to upset the boat and he would be free from me forever, my drowning just another accident of the storm. From a great distance I imagined I could hear Rupert's voice, "And always somebody's drowned. They go out in the storm, the boat turns over—pouf!"

Yet even as I thought of this I warned myself. Careful—careful, lest the evil prying mind reach in and read what lay in mine. I forced my eyes toward the shore, searching in vain for sight of another boat, another living being; but there was nothing. Only the desolate shoreline and the rolling saffron water under the saffron sky. And Saint Clair who, even as he worked the oars, seemed to sit motionless, his bright, mad eyes upon me.

If only he would speak! If only I could speak—speak of the storm, the safely stored rice and cotton, anything to bring everyday normality to dull the brightness of those eyes; but I could not and even as I despaired of my inadequacy I realized the futility of despair. Even if I spoke, he would not hear me.

But now hope, which I had believed dead beyond recall, revived again. We were approaching the place where we must turn into the channel, we were nearing home. And nothing had happened. Perhaps if I continued to sit passive and unspeaking nothing would happen.

But now the sky changed. The yellow light was being vanquished by thunderous black clouds once more, the stillness broken by wind which moaned and began to whip the water to fury. The boat danced grotesquely, almost standing on end at times; and Saint Clair must labor to buffet the swells which, rising higher and higher as the wind gained velocity, threatened almost to engulf us.

Perhaps it was the struggle which gave him a measure of release, freed him somewhat from the tenseness which had held him, or perhaps battling through the water renewed his sense of power; whatever the reason, he began to speak. And I, who only a short time before had wished him to speak, now wished for nothing so much as his silence, for his emotionless voice was deadly and the too bright eyes rested on my face unwaveringly.

"You thought you were clever, didn't you? Well, you're not quite clever enough."

"I don't know what you mean." I forced the words through stiff lips.

"Oh, yes, you do." He paused, waiting for the boat, flung high by a swell, to settle to keel again. "And I've known from the first. I've watched you wriggle like a bitch in heat to get what you wanted." An acid smile flitted over his face and was gone. "But you won't get it. And now"—the eyes lost some of their brightness, became the glazed narrow eyes of an animal—"now you'll do as I say."

I did not answer; I dared not answer. For in the drawn face, the controlled tenseness of the hands, the whole body, I saw that which made me fear him; and he knew I feared him.

"You are frightened, aren't you? You know how easily the boat could capsize, how easily you would vanish beneath the water."

I knew, and I knew, too, that to remain silent was the wiser part. But his taunting voice, his gloating eyes goaded me beyond the point of wisdom.

"You wouldn't dare," I told him scornfully. "You would never get away with it as you got away with Bob Kingston— and Lorelie."

His voice slid over mine. "It is surprising what you can get away with when the law is composed of crooked Yankee bastards. You need only to grease a few pockets. And I will have money tomorrow, a great deal of money."

Perilous as my situation was, the word "tomorrow" brought me a ray of hope. "Tomorrow," he had said. So Seven Chimneys had not yet been sold. Perhaps . . .

He misread the expression in my eyes which even slight hope had inspired.

"I may as well let you know—if you think you will benefit from that money, you are a fool."

"I want none of your money."

He laughed at that, the horrible silent laughter which held madness in its mirthlessness. "Not want money?" he jibed. "You'd sell your soul to the devil for it, you greedy slut." The laughter ceased like a light put out. "But you'll get none of it. Tomorrow I send you and your filthy brat packing as you sent Tawn, and without a penny."

I told him slowly, angered now beyond fear, beyond reason. "And if you do, I'll blast your infamy and your perversity to the world. I'll tell them of the money you stole from Cecile, how you killed Bob Kingston and Lorelie—"

I had spoken swiftly and in anger, but now, seeing his face, I halted. It was livid and contorted and suddenly I grasped the sides of the boat, rearing backward as if to flee, for he had dropped the oars gently in their locks and regardless of the tossing boat he stood and came toward me, those pale hands reaching.

Then as I reared back, staring up into the livid face, expecting to feel the reaching hands on my throat, a swell higher than the others lifted the boat and spinning it like a leaf, dropped it again. I had a confused impression of Saint Clair staggering, his hands clutching at air, then his tall body plummeted into the water. Still rearing backwards, still grasping the sides of the boat, I saw him disappear and the water close over him. Yet I sat there, still fearing those insane eyes and pale hands.

With the boat swirling and near capsizing, the will to survive asserted itself again. And crawling to the bow of the boat I seized the oars. Then I saw him emerge from the water, his face turned toward me, his arms reaching for the boat across the space which lay between us and yet not quite able to gain it.

His eyes commanded mine across the water. "Use the oars," he shouted impatiently. "Bring the boat this way."

Automatically my hands tightened on the oars. A few strong strokes and I could reach him. But I was not quick enough for him. "Hurry, you fool," he called again. But struck by a sudden thought I sat motionless, looking across at him, for that thought was, "Why help him? Help him and tomorrow David and I will be homeless—"

But even across the distance which widened as the unguided boat drifted farther from him and nearer shore, he read my thoughts. And now he ordered again and with utter confidence that I would obey, "Bring the boat, I tell you."

Still I did not move. I only sat staring at him and then, as if knowing he could expect no help from me, he tried to swim, nearing the boat now but then pulled back by the undertow as the waves receded. Then, realizing, there burst from him a scream, an insane scream that rang in my ears like the cry of a maddened beast; and I sat there motionless and watched his pale face vanish again. When it failed to rise I took the oars and turned the boat up the channel.

Chapter Twenty-eight

THE days that followed were like the distorted happenings of a nightmare with no incident clearly drawn but all merged into a shifting panorama without sense or reason—a nightmare in which I was the central figure. It was as if I stood and watched myself moving through a series of scenes totally lacking reality and without effect upon me. I saw myself standing in the hall at Seven Chimneys, the water dripping from my cape, heard my voice announcing that Saint Clair had been drowned. Margot's suspicious eyes met mine above the wheel chair where Old Madame's figure crumpled grotesquely, as if her sudden scream had pulled the marrow from her bones. Later, but how much later I will never know, I saw Genevieve Cram on the stairs (strange I should recall so clearly the fresh pink rosebuds which spattered her wrapper) her eyes staring, her mouth a silly O. Then her father drew her back protectingly, but not before he looked down at me, his eyes, too, unclean with suspicion—or so it seemed to me.

All day I sat in my room tended by the awed but loving Tib, conscious of the stealthy quiet—that quiet which is camp follower of death. It pervaded the house in spite of Old Madame's soft moaning which had never ceased since her first scream. I was like a swimmer who had struggled for hours against a heavy sea, come at last to rest upon a lonely beach, too spent to be either glad or sorry. But I had no sense of guilt. I knew that later the thing which I had done would rise to accuse me with that pale, dead face, but now I had only a fatalistic conviction that I had done what I must do. Every word, every act imposed upon me by Seven Chimneys, indeed by my entire life, had driven me toward it unerringly, and wearily I wondered if the guilty always feel so—caught in a monstrous web from which there is no escape.

Later at Tib's persuasion I threw myself across the bed in my clothes and slept and dreamed. And in that dream Roi and I walked beside a quiet pool of blue. It was the sweetest of spring days, the sun was gentle, the trees wore the tenderest green. I was happy as never before in all my life had I been happy. There was no past, no future. Only the pool and Roi's eyes laughing teasingly into mine. But my happiness was soon vanquished and horror returned. For looking deep into the pool I saw that Saint Clair's still, dead face lay there. Even in my dream I recognized the truth. I, who had longed to be free of Saint Clair, would never be free of him. I was bound to him irrevocably by that pale, dead face.

The opening of my bedroom door ripped the fabric of the dream and I awoke to instant alertness. It was Tib. When I sat up and instinctively smoothed my hair, she told me, round-eyed, that many men were searching the water for Saint Clair's body. She was, I thought, like a faithful retriever, bringing me news as a spaniel lays the spoils at his master's feet. It was she who told me later how the Crams had fled, risking the stormy trip to Darien rather than remain at Seven Chimneys; and it was she who told me next morning that Saint Clair's body had been washed up on the Mary-de-Wander. They would not bring it to Seven Chimneys, she said. They were taking it to Darien. There was to be an inquest.

For that inquest, which was to be held on Monday, I prepared carefully. With Tib's help I remade a black dress in which I would present to the suspicious and distrustful towns-people an exterior, at least, which they could not criticize. Yet even as I cut and stitched I felt the garment of mourning was a mockery, that it would deceive none into believing that my heart had been lost with Saint Clair.

That it did not deceive was confirmed upon my arrival at Darien. For as I stepped upon the wharf, four men with shot-guns lying negligently across their arms closed in about me. And when I turned to one of them and asked if I should consider myself a prisoner, he spat brown tobacco juice in the white dust and jerked his head toward the rabble of poor whites gathered across the way. Looking toward them I saw that they seemed to strain forward like tethered hounds, avid for the first glimpse of the woman who returned in ignominy to a place where she had once walked with such disdain.

"Consider it anyway you please," my guard told me, "but while you're about it consider yourself lucky the sheriff didn't leave you to the likes of them."

The insolence of his answer and the look of the mob, greedy to enjoy my humiliation, clearly showed me the perilous pass to which I had brought myself. Yet this was not the cause of my greatest bitterness. That came a little later when, as we went toward Angus McCrackin's store, hooted and jeered at by a scattering of young ruffians running before and behind us, I saw Roi. He leaned in a shop door apart from the crowd. His eyes met mine over their milling heads as cold and dark as if I had been a woman of the streets. More than anything that had happened those expressionless eyes kindled anger in me. It flashed through my mind, "He lets me endure this and doesn't come near me, or even lift his hand in greeting!" And seized by the impulse to force recognition from him, I paused and faced him. But as if sensing some weakness, the surging crowd immediately narrowed the circle which the guards held about me. So close they pressed that I caught the odors of their sweat, the stale sweetness of corn liquor. And my impulse of defiance directed itself against them. Deliberately I looked at those who had thrust their faces nearest mine. They must have sensed my contempt, for they pushed back somewhat as if ashamed, as if they would have me believe their nearness was the fault of those behind them.

I went on then, my head high with the scorn I felt, and though the rabble continued to push and scrouge, I was hardly conscious of them now. Within me there was gathering sick despair. Roi had deserted me. Aware as I was that this community, however crude, was to judge me, would condemn or find me innocent, I felt more alone at that moment than ever before in my life.

I hardly knew how we came to Angus McCrackin's store or when I went through the doorway. The store had been transformed for the occasion. A counter dragged to the center of the room would do duty as coroner's bench, with raw pine boards supported by boxes forming makeshift benches for spectators and witnesses. Already these were filled, and rows of figures lined the walls. As I followed a guard to a place on one of the forward benches I heard the murmur which swept the crowd. I knew the meaning of that murmur; it sprang from the relief of those who have waited for a show to begin, the anticipation, the cruel hunger for a victim that is born of mobs.

At first as I sat quietly in my place, I was most aware of the mob and of their eyes, which seemed to pierce through my clothes and touch my naked body. But then I became aware of other things. The coroner, a paunchy, sweaty man in shirt sleeves, fumbling through a sheaf of papers on the counter as if he drew from them some reassurance of his judicial importance. The coroner's jury of six men, dirt farmers, crackers and such, who would decide how Saint Clair had died and if they so found, would bind me over to the county court for trial. Yet to these I scarcely gave a glance. For Roi had entered, pausing at the doorway to talk with loungers, laughing easily and slapping his crop against his booted leg as casually as if joking with drinking companions in a barroom.

A sudden stirring and then a settling told me that the coroner had summoned the assembly to attention. But the words with which he instructed his jury were lost upon me. Vaguely I heard him explain that this was not a trial but merely the effort to determine the manner in which Saint Clair LeGrand had died, that he demanded order and would hold accountable anyone disturbing the proceedings. As he talked, peering out into the room over the top of his spectacles, the crowd chuckled. He was known to all present for his arrant cowardice and for his fondness for the bottle.

In haphazard fashion the hearing proceeded, coroner and witnesses talking back and forth with an informality that stripped the law of its dignity and meaning. Somehow it was established that Saint Clair LeGrand was a citizen of Glynn County in the State of Georgia, that he had met his death in the same county in a manner yet to be established. His body had been washed up on the Mary-de-Wander, and the fisherman who had recovered it recited—and with morbid zeal—the circumstances of the recovering and the appearance of the body.

I sensed the crowd was becoming restive. I knew well enough why. I was the one they wished to hear, to have recount for them the story of Saint Clair's death, perhaps to make some slip that would admit my guilt. And when the coroner called my name silence hushed them, a silence that persisted as I moved to the kitchen chair that had been placed beside his counter.

That silence continued to prevail while I told my story, and their eyes never wavered from me. Yet I knew that they were disappointed, for I told my story clearly but almost in a monotone and failed to give them the melodrama they desired. I refused them that. I did not weep, though I knew it would have impressed them more favorably had I done so. But to make a false plea for sympathy, to pretend an emotion I did not feel, was beyond my histrionic powers. As I finished I could feel disappointment turning childishly to anger, then suspicion.

The coroner, I realized, was experiencing the same reaction. His small eyes glared at me behind the spectacles and when I had finished he rubbed his veinous nose with a thoughtful forefinger, as if the gesture would somehow indicate that he would not be taken in by my Yankee craftiness.

He cleared his throat importantly. The pretended friendliness of his voice deceived neither me nor the spectators.

"Now, ma'am, I know you've been through a trying time," he said, "but there's a few questions I'd like to ask if you think you can stand the ordeal of answering them."

His poorly veiled sarcasm would have brought the red to my face had I not despised him. "You need not be concerned as to me," I answered. "I am prepared to answer any questions you may ask."

For a second he was discomfited and attempted to cover it by a pompous clearing of his throat.

"You said your late husband was thrown into the water by a wave, unexpected like?"

I agreed that I had so stated.

"But at the same time *you* were not thrown from the boat. Now I wonder if you can explain that to us, ma'am?"

"Certainly. I was seated. My husband was standing, as I told you, or to be more accurate, half standing."

He rubbed his veinous nose again. "Half standing, ma'am?" His voice was gently unbelieving. "Now that's a queer business. And the water running so heavy, too."

I shut out the swift memory of Saint Clair coming toward me in the pitching boat. "Not at all queer. As I told you before, one of the oars had slipped from his grasp when we were caught by the riptide. To retrieve it before it floated away, he was forced to rise quickly, almost to stand—"

It was the explanation I had offered in my first telling and I wondered if he hoped to lead me into an admission of guilt by forcing me to repeat my statements. If so, his was a futile hope. Too carefully I had rehearsed my story. This stupid little man with his obvious subterfuges would hardly shake me from it.

His next question was as gently unbelieving. "And did he retrieve the oar, ma'am?"

"He did."

"And it was then that he was heaved into the water?"

"Not that instant, sir. Not until he—and he was still half-standing—had placed the oar in the oarlock again. Then before he could seat himself it happened."

"And he sank at once, did you say, ma'am?"

I almost smiled but forced myself to answer patiently.

"Oh, no. I could hardly have made such a statement. It would not have been true. My husband struggled for a moment in plain view before he—disappeared."

"And while he struggled, ma'am, how far away were you and the boat?"

I shrugged. "Perhaps fifteen, perhaps twenty feet. You can hardly expect me to be exact."

He fumbled with his papers and almost I could have laughed. He hoped to confuse me, I thought, hoped to prove to his audience his ability as a stern instrument of justice. But so far he had failed of his purpose. And I saw that his failure angered him. Now his whole face tightened, the eyes behind the glasses turned cold. I braced myself for his next question.

"You say, ma'am, you were only fifteen or twenty feet from your husband while he struggled, but you couldn't row the boat close enough to help him." He paused significantly as if to invest his next question with grave importance. "But after he had drowned, you took the oars and rowed the same boat all the way up the channel. Is that correct?"

I felt the crowd waiting for my answer, waiting as if they knew I could find no way out of the trap he had set. And then I realized suddenly I could not escape this trap. Not because it had been cunningly laid but because, regardless of what answer I gave, it would not be believed. The shock of Saint Clair's being thrown from the boat, the high winds, the time it required to scramble forward and seize the oars—none of these would serve. In their minds the stark fact remained. I had been as near to Saint Clair as I was to them, yet I had not managed to reach him, even thrust out an oar for him to grasp.

Quietly, breathlessly they waited for my answer, wondering what explanation I would give, hoping no doubt that I would stumble. At least I could withhold that satisfaction from them.

I met the eyes behind the spectacles steadily.

"You are correct, sir. I could not reach my husband," I said coldly.

I was aware of their condemnation as I walked from the chair to my place on the bench, and knew that before them I stood guilty, if not of actual murder, of deliberately and maliciously allowing my husband to drown. But with a sudden revulsion of feeling I did not care what they thought or what decision they rendered. I was conscious only of utter exhaustion. It was only by summoning every scrap of will that I managed to sit erect. I cared nothing for them, for their stupidity or their condemnation. I cared only for Roi. And desperately my eyes went seeking him. He still lounged carelessly against the wall, the crop flicking lazily at the top of his boot. But his eyes evaded mine.

Only when his name was called did he stand erect and stroll to the kitchen chair. He sat in it, one leg swung over the other as easily as he would sit in a drawing room after a long ride. And when the coroner asked if he was the brother of the deceased Saint Clair LeGrand, Roi corrected him with a half-raised hand. "Only half brother, Gus," he said briefly.

The coroner brushed this difference aside impatiently. "Of course, of course, half brother. You and he were on good terms, weren't you, Roi?"

Roi's eyes lit with deviltry but his body remained relaxed; his crop scraped at a crust of mud on the heel of his boot.

"On good terms?" His repetition was offered lightly. "The devil, Gus! You know the answer as well as I do. We got along about as well as two hounds over a side of bacon." He had answered with mock ruefulness, and laughter rippled through the crowd. It was as if he and they shared a mutual secret and they gloried in his frankness. Even the coroner could not suppress a grin, though he made an effort to cover it with another judicial cough.

"Just so, just so. Guess there wasn't ever much secret about that. Anyhow it's beside the point. How well do you know your brother's wife, Roi?"

For the first time Roi's eyes swung toward me, passed over me casually.

"About as well as most of you know her, I imagine. I've talked with her a few times."

"Would you say you were more—er—intimate with her than with your brother?" The voice of the coroner was sly again but Roi's grin disarmed him.

"I'd say I was more intimate with the devil than I was with Saint, Gus. But if you mean do I know Mrs. LeGrand better than twenty other women hereabouts, the answer's no." His eyebrows quirked, "Come to think about it, perhaps you'd better make that twenty men. You might find women enough to win your point."

This time the laughter rang out unguarded and I felt the blood rushing to my cheeks. It was well enough for Roi to dissemble our relationship, but I could not understand why he should make me a laughing stock.

The coroner was hammering with his mallet. "Very well, very well. That's beside the point again. The point is—do you know your brother's wife?"

"I do."

"Would you say she made him a good wife?"

Roi's eyes passed over me again, as casually as before. "As good as most, I expect. I've not too much to say for wives—any wife. But then, I speak as a man of slight experience."

"Would you say that your brother—your half brother," he corrected himself, "was happy with Mrs. LeGrand?"

Roi shrugged. "Saint happy? Hardly. An angel from heaven couldn't have kept him content."

"But you would say, Roi, that she was a good wife? That she had his interest at heart? That she conducted herself as a wife should?"

"I would." The answer was drawled. "I would say that she made him a good wife. She worked like a nigger. It's common talk, what she accomplished with Seven Chimneys. She was good to his son." The riding crop gouged again at the mud on his boot. "As for the relations between my brother and his wife, I neither knew nor cared about them. But then, as I pointed out before, my brother and I disagreed on many matters. This was one of them. Between us, I could never understand how he found it possible to marry a carpetbagging Yankee schoolmarm even to get a good overseer."

The laughter shook the room now. Dazed, I knew that I had been absolved, for this was easy laughter, stripped of the tenseness and animosity it had held before. Yet even the verdict that Saint Clair LeGrand had met his death by accidental drowning did nothing to lessen the sick disappointment in my body. True, by turning the hearing into a farce, Roi had dissolved into ridicule the smoldering suspicion that I had allowed my husband to drown. But the device he had chosen left me scant consolation. He had made me a ridiculous figure, a "carpetbagging Yankee schoolmarm," unloved and unlovable, married because I was a good overseer, someone to drive the Negroes in the fields. He had left me nothing of womanhood or grace or even pride. And as I made my way from the place, jostled by the crowd, smelling again the sweaty odor of the herd, I felt it would have been far better to have been held for murder than to be a figure of contempt and scorn before the world.

I came out of Angus McCrackin's store and paused again upon the streets of Darien, confronted with an unknown future, as empty and barren of happiness and prospect of fulfillment as the one I had faced when I first stood here waiting to be conducted to Seven Chimneys.

Now I was returning to the house of the LeGrands, to Rupert and Old Madame and my child, to the struggle to win some measure of security. I was confronted by greater odds than ever before. My wages money lay at the bottom of the river. I must draw on my small reserve to settle with the hands. The new Negroes must be contracted for. I would have to manage the same amount of work with fewer hands. Even the house servants must be reduced; Margot and Maum Lucie must go. Between us Tib and I must cope with the house and children and care for Old Madame, with Vene to ferry me back and forth. However much I had come to despise this mainland some communication with it must be preserved if ever I was to make another successful crop.

All this struggle, all these problems lay ahead, yet now they melted into insignificance. Roi had betrayed me! I knew if I could but have him at my side these burdens would be lightened and seem as nothing. I might, I thought tiredly, even have found happiness and the fulfillment that my flesh demanded even as my will resisted.

This was to be my punishment. I had gone my dark and devious way, employing any method that came to hand to gain my ends even—now for the first time I admitted it—murder. I had thought no price too great to pay for security, yet I had failed to grasp it. And I knew why. In my struggle for material security I had ignored the only true security beneath the sun, security of the soul. What contentment could I ever know though Seven Chimneys be mine? Saint Clair was dead and I had let him die, and Roi, Roi who had seen me clearly as I was, had abandoned me.

Immersed in these thoughts I was hardly conscious of my surroundings as I walked on my way to the wharf, or of the scattering of young hoodlums lounging against the walls, their gap-toothed grins impudent and insulting. Only when one, larger and bolder than the rest, slouched toward me and barred my path, did my head jerk erect.

"If you've got a little time, ma'am, you might give me a lesson or two. I never did get as much schoolin' as I could use."

His leer, his narrow hateful eyes, made me feel soiled. I was without the defenses that decent women have to guard themselves against the insults of louts and wastrels. Yet I perceived that he was hardly more than a boy.

"Please move aside," I said coldly and walked on. But he ignored my request. He fell in step with me, still grinning. And now his cronies were slipping forward, trailing me, offering to one another opinions upon my appearance and behavior. Their comments grew more and more brazen until the bolder one barred my way again.

"Now sure 'nuff," he mocked, "that ain't no way for a lady to act when a fellow comes courtin'. Anyway I guarantee I'll be warmer than your last husband."

This produced ribald laughter from his fellows. Emboldened by that laughter, he put his hand on my arm.

"Take your hands off me," I ordered, and my voice shook with the loathing I felt.

He grinned again. "Now this ain't no way to act, ma'am. We just aim to see you to the wharf. Ain't as if you could be too pertic'lar who you walk with."

"Get out of my way," I ordered again and then halted, for I felt I could not go on. The wide gaping grins surrounded me, the unclean eyes moved over me, and though I repeated "Move aside," once more, I knew that my voice carried no conviction, that it trembled. And I was ashamed for its trembling. A sick nausea rose up in my breast. Still they clung jeering and jibing, their hands reaching. And the hand which had lain on my arm now moved up to my shoulder.

So swiftly it happened I did not know what brought the sudden welt of scarlet across his cheek. I saw his frightened eyes and then they, all of them, were scattering and running, calling back vulgar taunts. For the first time since I was heavy with child I was near to fainting. I was slipping, slipping. A fog of dazzling light enfolded me. Then an arm was around me, holding me firmly. It was Roi. Roi with Sans Foix's bridle over his arm and the riding crop with which he had slashed the cheek of my tormentor still in his hand. His face when it emerged clear for me was white and strained and there were beads of sweat on his forehead.

"Dear God, Hester! Will you never get over being a stiff-backed damned fool? Why didn't you simply walk on? Those youngsters would have done you no harm."

Somehow I managed to draw myself free from his support.

"Why do you bother?" I asked. "It is only what I deserve in your opinion. You made that clear enough at the inquest."

His hand slashed the air impatiently. "What did you want me to do? I had to make them believe there was nothing between us—between you and me."

"I didn't care what they believed."

He nodded. "You didn't. That was plain enough. You were ready to put your neck in a noose rather than bend that stiff back of yours so much as half an inch. By God, we southerners are supposed to be proud. But damned if I've ever met one who could hold a candle to a Yankee schoolmarm."

I managed a smile now. For it was beginning to dawn upon me that Roi, no matter how he railed at my stubbornness, was still, perhaps, concerned for me and cared whether or not my neck was placed in a noose.

"Then you were lying when you said you disagreed with Saint in his taste for a Yankee, carpetbagging schoolmarm?"

His dark eyes bored into mine, his lips were grim.

"Yes, I lied, Hester. If you were not sometimes the fool of the world you must have known it. I had to save that stiff neck of yours. Did you not feel it, Hester? In Angus' store? How they were ready—" He broke off and his eyes were somber. "Yes, Hester. I lied."

He stood there, his face so close to mine that merely by raising my hand I could have stroked his cheek. And triumph surged through me. I had not lost Roi. He was still mine. And with the realization that this was true, the misery that had enveloped me for so long dissolved into nothingness. Happiness which I had given up for lost swept through me, dizzy and sweet.

I raised my eyes to his. "Roi—" I began.

He moved away, a quizzical smile on his lips. "Come along, Hester. A schoolmarm mustn't stand here being courted in the square even if she's just escaped hanging by the skin of her teeth."

Chapter Twenty-nine

WALKING over the land I thought I had never seen the place so fair. The harvest-stripped fields lay cool and sweet in the early morning. The girdle of forest which bound them gleamed with the fiery tongues of sumach, flashed with the orange and lemon and brown of the trees. Raindrops, touched to iridescence by the rising sun, jeweled bush and shrub. And somewhere within the dripping forest a mockingbird bade goodbye to autumn. Recessional, I thought, for Hester Snow. For this was my farewell to Seven Chimneys.

Once I had said, "It is mine, it is mine, I will not give it up," though I had no claim on it. Now that the law proclaimed it mine, I could not accept it. For on that day two months ago when Roi had come back to me, he had convinced me that we could never live at Seven Chimneys.

"We have no right," he had said, his eyes on mine, steady and somber. "We have no right—you know why."

Even as I stared back at him wondering what he knew—if he guessed—his eyes gave me the answer. They were tender now, and compassionate. "Saint was—a devil."

Standing in the little cove I looked out over the Sound. The marsh grass brown and sere quivered delicately on its breast; above it a V of wild geese sped, uttering their rasping cry. And gradually, gently the weeks just past slipped over my consciousness, reliving themselves once more. Again I saw Saint Clair lying in the drawing room, as alone beneath the tall tapers as he had been in life. I heard again the creaking buckboard lumbering over the land, bearing the long black coffin, the chanting of the little priest as he said his prayers for the dead. Heard too the high sweet voices of the Negroes at the grave lot, their voices

273

mingling with the murmuring of the Altamaha. And I remembered Tawn—Tawn facing me across the open grave as if she dared me to question her right to be there.

Between that day and this one there was so much to be done. . . . The settling up with the Negroes and their departure, saying goodbye to Shem, shocked at the tears on his earnest face. The hiring and breaking in of the McAllisters, the kindly Scottish couple who, under the watchful eyes of Stephen Pearsall, would serve as caretakers and look after Old Madame, who continued to lie like a clod, hardly more alive than the son whose death had broken the mainspring of her life.

But now it was all done. The dishes and bric-a-brac packed, the inventory complete, my accounts settled with Stephen Pearsall. The boxes holding our clothes—Rupert's, David's, mine and Tib's—had been rowed to Darien yesterday by Vene. In but a short while he would take us over. Yes, this was my farewell to Seven Chimneys.

I left the cove and went along the path that led to the cabins, empty now. And even as I went I sensed an oppressive change in the air. Already the taint of neglect lay upon the place. Weeds had sprung up in the gardens, in the cotton rows, along the paths, and I had a frightening picture of nature's will opposed to man's, obliterating ruthlessly the work of man. Remembering the time when swish of scythe and clank of plough had resounded on the air, when the Negro voices had called and laughed, I now sensed something fearful and akin to death in the stillness.

Entering the "street" between the rows of cabins and walking almost furtively, I peered through the open doors. Only disorder and emptiness met my eyes. The cabins had been stripped of everything that could be toted away. Even the calico curtains had been ripped from their poles. And the windows stared out blankly with the emptiness seen in the sightless eyes of the blind.

I stood in the "street" beneath the pines whose whispering was less a sound than part of the stillness, recalling those who had trod this ground into satin brownness. Stella, Big Lou, Uncle Early, Linette, John Eaton, Clarence. How nimbly their feet had danced the night of the rice claying. And now they belonged to the past. Never again would dark agile feet tread this spot. Never again would the cabins ring with their carefree laughter. The river would take over the rice bottoms and encroach on the front gardens; the weeds and undergrowth would devour the house; in time the house itself would stand gaunt and desolate, deserted except for the unhappy ghosts which might wander there.

Saddened, I made my way back toward the house, telling myself as I went, that I would never forget the little cove or how quiet the marshes lay, trying to impress forever on my memory those places I had loved. For there was pain in my leave-taking. At Seven Chimneys I had dreamed high dreams, had aspired to transcend my fate. I had not won. I was leaving it all behind. And despite the pain I was glad.

An hour later with Rupert's hand in mind I preceded Tib, carrying David, down the path to the landing where Vene waited with the longboat. A moment later we pushed down the channel.

As Tawn had done on that long ago day, I kept my eyes on Seven Chimneys. It rose sturdy and high, the chimneys tall against the sky, and as I looked a great wrench twisted my heart. The sun, now fully risen, had transformed it, lighting it with splendor. It might have been a magic house, so wondrous it appeared. Yet not for this transient splendor alone did my heart ache.

For me Seven Chimneys had possessed another splendor, the splendor which flames in every heart when it hears the word "home." For a while it had been my home, the only home I had ever known. And I would never cease to love it and to mourn it.

Rupert, too, felt the pain of parting. Suddenly, as if seeking comfort in nearness, he moved close to me. "Are you sure we'll like it out in Missouri, Hester?" His voice was wistful.

"I'm sure, Rupert."

"Shall I ever come back to Seven Chimneys?"

"You will come back, Rupert. It will always be here waiting for you. When you are grown up—"

He interrupted me eagerly. "But we'll have a home in Missouri, too—won't we?"

"Yes, we'll have a home in Missouri, too." As I spoke I saw the cabin in the clearing, knew as surely as if already I endured them the long cold winters, the hot dry summers, the never-end-ing toil. And reaching out I took Rupert's hand and held it tightly. I too was desolate and afraid.

But as we neared Darien my desolation and fear were eased, for I saw Roi waiting on the wharf. And as the boat went toward him through the sun-dappled lane of water, he flung up his hand in greeting. With his hand held high he waited for us.